Colin MacInnes (1914-76), son of Angela Thirkell, cousin of Stanley Baldwin and Rudyard Kipling, grandson of Burne-Jones, was brought up in Australia but lived most of his life in London, about which he wrote with a warts-and-all relish that earned him a reputation as the literary Hogarth of his day. Bisexual, outsider, champion of youth, "pale-pink friend" of Black Londoners and chronicler of English life, MacInnes described himself as "a very nosey person" who "found adultery in Hampstead indescribably dull". He was much more at home in the coffee bars and jazz clubs of Soho and Notting Hill, which provided the material for his three acclaimed London Novels, *Absolute Beginners, Mr Love and Justice* and *City of Spades.* His first novel, however, was *To the Victors the Spoils,* originally published in 1950 and closely following his own wartime experience as a sergeant in the Intelligence Corps after the Normandy Landings. His other books include *June in her Spring* and *England, Half English.* A selection of the best of his fiction and journalism is available in *Absolute MacInnes,* edited by his biographer Tony Gould and published by Allison & Busby.

Also by **Colin MacInnes**
and published by **Allison & Busby**

Absolute MacInnes: The Best of Colin MacInnes (edited by Tony Gould)
Absolute Beginners
City of Spades
Mr Love and Justice
The Colin MacInnes Omnibus (the three "London Novels" in one volume)

Colin MacInnes

To the Victors the Spoils

ALLISON & BUSBY
LONDON • NEW YORK

This edition first published 1986 by
Allison and Busby Limited,
6a Noel Street, London W1V 3RB
and distributed in the USA by
Schocken Books Inc.,
62 Cooper Square, New York, N.Y. 10003

British Library Cataloguing in Publication Data:

MacInnes, Colin
To the victors the spoils.
I. Title
823'.914[F] PR6063.A239

ISBN 0-85031-670-7
ISBN 0-85031-659-6 Pbk

Set in 10/11 Times
Printed and bound in Great Britain by
Richard Clay (The Chaucer Press) Ltd, Bungay, Suffolk

CONTENTS

PART ONE THE END OF THE LIBERATION

The Reinforcements 9
The Rehearsal 74
The Frontier 129

PART TWO BEHIND THE ADVANCE

The Rhine Villages 144
The North-German Plain 178
The Baltic City 249

PART THREE THE OCCUPATION BEGINS

The General 256
The Visitors 276
The Prison 290

TO MY BROTHER GRAHAM

TO THE VICTORS THE SPOILS

1

The End of the Liberation

THE REINFORCEMENTS

In the last days of autumn, we had moved into a house overlooking the junction of a main road and a canal. The canal, which was almost drained of water, ran north towards the provinces of Holland that were still held by the enemy. The road led eastwards to the marshes where our soldiers were fighting a German rearguard beside the Maas; but most of the enemy troops had fallen back across the river to the frontier of their country, where they had halted and turned to face our Army.

From the windows of the house, we could watch the convoys of armoured and soft vehicles which passed daily over the metal bridge that spanned the canal. This bridge wasn't wide enough for two-way traffic, and a Military Policeman stood at one end of it, signalling the vehicles east or west. At slack moments in the day he would wave to us, and we'd send him out cups of hot, sweet tea. 'Why Gerry doesn't bomb this lot is a mystery to me,' he'd say. 'In their place, I'd not hesitate. And if ever they do pay us a visit,' he'd go on, handing us back the empty mug, 'I'm coming over to join you in your cellar, if you don't object.'

Except for its being so near the bridge, our billet had many advantages. It was the largest we'd been in since we'd come into Holland, it had running water and even electric light, and the muddy remains of a garden made a parking place for all our transport. The owner, who called on us soon after our arrival, explained he'd not been able to live there himself since 1940.

'Formerly, as you can see,' he told us, waving his hand around, 'it was one of the principal residences of the town. So much so, unfortunately, that first the Germans, and now yourselves, have requisitioned it.' He paused, sensing he'd given us the wrong impression. 'Of course, I am delighted to have you here,' he went on, 'and if your soldiers, when they freed the town, also removed most of the furniture and fittings'—he gazed despondently about the room—'that is of course to be expected in time of war. But now, at least, I know responsible persons are once again in charge of it.' He looked at us encouragingly.

It was true the house was cold as well as bare, and as its three storeys were more than a dozen men needed, we tried to keep the ground floor heated, and we set up our mess and offices there. Most of the Sergeants slept in the basement, which was warmer still; and only our Lieutenant lived upstairs in a suite with a private bathroom whose pipes had frozen. But this Lieutenant had left us a week before, summoned away to Brussels in one of the transfers our Depôt there decided on from time to time. And we didn't yet know whether the new officer, whom we now expected, would prefer the communal warmth below, or the chilly solitude up above.

We were looked after by two young Dutch women who arrived early, usually before we were awake, cooked all the meals, and left late in the evening. These two had attached themselves to the Unit who'd been in the building before us, and when we'd taken it over, they had decided to stay on. Both of them were cheerful and obliging, and the only material advantage they had from working for us, was that they could take home whatever was left over after the meals; and as there was hunger in the town, this meant a lot to them and their families. They also sampled their own cooking in the kitchen, and invited friends through by the side door to share it.

It was certain they liked our company too, because we were all young, well-fed and optimistic, and we came from the world outside the occupied zone that they had long been so curious about, and with which they were now so much in love. Though the liberation of south Holland was already more than two months old, and we had taken no active part in it, they still felt for us some of the tenderness and admiration with which the Army had been greeted by civilians all the way up from France.

We were glad to be in a town again after spending the earlier part of the autumn in ruined and disconsolate villages dotted about the corridor of territory our Army held. And though the winter was bleak and most of the citizens were oppressed by uncertainty about their relatives in the north, and by the fear that the Germans might even now return, there was a lot of gaiety of a straightforward kind. The door of any house would open readily at the sight of a khaki uniform, and the local girls, wearing white knitted stockings on their pink legs, were very ready to enter into conversation and ask us home. The men in the town whose work during the occupation made them more entitled to be fêted than we were, kept quiet about what they had done. The more exuberant were in the citizen Militia, and many joined the Dutch army that was being recruited once again.

We hadn't much work to do, because most of the people we wanted to arrest had already been captured, or had fled across the river into Germany. The collaborators who were still at large were being hunted out by the Dutch Resistance, and as these pro-German groups weren't thought to be of much danger to the Army, this job was usually left to our Allies. The only fear our own Intelligence officers had was of the German agents who might still be in the area, or whom the enemy might send back over the Maas to hide among the refugees streaming out of the combat sectors on its left bank. So we were ordered to go down to the camps where the evacuated villagers were being gathered together, and question them in the hope of finding spies among them.

These camps for Displaced Persons—as they were already being called—were administered by Civil Affairs teams attached to the same Corps as ourselves. We all felt that the job we were doing in a friendly country was a preparation for the real task that lay ahead once the Army entered Germany.

I went into the office and found Norman, our Detachment clerk, rearranging the contents of his metal boxes. He was squatting on the floor among piles of military handbooks and files, and he looked up and said, 'We'll have to dump some of this stuff. It simply won't go in the boxes any longer.'

'Couldn't we get some more boxes?'

'Then they wouldn't all fit on the trucks when we come to make our next move.'

'There's still room in the trucks, isn't there?'

Norman was stout, and he crouched there with his hands between his knees and with his pale blue eyes blinking at me. He rose slowly to his feet, pulled down the front of his battle-dress blouse and said, 'Now, Mac, you know as well as I do, from previous experience, that by the time we've loaded on the petrol and rations and stores and office furniture and all the private bed-rolls and other bits and pieces everybody's begun to accumulate, there'll be no room left on the trucks for extra boxes.'

'What were you thinking of dumping, Norman?'

He pointed to a pile of documents set on one side, and I sat down and turned them over. The files related to cases the Detachment had handled in France, and there were some of the counter-Intelligence manuals which had interested us so much in England, but which we'd not consulted often since.

'We could keep the ones that refer to Germany, and burn the rest.'

'I'll do it right away, here in the stove. I've got to run this office systematically, or it might get on top of me.'

If ever any of the other Sergeants came in and asked Norman for a report, he would glance at this person and tell him to look it up in the card-indexes. The Sergeant would pretend to do so until Norman, watching him over the top of his glasses, would get up and show him how simple the system was. He kept a chart showing which of our vehicles was in or out at any time, though a glance through the window would reveal this. In a special file marked 'All to See,' he put those orders from our Staff officer at Corps headquarters, Major Benedict-Bane, which he felt to be of general interest; and he would remind us, with patient impatience, if we forgot to initial each of them.

He paused from making his bonfire and said, 'You're going in to Corps this afternoon for the pay? Then try and get some more coal, will you? We'll soon all freeze to death, otherwise.'

'I'll take Walter with me. He knows how to talk to those supply people.'

'Walter, like all old soldiers, can be very convincing when he wants to,' said Norman, dropping a manual into the fire. 'And what about the men we've sent down to the refugee camp? Do any of them need paying?'

'Only Cuthbert. He 'phoned through from there just now.'

'I wish you'd tell me these things straight away. And how do you propose getting Cuthbert's money to him?'

'I'd like to see what's going on at the camp, so I'll drive out tomorrow and take the cash there with me. I'll get the Civil Affairs Major to pay him. Will that suit you?'

'I suppose it will.' Norman tore up some more documents in silence, then looked round at me with a frown. 'When you're in at Corps,' he said, 'make sure you find out if there's any news of our new officer. It's high time an officer of some sort got posted to us here. I know you do your best, but a senior Sergeant hasn't the same authority. Some of the others take advantage of your position.'

'Oh.'

'Yes. And let's hope they send us a Captain this time, not a Lieutenant. It wasn't his fault he was a Lieutenant, but if I ring up a Unit and say, "Lieutenant So-and-So to speak to you," they're not impressed.'

'No. Well, the Depôt promised us the new officer would arrive before the Lieutenant left, didn't they?'

'The Depôt have made lots of promises. They know we've been two Sergeants under strength for a long while as well. Being short-handed means more duties for everyone and fewer evenings off, especially when we have to send out parties of men to these refugee camps.'

Norman gazed at me severely. 'True enough,' I said.

'When those two new Sergeants do come,' he went on, 'let's hope they're the right type for us. People who fit into our *esprit de corps*.'

'I hadn't noticed we had much of a one.'

'Well, your not getting on with the Lieutenant certainly didn't contribute to our morale. Before you were transferred to us in Brussels, we'd been a happy family all the way up from the beaches.'

'I've got on with the rest of you, haven't I?'

'I grant you that. But I can't see what you had against our former officer. He did his best.'

I thought about the Lieutenant, and remembered a scene that had taken place just before he was posted away from us. On one dull, late afternoon, he had sent for me to his room on the first floor; and when I'd gone in, I'd found him sitting at the table with his head on his hands, gazing out of the window. 'Sergeant,' he'd said, without looking round, 'do you know those lines that go "Tomorrow, and tomorrow, and tomorrow rolls on this dreary life from day to day?" Well,' he'd continued, turning round and staring at me, 'that's what I feel when I sit here, looking out on that empty canal.'

The trouble was I couldn't take him seriously. When a man is put in authority over you, there has to be an almost animal relationship between the two of you that makes you feel it is natural he should tell you what to do. But the Lieutenant, who had none of the magic needed in a leader, felt he owed it to his background to become one; and patterning his conduct on that of the regulars, he tried to outdo them in dash and confident assurance. Everyone who served with him soon realised this, and most of our men were nice about it, playing the parts his imagination had assigned to them. But I would needle him whenever the conflict between his aspirations and his capacity put him in a false position; and this was often.

So our relations had grown sour. In a larger Unit, with stricter discipline, he could have kept me in place. But in a small Detachment like our own, he was so dependent on his senior Sergeant that there wasn't much he could do, particularly as he messed with us, and had no brother officer to support him.

At meal times, we would have acrimonious discussions on topics about which neither of us knew much. My vindictive insolence would come further into the open, until he'd get red in the neck and sit glaring moodily at his plate. Then he would suddenly get up and say, 'I've decided these subjects will not be discussed any further in the mess,' and there would be an awkward silence round the table.

When we rode together in a vehicle, we would sometimes have an open argument. 'The trouble about you,' I'd tell him, 'is that you take on too much for yourself and never finish anything you begin.'

'And if you want to know what the trouble with you is,' he'd answer, gripping the steering-wheel, 'you're afraid to take responsibility. You like to have your own way and try to get me to do things you want done so that you can claim the credit if they succeed, and shelter behind me if they don't come off.' And we would lapse into a spiteful silence as the car sped along in the flat country.

But now I was wondering whether, when the new officer came, it might not be a change for the worse. I hoped that if he was the man who would be taking us all into Germany, he would know how to get a firm grip from the start, and perhaps have a pleasant nature as well.

Walter was in the garden, tinkering with his truck, and he turned to reveal his bony features with their friendly, menacing expression.

'We've got a job on, Walter,' I said.

'Who has?'

'You and I. We're going up to Corps in your truck for the pay and one or two other things.'

'Can't you go in your utility? I've got an inspection of this vehicle coming off in a day or two's time.'

'We're short of coal and the utility's too small.'

'Coal? They'll never give you any of that, you know. They keep it all to heat the headquarter messes.'

'That's why I want you to come too. You'll talk to them as one old soldier to another.'

Walter put his hands in the pockets of the twill breeches that encased his lean legs, and gave me a condescending smile. 'So I am of some use to you?' he said. 'Even though I don't know French or Dutch or ancient Greek?'

Walter was our only regular, and he treated the rest of us with cordial scorn, though this had diminished slightly since his first arrival among us from the Guards. Then he had made us feel that men as ignorant as we of military etiquette, and who'd never known what a bake it was in India, hadn't really any business to be campaigning at all. But when he saw he would have to deal with civilian officials who didn't always speak English, he reluctantly admitted that even our most makeshift, bespectacled Sergeants had an advantage over him. And he had begun to take German lessons from one of them, so as to be sure that when it came to dealing with the enemy, he wouldn't be handicapped in telling them what to do.

'Put some rations in the truck,' I said, 'and we'll call at one of the farms and trade them for vegetables.'

'So you've made up your mind I'm coming with you?'

'Well, are you?'

Walter grinned. 'About that coal, Mac,' he said. 'Would you be satisfied with coke? I've heard where there's a lot of it in an abandoned Gerry camp down near the river.'

'Do you know how to get there?'

'Yes, I expect so. We could go and have a look.'

'Well, so long as it's abandoned.'

'Oh, definitely. We don't want to start a private war, do we.'

We drove out of the front gate and took the cobbled road beside the canal. Walter's legs were wrapped round the steering column, and he swayed with the motion of the truck, as though he were driving a bobsleigh.

'What you need, you know,' he told me, 'is an experienced man to act as quartermaster permanently. Take him off all other work.'

'You mean yourself?'

'Oh, no. I've quite enough to do as it is, in charge of all the transport.'

'Well, there is no experienced man, apart from you.'

'That's just it. You're all too easy. The crafty sods that issue the stores and rations see you coming, and know they can blind you with science.'

'Perhaps one of the new men we're expecting will be able to take it over.'

'Perhaps—but they'll most likely be some more of these Masters of Arts they keep sending us.'

'There isn't a Master of Arts among us.'

'Well, nicely educated kiddies, I mean, with no common sense.'

'Listen, Walter. To do Intelligence work may need educated kiddies.'

'That remains to be seen. But I don't imagine Norman or Cuthbert or some of the other lads putting the fear of death into the Gestapo, do you? I tell you. I'd give a month's pay for every Gerry agent young Cuthbert and his crew catch down at the refugee camp. What's needed for that is less dead languages and a bit more savvy.'

'That's why they posted you to us as well.'

We passed through one of the villages, so like the others we had been in earlier on. Those that were undamaged were dull and rather shapeless, with little model estates on the outskirts that had a temporary appearance. Somewhere in the centre there would be a baroque Madonna, surrounded by an iron grille. And the wet, flat fields lay all round the edge of the outer houses like a grey-green lake seeping gently into the back yards.

As we drove by a gang of Dutchmen mending the road,

Walter nodded at them and said, 'They're a tired lot. They don't over-exert themselves. We come here and liberate them and pay them Army rates, and do they care?'

'We didn't come here to liberate them. We came up into Holland because the German Army retreated there. The liberation was incidental.'

'Oh? We're called the Liberation Army, aren't we? And you can't get away from the fact that we set them free, and all they do is lean on their shovels and take our money.'

'Have you ever known anyone do a day's work in the Army like a civilian has to?'

He laughed at me. 'A soldier's on duty twenty-four hours in the day.'

'So I've often heard. And most of that time he's swilling tea or lying on his back.'

'Not in peace time he wasn't. War's a bit different, I admit.'

We had reached a smashed village near the edge of the combat area. The newly ruined houses had an ashamed, pathetic look, and the outrage that had been done to them was emphasised by the presence of a really venerable ruin—a large red-brick castle, whose smoothly broken walls were half hidden with creepers; and which, nestling snugly into an oily, leaf-covered moat, gave a contrasting impression of age-old, self-satisfied resignation.

At the top of a grassy track, we saw a group of soldiers gathered against the horizon and, beyond them, a jumble of wooden huts beside a forest. They were Engineers, dismantling a German gun. Walter raised his voice above the clink of the metal. 'What about this camp? Is it mined?'

They waited for one another to answer. A Corporal said, 'Not so far as we know, matey.'

'Have you seen anyone going in there?'

'Oh, yes. They didn't say anything about mines.'

We drove through the gate, and stopped at the edge of a clearing. Dead horses lay around, looking enormous on the ground. We walked gingerly over to the first hut. The sound of the dismantlers could be heard from not far off.

Walter kicked open a door. Wooden beds and straw mattresses were lying about in heaps, and there were large piles of coke.

'So long as old Gerry doesn't send out patrols this far.'

'There's still a lot of stuff between us and them, isn't there?'

We started loading.

The 'lot of stuff' there was between ourselves and the enemy were the fighting troops and their armour. Technically, we, too, were 'fighting troops,' but none of us, except for Walter, had ever fired a shot at anyone or had to defend himself.

Of the soldiers on the continent at that time, there were those who were stationed with rear formations, along the lines of communication with the sea, who read about the progress of the war when the newspapers reached them from England. Then there were those, like ourselves, who were attached to a Corps or a Division, just behind the combat area. We were near enough to the enemy to see something of what was going on, but far enough to be out of harm's way.

And then there were the fighting troops, who lived in a different world of which most of us knew nothing. When we met them while they were resting out of the line, we noticed how they kept together and seemed to regard the life we led as being cut off from a greater reality. If we drove up among them to the forward areas they were quite friendly, but they made us feel there were secrets which could be known only to those who shared their existence. As we looked at them from the comfort of our soft vehicles and clean clothing, their eyes returned our glance and said, 'We don't hold it against you that you're not here with us, it's all a matter of how you're posted and it might have happened to you. But since it hasn't, don't try to understand what you can't.' Most of us admired them, and even envied them; but this, half-heartedly.

They, at any rate, knew the German army in an intimate, physical way, while to us it remained an unknown juggernaut, badly shaken, but still the object of foreboding.

So we hurried to load the coke and looked curiously at the printed notices in German that were nailed up on the walls. It seemed that a Band Unit had been living there at one time, for dirtied scores of military music were lying about on the floor.

The dismantling team had disappeared by the time we drove out, and passing by the end of the last hut we saw large German words chalked hurriedly up on its wooden wall: 'We shall come back again,' they said.

Before we took the road on to Corps, we started looking out for a farm we could stop at to get vegetables. We picked out one that stood by itself among brown furrows and thin trees, and which seemed to have no Army vehicles near it.

Walter got out the box we'd filled with tins of unpopular rations, and we went into the farmhouse. A family of children gathered round us, and Walter talked pidgin English, smiling and telling them about himself and his own home. They seemed interested, and coming to within two feet of him, stood staring intently at his face.

The farmer didn't care for what we had to offer, and tried to persuade us to part with some petrol. But this was contrary to Walter's code; the rations were personal property, but petrol belonged to the Army. So we compromised on tins of meat and sugared tea in exchange for potatoes and red cabbages.

I asked the farmer whether he'd been troubled by the Germans. He answered guardedly, but gave the impression he hadn't altogether disapproved of them. They had bought his produce at good prices, but now he was being told to hand it over for a fixed sum. 'Yes, it will be well when the war is ended,' he said. 'It is not easy for us with your camps and gear all over our barns and fields.'

Walter was indignant when we started off again. 'There you are,' he said, 'it's just as I told you. That swede's more interested in selling his turnips than in who wins the war. What a mentality.'

As we got nearer to the village where Corps was located, we were held up by convoys of vehicles, many of which had been strangely altered throughout the autumn. Some of the trucks had been designed for Spartans, with seats open to the winds. So the drivers had enclosed their cabs with three-ply, and even built caravans onto the body-work behind. In England, all these vehicles belonged to a Unit, not to individuals. But during the campaign, the drivers must have felt a growing affection for the trucks that housed and carried them; and to show that each had now its personality, they had painted the names of their wives or girls over the windscreens.

Authority had tried to stop them at first. But as happened in so many ways once the Army was in movement, the men found out how far they could go in adapting peacetime regulations to their advantage. Sometimes their innovations were sanctioned by custom, so that a modified discipline came into being, a compromise between Army rules and the longing for comfort and freedom of the soldiers. And now we understood why veterans in barracks at home had been so restive, and had spoken with such regret of past campaigns. In conditions of war, they fought it out with King's Regulations on equal terms, and could feel the debt the Army owed them, was repaid.

'We might call on the Camp Commandant and see about those leather jerkins,' I said, as we drove into Corps headquarters.

'Did he promise you some?'

'More or less, he did.'

'I don't fancy your chances with the Camp Comedian. He's only interested in headquarter troops.'

The Camp Commandant had a well-scrubbed face and a brisk, impatient manner that hinted at big tasks from which your visit had disturbed him. As some mothers address you indirectly by speaking to their babies, so did he repeat our request to his office clerks, calling loudly for their comments which they forebore to give, preferring a sycophantic smile.

'Now what do you think of this?' he asked them, in tones of ponderous astonishment. 'Here's two Sar'nts come asking me for leather jerkins of all things, when they of all people ought to know how difficult to get they are.' Then he wheeled on us. 'No,' he shouted, 'not for you. Fighting troops come first.'

Walter swallowed and stood his ground. 'Meaning what, Sir?'

'Meaning what I say. People like you can wait your turn.'

'You mentioned fighting troops, Sir. That's something I know a bit about, as it happens.'

'Do you want to start an argument, son? There's no call to flash a Palestine ribbon at me, I've got one myself. You're not in the line just now, remember.'

'I'm not alone in that, Sir.'

'Look. Run along, will you? I don't want to lose my temper with you. I might say something I'd regret.'

He gazed at us with pitying distaste, and Walter, feeling he'd gone too near the edge, began to head the conversation off on a meaningless tangent in a way that amounted to an apology; his tone apologised, if not the words he used. Hearing his assured and soothing voice, the Camp Commandant began to listen, and his rage subsided. 'Well, I dunno, I'll see what I can do,' he said, as we went out.

'A nice old bullshitter,' Walter told me. 'Still, I was wrong to argue. Never argue, that's the golden rule. Agree with all they say, and then do what you wanted to.'

'I'm going over to the Intelligence office now. Will you call at the Pay Corps for the cash?'

'I'll do that. And when that nasty article's gone for his tea, I'll drop back there and talk to his quarter-bloke. They've got bags of those jerkins. He'll give me some, or else.'

Walter drove off in the truck, and I walked along the curved streets of the village. The dim lights of the passing cars were caught by the white skirts of the Dutch girls strolling arm in arm up the middle of the road, or standing talking to groups of soldiers in the friendly gloom. I opened the gate of the Staff officer's billet and went through the front door into the room that was used as an office. 'Hullo, Harry,' I said to the clerk who was sitting alone there.

'Oh, it's you. A signal's come through from Brussels this afternoon about your new officer. He's on his way up tomorrow, and they're sending you the two Sergeants this week as well.'

'I'll believe it when I see them. Any other news?'

'Well, no . . but did you hear some Gerry pockets this side of the Maas have been counter-attacking?'

'So we won't be going over the river just yet.'

'Not till the spring, I don't suppose. That'll suit me, though, I shan't complain.'

'You like it in this dump, then?'

'Well, it was better when Corps headquarters was in that town where you are . . . and that reminds me. You're taking us in there this evening, please. Me and the Major—his car's in workshops. Do you want to see him?'

He knocked on the door to the next room and beckoned me through. Major Bane was telephoning, and he smiled and waved me to a chair. I was struck by his round, boyish face, which was even redder and more swollen than usual. He saw me looking at it during a break in his conversation, and putting his hand over the mouthpiece, said, 'Good evening, Sergeant. Excuse my flushed appearance. There was a bit of a party last night.' Then he went on telephoning.

Major Benedict-Bane was born to a staff job, for in addition to his natural gifts, he had all the instincts of a courtier. In spite of his youth, he could simulate the gravity of an older man, and he had just the right mixture of deference and eager bonhomie when dealing with his superiors. But he also paid court to those below him. To us he was always affable, he listened patiently to what we had to say and gave a prompt decision of some sort to all the problems we brought him. But though he was such an agreeable man to work for, he gave the strong impression of a complete indifference to any of us as individuals.

He put down the receiver.

'I've got good news for you, if it is good news,' he said. 'I'll be sending you down to Belgium in a few days.'

'Oh, really? How's that, Sir?'

'The Corps's taken over a small chunk of territory down there, and I have to send one of the Detachments. I thought of yours.'

'Well, it'll be a change to be back in Belgium again.'

'That's what I thought. Mind you, I don't want to paint your prospects in too glowing colours. I mean, it's a rather dreary area of country you'll be going to, just over the Dutch frontier. Not like the fleshpots of Brussels. Still, the beer will be better.'

'We'll remember to bring you up some.'

'I'll hold you to that. Now, you've heard about your new officer? No name signalled, so I don't know who it is. However, when he arrives, I'll tell him how lucky he is to be going to you.'

'That's very nice of you, Sir.'

'Not a bit. And have you any worries? What about this refugee camp? Any arrests?'

A slight gleam came into Major Bane's frank and treacherous eyes. 'None so far,' I said. 'We've only just started there.'

'Well, that's all right . . . Ferret them out, though . . .' The gleam was switched off. 'And Sergeant,' he went on. 'You're taking me and my clerk in to town this evening, aren't you? If you hang on about half an hour, I'll be with you.'

I went back to the outer office, and found Harry polishing his shoes with one foot up on the chair. 'Shoes?' I said. 'Where did you get them from?'

He looked up and smiled. 'I had a week-end in in Brussels.'

'How are things in Brussels, now?'

'Oh, it's all highly organised, Army signs everywhere, and they've even brought the Women's Services over. It's changed a lot from how it was the first few days we got there.'

'You weren't in Brussels then, were you?'

'Oh yes, I was. They only posted me to this mob when the Battalion was moving up to Holland.'

'Were you on the same job in the Battalion?'

'Me? A clerk? I don't know a thing about it. No, I'm a despatch rider, by rights. But one day it was, "Three volunteers, you and you and you," the usual caper, and they attached me here as a clerk on loan. But I still go out on the bike.'

'So you were in Brussels on the first day.'

'No, no, the second. What a sight, I'll never forget it. You couldn't do a thing wrong . . . Well, I mean they were so glad to see you. Wherever you went, the kids took hold of your hands and the women wouldn't even leave you alone at all. I thought it was just they were a bit excited, but it was more than that, it was like as if they'd been waiting for us all their lives. I was only there three days, but it was worse the third day than the first.'

'What do you mean, "worse"?'

'Well, I mean better. Do you know? They were buying you drinks all the time, offering you meals and hot baths, and one place I went to, they made me stop the night—the women there, there were two of them. One sang songs all to herself, and the other one, the fair one, she wore carnations in her hair and cut all the Unit signs off my battledress and sewed them onto her sleeves. I had a lot of trouble replacing them afterwards.'

'Did you see her again this time?'

'Well yes, I did, but it was different. For one thing, her husband had come back, but it wasn't only that. It was the way she looked me over. The first time I was there, I couldn't do anything wrong.'

He had stopped polishing, and gazed ruminatively at the wall.

'Some of them seem to think the war's ended now,' he went on. 'They've started to charge you for everything, and when I was buying these shoes the man said, "Well, how soon are the English going to export us their wonderful shoes again?" You see what I mean? And of course, they're getting short of food . . Well, you can't blame them, I suppose.'

Walter came in, carrying two leather jerkins over one arm. 'The best I could do,' he said. 'Hullo, Harry, what are you dressing yourself up for? Are you coming in to town to see your girl?'

'As a matter of fact, I am.'

'I don't blame you, my lad. Mind you behave yourself, though.'

When we started off, Major Bane got up beside Walter in the cab, and I rode with Harry among the coke and cabbages. 'It's just near your billet where this girl of mine lives,' he said. 'Her father's in charge of the lock there—do you know the house?'

'Yes, I know it. I think I've seen your girl, too. She's fair and wears a pink woollen sweater—is that her? I've seen her going by.'

'That's right, on her way to the Town Hall. She works there.'

'Have you known her long?'

'Well, I met her when Corps used to be in the town. Since we moved down here I've got the Major to let me come in on evenings I'm not on duty.'

'You see her quite a lot, then.'

'Yes, I do. I told him I might be marrying her. You never know.'

'What did Major Bane say to that?'

'He says there's no objection, I mean he was best man himself to one of the Staff officers who married a Dutch girl. He said I'd probably get permission, but in his opinion, I'm too young. So I told him if I was old enough to be at Dunkirk, I was old enough to get married. I've been in the Army longer than he has.'

'Were you at Dunkirk, Harry?'

'Yes. I was a National Service victim.'

'I didn't know that.'

'Yes, I've been in since '39.'

'And you haven't asked her yet.'

'No, not yet I haven't.'

'Would her parents agree?'

'Oh, yes, they're all for it, you can see that. I haven't said anything to them, though. There's my own folk too, of course. My Dad would be all right, but my mother doesn't care for foreigners. She doesn't see everybody's a foreigner to somebody. Well, I expect I'll make up my mind about it.'

We were nearing the outskirts of the town, and at the Officers' Club, Walter slowed down to drop Major Bane. 'Thanks for the ride, I'll make my own way home,' he cried out. 'Good evening to you all.'

When we went on again, Harry said, 'I'll tell you what you

could do for me, though. I want to take them in something this evening. I've got my fags and chocolate, but could you let me have some tinned stuff if you've got it to spare?'

'Yes, if you stop off at the billet, we'll fix you up.'

'You couldn't give them a bit of this coke, could you?'

'Yes, I expect so. I'll run some of it round there for you after supper.'

'Thanks. Some of the other lads that come in there evenings always take them a lot of stuff.'

When I went into the kitchen later on to get the tins for Harry, I found an argument going on. Norman, who was helping our two Dutch women wash up, was trying to prove to them that Belgium was a gayer place than Holland. The younger one, a serious, dark-eyed girl, had put down her dish-mop in her eagerness to refute him and stood wiping her hands on her apron, waiting for the moment to break into Norman's self-confident flow. The other woman, a jovial potential spinster, was taking little part and smiling at them both.

'You cannot judge things as they are with us now,' the dark girl exclaimed. 'Here is all ruin and disaster, while in Belgium, so much was spared.'

'Yes, yes,' said Norman, 'I grant you that . . .'

'If you had known Amsterdam and Rotterdam before the bombing and hunger, you would not say as you do.'

'Oh yes, we all know you've had a bad time of it. But everyone round here's got such a long face, they're so solemn about it all.'

'Solemn faces?' the older one broke in. 'Why! Prior to the war, here in Brabant, or Limburg, were considered gayest parts of Holland by our soldiers. They were delighted to do their service here. It is in the north perhaps that the faces are longer.'

'They must be quite a length, then.'

The dark girl took Norman by the sleeve.

'Listen to me, young man,' she said. 'The Belgians are very delightful people, but they are not serious. They may be gayer perhaps, but they are also sly and not responsible persons, you must remember. They throw some flowers on you, but will not give correct change to a banknote. With us, it is the other way about.'

She spoke quite heatedly. 'Well it takes all sorts to make a world,' Norman conceded.

I got the tins and went out to Walter's truck, on which we'd left some of the coke. Then I drove a hundred yards along the canal to the lock-keeper's house. He was on the *qui vive* for my arrival, and came into the yard before I'd got out of the car. After shaking me by the hand, he began carrying the coke over to a shed. 'Better to be prudent,' he said. 'Civilians have been in trouble for taking stores from you soldiers.'

'This isn't Army coke.'

'No doubt. But how could I prove that to an official?'

When I saw him in the light, he was a weather-beaten man with cropped hair and a self-effacing manner. He took me into the living-room. The mother, a well-padded woman in a dark brown dress, was sitting knitting in a leather arm-chair. Harry and the girl were together on the sofa, looking through a pile of magazines she held on her lap. Two other soldiers were playing solo whist with her elder sister at the table; and after he had introduced me round, the father went and joined them again.

The mother handed me a cup of tea. 'Then you are one of those who cause all the noise in the big house?' she said. 'But when the Germans had dances there, it was an even greater noise.'

'Did they have many dances?'

'At first yes, but later not, owing to difficulty in finding partners. Some German girls there were, of course, but few of the local people. All through the occupation our girls could not go dancing, you see. That is why they are so fond of it at present.'

'Do your daughters like dancing?'

'Oh, yes, both my daughters like it, but also to sit quietly at home,' she told me, glancing at Harry and the younger girl.

Sitting side by side on the sofa, they were turning over the pages of the magazines and teaching each other their languages by pointing to the photographs. He had one of those faces that are nondescript and rather shapeless, and tranquil because of an habitual certainty as to what to do and how to behave. She was fair and pink and wonderfully material, like a lot of the girls round there, but she still had the freshness of one not yet worn by a long succession of similar days. Her lower lip hung open with pleasure as she listened to him, for Harry, as the man and the Englishman, was doing most of the teaching. He had a preoccupied, sensual expression, and it was clear that their low, steady chatter about photographs and languages was the outward form of deeper thoughts they were exchanging. Sometimes they both spoke at once with serious faces, not listening to each other, or listening only to the sound each other made. With their heads touching and hair just mingling, their occasional smiles and sudden upward, identical glances showed that they had withdrawn from the rest of the room into the warmth of their own proximity.

The game of solo whist came noisily to an end, and the father got up and cried, 'Well now, refreshments for all these young people.'

Harry took the magazines off the girl's knees and they got up too. 'We're going out for a bit of a walk, Ma,' he said.

'But there is now to be food and drink,' the mother told him.

'We won't be long. Just up to the bridge and back.'

They put on their coats and scarves, stood a moment in the doorway, holding hands, then waved and said they'd soon be back. There was a short silence after they'd gone out, as though some felt older, some anxious, some half envious, and yet as though in everybody's mind there was a part of happiness and agreement.

'Now, the cakes and sandwiches and fresh tea,' the lock-keeper said.

The women brought them in, and we all sat round the table. The mother kept the plates replenished, and when the other daughter handed the soldiers cups of tea, saying 'Just the job?' in English, and gazing expectantly at their faces, they both nodded and laughed with tolerant approval. It was evident they were regular visitors and perfectly at home there, and that they regarded it as natural they should be made much of; and perhaps it was this assurance and almost animal friendliness towards those strange to them, that increased the pleasure these Dutch people clearly felt in having them.

Most soldiers had this homing instinct for finding themselves a family who would wash their socks, cook them fried potatoes and listen admiringly to their conversation. The fellowship of an Army billet, so attractive by the possibilities it gave for the rapid growth of friendship, was blighted by the absence of women which makes a soldier's sentimental life both rich and arid. So when their Unit came to a new village, the men would find a fireside to which they could transfer their longing for their own. It was best if there were girls there, but other important elements were the presence of an alien version of Mum, the dispenser of cups of tea and uncritical kindness, and the measured, soothing and fuggy rhythm of a friendly family inside its home.

Coming down to breakfast next morning, I was surprised to find Cuthbert sitting alone at the table, dressed in his motorcycling kit and drinking tea. 'You're in a hurry for your pay, Cuthbert, aren't you? Didn't I tell you I'd bring it out to you at the refugee camp this morning?'

He looked at me solemnly. 'It's not on account of pay I came in here so early to see you. It's because there's been a big scare I thought you ought to hear about right away. I've just this minute arrived.'

'What scare?'

'German armour has been advancing towards the camp. We were all up half the night. I tried to 'phone you, but the fighting troops were monopolising the camp lines.'

'Which fighting troops?'

'Our armour that's been moved up to hold the Germans.'

'Are they holding them?'

'It would seem like it. But nobody could tell us for sure how near the Germans are. So the point is, whether we should stay down there or not. I discussed it with the others, and as you put me in charge of them, I thought I'd better come in at once on my bike and ask your opinion.'

Cuthbert's candid red face, surmounted by its fair, curly hair, was wearing its customary expression of a man used to finding his own conscience clear. And his small, compact body, draped in an outsize waterproof coat that trailed upon the floor, was bent forward towards me, hands planted on the knees, in the posture of one who has done his duty, and waits for you to do yours.

'What about the Civil Affairs people?' I said. 'Have they any instructions what to do if enemy troops get near the camp?'

'I went and saw Major Parsons, who as you know's in charge of them, as soon as the scare started to develop. He told me he hadn't the faintest idea what was happening, that nobody had told him to evacuate the camp, and until they did, he was going to stay there. He seemed very calm.'

'Did you ask the fighting troops?'

'Yes, I spoke to a Lieutenant. He said he thought it was a false alarm. But in my experience, the fighting troops usually don't know what they're doing themselves, or if they do, won't tell you.' Cuthbert paused. 'So the question is, Mac, what those of us who are stuck down there should do.'

There was an as yet unspoken thought at the back of our minds: if we were taken prisoner, we would be handed over to the Gestapo, or its military equivalent, as soon as they found we were doing the same work as themselves.

'If you think there's danger of the Germans over-running the camp,' I said, 'make sure you get out in time.'

'You mean leave before Civil Affairs? Shouldn't we at least stay on as long as them? We may be doing Intelligence work, but we're still soldiers.'

'You could tell that to Himmler if you meet him.'

'But how would the enemy know what we're doing at the camp?'

'Apart from anything else, some of the refugees you've been questioning would be sure to tell them. So remember. You're to come back here at once if there's a serious threat.'

Cuthbert blinked once or twice and said, 'As a matter of fact, we had a consultation about it down there, and the others agreed with me that would be the right course.'

'We'd better get down to the camp now.'

As we walked out to the car park, I asked him if they'd found any suspects yet among the refugees.

'There's been nothing positive to date,' he told me. 'But we have to check several hundreds through a day, and we can't spend more than a few minutes on each. Some collaborators have been denounced to us, no doubt from motives of personal spite, and there are certain people, as usual, who nobody knows and who can't account for themselves. But so far we've discovered no positive cases of infiltration.'

'And apart from this scare, our Sergeants are getting on all right, are they?'

'Oh, yes. I've worked out a method of work. We take it in turns, two on at a time, one asking questions and the other stamping documents. You'll see.'

He climbed onto his bike, and I got into the utility. There was a traffic block at the canal, but Cuthbert edged through it and shot off ahead at a furious speed. Once over the bridge, I took the road leading straight through a long, sodden wood towards the Maas. When the car had begun to drive itself, my thoughts followed Cuthbert from afar.

He was one of those men who are honest not because they have overcome their vices, but because they hardly have any to overcome or, at all events, none of which they are themselves aware. It was not so much that he was above wrong-doing, as that it didn't interest him.

He had all sorts of ideas about life, the war and the work we were doing—most of which struck me as ignorant and ungenerous, when not footling. But as both of us were surrounded by men who were doing things more than thinking about what they were doing, we were sometimes drawn together like gnostics among a crowd of unbelievers. Sterile arguments resulted. With a frustrated longing to talk to anyone who'd listen, I was encouraged by the very blankness on his face to pour my ideas out all the more emphatically. Cuthbert, who regarded an 'idea' advanced by another as a sort of ticket entitling him to their silence for an equivalent length of time, would then put forward an irrelevant proposition of his own.

His positive points were that he was persistent, never bore malice, and that his spirits always stood at the same buoyant, predictable level. All this gave him a tortoise-like strength.

I had reached the village near which the camp was located, and passing by some fields with tanks embedded in them, turned off down a sandy track lined with firs. Skirting a line of huts, I came out on the camp's enormous central square. Crowds of refugees were wandering all over it in an aimless, dejected way. Of those who turned to watch me, some looked resigned, but others gave me a hostile glance of reproof. Their eyes said clearly, 'All this should be an affair between soldiers. Wars should take place far away from home.'

I went over to the reception hall. Cuthbert, who had arrived some time before me, was sitting there with two other young Sergeants behind a trestle table. Beside them were piles of forms, a stack of identity cards, some rubber stamps and pads, a packet of labels and several cartons of powdered insecticide.

Cuthbert rose and stared unblinkingly at me as I came up.

His expression invited the words, 'Well done, thou good and faithful servant,' but I said, 'The camp looks fairly normal to me. Is everything under control in here?'

'Yes, I think I can say so. Though there's not much to control for the moment. No more refugees are expected now until this afternoon.'

'Is this the new method you've got going? What are all these lists?'

'These? They're Nominal Rolls. We write down the names and particulars here, and then in the Remarks column, we put an A, D or X.'

He looked up.

'Go on,' I said.

'A means—seems all right. D's are doubtful; X's, suspect.'

'And how do you tell which is which?'

He looked at me with the kind smile of one who has detected a frivolous question, and said, 'By checking whether their documents are in order and whether they have anyone who can vouch for them.'

'And suppose two friends arrive with forged papers and vouch for each other?'

'We also go by whether they make a favourable impression on us.'

'And if they don't, they get an X?'

'Or a D, as the case may be.'

'You don't give them an A unless you like their personalities.'

'We don't pretend to be infallible, but as I've already explained, we haven't got much to go on.'

'And what happens to the D's and X's?'

'If there's time, we have them back and ask them questions and make out reports about them for Corps. We also stamp their identity cards to show we've seen them.'

'To show who?'

'To show anyone. Anyone who interrogates them subsequently will get in touch with Corps to see our reports, or should do.'

'You're like Gabriel, Cuthbert. You know how to separate the sheep from the goats.'

'There's no need to make a remark of that kind, Mac. Your method, as far as I could see when you were here the other day, was to wave everybody by and just talk to whoever happened to interest you personally. That may be less exhausting, but at least we're trying to make a serious attempt.'

'And what's all this insecticide for?'

'To spray new arrivals with. The Red Cross do it, of course, not us.'

'How do they do it?'

'The sexes are split up, stripped down, and the powder applied to them and their clothes with a sort of bellows.'

'And these huge labels?'

'They're supposed to wear them round their necks. But most of them lose them.'

'I'm glad to hear it. Look, here's the Major. Perhaps he'll be able to tell us what's going on.'

Major Parsons, who was now coming into the hall, was a large-limbed, big-featured man who affected a blunt and friendly manner to all comers. Like many of the officers in Civil Affairs, he had been transferred there directly from the Police force, without having first been processed in the military machine. As a consequence, he had none of the hauteur with which conscript officers sometimes masked their lack of conviction about themselves, and he treated you openly as one disguised civilian to another. But his friendliness was of a professional kind, it proceeded from cunning, not good nature. It was the bedside manner of the Station Sergeant to whom you have come to report the theft of a bicycle and who, as he blinks and grins at you amiably, makes you realise uneasily that he thinks you have stolen it yourself.

'Well now, Sarge,' he said, as soon as he saw me. 'What is it we can do for you today?'

'What about this flap, Sir? Is there anything in it?'

'I couldn't really tell, laddie. My Staff officers never know what the fighting troops are up to any more than I suppose your own do either.'

'So we're staying put here, are we?'

'I am —yes. But judging from my seeing one of your young Sergeants haring off to the rear area on his bike early this morning, I take it you people may be thinking of pulling out.'

He shot us all a glance of frankly-revealed duplicity that was probably intended to mask deeper layers of guile that lay beyond.

'Oh no, Sir,' I said. 'We'll be around so long as the Germans aren't.'

He nodded; and coming up to the trestle table, put his hands in his pockets and rested his belly against the edge of it. 'And how's the snooping been going?' he said. 'Found any Gerry spies yet? Don't forget now, if you do, send them over to me. I'll know what to do with them.'

'According to you, Sir, there's only one kind of good German, isn't there,' I said.

'Oh, I know you're another of these Hun-lovers, Sarge, but you weren't in Flanders in '14-'18, were you. As for our young friend here,' he went on, pointing at Cuthbert, 'he knows better, he knows they're a bad lot, but the trouble is, he imagines he can cure them.'

Cuthbert said patiently, 'All I've maintained is that there's no disease, however bad, that hasn't got a remedy.'

'And you're going to be the doctor are you, son?' said the Major, winking, grinning and nodding at the rest of us. 'Well, mind you know the difference between a sick man and a malingerer.'

All this was a reference to a discussion we'd had during my last visit to the camp, about 'what we were going to do with the Germans.' Major Parsons had been for killing them, Cuthbert for bringing them up to his own level, and I had spoken against both solutions, without putting forward an alternative. Everyone had assumed they'd have a free hand, and that the Germans were made of putty.

Now Major Parsons, suddenly looking serious and severe, asked, 'Are my copies of those lists of yours ready for me yet?'

'Not quite yet, Sir,' Cuthbert said.

'I'd like them over at the office in time for my outgoing mail, you know.' He turned to me. 'Perhaps you'd bring them to me, would you, Sarge? There's one or two further points I'd like to have a bit of a chat with you on.' He averted his eyes, gave us a wave with the whole of his arm and went off towards the door.

Cuthbert told the other Sergeants he'd finish the lists himself. 'And to think Civil Affairs are going to become the Military Government when we get to Germany,' he said to me, as soon as we were alone. 'Well, I don't like the Germans, and I believe they should be punished, but I must say persons of Major Parsons' type are a most unsuitable choice to govern them.

The Germans have a lot to answer for, but it's useless hating them like he does. One should never hate; one should try to understand, so that one can judge them fairly.'

'Are you going to understand the Germans, Cuthbert?'

'I shall try to. I know you think that having once lived there, you've got a monopoly of understanding them. But despite all they've done, I've an open mind and some confidence in my own powers of judgment. More, at any rate, than I have in Major Parsons'. Why pick such a man?'

'It's probably thought policemen make good governors.'

He paused from his writing and reflected. 'I suppose in a sense they do, the more suitable ones.'

'The Germans have been governed by policemen for the last twelve years, and it hasn't done them much good.'

'Yes, but by German policemen. Their methods are different from ours.'

'Oh, quite different. You wait and see.'

He shook his head. 'You're always telling me to wait and see when you can't prove your point.'

I left the hall, and went out onto the gravel square. Herded together in the huts with a few cooking pots and with their animals tethered outside, the villagers looked even more uprooted than townspeople might do, even further removed from their natural rhythm. Dwellers in cities may feel that they are lodgers anyway, and the camp might have been for them another inconvenient halting-place. But these farmers looked undignified and despoiled.

I followed some of them into one of the huts. There was no furniture, but families had marked themselves out little territories on the floor. It was soon possible to see what areas were left for general congregation, and others to go into which you would have to knock at an imaginary door.

As I was passing one young family, the woman called out to me and came hurrying over. 'Now listen, Mister,' she said, standing in front of me and taking hold of my arm. And she began to explain, in an insistent, dogged fashion, how I must take a letter for them to an address of relatives they had in our town. 'Then, you see, if they will receive us, we shall go and live with them instead of remaining in this camp.' She told me this as though I would benefit by the arrangement, and as if she considered me to be under an obligation to them.

She led me over to their sector of the room. Her husband stood looking as if he felt useless, and angry about this, and there were three dirty children mixed up with a heap of belongings on the floor. 'Now let Mister have the letter,' she said to him, but he stared at me suspiciously, and handed her the letter to give me. When I'd taken it, he looked me over a bit more, then got down a sack from a hook and pulled out a string of onions. 'Yes, take them,' he insisted.

His wife began telling me more about their troubles, and she was intensely preoccupied with the cottage they had had to leave, and with what they could have done to deserve it all. A child with a cross, lethargic face climbed onto her knees, and she kept brushing its scanty hair into a gnome's curl up the middle of its head. Her husband listened admiringly as she confided in me without pausing for breath, watching the other children out of the corner of her eye.

I went out again onto the square, and saw files of refugees climbing slowly onto the lorries that were parked there. Cuthbert came up with the completed copies of the Nominal Rolls, and stood beside me, watching them. 'Yes, they all ask when they can go back home,' he said, 'but the plan is to evacuate them even further west for the present. This is only a transit camp, you see.'

We went up closer and saw them huddled promiscuously together, grabbing hold of one another as the lorries jolted off.

'Poor sods,' I said, 'it's not very nice for them.'

'They've certainly had a raw deal, poor people, but everyone's doing all they can for them. And I must say, it's been a bit disappointing to see they don't show much signs of gratitude.'

'For what?'

'For our evacuating them to safety.'

'It's a military measure. Left to themselves, they'd have stayed on at their farms, fighting or no fighting.' Cuthbert was silent, and I went on, 'Yes, the general idea seems to be that once they're sprayed with insecticide and asked a lot of nosey questions by you and me, then all's well.'

'That's not the general idea at all. Those are necessary precautions in dealing with Displaced Persons.'

'We're displaced persons too, when you come to think of it. But if you call another man a Displaced Person, it means he doesn't matter as much as you do, because he's destitute. That's one of the advantages of being in the Army. Once you've lost your liberty, you're better off in times like these.'

'That's a bit superficial and cynical, I think,' said Cuthbert, restraining himself. 'I also think it's time you took these lists to Major Parsons.'

Over in the Civil Affairs office, I found the Major sitting in front of some maps with coloured pins stuck in them in clusters. He spread the Nominal Rolls on the table without looking at them, and asked me deliberately stupid questions about their contents. And as he sat listening to my answers, I got the impression he was sizing up what I was saying not in terms of its meaning, which didn't much interest him, but to determine my rating as the eventual occupant of some vast, imaginary jail.

Then abruptly he stopped staring, leant back in his chair, pulled out a silver case and offered me a cigarette. 'It would seem these interrogations of yours haven't been bearing much fruit,' he said.

'No, there's not been much fruit, as yet.'

'Well, if you ask me, Sarge,' he said, assuming a confidential expression and leaning forward, 'I know it's none of my business, and I'm only Civil Affairs, but the reason is that your young Sergeants don't know whether they're going or coming. They're nice lads, we're glad to have them with us, but I've noticed them questioning these Dutchmen, and if my experience counts for anything, they've got as much chance of finding a German agent as I have of understanding Dutch. Of course, they've that in their favour, they know the language, but they're far too mealy-mouthed and trusting. It makes me weep to see them. And Dutch or no Dutch, if I was sitting with them at that table, I'd back myself to spot the dubious cases against the lot of them.'

He rose to his feet and sat on the edge of the desk.

'Yes, in police work, Sergeant,' he went on, 'there's only one sound principle to go on: everyone's a potential criminal until he's proved the contrary.' He paused. 'Of course, some would say, regard everyone merely as a potential suspect, but I say, criminal. Don't trust anyone. Don't trust your own brother.' He gave me a sharp look. 'Now no offence, but take yourself. You've come into my office here on several occasions, and as far as I know you're an honest sort of a fellow, but until you've proved that to me, clearly and unmistakably, I wouldn't trust you an inch.' He stuck his face forward. 'Not an inch.'

'You've got to remember we're beginners.'

'Oh, don't I know it!' he cried, rising and walking up and down. 'But just consider. Have you imagined those boys of yours in the middle of the Ruhr, say, chasing after werewolves and Nazi fanatics and the Gestapo?' He stopped, faced me and grinned. 'Who'll do the chasing?' he said, holding out his big, red hands.

'You think those German organisations will still be active, once we get there?'

He nodded, but then, reflecting, raised his brows in an expression of cautious doubt. 'Yet who can tell?' he said. 'Old Gerry's a queer customer. In '18, he had us all on the run up to the last moment and then, when everyone was least expecting it—wallop! He'd packed in.' The Major contorted his mouth, pulling it down at the ends. 'Still, this time's a bit different. It's a different sort of bug that's biting him now. So, as I say, you'd better watch out.'

'Well, I don't think they'll pack in,' I said. 'I think they'll fight right on to the end, and this time there'll be a civilian resistance movement, too. It's everything or nothing with them now.'

He rubbed his face with one hand. 'I wonder if you're right?' he said. 'I mean about the civvies mucking in as well? No, as I see it, that's unlikely. What we're probably going to find, once their army's had it, is quite a bit of that nothing you speak of. Collapse and apathy, I shouldn't be surprised. Gerry, you see,' he continued, starting to walk again, 'is not a bad chap in his way, despite my having kidded you all a bit about him. He knows his own interest once you've got him down. But until you have, he's not much more than a raving lunatic, and has to be treated as such.'

I found there was half an hour till lunch, so I walked down one of the lanes through the planted forest that grew up to the edge of the camp. When I was surrounded by trees and silence, I thought over Major Parsons' words.

In one sense, he was right about our Sergeants: we were quite unsuited to the job we were doing—either by temperament, or because of a happy ignorance as to what Intelligence work was all about.

The younger men were really boys, gently nurtured in decent homes, and their only qualifications for detecting spies were boundless confidence and the knowledge of a foreign language. Sitting behind their desks with the novel powers of a rubber stamp and the absolute right of asking strangers personal questions, you could see how important they felt. You could also see that they were amateurs, playing a parlour game.

It was rare that they had an idea of how to make personal contact with the man they were interrogating. If any of the refugees was a German agent, they felt it would be his duty to admit it to such righteous men as they. They didn't realise that to find out a man's secrets against his will, you have to be treacherously sympathetic and calculatingly brutal. That you have, at any rate, to be interested.

My own inefficiency was due to facing two ways. What attracted me about our life was the comfort it offered compared with slogging in the Infantry, the gratification it gave to crude curiosity about human lives, and the exciting amorality with which the mental climate of Intelligence work is saturated. I was fascinated by the human weaknesses this work disclosed (in oneself and others), and eager to understand the motives and methods of those involved in it. But all this was equally disgusting. So I wavered around the edge of these experiences, wishing for the knowledge that can only come from a full participation which, anxious for my spiritual virginity, I wanted to avoid.

That was why I was hoping the Depôt might send us one or two hard-headed men who would do the dirty work that would have to be done. Not just strong-arm men like Walter, but men crooked and capable as those they would be hunting. This would save the younger Sergeants from having to learn what lay behind their work, from taking themselves seriously and growing to believe in it. And I would be able to see the sights our life uncovered, without being implicated in all the acts that made them visible.

At lunch, Cuthbert pointed out that in our haste to leave town, I'd forgotten to bring his pay, so it was decided he'd have to return with me to the billet. 'If I put my bike in the back of your utility, perhaps you'd let me drive,' he suggested. Once we were on the straight road home, he opened up the throttle, his small body leaning forward on the extra cushion he'd put there for himself. 'Cuthbert,' I said, 'do me a favour and slow down a bit.' He lifted his foot and, glancing round in an injured way, said, 'I don't drive fast.'

'You drive much too fast.'

'Well, it's not fast drivers who have the accidents.'

We reached the billet in the late afternoon, and as Cuthbert pulled in beside Walter's truck, I noticed the tarpaulins at the back of it were closed and bulging. We opened them and looked in. The truck was filled with piles of Army clothing and boxes of rations and canteen goods. 'Good heavens,' Cuthbert said, 'that can't all be for us. Who does it belong to?'

'We'd better find that out.'

Walter and Norman were standing arguing in the office. Norman was red-faced, and Walter had a defiant, but rather sheepish look. 'You'd better explain to him, Walter,' Norman said. 'I'm not one to tell tales.'

'Don't get excited, Norman. You've seen that clobber, then?' Walter said to me. 'Well, it's the stores I and the reinforcement have got for you.'

'What reinforcement?'

'The new Sergeant.'

'Have they arrived already?'

'Only one of them so far, and the new Captain's here, too. They came up together from Brussels last night. The Captain's spending the day at Corps with Major Bane and driving over in the evening. He sent the new man on ahead this morning.'

'Where is he, this new man?'

'He's having his tea.'

'And what about all these stores?'

Norman stood with his plump arms akimbo, watching Walter. Cuthbert also peered at him, listening intently. Walter put his hands in his pockets, and spoke in a defensive drawl.

'Well, this bird arrived, you see, and I was showing him round, and I explained the difficulty we'd had getting certain things, and he asked to see what stores we'd got and when I showed him, he said it was disgraceful.'

'What was?'

'That we had so little of everything, of course, and in a way I agreed with him. So he said, "Make out a list of all the things you need, and I'll get them for you." Well, then we needed indent forms, but Norman here refused to part with them at first.'

'He was quite right. I'm supposed to sign them. Who did sign them?'

'This new man,' Norman told me indignantly. 'And what's more, he signed them in the new Captain's name and put the Detachment stamp on them while my back was turned.'

'Go on, Walter.'

'Well . . . then we called at one or two of the supply points and got that stuff.'

'How did you get all that on an indent for a dozen men?'

'There I admit he worked a bit of a flanker on me. Before we got to the supply point, he'd altered all the numbers to twenty, and it wasn't till they'd started off-loading it into my arms that I was on to what he was up to. I couldn't very well say anything then.'

'But there's more kit out there than even twenty men are entitled to.'

'Yes. Well, you see, that was another idea of Dennis's. He suggested all we had to do, after we'd left the Corps supply point, was to call at a Divisional supply point as well. So we did that.'

'We're not attached to a Division.'

'No.'

There was a silence.

'Is Dennis this person's name?' said Cuthbert. Walter nodded. 'Well, if you want to know what I think, it's stabbing the Army in the back. The extra stores you've taken means some other Unit will go short.'

'I've told you my opinion,' Norman said. 'I don't mind your getting all you can for us, but what I object to is this faking indents and misusing the Detachment stamp.'

'We'll have to give it all back,' said Cuthbert.

'What, and land ourselves in a court-martial?'

'I'm not vindictive, Walter, but if this man's going to start off like that, we'd best get rid of him right away.'

'Oh, no. If they catch up with him they catch up with all of us—me and Norman, and you too,' Walter said to me. 'They'll say you were in on it.'

'Well, you've both let me down,' I said. 'You'd better get that stuff off the truck and stowed away before someone sees it.'

'Perhaps we'd better, at that,' said Walter.

When they'd gone out, Norman said, 'I didn't like that remark of yours about letting you down. What you've got to realise is that after he'd talked Walter into it, the two of them gunned up on me and practically snatched the stamp and papers out of my hands.'

'I was a bit surprised, that's all. You're usually so careful.'

Norman irritatedly tidied his desk. 'I'm ready to hand over this job to someone else any time,' he said. 'If you ask me, I'm the only one who does any regular work at all. I sit cooped up in here taking the can back for all the others.'

'Well, all right, Norman. Will you tell this Dennis to come to my room when he's finished his tea?'

As I passed by the store-room, I saw Walter and Cuthbert putting the last of the things away. Cuthbert was stacking tins of food neatly in rows, with a great air of disfavour. 'Pure waste,' he said, 'when you think of all those refugees and the miserable meals they get.'

'We'll take them out some of it.'

'A good idea, provided we make sure it's fairly distributed.'

'Six new battledress suits,' said Walter, holding one up against himself. 'Here's a biggish one would fit you.'

I looked at it.

'Well, lock all this up and give me the key,' I told him. 'We'll issue some of it out later in the evening.'

I went along to my room, and in the passage outside the door I saw a lean man with slightly rounded shoulders whose arms were swinging by his side as he walked up and down with his head bent, looking at the floor. He turned round as I came up. He had a long, sallow face, a pointed nose, a sharp chin, a thin, curved mouth and two large, gleaming eyes. He threw up a salute and said, 'Hullo, Colonel.'

'You're the new arrival.'

'That's it.'

'Come in, will you?'

He opened the door for me, waited till I sat down on the bed, then seated himself on the table with his hands on his knees, looking at me.

'They tell me you got up to Corps last night with the new Captain?'

'Correct.'

'What's he like, all right?'

'Oh, yes. He's quite a gent.'

'We were expecting another Sergeant to come with you.'

'Yes, he's on his way. He's stranded in Brussels just now. Our Peugeot broke down, you see.'

'Oh, did it?'

'Yes. Gordon and I came up from France in it—from the Detachment we were stationed with down there. When the signal came through from Brussels that we were transferred to you, we started off in our Peugeot to get here.'

'It belongs to you personally, this Peugeot?'

'Oh, yes. But we had some trouble on the road up to Brussels, and had to get a tow. So Gordon put up at a hotel while the car was being mended, and I went in to the Depôt to report.'

'This Gordon stayed at a hotel in Brussels?'

'Yes. He doesn't like the Depôt.'

'I see. Well, go on.'

'At the Depôt, I met the new Captain and heard he was posted here too, so I came up with him last night.'

'And when should we expect this other Sergeant?'

'In a day or two—as soon as the Peugeot's repaired.'

He told me all this in an emphatic, serious way. I didn't know what to make of him.

'Well,' I said, 'we're glad to have you as we're under strength, but you seem to have taken rather a lot on yourself since you arrived.'

He raised his eyebrows and smiled. 'You mean the trip today?'

'Yes.'

'Do you object?'

'Yes.'

'Why?'

'Do I have to tell you that? You arrive here, and without waiting for any orders you swan off with Walter and get this stuff on your own responsibility.'

He said nothing.

'And you seem to have taken forms and stamped them without my clerk's permission, made incorrect entries in them and got a lot of things that aren't needed.'

'Aren't they needed? Won't you find some use for them?'

'Perhaps we will, but that's not the point. The point is that you're not expected to show all that much initiative. You wait and do what you're told, more or less.'

He was silent again.

'They're not as dim as that at the supply points. You may get away with it once, but if they catch up with you, we'll all be in the dirt.'

'They won't catch up with us.'

'Perhaps they won't, but they may. Why should we run a risk on your account?'

He got up, frowned slightly, then began walking about the room shaking his hands round from the wrists as if they were ball-jointed. He stopped abruptly and faced me.

'Now listen, Sergeant,' he said. 'In a campaign, they don't bother about all that. Everything's in a state of flux, nobody knows who's who, you can practically do what you want to, provided you do know what you want. This isn't a manœuvre in England, it's an international battle. When you're at home, they've got you more or less, because they can spend as much time chasing you up as they can telling you what to do. But once you're over here, they're only interested in the German army, and so long as you go after that, they don't much mind about anything else.'

He broke off and stared at me.

'Besides,' he went on earnestly, 'the Provost people are much too busy signing roads and guarding prisoners to worry about minor raids on War Department property.'

'You're wrong, you know. They've pulled squaddies in up here just for flogging cigarettes.'

'Well, of course you have to use your loaf and not do anything too obvious. But I can tell you from experience every Unit in the Army over-indents. And though they don't admit it, the boys in Whitehall add a percentage to allow for it. So why live like paupers when there's no need to? You want to be comfortable, don't you?'

He stopped and stared at me expectantly.

'That's all a lot of nonsense,' I said, growing more and more fascinated and convinced. He shrugged his shoulders, raised his brows high again and shook his head in a kindly, disappointed way.

'The thing is,' I went on, 'you took far too much for granted, going off like that before I'd even met you, and you overdid it, getting all those piles of stuff.'

He reached out an arm and patted me lightly on the shoulder. 'Excuse me, Colonel,' he said, 'but I meant it for the best.'

'Well, go easy, Dennis. Don't exaggerate.'

He nodded, closing his eyes so that his face wore a mixed expression of spurious deference and guile.

'What time is this Captain of ours coming, do you know?' I asked him.

'Oh, after supper, I should think. He'll probably be dining and wining with Major Benedict-Bane.'

Everyone was rather on tenterhooks for the new Captain's arrival as we sat about in the mess during the rest of the evening. Dennis, whose personality was making quite an impression on the other Sergeants, was telling them stories of his exploits in France.

'Now what about this Peugeot you talk of?' said Cuthbert, who had stayed on for supper. 'How did you manage that?'

'It's captured enemy equipment, my boy. We found it at the time of the break-through at one of the enemy headquarters in Amiens.'

'And you just took it? But it's a civilian car, isn't it?'

'That makes no difference. If you can prove that a vehicle was in regular use by the enemy, even though he requisitioned it from an Ally, then you put in an application for a Retention Certificate and if you get one, the vehicle's yours.'

'You mean the Army's.'

'If you prefer to put it that way.'

'And have you got a Retention Certificate for your Peugeot?'

'Oh no, we didn't apply for one, of course. If we'd done that, some Staff officer would have seized it from us for himself.'

'So you're not entitled to drive it at all, then?'

'We got over the difficulty this way. We made out a document certifying that a Certificate has been applied for, and we keep that in the car to show the Military Police, or anyone else who's interested.'

Cuthbert reflected on this, impressed despite himself, for anything connected with motor transport had a great fascination for him. 'Well, it's ingenious,' he said, 'but it's not exactly scrupulous.'

'Now look here, my lad,' Dennis said to him. 'Don't you know the whole British Army's starved of transport? And who likes riding about on those ridiculous and dangerous motor-bikes most of you have got? The trouble about you people, you know, is that you've got a Lines of Communication mentality. It's not in the rear that you get the opportunities, but up in the front—or rather, just behind it. That's why I'm glad to be posted up here. The fighting troops clear the way and then the carrion crows descend to get the pickings. And when the Lines of Communication people come lumbering up to try and straighten everything out, that's the time to move on to fresh pastures out of their clutches.'

A summons now came from Norman for Dennis to go to the office so that his personal particulars could be noted down in Norman's records. I went along there too, and watched him labouring to restore his credit with Norman by initiating and then yielding in a discussion about ways of manipulating Army forms. 'Fair's fair,' Norman said at last. 'All I ask is that you don't make my job impossible for me.'

We heard the sound of a car driving up outside, and Dennis crossed to the window and said it was the Captain. I went out to put on a jacket, and as I came back into the office, the far door opened and a young officer, wearing a mackintosh and carrying a hold-all, and with his cap slightly tilted onto the back of his head, came into the room and advanced towards us with a fixed and apparently friendly smile.

'Good evening, Sir,' said Dennis, giving him a capable salute. 'Welcome to the Detachment.'

The officer reached the table, put his hold-all down and undid the belt of his mackintosh, still fixing us all with the same rather toothy smile.

'This is the Sergeant-in-charge, Sir,' said Dennis.

He waited for me to come over and shake hands. 'How do you do, Sergeant?' he said, with something still left of the smile, but with a beady glint in his small, almost triangular eyes.

Dennis introduced Norman, who was standing behind his desk at semi-attention gazing at the officer with a respectful, obliging air, but one that also hinted at the consideration due from a newcomer to an old hand. 'How are you, Sir?' he said, shaking hands across the table like an executive welcoming an important client.

The Captain slowly took off his mackintosh and started giving us a long, dull account of his journey up from Brussels, addressing himself particularly to Norman, to a lesser extent to

Dennis and not at all to me. I saw his pointed face in profile, with its general cast of countenance that projected foward to the tip of the nose, and receded gradually to the chin. He was speaking with steady insistence and passing over Norman's polite interjections with a series of slight nods, as though the commonplace facts he was relating must be of the utmost interest to us all. Standing there holding his mackintosh over one arm, leaning forward and talking away, he looked rather young and inexperienced; though there was an air of deliberation, of control over all this affability, that put me on my guard.

'And you can imagine what a bind it was having to leave Brussels,' he went on. 'I was beautifully dug in there with a flat of my own, and we had some wonderful parties. However, Major Bane tells me it's not too bad up here, and that it may be possible to get in to Brussels for week-ends.'

He now looked round at me.

'Well, perhaps you could show me my room, Sergeant,' he said. 'And I'll be asking you to tell me more about the work you're doing on the way down to Belgium tomorrow.'

'We're going down there at once, then, Sir?'

'Yes. Major Bane wants us to move as soon as we can, so I think you and I had better reconnoitre there tomorrow, contact the Town Major and find ourselves a billet.'

I picked up his hold-all, and we walked over to the door.

'Major Bane told me a bit about you all, and I met your former Officer Commanding for a moment in Brussels,' he went on. 'But of course, there's a lot I don't know as yet.'

'Oh, you met the Lieutenant, Sir?'

'Yes, I did,' he said, and he eyed me sharply.

Early the following morning, I drove out on several errands, and when I got back, was told the new Captain wanted to see me. I went into his office and saluted. 'You've taken the utility out, Sergeant?' he said.

'Yes.'

'In future, it is not to leave the grounds without my permission.'

I tried to hide my annoyance. 'Not to get petrol, Sir?'

'All right, to get petrol. But otherwise, not without my permission. I might need it any time to go to Corps. I've also been looking at the rest of the transport, and I find it's in a filthy condition.'

'There's a lot of mud just now.'

'I'm well aware of that, and I want the men to remove it rather more frequently.'

'They all clean their vehicles up before they go in for the monthly inspection.'

'Well, in future they will clean them weekly and show them to me on Friday mornings.'

'That may interfere with the work quite a bit.'

He looked at me, opened his mouth without speaking for five seconds or so, then said, 'Are you ready to start now?'

'Yes.'

'All right, we'll go.'

He picked up a map-case and a board with sheets of paper held on it by elastic bands, put on his mackintosh, and we walked out to the car. I went to the driver's seat. 'No, Sergeant,' he said. 'I'll drive.'

'Are you taking the vehicle over, Sir?'

'I beg your pardon?'

I gave him as insolent a look as I thought prudent. 'It's one car one driver in the Army, isn't it?'

'What do you mean by that?'

'If you're driving, I should sign the car over to you in the vehicle-book, and make out a new work-ticket for the journey in your name.'

'Why? Officers drive cars.'

'If they do, the documents should be in their own names—unless they're overriding routine regulations in an emergency.'

'What do you mean, an emergency?'

'They might take over to relieve the driver from fatigue after a long journey, or in some other case where the exigencies of the Service demanded it.'

We stared at each other.

'Well, I'll drive there and you drive back,' he said. 'Just show me the way to the canal road.'

After that, he didn't ask any questions, but followed a route he'd evidently worked out for himself in the office, and marked in blue pencil on the celluloid that covered his map. But he hadn't allowed for the Assistant Provost Marshal's system of one-way routes in the Corps area. The purpose of these was to make driving safer, and, for big convoys, faster, but they often resulted in an individual driver having to travel ten miles to go one. Our men ignored them, relying on charm if they met a Military Policeman. The Captain soon had an opportunity of showing his skill, for we were stopped by a Redcap at a check-point. 'Not that way, Sir,' he said, coming over and leaning against the car. The Captain assumed an amiable, obtuse expression, and by pretending not to understand the Redcap's objections and relentlessly repeating what the object of his journey was, he wore this man's patience down. He managed to give the impression it would be a great nuisance to make him change his mind, and something of a privilege to wave him on the wrong way. 'Well, all right, Sir, but when you reach the bridge, turn left,' the Redcap said at last.

The Captain turned right onto a cracked-up road with small, deep ruts close together, and we rattled along it very uncomfortably. He frowned and made impatient noises, as though these pot-holes had been put there to annoy him. He handled the car carefully, however.

'About that remark of yours just now,' he said, breaking a long silence. 'I'm not referring to the present case, but suppose an officer wants to drive and the exigencies of the Service don't demand it. Suppose he just wants to drive.'

'He can always give a direct order.'

'And if he gives a direct order, what can the driver do?'

'The driver obeys the last order and reports the matter on returning from the journey, if he feels like it.'

'Reports it to who?'

'To his Officer Commanding.'

'To me, in other words.'

'A Unit like ours with only one officer is rather exceptional. But you said you weren't referring to any particular case, didn't you?'

'Oh, of course. I was merely interested to know what you thought.'

We now saw ahead of us a main road running along an embankment lined with tall trees on either side. It was the highway that followed the course of the Maas some miles west of it, and in this sector, there were no German pockets left on our side of the river. We turned on to the highway and headed south, catching occasional glimpses of the river across the meadows. When we reached a shell-pitted crossroad, a Sergeant signalled to us to stop. 'Do you have to go down this way, Sir?' he said.

'Certainly,' the Captain told him.

'Well, you know, if you do, Gerry will see you and send a few bursts over the river. We don't mind as far as you're concerned, Sir, if you see what I mean, but being stationed here ourselves we have to take cover, and it interrupts our work.'

'They don't fire unless the road's used?'

'That's it.'

The Captain agreed to take a more roundabout route, and we set off inland. 'We'll be reaching the frontier in a minute,' I said.

'What happens there?'

'Nothing. You just blow on the horn and sail by.'

We were soon in sight of it, and a Dutch official came running out of a forlorn brick customs-office to raise the barrier. On the Belgian side, the barrier wasn't even down. A Gendarme sitting at a café table watched us as we accelerated past the zig-zag coloured posts.

It was one of the futile pleasures of the campaign to be able to ignore the frontiers which, in time of peace, had seemed so absolute. Everyone felt that dotted lines on maps had no significance, and that the only nation just now was the Allied Army, whose expanding territory spread all over national boundaries. These still had some validity for civilians; but for soldiers, the real frontier was the one on which our own troops faced the enemy.

We coasted along a straight road and crossed a Bailey bridge into our new town. Its most striking feature was an enormous tower, almost of the proportions of that of a cathedral, which rose by itself without any building attached to it. Crossing an untidy square from which streets straggled casually away, we noticed how very full the houses were of troops. We found our way to the Town Major's billet, and after waiting a moment among a queue of civilians in the corridor, were ushered in.

It seemed, from the Town Major's sly, life-furrowed face, and from his practical, familiar manner, that he might be a regular who had come up from the ranks. His grey hair was brushed back from his red forehead, and his features were coarse and distinguished, like those of a provincial actor. He greeted us with jovial informality, and asked if there was anything he could do; at the same time giving the strong impression that unless we were going to be useful to him, he wouldn't do much.

The Captain bore down on him and told him at great length about ourselves and what we wanted. The Town Major listened non-committally, until the Captain mentioned that we would deal with issuing permits to civilians going into the military areas.

'Then you're just the people I want,' the Town Major said. 'Did you see all those locals in the corridor? They come pestering me for permits all day. Some are farmers, but others are smugglers or people who just want to visit their families. Could you sort them out for me?'

'Oh, yes. But not today, of course. We must fix up a billet first.'

'Well, as regards billets, we're in a bit of a fix, too. There's an Armoured Division resting here at present, and we've put so many in among the civilians that the Burgomaster's getting restless. Lieutenant!' he called out to a thin, beak-faced man who was sitting at a nearby table. 'Where can we fit this Unit in?'

The Lieutenant, who wore the uniform of the Belgian army and a great many medal ribbons, came over to the desk. 'Why take such notice of the Burgomaster?' he said, with tight-lipped emphasis. 'He thinks only of the coming elections. Requisition whatever houses you require.'

'The Lieutenant's a terror, he's worse than I am,' the Town Major told us. 'He's spent all his life in the Congo, and he treats his own people like kaffirs.'

'Not at all. But it is war, Major, and some of these farmers do not realise it.'

'Well, I dunno . . .' said the Town Major gloomily. And then, as if inspired, 'But there might be a way. Just up the road there's a nice house with central heating and a bathroom, I don't know why I haven't taken it myself. The proprietor's a big collaborator who's gone off with the German army, so you'd have no landlord trouble like the rest of us. Now, there's a Civil Affairs team in it, but the thing is, they're not attached to your Corps.' He stopped and gazed at us to see if we saw the point.

'So this isn't their area any longer, and they're not operational here,' the Captain said.

The Town Major nodded. 'They keep saying they're moving back into their own formation area, but they're very comfortable, and taking their time about it. Now, if you were to go along and say you're posted down on duty, they'll have to move out—or according to the book, they'd have to.'

'I see,' said the Captain, picking up his map-case. The Town Major rose and saw us to the door. 'You'll like it here,' he said. 'It's a small sort of a place, and a bit of a thieves' kitchen so far as I can see, but we've one or two decent bars, and the women are co-operative. Well, there it is. Let me know the result, and don't make use of my name, please.'

The smile left the Captain's face as he walked grimly up the road towards the Civil Affairs billet. When we went in, we found two officers huddled together over some papers on the table. The younger one, who wore spectacles and had a bright, impatient manner, was evidently explaining something to his rubicund, heavily-built companion. They both looked up.

'Good morning to you,' the Captain said, beginning his explanations. They gazed at him in growing amazement. The older officer leaned against the mantelpiece and said nothing, but the younger one was soon bubbling over to reply.

'Well, really,' he said. 'I've never known anything like it. You're trying to evict us as if we were civilians.'

'Not a bit of it,' the Captain told him. 'The point is, you see, we're operational and you don't seem to be, so naturally, we take priority.'

'Take? But you can't take what doesn't belong to you. This is a Civil Affairs billet and we're engaged on important work.' The Captain nodded, not taking his eyes off him. 'Do you realise,' this young officer went on, 'that we're making plans for coping with the millions of Allied Displaced Persons we're going to find in Germany?'

'No.'

'Well, we are.'

'Now look here, Captain,' the older officer said, 'you're pushing us round just a bit, aren't you? You want a nice place for yourself, I quite understand that, but do you have to march in here and threaten us?'

The Captain was slightly abashed, but calling up reserves of egotism, he recovered himself and repeated his case. The older officer listened a while, then interrupted, 'Yes, we've heard all that, and I don't say we wouldn't be willing to oblige you, if you give us time to turn round. How soon do you expect to be coming here?'

'As soon as can be,' the Captain said. 'I'm sending an advance party down forthwith.'

'Well, tell them to contact me and we'll come to some arrangement. There's no need to make any sort of a fuss. After all, your people and ours will be seeing quite a lot of each other once we get to Germany, and we might as well start off on the right foot, don't you think? So what about coming in next door and having a glass of something? It's no use asking Lieutenant Adeane here, he doesn't touch it before sundown.'

I was left alone with this Lieutenant Adeane, who began to rearrange papers on his desk. He didn't speak to me at all, so I sat down and offered him a cigarette.

'Oh, thank you,' he said, after hesitating.

'You're going to be very busy in Germany, then,' I said to him.

He eyed me to decide whether I was being impertinent, and perhaps to determine whether I deserved his confidence, till reassured by my serious, frank expression, he said, 'Oh, yes. There's a big task ahead of us, full of responsibility and full of opportunities.'

His eyes began to shine. He had an honest, youthful face, rather pinched and marked by self-sufficiency.

'Think of it,' he went on. 'Teeming millions of Allied nationals will be dependent on us, and the whole German nation waiting to be re-educated.'

'It'll be a big job.'

'Yes. But it must be tackled. That's what we're here for.'

'Are they making up Civil Affairs teams to handle Allied nationals in Germany?'

Yes, that's so, we're being specially selected for the job. As a matter of fact,' he went on, glancing towards the next room, 'I'm parting company with my present Officer Commanding and being posted to a refugee camp to get experience of field work.'

'You're not going to Major Parsons' team, are you?'

'Oh, you know him? Yes, they tell me he's had great experience of refugees.'

'I should have thought they'd make a policeman like Major Parsons a Public Safety Officer in Germany.'

'Really? Well, perhaps later on, when we go on to Civil Administration work proper. But at the outset, we'll be dealing with German refugees and Allied Displaced Persons. First-aid to begin with, you see, before we can start on the cure.'

He took off his spectacles and stared at me intently. His earnestness reminded me of Cuthbert, though he didn't seem to have Cuthbert's redeeming fund of uninventive common sense.

'And you think a cure is possible?' I said.

'Oh, yes,' he answered quickly, laying his spectacles on the table. And throwing another sharp glance towards the next room, where a clinking of glasses could be heard, he continued, 'Some think only of revenge and punishments. But if we're to get anywhere, we must rise above all that and put ourselves in the position of the Germans. They're a great people, you see, however much they've been misguided. And whatever others may say, I intend, when we get there, to admit our own mistakes before I point out their errors to them.'

'That's not official policy, is it?'

'Oh, no. Non-fraternisation and unconditional surrender will be the order of the day. But we can do better than that, although of course,' he said with a slight smile, putting his spectacles on again, 'being in the Intelligence, you wouldn't agree with my point of view.'

I advanced some specious arguments in favour of our duties, but Lieutenant Adeane went on to make it clear he disapproved of Intelligence work so much he'd rather not discuss the subject at all. He was evidently one of those who thought what we did so distasteful that however much they might make use of us, it was best to pretend the need for our services didn't exist.

'Well, I expect we'll meet again some time, Sir,' I said, as the two other officers came back into the room. But perhaps regretting his condescension, Lieutenant Adeane gave no more than a thin grimace in reply.

'You can get a meal over at the Universal Hotel,' the older officer was saying to the Captain. 'The Armoured Division have their mess there, it's up on the first floor.'

We rode round to the square and parked the car in front of the hotel. 'What about you?' the Captain said.

'I've brought some sandwiches. I'll have them in the café here downstairs.'

'Have you got enough for two? If so, I'd prefer to join you, on the whole.'

We went in and sat down at a table. The Manager, who was surprisingly dressed in smart city clothes, came up and told the Captain about the military mess. He was offended when the Captain said, 'Yes, yes, I know, can you bring us some beer?' To show his disapproval, he repeated this order to a waiter in a loud voice. The Captain stared round at the company, then ignored them.

'You seem to have got that billet,' I said.

He nodded, as though this had been a foregone conclusion.

'What a typical Civil Affairs pair,' he said. 'They're either coppers, or old gentlemen dragged out of retirement or Lieutenant Schoolmasters with strange theories.'

'They're not all like that, are they?'

'All I've met so far have been first class wafflers. Their trouble is they don't know what they're up to themselves. Their job here in Allied territory is to deal with civilian questions affecting the Army, nothing more, but they can't resist trying out their hands at governing.'

'They'll need to have theories if they're going to govern the Germans.'

'You mean a policy? I suppose so. Yes, I suppose it's a difficult job, and they haven't been briefed for it properly. I expect the higher-ups haven't really made up their minds about Germany. So what will happen later on to them and to us, let alone the Germans, I tremble to think.'

He opened a sandwich, looked inside it, and munched methodically.

'What about the advance party?' I said. 'When should they come down?'

'Send two Sergeants here some time tomorrow and tell them as soon as those Civil Affairs people move out, they're to get into that house and hold it against all comers. If the Armoured Division hear it's vacant, they'll be in there like a shot.'

'Which men shall I send?'

'I leave that to you. And I'll have a word about it to Major Bane at the Corps dance this evening, and see he backs us up. Are you going in to the dance yourself? No? Well, he's invited me, so I'll stop off there on the way back.'

The Captain reached the car ahead of me and got behind the

steering-wheel. After consulting his map, he decided to take a road running along the banks of yet another canal. 'We can cross by this bridge,' he said, pointing it out. 'It'll be a short cut to Corps.'

'That bridge may be blown. A lot of them only exist on the map.'

He nodded in disagreement, and as we drove along this road, I noticed it wasn't signed for military traffic. Being made of yellow clay it got muddier every mile, and as he was trying to accelerate up a greasy slope, the utility slipped back and was bogged up to its axles. We got out.

'These feeble little vehicles!' the Captain cried. 'How does the Army expect us to do our job if it doesn't give us a car with a bit of power in it? Utility! What a word. These things are only fit for women officers in Whitehall.'

'There's a farm over there. Shall I get a horse to pull us out?'

He nodded, and I set off over the fields. When I turned back a moment, I saw him on the bank of the chilly canal, gazing across the water at the thin, misty trees on the further side. He looked almost exotic, standing in his military mackintosh beside the broken-down truck in the middle of the lonely Flemish landscape. But holding a cigarette in one gloved hand, and swinging his map-case slowly by the straps with the other, he seemed unaware of this. Generations of captains had come this way before him, and in whatever place an English soldier finds himself, he is cloaked about with the confident assurance that where he is he should be, and that it is the alien land, not he, which is strange and foreign.

I got back alone in time for tea, after dropping the Captain off at Corps. I'd seen Harry a moment, and he told me he'd 'phoned through to Walter and asked him to bring his girl in to the dance. I found her sitting in the mess, wearing a flamboyant red dress and carrying her shoes in a paper parcel. Knowing she was Harry's sweetheart, the men were painting a lurid picture of the life that might await her in England, should she marry a soldier. She listened turning from one to the other with a smile of foolish joy, and it was clear that, in Harry's absence, some of the feeling she had for him was transferred to the men who were good-humouredly teasing her.

'Mark my words,' said Walter, staring at her grimly. 'One glimpse of a smoky English town and of Harry's Ma over the kitchen sink, and you'd come flying back to Holland.'

'Oh, anything where he lives would be excellent to me,' she said, and she waited for Walter to go on, since any description of Harry's background, even a fantastic one, was a delight to her.

After tea, I went into the office where Norman was having his, as was his custom, alone. He greeted me with the news that Gordon, the second reinforcement, had sent word from Bourg-Leopold, where his Peugeot had broken down again, to say he expected to arrive next day.

'He's taking a lot for granted, isn't he?' said Norman. 'Now as regards Belgium, who will this advance party consist of?'

'Dennis and Walter would be best, I think. I've told Walter.'

'You know Dennis was out at the refugee camp today?'

'Yes. I said he was to go and have a look round. Is he back yet?'

'He's in the Captain's office with two Dutchmen.' Norman looked at me with heavy resignation. 'I told him it wasn't the proper place to interrogate people in, but he brushed my objections aside. And if you want to know who these Dutchmen are, I suggest you go and find out for yourself.'

Dennis was sitting in the Captain's chair, pointing accusingly with a ruler at two young men who were standing with their hands behind their backs, facing him. One was dark and bulky, and he was looking disdainful and annoyed. The other, who was slender and had a mop of fair hair, was gazing at Dennis with polite irony.

'What's it all about Dennis?' I said. 'What are you doing in here?'

'In my opinion, this pair are possible enemy agents,' he told me, giving them a malevolent look.

'Do they speak English?'

'Oh yes, we do,' said the fair one.

'Are they armed?'

'No, no, we are unarmed, since you are not Germans, although your friend behaves to us like one,' the bulky man said.

'Dennis, park them with Norman a minute, will you, and come and tell me a bit more.'

Dennis shrugged his shoulders, escorted the strangers out of the room in silence and then came back and sat down on the table. 'It's a pity you interrupted,' he said. 'I may have been about to extract an admission from them.'

'Why did you choose the Captain's office to extract an admission in? There are plenty of other places.'

'Is that important? Don't you want to hear all about them first?'

The gist of his involved explanation was that while he was driving back from the refugee camp, these men had asked him for a lift and had hinted that they'd just come over the frontier from Belgium. 'Naturally, that was a suspicious fact,' Dennis went on, 'because civilian travel's restricted as you know, so I demanded them to produce their papers, whereupon they showed me these phoney-looking documents which say they're official couriers for the Dutch Forces of the Interior. Well, I ask you, do these things look genuine?'

He handed me the papers. They were of a kind that anyone with a typewriter and a passport photograph could have made.

'What did they say they were doing?'

'Visiting Belgian contacts in connection with hunting out collaborators is their story. I told them I didn't believe it, and they had the cheek to say if that was my attitude, they declined to discuss the matter further. Well, by this time my suspicions were thoroughly aroused, and it seemed to me they might easily be Gerry agents, posing as Dutch Resistance.'

'That was leaping to conclusions. Did you check up on them with the Militia here?'

'Of course not. I've no confidence in the Militia.'

'Why not?'

'Because they're not official. I mean they're not part of the regular Dutch army. No, I did better than that, I went straight to the source. I whipped them both up to the Dutch Military Mission. They interrogated them a bit, and said they'd check up and let me know, and meanwhile I was to hang on to them. So I brought them back here for further questioning.'

'Why go all the way to the Military Mission? Why didn't you ask the local people first? It's the men who were here all through the occupation who'll know about the secret organisations.'

'That wasn't what the Liaison Officer at the Mission thought. He has a very poor opinion of the Militia. And my experience is, that Allied personnel who came over with us from England can be relied on to give a more accurate opinion than any locals can.'

'What are you going to do when you get to Germany, Dennis? You won't have a German Liaison Officer to help you then.'

'When I get to Germany, I shall go straight to the source in the same way, i.e., to the German civil servants and regular police. If I want to find out anything about the Gestapo and the Nazi Party officials, they'll be the people to tell me.'

'Most of them will be Nazis themselves.'

'Oh, I don't mean the fanatics. I'll arrest them. I mean the regular officials who are always there whoever's ruling the country.'

'What about the anti-Nazis, won't you take them into your confidence?'

'If I can find any, yes. But they'll have been in the concentration camps so long that there'll be a lot they won't know about. The regular, permanent officials are the best people to tell you what's been going on.'

He expounded this doctrine with great conviction.

'Look, Dennis, I haven't told you yet, but you're going down to Belgium tomorrow with Walter. You'll need to pack this evening, so you'd better hand these two over to me.'

I explained to him about the Civil Affairs billet. The prospect of a journey to secure it distracted his attention from the Dutchmen.

'Excellent,' he said. 'And you know Gordon's expected tomorrow? Can't I wait till he comes, and go down there with him? It'll be much more convenient travelling in the Peugeot, and Gordon's just the man for negotiating with Civil Affairs. Besides, Walter will be feeling tired after the dance.'

'No. I can't rely on this new man being here in time, and I can't ask Walter to load up a truck and then unload it again if Gordon does arrive. So be ready to leave with Walter in the morning, will you?'

'All right, it's a bargain. But as regards those two individuals out there, it's just as you prefer, but I think they ought to be arrested on suspicion.'

'Suspicion of what? Of course not, till we've checked with somebody reliable who knows them. Why be in such a hurry to arrest them?'

'Because it's better to arrest a man and then let him go, than let him go and not be able to arrest him again.'

Crossing the stone corridor between the Captain's room and the office, I thought how I had not arrested anyone yet. I'd often seen it done, but in the countries we'd passed through up till now, the Allies had usually jailed their nationals themselves. But in Germany where, according to the Army manuals, hundreds of thousands of members of the Nazi organisations belonged to the Automatic Arrest Categories, it would be we who would have to find these men and bring them in. To arrest a Gestapo agent or a guard at a concentration camp would be one thing, but what about the thousands of dubious persons police call 'suspects'—people concerning even whose technical guilt they are not certain? In time of peace, the laws and courts may protect them from the absolute whim of those who make the arrests; but in Germany, we were to be the judges as well as the jailers. Dennis's principle, 'When in doubt, sling 'em inside,' was one I couldn't apply with his conviction, because it seemed to me to be criminal to put a man in a cell on a flimsy pretext; and even wrong to arrest all those who had been classed in the Automatic Categories, irrespective of their individual histories; and deeper down, I felt that to take away any man's liberty—any man's—was no solution. Still, Dennis's attitude was logical—he accepted the job and its conditions. And it was certain that in spite of my 'wrong' and 'criminal,' I wouldn't be able to avoid what I disliked the thought of doing much longer.

In the office, I found that Norman, always sociable, had offered the suspects a cup of tea and was practising his store of Dutch on them; while they were patiently correcting him, at which he would remark, 'Oh, that's how you say it, is it?' and repeat the phrase as he had pronounced it before.

'You say you were working for a Dutch organisation,' I said to them. 'Is there anyone in the town who can speak for you?'

'Almost anybody. But if you wish it, you could come with us to our local leader.'

'Is he in the Militia?'

They smiled.

'Oh no, he is a doctor. Few of our people have become soldiers, our work is more important. But if it is a man in uniform you need to convince you, we could ask the Militia Commandant to come. He knows us also, of course.'

'That won't be necessary. Shall we go round to this doctor?'

'May we now have our papers back?' the burly man said.

'When I've met this doctor you speak of.'

'Of course,' the fair one said as we went out, 'we know these papers do not look impressive, and we made better ones to deceive the Germans. But we did not think our Allies would trust more to papers than to our words.'

We drove into the town, and they directed me to an old house in the market square, with a blue and white enamel plaque on the door. It was opened by a blonde nurse who showed us down a long corridor past a surgery and into a sitting-room. This was decorated in an occidental-oriental style with low couches, too many carpets and hammered metal-work. 'The doctor was in Java,' one of the Dutchmen said.

After a short wait, a man with rounded shoulders, greying sandy hair and a tired face, came shuffling down the corridor into the room. He glanced at me and listened while the young men explained what my visit was about, speaking both at once and laughing slightly. Then the doctor nodded and said, 'Well, it would be best if you left us here alone.'

He offered me a cigarette and, talking of other things, took some time to come to the point. It seemed he was weighing up how little he would have to say to get rid of me. Then he began a guarded explanation of the work his organisation had done, and I interrupted him to say, 'Yes, but what was the reason for their visiting Belgium?'

'Please remember that we have had the Germans here for many years and that their army is still a short distance from this town. Until they are quite defeated we shall not be secure. For unfortunately, since the liberation, some have foolishly spoken of things we did, and the names of many of us have become generally known. If the Germans were to return and find us, we would be treated without pity. Until the war is over, we must remain in contact with our friends here and in Belgium, so that we can make arrangements for such an eventuality.'

'You think the Germans might return?'

He raised his hands in the air and dropped them on his knees.

'Probably they will not, of course, but if they did, your soldiers would fall back to new positions, but we would be left here, should we not? And since many in the town have learned that Allied airmen were hidden in this house, it would be one of the first places for the Gestapo to visit. I should not like to be found here when they came.'

'Allied airmen were in this house during the occupation?'

'On the chair where you sit they have also sat, drinking gin. And on the sofa there, many of them have slept.'

I looked round the room.

'Gin is scarce now,' he said, after a pause. 'But I have some for you, if you wish it.'

He got up, opened a lacquer cabinet and poured out drinks. I asked him to tell me more about the Gestapo. 'When we get into Germany,' I said, 'will they try to go underground?'

'Not they, at any rate. Evidently they were most dangerous to us here, but once it becomes clear to them that Germany is defeated, they will fall completely to pieces, I would say. They are men who never fought from principles, and who now are kept alive by force and fear.'

He sat sipping from his glass, smacking his lips with a sound of distaste.

'And those two who brought me here. What sort of work did they do?'

'They were couriers. Being students, they were able to travel from city to city on the pretext of their sports. I fear they have not learned much of their books during the war.'

'How did they travel?'

'In usual ways, by 'bus or train, or sometimes in the canal boats to avoid controls that were made on public transport. Among canal workers we had many helpers.'

'Among the lock-keepers?'

'Why do you ask?'

'I know a lock-keeper here.'

'In the house near where you live? Yes, he was with us. Did he tell you so?'

'No.'

'He was right. Yes, it was he who sent messages for us on the canal telephone, which the Germans neglected to cut.'

'Why didn't they cut it?'

'We were not sure. Perhaps due to ignorance, perhaps to penetrate our organisation with the help of traitors who also listened. And that is another reason why we remain in contact with friends in Belgium. For some who betrayed us have fled there, and we are anxious to find them.' He glanced at me, then down at the floor. 'Many of our best men are dead, and others have been taken away to Germany, which is perhaps the same thing. The lock-keeper you speak of: his son was taken away—did he mention this?'

'No.'

'Yes, his son. And another of the students who worked for us, the best of them. He also was taken.'

The doctor put his empty glass on the table with a slight bang, and I got up. 'I'm sorry we troubled those two,' I said.

'It is understandable. One must be careful.'

'When you meet a stranger, it's not always easy to imagine he did work of that kind. The lock-keeper, for instance. I shouldn't have guessed it.'

'And why not?' said the doctor, getting up too and unbending slightly now he saw I was going. 'Men often hide their characters behind their faces, and a good man may at first be indistinguishable from another.' He put his hands in his coat pockets and looked at the ceiling. 'But it is also true that even in an organisation like our own, I have noticed that many who came to us, and did fine work, were in no way outstanding. One might expect all such men to be unusual in some way, but it was not so.'

'What made so many come and work with you?'

'Each man had his motive, I suppose. Some came for patriotic or political reasons, some by desire for excitement, some by curiosity and the wish to know secrets, and some, perhaps, from a feeling that, at such a time, it was a man's duty. In many, these motives were no doubt mixed, but once they began working for us, even if they were ordinary people to begin with, they were bound to become what the newspapers now call heroes, or else traitors.' He slapped his pocket and held out his hand. 'You will excuse me?' he said.

He went to the door and called out, and the fair young man came in and led the way along the passage. When we were half way up it, he stopped and said, 'You have a moment?' He opened the door of a waiting-room, and I saw that the nurse who had shown us in was standing there. 'This is my sister,' he said.

Although she was blonde, she had dark eyes and eyebrows. She was an elder sister, it seemed. I shook hands with her.

'Listen,' the brother said. 'I must tell you. My sister's fiancé has been taken to Germany. She wishes to speak to you about him.'

'I only thought,' the girl said, 'that when you go there, you might possibly find news of him. I know it is unlikely, but perhaps it is possible.'

'Was he working with you here?'

'Yes, he was with us, a fellow student of mine,' the brother said.

'What was his name?'

'Maarten,' said the girl. 'He will be in some prison or concentration camp. I know it is doubtful, but perhaps if you were to find news of him later on, you would tell us.'

'Is that his family name?'

'No, a first name.'

'You would find he speaks English,' the brother said.

I asked for his full name and for other details, which the brother gave me, and I wrote them down with as great an air of conviction as I could muster. The girl said nothing more, nor attempted to establish any contact, yet looked at me with an interest arising from thoughts directed elsewhere.

The brother came out to the front door, and we stood a moment talking on the doorstep. When he heard we were going down to Belgium, he said, 'Well, perhaps it would be useful to you if I sent some of our friends there to see you? They could be ears for you.' I thanked him, and told him our new address. 'Good-bye then,' he said. 'All that my sister asks concerning Maarten may be useless, and you are not in Germany yet. But it will give her greater optimism to have spoken to you.'

I said good-night to him and got into the car. As I was driving back through the town I saw soldiers coming out of the cinemas and canteens, and waiting for the lorries that would take them back to camp. There was a big moon up, and standing together in casual groups, with the patience of men who live restricted lives together, their faces were lit with sudden brightness by their fags and, more generally, by the shallow light from overhead.

Except for a light burning in Norman's office (where he also slept), the billet seemed deserted when I got back, but as I walked into the hall from the side door, I heard a clatter of feet on the floor above. I was going up the stairs to look, when the light of a torch came down them and, turning at the landing, it shone full into my eyes. 'Don't look so suspicious, it's only me,' said Dennis's voice, and he swung the beam round in an arc to illumine the diplomatic smile on his face.

'What are you doing up there? Examining the Captain's quarters?'

'Now, Colonel, no heavy irony, please. Let's go into the mess, revive the fire and crack open a bottle of the whisky you disapproved of me getting.'

'Well, those two Dutchmen were all right.' I said, as we went in there. But he'd lost interest in them. 'Were they? So that's one up to you. Meanwhile, look at the dismal state this mess is in. No proper fire, crumbs all over the floor and no one to bring in the drinks on a tray.'

'This isn't an officers' mess, you know.'

'It should be better than one, with our opportunities. At present, it's little better than a slum.' He half filled two beer glasses with whisky, handed me one, and went and squatted between the stove and the wall, holding his own glass and the bottle in either hand.

'When you were down at the camp today,' I said, 'did you remember to tell Major Parsons we'd be turning the job over to another Detachment?'

'Yes, and I must say he bore up bravely.'

'You don't think he'll miss us.'

'I should sincerely doubt it. But I think young Cuthbert will be sorry to go. He's the uncrowned king of the place, as far as I could see. He utters Dutch so fluently the farmers stand staring at him in amazement.' He topped up his glass, and added, 'And tell me your impressions of the Captain. Do you approve of him?'

'He seems like the rest of them on the surface, but I don't think he is.'

'Quite promising, you'd say.'

'Yes, I think so. And what were you doing up there on his floor just now?'

Dennis replenished my glass, and said, 'Oh, I only gave his rooms a cursory inspection. My real objective was to examine the upper regions. It's a principle of mine not to sleep in a house I haven't thoroughly explored, you see. And everyone being out seemed a suitable opportunity.'

'Did you find anything up there to interest you?'

'Yes, as a matter of fact, I did. In the attic, I found this, left behind by one of the previous tenants,' and he handed me a photograph across the stove.

It was of a young German soldier with his arm round a strong country girl, and they were leaning their backs against a wall, looking up at the person who'd been holding the camera. The soldier's arm was thrown over the girl's shoulder in a possessive gesture, and his face wore a coarse, energetic, contented look. The girl was holding her hands together in front of her body, and her expression suggested she felt herself to be the real possessor. Both of them had their lips half open, as if they'd turned away from kissing.

I looked up from it to find Dennis eyeing me. 'Now the question is,' he said, 'was the girl there his *Fräulein* at home, or is she one of the local *mejuffrouws*?'

'If it's a local girl, you want to make sure they've cut her hair off?'

'Now, don't misjudge my chivalry. No. Just as a matter of interest, which would you say it is?'

'I don't believe she's German. She looks too thoroughly aware of herself, too reasonable.'

'German women aren't reasonable, in your opinion?'

'Some are, but there's usually something simpler and more spontaneous about them, something more absolute.'

He reached over, took the photograph and studied it. 'You know the Germans?' he said, without looking up.

'I've seen very little of them during the war, but I lived over there a while in pre-Hitler days, just after I left school. You've been in Germany too, haven't you?'

'Me? In my youth, I actually went to school there in person. In many ways, I'm practically a German myself.'

He smiled and threw the photograph in the grate. I picked it up again and said, 'The soldier looks the part, doesn't he. A real warrior. Not like our friendly, scruffy squaddies.'

'You don't think our soldiers look the part?'

'They do in their own way, but it's not the same way. You can see it in this man's face and whole bearing. It makes you feel he was born to wear that uniform, and look how well he wears it, how sure and successful he looks. For them, being a soldier isn't a job, it's a vocation.'

'It's a vocation for our regulars, isn't it?'

'Yes, for some of our regulars, but not for our men in general and anyway, with them it's more than a vocation, it's a fulfilment—something so many of them do well instinctively.'

Dennis had moved onto a wooden stool, and he sat swaying slightly, though blinking occasionally when in danger of losing his balance. He didn't seem to be taking in the words I was saying, but to be extracting their drift and assessing its value by what they revealed to him of my personality.

'So you like the Germans,' he said.

'Like? No, not really. Well, it's not a question of liking. You can't like the Germans as you can the people here, for instance. The word doesn't fit. You can be attracted, or repelled, or both, but if you know them at all, you can't just like them. What's wonderful about them is so deeply involved with what's horrible.'

He nodded his head, still staring. 'Personally, I'm a quarter German on my mother's side,' he said, in a way that seemed to express some agreement and offer a gage of confidence. He got up, filled his glass to the brim, handed me the bottle and said, 'Well, since you're sending me off to Belgium at crack of dawn, I'd better get my head down before that beery crowd of rowdies return from the dance.'

When he'd left me, I turned out the lights and pulled back the curtains from the window. I wished I'd known Dennis longer and well enough to have told him more of what was in my mind. I looked out across the park towards the lock-keeper's house, and spoke to an imaginary companion.

'I was seventeen when I first went there, just the right age. I fell in love with Germany then, because I found everything I wanted.

'I got there at the beginning of the spring, the sort of lad you can imagine. My instincts were sensual and my real feelings tender and melancholy, but they hadn't had an outlet up till then. So to lessen my despair, I had smothered my longing, which bubbled up in the form of a perpetual flow of heady and tiresome chatter.

'But as soon as I came into Germany, I found it was all right to have sensual instincts and all right to feel tender and melancholy. I wasn't there long before I met a girl who came walking with me in the woods to exchange German conversation for

English, and we'd lie on the side of a sunny slope overlooking a lovely vista of the river valley. And boys of my age would be ready to start off in the middle of the night, stopping on a hill-top to sing songs in parts, and tell their troubles to one another very seriously. We all used to go camping up by the lakes in the mountains, sleeping in barns in the forest villages, or down to swim in the river, travelling in railway carriages that smelt of varnish and the sweat of both sexes. The landscape was poetic and smiling, or else romantic and rather gloomy, and it perfectly suited the mood of exaltation we lived in.

'The atmosphere I'm trying to convey to you is one that was serious, animal and lyrical. The country and the people made me feel I should yield myself up, be natural, be like a tree or a bird in the air. It was so attractive, because I was in love with life and felt it had eluded me before.

'But there was another part of this I hadn't realised.

'On top of the highest mountain in the forest we used to walk through, there's a cairn. The summit itself is bare of trees, so that if you stand by the cairn, you have a splendid panorama of hills, lakes and sky, stretching away to the horizon in every direction. We'd spent the night at an inn a mile or two down the rise, and on a wonderful June morning, I got up early and climbed to the top of the hill and sat looking at this view in the warm air.

'A bit later, I saw my friends coming out of the wood and across the open slope that led to the hilltop. I waved to them and called out, but they didn't answer. They came slowly on, and before they reached the cairn I got up to greet them, but they nodded and more or less ignored me. So I went a little further off and sat down there. When I looked round, I saw they had formed up in two circles round the cairn, the girls in the centre and the men around them, all looking out at the landscape. Then they began to sing perfectly together, the women, then the men, then in chorus. It lasted about ten minutes. After that, they broke up and drifted away and sat down in threes and fours in silence. I felt it was a rite, and that I shouldn't have been there.

'Back at the town a few weeks later, I was walking towards the railway station, and getting near the point where the main road was intersected by another, both made on concrete. Down one of these roads came two young lads on bicycles, travelling at speed, and down the other, a closed car driven by a chauffeur, with two elderly women in the back. There was nearly a collision, both parties swerved, and the cyclists dismounted to get back their breath. Meanwhile the car had pulled up about a hundred yards further on. The chauffeur got out, didn't say a word to the old women who went on looking straight ahead, slammed the car door and walked briskly back up the concrete road in his boots and leggings towards the cyclists. He went up to the first, grabbed him by his shirt, and smacked him across both cheeks. Then he did the same to the other. And still without a word, he turned round, marched smartly back to the car, got in and drove off. The cyclists muttered a bit, and did nothing.

'I suppose these were small things, but now I began to feel that behind the animal freedom and exaltation, there were magic and violence. I thought that if what I loved was inseparable from what I'd begun to fear, then I'd been enjoying myself under false pretences. I couldn't be as wonderful or as terrible as they seemed to me to be. But I remained deeply attracted, and still am, though now I know what I'm attracted by. When you cross the German frontier, you go into another world; you find it's like entering a deep forest, peopled with unpredictable spirits. As in a fairy tale, and perhaps that's why they've invented such wonderful ones . . .'

In the office next morning, Norman buttonholed me with a self-satisfied look, and said, 'Have you thought of our two Dutch women at all? I broke it to them yesterday we were leaving, and they seemed quite cut up. But what I thought was, instead of their waiting at table this evening, why not invite them to be our guests and wait on them ourselves? A sort of farewell banquet, it would be.'

'A nice idea, Norman. Will you fix it up with them?'

'Yes, I will. I think they'd appreciate it. It's a pity the Captain won't be here, he's got a conference at Corps all day in connection with the move. But perhaps it's a good thing in a way, because we ought to give them two really decent loads of rations from that stuff Dennis got, and the Captain mightn't approve.'

'I don't think he'd mind at all, but that's a good idea too. Where is Dennis? Is he ready to move off to Belgium yet?'

'Oh, didn't you know? He left early on a motor-bike for the

refugee camp. He said he had to go back there for a few hours for a special purpose.'

'A special purpose, I'll bet it was. Where's Walter?'

'In his room, I expect. How should I know where everybody is?'

I found Walter standing shaving in the striped civilian shirt he wore as pyjamas. 'Hullo,' he said, pulling down his jaw and scraping it. 'Sorry I'm a bit late getting up, but you must blame the dance for that'.

'Dennis has shot off to the refugee camp. Do you know anything about it?'

'He came in here before I was properly awake and muttered something about not having to start till after lunch. Wasn't that right?'

'No. I wanted you to leave straight away.'

'He mentioned the refugee camp, too. He was going to fetch somebody from it, he said. Some Dutchman.'

'I don't know. He's beginning to get me down.'

'Cheer yourself up and have a cigarette,' said Walter, wiping his face as if he was polishing a boot. 'Well, that was a grand dance last night, even though the beer ran out.'

'Did you get Harry's girl home all right?'

'I did, but it was all I could do to tear those two apart.'

'Well, as soon as Dennis gets back, start off, Walter, will you? I've got to go out for rations.'

But when I returned in the afternoon, Walter's loaded truck was still standing in the car park. I looked all over the house till in the store-room, I found Cuthbert and Dennis examining a small, bony man who was changing into a khaki shirt and trousers that were too big for him. Dennis stepped forward, put one hand on the small man's shoulder and said, 'Meet Cornelis, our new mess waiter.'

He had curly hair well oiled, and oriental features with large, brown eyes. He looked at me in an ingratiating way. 'Who is this?' I said.

'He's coming to work for us.'

'Who says he is?'

The smile left Dennis's face. 'Now listen,' he said. 'Is it or isn't it a fact no self-respecting soldier likes to sweep and dust? So what's the answer? To have a regular domestic assistant on the strength who'll travel with us wherever we go. And here he is—Cornelis.' He patted the Dutchman on the shoulder.

'What is all this, Cuthbert?'

'The young person came through yesterday among the refugees and told us he had no family or anywhere to go, and Dennis took a fancy to him.'

'Why didn't you tell me about that last night, Dennis?'

'The inspiration of getting him only occurred to me in the small hours, and then I realised I'd have to act quickly before I left for Belgium, and didn't like to disturb your slumbers.'

'And it took you till now to get back from the camp?'

'I had to stay on there for lunch, you see, so as to persuade Major Parsons to part with Cornelis. And he only agreed at last when I told him I believed Cornelis to be a high-grade suspect, which was not, of course, quite the case.'

'But who is he, this person?'

'If you ask me,' said Cuthbert, 'he was down in one of the bombed villages, looting.'

'And the idea is to have him live with us?'

'Correct.'

Cuthbert and Dennis watched me. The Dutchman had withdrawn discreetly to a corner of the room.

'Now I think you're making a mistake,' Dennis said soothingly, 'if you imagine that because this man may be a bit of a thief, he'd rob us too. On the contrary. We're the last people in the world he will rob. First, because we've done him a good turn and he's dependent on us, and second, because he'd be far too scared to.'

'He may rob somebody else,' said Cuthbert.

'All the better, so long as he brings us our share of the proceeds.'

'Quite apart from anything else,' I said, 'the new Captain would never wear it.'

'Then it's up to you to put it to him the right way.'

'I don't like it. We've got on all right with voluntary help so far.'

'Voluntary help! What's the use of that? Don't you know a small Unit like ours is entitled to employ civilian labour?'

'Are we?'

'Of course we are. It's just a matter of getting hold of the right forms so that we can pay Cornelis his wages. And then, as soon as we engage any further domestics, Cornelis can supervise them for us. He'll be our major-domo.'

'Dennis, you're a character. Don't you realise you're in the Army?'

'Don't talk like a recruiting-sergeant. If there's one thing the Army teaches you, it's not to be bashful. The way to do these things, is to do them.'

'What do you think, Cuthbert?'

'I realise you're only asking my opinion as a formality, but if you want to hear it, I'll tell you I think it unwise for obvious reasons to take this man, though not necessarily a wrong idea to have a civilian help if we're really entitled to one as Dennis says we are. All I insisted on coming up here for was to make sure Dennis didn't disguise the true facts about his background.'

'Well, let's have a talk with him.'

Dennis called Cornelis over, and I asked him if he'd be willing to work for us. He smiled and nodded vigorously, though making it clear he regarded the matter as settled.

'I knew you'd see the light,' Dennis said. 'I've already fitted him out with some of his kit, and as soon as he's got the rest of it, we'll set off together for Belgium.'

'No, you can't take him yet. I'll have to show him to the Captain first.'

'Now, why? The thing to do is to present the Captain with the accomplished fact.'

At this juncture, Norman's head appeared round the door, and frowning suspiciously at Cornelis, he said, 'I think the second reinforcement is arriving. You might come out and identify him, Dennis.'

We went onto the front porch, and saw the Military Policeman by the bridge leaning through the window of a blue civilian car. The Redcap waved towards our billet, and the car, which was heavily stacked with luggage, came grinding horribly through the front gate. Dennis slapped his thighs. 'I knew the old Peugeot would hold out,' he cried. 'Good evening to you, Gordon. So you made it.'

A stout man stepped briskly from the car, pulling off his motoring gloves. 'Hullo, Dennis,' he said. 'Oh yes. Rely on me, you know.'

'Well, come over and meet the Detachment notabilities.'

The newcomer came walking towards us, taking little steps

on the edges of his feet and rolling slightly from side to side like a mariner. A pistol hung loosely against his flank in cowboy fashion, and he wore a semi-military jacket, cut to resemble a regulation leather jerkin, but evidently home-made out of a patterned blanket. His pale blue eyes gazed at us with a show of disinterest from out of a big, pink, asymmetrical face. He raised his gloves in a general salute as he came up.

'Now, let me introduce you round,' said Dennis. 'This is our senior Sergeant . . . .'

Gordon waved his gloves again. 'The big cheese, hullo chummy,' he said, shaking hands.

'And these are Cuthbert and Norman, and you'll meet the others inside. Don't unpack, Gordon, we're leaving for Belgium immediately.'

'What, back to Belgium again? Well, I'd like a bite to eat first, if you've got such a thing.'

'Just a minute, Dennis, you're going down there with Walter.'

'Now look,' cried Dennis, walking about and shaking not just his wrists at the joints, but his arms from both shoulders. 'Why make Gordon unpack when he's all ready to leave again? He can come with I and Walter—don't you see we're the obvious people to represent the Detachment's interests there in Belgium?'

The new Sergeant put his hands into the top pockets of his blanket-jacket, threw the weight of his body on one leg and listened judiciously with his head on one side. 'Come on, do be reasonable,' Dennis urged me.

When Norman pointed out that it was so late they might as well stay on for his farewell banquet, Cuthbert and the party for Belgium decided to join us and leave afterwards. And so the two Dutch women were enthroned at either end of the table while Norman and Cornelis did the waiting; but from time to time they would leave their seats of honour and rush off to see to the progress of a dish in the kitchen. Norman's speech in Dutch which nobody understood, and Dennis's imitation of Dr. Seyss-Inquart looking under his bed for time-bombs, sent them into screams of laughter. But when we all went out to help wash up, we found them crying. We said we'd go and fill the boxes with rations, and see them home after the coffee.

I drove the tall, jovial girl, and she directed me through the town to a small house in one of the circular avenues on its outskirts. 'Here I share a room with a friend,' she said. 'She is also from Rotterdam and, like me, was cut off from home at the liberation.'

I followed her carrying the box up a narrow, carpeted staircase, into a neat, low room full of ornaments and brittle furniture. She asked me to stop for a cup of tea.

While she was out getting it, I thought of these two women and of how kind they had been to us. At so many other places where we had stayed on the way up from Normandy, the same sort of thing had occurred. We would arrive among a fresh group of civilians, and well aware of the attraction of soldiers and liberators, would impose on their friendliness in a hundred ways. Everyone has imagined a world in which he can open any door and be quite sure of being made welcome; and during the campaign, this had really happened, again and again. The conditions of the war, the uncertainty as to what was coming next and the urgency of immediate tasks, created the illusion that the passage of time was suspended, and everyone was filled for the moment with an extraordinarily potent sense of perpetual youth. Friendships were rapidly born, and people revealed themselves in a day as they would not usually do in a year. As we moved on, renewing the experience before it had had time to stale, we lived in what seemed to be an expanding and eternal dream: a paradise to the restless, for our halts in each place were so short that if no relationship could develop in depth, we were also protected, so long as the advance continued, from the disillusionments of day-to-day reality. But for those we left behind each time, and who loved us not really for ourselves but because we were the liberators who made them feel young again, there was a sudden awakening when we cheerfully said good-bye to them and moved on.

She came in again with the cups on a tray. 'It is your English tea,' she said, sitting down. 'We are very fond of it.'

'Let's hope it won't be long before you can get tea regularly again.'

'We, yes. But what of our relations in Rotterdam? What are they living on? How often have I wished, seeing all the plates and cups not emptied at the washing-up, that they could eat and drink some of it as well.'

She started to cry again at the thought of this, and her body relaxed into weakness with the same grief that was in her eyes.

THE REHEARSAL

As soon as word came through from Dennis that his party were in possession at the new billet, Norman and I set out there one afternoon ahead of the others. In earlier times, we'd tried to travel all together in convoy, with flags on the front and rear cars and an even space between each vehicle. But as moves became more frequent, the need for advance parties and rear parties, and the general inclination to ride in groups or even singly, had led to these piecemeal migrations.

We crossed the frontier by the main route which carried the heavy convoys up from Antwerp and the French ports beyond. The change from Holland was again immediately noticeable, and we had only to reach the first Belgian village to sense what seemed an almost Mediterranean atmosphere of greater relaxation and good cheer. This may have been partly so because the Belgians, whose territory was now cleared of the enemy, must have felt themselves further from the centre of the war. But it was also that they seemed to take their troubles more easily, and perhaps a greater habit of occupations helped in this. Faced with a problem, their first idea was how to solve it, however unorthodox the means, and this practical instinct also emerged in their different attitude to ourselves. The Dutch treated us as soldiers and men of principle, but wouldn't necessarily give us what we wanted unless we could clearly prove we were entitled to it. The attitude of a Belgian would usually be that we were fallible human beings in uniform, and that we might certainly have what we asked for, provided we showed him we were strong enough to take it anyway if he said no, and could offer some advantage in return if he said yes.

As soon as we saw the tower of our new town, I overtook Norman and led the way to the billet. We ran the vehicles up the alleyway to the garage. The Peugeot was parked there.

In the front room where the Captain and I had met the Civil Affairs officers, we found Gordon sitting with his feet on the glass-topped desk and with a bottle and some dirty glasses on the floor. He winked at us from this position. I said, 'You got in all right, then?'

'Yes, no difficulty. We had a tussle with one of the officers about some furniture he tried to take with them, a Lieutenant Adeane it was, but we got the Town Major to sabotage that little plan.' Gordon tilted his chair back. 'Walter was telling me you need a full-time Quartermaster to see we're well supplied with everything, and if you've no one else in mind, I might do it for you.'

'I thought of asking Dennis, as a matter of fact.'

'Dennis? Well, it's just as you like, but I don't think you'd find he'd stick it. He starts a thing all right, you know, but you have to tidy the ends up after him. Anyway, I mentioned it to him, and he's not interested. So what about it?'

'Well, I don't mind, so long as you let me know what you're doing from time to time.'

'Fair enough, chummy. I'll make the necessary arrangements.'

Norman had caught sight of some lettering incised on the surface of the desk. It was the word PARTISANEN. 'Who did this?' he demanded, pointing.

'There was a Resistance headquarters here at the liberation,' Gordon said to him.

'Need they have defaced valuable property? It's pure vandalism.' Norman rubbed the letters with one glove, as if to efface them.

'There's a rumour around that the owner of this place didn't really go off with the Germans. Some say he's hiding in the town.'

'Who told you that?'

'Lieutenant Vroons for one, but he doesn't believe it. He's the Gendarmerie officer here. Dennis is taking you round to see him later this evening.'

Dennis came down from the bathroom, rubbing his scanty hair into a tuft with a towel. He gave us a beaming smile and said, 'Welcome to collaboration villa. Let's have some imitation brandy while I tell you new boys all about it.'

He called out for Cornelis, who came in with more glasses, miming an expression of delighted recognition when he saw us.

'Did you have any trouble with the Captain over him?' Dennis asked me.

'No. His only real condition of keeping Cornelis was that we must get him an identity card.'

'The Captain likes to preserve the outward forms. Well now, here's what we've arranged. Lieutenant Vroons is sending us a hand-picked cook and two cleaning women tomorrow, to do the lunches for us and supper for anyone who wants to live here.'

'We're all going to live here.'

Gordon and he expressed varieties of surprise. 'But we've arranged private billets in the town for everybody,' Dennis said.

'You're not going to try and pack us all into this place, are you?' said Gordon.

'Everyone will be much more comfortable with their own family to look after them,' said Dennis. 'You must consider the men's morale, you know.'

'And they'll all be here at nine in the morning? And within call when they're wanted for duties? No, this house is big enough, there won't be more than two to a room.'

'Perhaps you could find a barracks for us somewhere,' Gordon said.

There was a silence.

'On occasions when we've tried private billets before,' Norman told us, 'I've found myself stuck in my office without an evening relief for days on end.'

'That should have made you happy,' said Gordon. 'What we could do is talk to the officer and see if he thinks differently,' he said to me.

'Don't swing the officer on me. I'll tell him what I think, and if you want to try and persuade him, go ahead.'

'Ah well,' said Dennis, throwing out his arms, 'we'll let the Colonel have his way. We'll stay on in our private billets till the others get here, and if there's any room then, we'll come in too.'

'You'll come in in any case.'

Dennis raised his eyebrows up to his forehead, and Gordon kept nodding as though to say, 'Would you believe it.'

'What about a British compromise?' cried Dennis. 'There's another house next door—let's fix up with the Town Major to take that too, and those who don't like to be near the powers-that-be, can move in there.'

'All right, we'll see about that.'

Dennis poured out some more of the imitation brandy, and we clinked glasses sullenly.

'Now,' said Dennis, 'the next thing is that tomorrow at 6 p.m., I've arranged for some of the local dignitaries to come in for a drink.'

'Have you.'

'Yes.' He began ticking names off on his fingers. 'The Town Major, of course, and his Belgian Lieutenant. Next, a most important person, the Regimental-Sergeant-Major of one of the Units of the Armoured Division, who says he's coming along here for a bath this evening, by the way. Then Lieutenant Vroons of the Gendarmerie, Slippery Sam and the . . .'

'Who's Slippery Sam?'

'That's the Town Major's name for the Burgomaster. He says shaking hands with him is like holding a piece of cod. And then, as I was saying, the Director of the Catholic Seminary here, who I thought might be a good influence on us all.' Dennis grinned in a way that seemed partly serious. Norman looked shocked.

'Well, bring him along, Dennis. Anyone else?'

'Yes. The former leader of the local Resistance.'

'Isn't he still their leader?'

'It's been disbanded by order of the British. But they're still more or less organised, and we ought to get to know them. Particularly as the cook Lieutenant Vroons is sending us is his brother's widow.'

'Who's brother's widow?'

'The Resistance leader's. They shot the brother just before our troops arrived.'

There was a pause.

'Well, we ought to create a good impression by our hospitality,' Dennis went on, 'and I think they're some of the right people to invite.'

Gordon offered to wait at the billet and watch our kit while Dennis took us to have supper at the house where they were staying. 'You're wrong to be obstinate, you know,' he told me, as we sat down to the enormous meal the family had prepared. 'Look what a pleasure we're doing these people by our company.'

Afterwards, he took me on one side and said, 'Are you in need of silk stockings to send home? They're the result of a trip we made this morning to a village near the frontier—by all accounts a sort of smugglers' den.'

I followed him up to his room, where he pulled a blanket away from a pile of cardboard boxes in a corner. 'Has Gordon got some too?' I said.

'Oh, yes. He's going to market them, he's got the real commercial instinct. Well, you can't altogether blame him, he lost his business through the war.' Dennis let the blanket fall and picked up some boxes. 'Gordon has to be handled carefully. He's very tolerant and matey, but he can get quite unpleasant when he thinks he's being treated wrong or that it's necessary for some purpose of his.' He opened a box and held out pairs of stockings like a street vendor. 'How many do you want?' he said.

'I don't know that I want any.'

'Come on, have this boxful. They might come in useful for corrupting female morals.'

He didn't hand it to me, but waited for me to reach out and take it. I looked at the box, but seeing the triumphant expression on his concave face, said irritably, 'What about a bit less fooling around? You were sent down here to get the billet ready, not to rob smugglers.'

He smiled and put the box away. 'Let me know if you change your mind,' he said, 'or if there's anything else you need.'

In all Dennis's schemes, the ulterior motive of making himself indispensable and of compromising you in the plot, stuck out a mile. And yet there was a real generosity of intention—in his way he was disinterested, though his gifts, like those of all Robin Hoods, were made at the expense of whoever he plundered. And I'd noticed that his impulse to tell you what he'd done wasn't only due to vainglory and calculation, or the wish to let you in on a good thing, but to a naïve desire for a confidant as well. The donor and tempter was also a penitent, as though he wanted to ward off the consequences of his exploits, in fact and imagination, by letting someone into the secret. But from these hesitations he'd soon fly back to action; the urge to confess the deed seemed no less than the urge to repeat it.

We dropped Norman off at the billet, and drove through the town to visit the Lieutenant of Gendarmerie. 'A very charming man,' Dennis told me, 'very ready to co-operate, and quite a perfect sort of rogue, I think.'

'Well, Dennis, you should know.'

'Correct.'

At the guardroom, they told us the Lieutenant was over in his house, so we walked across there and knocked. The door was opened by a man wearing blue breeches, leggings and a knitted jersey. 'Hullo, Lieutenant, here's some bribery and corruption for you,' said Dennis, thrusting a carton of cigarettes into his arms.

'Oh, good evening,' said the Lieutenant. 'Excuse my clothes, come into the sitting-room, and I shall dress properly.'

'Don't bother about that.'

But he hurried away, and left us in a best room hung with photographs of himself being married, on horseback and marked with a cross in a procession. When he reappeared, he was wearing a jacket with silver buttons and a white lanyard.

He gave us a drink of gin, and we began talking about the war and the Germans. Your first impression of Lieutenant Vroons was of an open and reliable young man, only too willing to do all he could for you in the line of duty. But then you began to notice the double glance in his eyes, the delicate wrinkles, and the way his smile would suddenly fall off his mouth, leaving an equivocal grimace.

I asked him how he'd got on during the occupation, and he said, 'Well, of course, we had to continue to serve under them—those were the orders our government left us with when they departed to France and, in any case, it was the best way we could help our people. How many times during the war did different men come to me and say, "Lieutenant Vroons, whatever you do, do not get dismissed by the Germans, or they may put a really bad man in your place".'

He looked at us candidly.

'So we had to serve two masters,' he went on, 'the Germans, whom we disobeyed as often as possible, and our own government, from whom we had secret orders.'

'Did all the officials stay on when the Germans came?'

'No, no. Not all. For instance, the Burgomaster fled—well, he was right to do so, as he was also a member of the Parliament. He went to France, and the Germans appointed the Deputy Burgomaster to his place. Then, after the capitulation, the former Burgomaster returned, but lived carefully in retirement. The Deputy did everything he could to protect the population but now, since the liberation, he has been deposed, and the old Burgomaster, who never did anything, is back in his former place again. But if there was an election tomorrow, the Deputy would certainly be chosen, despite some calling him a collaborator.'

He spoke as one who can see the reality behind appearances. 'What about our landlord?' I asked him.

'Oh, that is a different matter. He was a political fanatic. He enriched himself by German contracts, and could put a bathroom in his house when private building was forbidden. He also denounced Resistance workers, found men to go and toil in Germany, and so on.'

'Were there many Resistance workers in the town?'

'Oh, I think so. Some I knew, some I did not know, there were various organisations, good and not so good.'

'And do you think there are people here still working for the Germans?'

'You will hear many stories, everyone has spy fever after all these years, but I do not think so. So many were arrested, and others have fled into Germany.'

As soon as he could do so unobtrusively, he changed the subject. His attitude seemed to be that our business was to get after the German army, defeat them, and then go home and not return to Belgium unless as tourists.

'Well, what do you think of that Vicar of Bray?' said Dennis, as we drove back.

'I wonder how we'd have got on in his shoes.'

'Us? That would have depended on what our ideas were, also on what courage we had, if any. Being occupied must be a tricky business.'

When we got in to the billet, we found Gordon sitting drinking with the Regimental-Sergeant-Major from the Armoured Division. He was a large man with blue, blood-shot eyes, and a fierce, simple expression. As he talked, you guessed he knew a lot about leading men and killing them by instinct, and a great deal about the Army from experience; but that outside those spheres he had no pretentions, and was willing to listen to anybody if what they said happened to interest him.

Just now, he was telling us about the unpredictable behaviour of one of his Majors.

'He's a terror, you know. Good as gold and all for the lads, but flies off the deep end when you'd least expect it. You know that dance they call the Hokey-pokey? Well, right in the middle of the Other Ranks Ball, he steps into the middle of the floor and bawls out above the music, "I won't have that degrading dance danced here"—see? So the orchestra stopped and the lads stood not knowing quite how to take it because they were there with their girls, and it was no business of his, really, what they danced, so long as it was decent. So I walked up and told them to play a spot-waltz, which eased the situation, but it took me the rest of the evening to calm him down, and then I had to calm down some of the lads who spoke as if they wanted to make a complaint. Well, there it is. You can never tell with an officer, can you.'

Gordon filled up his glass.

'Still,' the Regimental-Sergeant-Major went on, 'I see the Major's point, he doesn't want the men in his Regiment getting slovenly habits. He's right about that—they're good lads, you know, the ones we've got, very few of them regulars, but still, good lads—and I only wish myself that when they're walking out, they wouldn't wear their caps at all angles like matelots. That's a way you can tell the regular soldier from the conscript, his pride in his appearance when he walks out. Well, I suppose you'll not agree with me, you're none of you regulars, I can see that.'

'We've got one regular in the Unit, 'Major. You haven't met him yet, he's out at supper.'

'What mob's he from?'

'He was a Guardsman.'

'Oh, a Guardsman.' It was difficult to tell whether the face he made expressed grudging approval or mild disgust. 'Well, anyway, he'd tell you the same. The Army hasn't been improved by conscription.'

'But 'Major,' said Gordon, 'the regulars could never win the war all by themselves.'

'And after all, Sir,' Dennis told him, 'the war's the regular's bread-and-butter, isn't it. It gives him his chance to display his skill and get promotion. As for the poor old conscript, unless he happens to have a taste for unrestricted killing, all he's got to fight for is to save his skin and prevent his home being treated the way he treats the enemy's.'

The Regimental-Sergeant-Major drained his glass and got up.

'Oh, granted,' he said. 'We need the numbers, and I dare say we even need the highly-skilled camp-followers like yourselves. Still, if you pour water into beer, it's no longer beer, is it. Well, thanks for the bath, it's set me up for a day or two. I'll be around again, and don't forget you're welcome in the mess, and I'll tell my Regimental-Quartermaster-Sergeant you'll be paying him a visit,' he said to Gordon. 'If you treat him right, he'll give you everything in his shop, though it's all I can do to get a pair of socks out of him.' But his expressionless glare all round suggested their relations were quite different.

'And when is it we're going to crack on into Germany, Sir?' Dennis asked him.

'Don't ask me, lad,' he said, putting on his beret and sheepskin coat. 'Sooner rather than later, I don't doubt. We'll all be in Berlin before next Christmas, I shouldn't be surprised.'

The Sergeants walked over for another drink at the Universal Hotel, and I went in to the office to write some letters. There I found Norman, who was bringing his diary (which he kept in a large, black exercise-book) up to date. The silence was unbroken till he sighed, closed the book, and said, 'Well, you met that Armoured Warrant Officer? The sight of him reminds me of my sufferings in my rookie days.'

'He can't get at you now, Norman.'

He shook his head. 'I may be wrong, but I don't really care for regulars. Most of those I've met are foul-mouthed, crude and brutal. Of course, I admit they can be relied on never to retreat, and that's something. Well, good-night. I can trust you to lock everything up, can't I?'

Norman was one of those who managed, while in the Army, to isolate themselves from experience like a larva that might decline to become a moth. And yet, I thought there was this much truth in his remark, that good soldiers are not always attractive human beings. Who was not struck, at the camps and barrack-rooms in England, by the devious, self-assertive and mean-minded nature of some of the old soldiers? By their turgid satisfaction in the knowledge of ancient customs that gave so strong an echo of dead patterns of life? Or by their low-comedian's performance, with bogus boot-stamping and spuriously smart salutes, of the role of sturdy and reliable veterans? But now these artful dodgers, they of the box-creased trousers and over-boned boots (from whose lace-holes the black paint would be scraped to reveal the underlying brass), were camping all along the Maas, while Norman lay to rest in the collaborator's veneered oak bed upstairs.

These thoughts were interrupted by the sound of a motor-cycle roaring up the road outside, and by the metalic whinny as the rider cuts the engine off to coast the remaining yards. Next came a banging on the door, and when I went to open it, I saw Harry there.

'Haven't you heard? The Germans have broken through.'

'Where?'

'Further south, in the American sector. The Yanks are falling back.'

We went into the office. He took off his crash-helmet and pulled his haversack over his head. 'Here's a letter from Major Bane all about it. There's things you've got to do in it right away.'

I opened the letter, which said:

> 1. Enemy troops under F.M. von Rundstedt have launched large-scale attack in Ardennes sector in general direction river Meuse.
>
> 2. Assist Area Commander in restricting movement of civilian traffic on all roads being used by troops moving south to reinforce Allied positions. (See attached map). In view possibility of enemy dropping agents or infiltrating across Maas in this area, prohibit entry of non-essential civilians into forward areas, set up check-points on canal bridges and other Vital Points.
>
> 3. Enlist help local officials, Gendarmerie and Resistance organisations, which are to be re-armed, in maintaining night patrols on all roads your sector. Additional troops and transport if needed from Area Commander, who will be informed.
>
> 4. First reports suggest enemy personnel wearing American uniforms. Contact any local American formations and arrange check-up on possible detainees.

At the foot Major Bane had written, 'Hope this won't disturb your Xmas celebrations.'

We went over to the map of Holland and Belgium whose sections Norman had pinned up on the wall.

'You see?' said Harry. 'It'd be a sod if they got through to the Meuse. If they did, they'd try to bash on to Antwerp, and cut off our armour in south Holland. They might attack us from the north as well, to divide the Army in two.'

'Will they attack over the river here, do you think?'

'Not yet they won't, unless they're lucky in the south or north. Then they might. But I expect they'll be held all right.'

'Is there much of a flap at Corps?'

'Yes, there's a certain amount of it, but you can never tell with Major Bane, he always makes a point of laughing a thing off. I don't suppose he knows what's happening, though. He's not a General, is he.'

'I can't see there's much for us to do till the Captain gets here tomorrow, but I'll warn the others when they get in. Have you time for a cup of tea before you go?'

We found that Cornelis had gone to bed, and went into the kitchen to make it.

'Anyway, you're going to have an interesting time,' said Harry, 'chasing after spies and mixing in with the civvies. I'm getting browned off, myself, up in that office, I can tell you. If I'd known they'd do that to me, I might as well have taken my Dad's advice.'

I asked him what that was.

'He wanted me to be a conchy.'

He swilled the tea round in the cup.

'Why? Was he one himself?'

'Yes, in the last war, he was. They turfed him out of his job and made him bash swedes for the duration, but he never weakened.'

'You didn't agree with him, then?'

'Yes, I did really, and I expect Dad was right in his ideas, but perhaps he was wrong not to find out for himself. It seemed to me you couldn t tell whether you were a pacifist until you'd been in the Army. I mean how can you talk about war until you've seen what it is? That's why I'd like to get back to the Regiment, really. I never saw a Gerry at Dunkirk time, though I saw plenty of the dirt he dropped on us. If it wasn't for that lass I'm going with, I'd ask Major Bane for a posting.'

'How's she getting along?'

'Oh, all right. I haven't put the question to her yet, though. There's something seems to be holding me back.' He put down the empty cup. 'Perhaps she loves me too much, I don't know . .'

We went into the office, and he put on his helmet and jeep-coat.

'Do you know what she told me a few days ago?' he said. 'She's got a brother there in Germany. They took him away before we came.'

'Yes, I'd heard a bit about that.' And I told him of my visit to the Dutch doctor.

'Did you know her father was in the underground too? That needs guts, doesn't it. Do you think her brother will be alive?'

'You can't say, Harry.'

'She says will I look out for him when we cross over. But what chance is there?'

I told him how the nurse at the doctor's had asked me to try and find news of the man called Maarten, too. He listened swinging his gloves, and said, 'It's a faint hope, our seeing them, isn't it? There must be thousands of Allied prisoners there in Germany.'

We went out to the road, and he climbed onto the bike and kicked down the starter, jerking it round as habitual riders did, who handled these clumsy machines as if they were pedal cycles. He waved and shot off, accelerated and tilted round the corner out of sight.

Very early next morning, we were awakened by one of Lieutenant Vroons's Gendarmes, who told us that a farmer had seen two German soldiers in the fields behind his barns. Leaving Norman at the billet, we set off in two of the cars, picking up the farmer at the Gendarmerie headquarters on the way. He led us along country tracks in the watery sunshine, and halted us in a lane from which his farm was visible about a quarter of a mile away.

'How do we go about this, Walter?' I said.

'Oh, no. It's for you to decide. That's what you're paid for.'

'What's needed is immediate action,' cried Dennis.

'I suppose some of us should go round behind the buildings as well,' I said.

'That's right, chummy, and cut off their retreat,' said Gordon. 'Come on, let's get going.' And carrying a Sten gun he had brought with him, he set off with Dennis across the field. The rest of us followed further in the rear, Walter and the Gendarme, the two professionals, having no false feelings about this. Walter, who was stalking slowly, lifting his feet high off the ground as if stepping over trip-wires, said, 'There's no point in getting shot at unless you have to.'

'When is it you have to?'

'To defend yourself, of course, or when you've got to attack.'

'Isn't this an attack?'

'An attack? Two Gerries hiding in a barn? Naow! An attack's when you've got to attack because if you don't they'll attack you. Who wants to get damaged rounding up stragglers?'

When Dennis was within hailing distance of the barn, he held his pistol at the ready and bawled out in German a summons to surrender. Gordon went steadily on with his rolling gait until, within a stone's throw of the wooden door, he let off a burst with his gun.

'My cattle!' cried the farmer.

With Dennis close behind him shouting threats, Gordon ran up to the barn, flattened himself in the doorway and fired another burst into the loft. While doves fluttered up in the sky; and when the noise of the shots had died away, there seemed an even greater silence. A woman came running out of the farm.

'The children!' she screamed. 'Do not fire in this direction!'

As soon as it was certain that there were no Germans in the building, the annoyance of some and the relief of others were vented by a general upbraiding of the farmer. 'You should be more careful about spreading false reports,' the Gendarme told him severely.

The farmer was indignant.

'Would I have ridden four miles on my bicycle and left my family alone with my old father, if it had been nothing?' he said angrily, eyeing the damage that had been done to his barn.

'Well,' said Dennis. 'there's nothing like an early morning outing very occasionally.' He shook hands with the farmer, and we walked back towards the cars. A rabbit started up as we drew near the road, and some of the party blazed away at it unsuccessfully.

At the Gendarmerie office, we told Lieutenant Vroons to turn back any civilians who might try to cross the canal bridge. When we reached the billet, we found the rest of the Detachment had arrived. The Captain was sitting at the glass-topped desk. 'Did you capture anyone?' he said.

'No, it was a wash-out.'

He nodded, and holding up the letter Harry had brought, asked, 'Well, you've read this thing?' And when I said I had, he began reading it aloud as though I'd said I hadn't. 'I'll go and see the Area Commander,' he concluded, 'and you'd better send some people round to these local officials, and tell them to come for a meeting here this evening.'

I mentioned the party Dennis had arranged for 6 o'clock.

'Oh. Well, if they don't mind mixing business with pleasure, you could tell them all to come round an hour earlier, before the drinks.'

'About the Resistance here. You know our Army's disbanded it?'

'According to this letter, it will have to reconstitute itself. These people must realise there's a sudden emergency. Now, Americans. Have we any in the neighbourhood?'

'Yes, Sir,' said Dennis. 'There's a Signals Unit down the road from here, all by itself among the British. Should I contact them?'

'Do that. Give my compliments to their Officer Commanding, and ask him if he'd kindly send a representative for a conference.'

The Captain got up and looked at his watch. I noticed one of his wrists was bandaged.

'It's that decrepit stores truck I had to ride down in,' he explained. 'The engine failed, and when we were trying to crank it, it back-fired on me.' He patted his arm. 'What about that Peugeot of yours?' he asked Dennis. 'Is it any good at all?'

'It's working life is practically over, Sir, but of course, what you need is a really decent car for your personal use. We'll have to see what can be done.'

The Captain nodded absently, and said, 'Well, I'll take the utility for now.'

I went out with him to see if it was fuelled. Dennis and Cuthbert were going in the Peugeot to deliver the other messages, and we spent some time towing them up and down to get them started.

Coming in again by the front door, I met Norman putting up the Detachment sign, and next to it, his notice reading 'Knock and Wait' in three languages. 'We'll need these now we've opened up shop,' he said. 'Did you know we've customers already?'

Gordon was interviewing two stocky men in leggings at the Quartermaster's table he'd set up for himself in the office. The three of them were deep in conversation and smoking fat cigars.

'They've been turned back by the Gendarmerie, and want to go down near the river to buy cattle,' Gordon told us. 'Does that qualify for a pass?'

'The drill is, only urgent government business,' Norman said. 'No personal or family visits.'

'Isn't buying cattle government business? Who are you buying cattle for?' Gordon asked them.

They looked at each other. 'To sell,' they said. 'Where, we do not yet know. Perhaps to the Food Office, or elsewhere. Who can tell.'

'That doesn't sound like government business to me,' Norman said. 'It sounds like black-marketing.'

'What of it?' said Gordon. 'With everyone in Belgium hungry, I don't see why we shouldn't let them through to buy meat. There's no fighting yet in this area, anyway.'

'There may be.'

'Then they deserve a helping hand for enterprise and taking a risk.'

Norman said, 'An Army regulation has been made, and it's up to us to see that it's enforced.'

'The Army's got a mania for issuing orders it just can't enforce. Any old soldier will tell you that. All he thinks of when he sees an order is not what it says, but whether it can be put into effect. My advice to anyone who wants to go into the forward area on reasonable business, is simply to go, and see what happens. There are plenty of other places where you can get across the canal. I'm going to authorise these two, anyhow. Where are those permits of yours?'

Norman looked at me appealingly, then unlocked his desk and handed over a pad. While Gordon was scribbling on the form, referring impatiently to Norman for guidance, one of the cattle-dealers took out his wallet, selected a note and put it on the edge of the table.

Norman saw it first, and stared with fascinated distaste. When Gordon saw it too, he picked it up, smiled, and handed the dealers their permits as he showed them through the door.

'And that's the man you've chosen for our Quartermaster,' said Norman. 'Are you going to let him get away with it?'

'What would you have done?'

'Me? About open bribery? I'd have sent them packing and made that note a prize exhibit in my "Would you believe it?" file.'

Our next visitor was a morose young farmer, who sat down with an awkwardness that seemed to show a contempt for offices. He pulled a wrist watch out of his pocket and handed it to me. I saw that it was a Royal Air Force issue.

'He came down in my fields two years ago,' the farmer said. 'He was dead, and the Germans took his body away. I wanted you to tell his folk.'

I wrote down the number of the watch, and other facts about the crash he could remember. 'Thanks,' I said, 'but how is it you didn't notify this before?'

'Well, I see that perhaps you may now withdraw from here. If that should be, I wanted to make sure they knew.'

He got up, reached over and took the watch, nodded to us and went out. There was nothing grasping about the way he'd taken it back, but it was clear his thought for the airman's parents didn't extend to giving them the only memento of their son's last flight. He may have felt that a watch, being useful, was for the living.

When the Captain returned from his call on the Area Commander, he brought in an American Lieutenant whom he had met on the doorstep. This officer, who wore a steel helmet and carried a brief-case, said that as soon as his Colonel had heard Dennis's message, he'd decided to send a representative right away. 'We're some distance from base out here,' this Lieutenant explained, 'and we've got to keep in touch with you to know what's what.'

'Jolly glad you came,' the Captain said. 'I was going to pop down to see you, as it happens, to have a chat about this break-through nonsense and these tales of S.S. types masquerading in your fellows' kit.'

Perhaps it was because the Lieutenant was a foreigner that the Captain had adopted a comic-Englishman style of speech. Or perhaps it was due to the perverseness that makes some

Englishmen talk idiotically to a stranger of whose qualities they haven't yet formed a favourable opinion.

But the Lieutenant was of the serious, efficient kind, he clearly didn't think it amusing to talk that way, nor care particularly if the Captain chose to. All that interested him was making arrangements for ensuring that his men weren't mistaken for Germans. The Captain, impressed by this impersonal briskness, abandoned the rôle of Algy and reassumed his own. He explained the measures we were taking, and before the Leiutenant left, insisted he should come and have a meal with us some time.

'Duty permitting, it'd be a pleasure, Captain,' the Lieutenant said with firm vagueness.

I was watching him drive away in his jeep, when I saw the Peugeot coming up the road with Cuthbert alone in it. A brown Buick, driven by Dennis, was following on behind. When they got out, Cuthbert said, 'It's a low trick, Dennis, and you won't persuade me of the contrary.'

'An addition to our transport,' Dennis said to me. 'Just let me get it out of sight, and I'll tell you all about it.'

Gordon and Walter were in the garage checking stores, and we all gathered round the new car.

'Well, you see,' Dennis began, 'when Cuthbert and I were coming back from the American Unit, we passed this Buick, and I happened to notice it had a military star on its door, which is illegal.'

'The owner explained that,' Cuthbert interrupted. 'His car was requisitioned by the Partisans, and it was they who put the stars on. He forgot to take them off when he got it back.'

'Forgot! He kept them on so as to deceive people into thinking it was an official vehicle. And anyway, next I noticed he had an Army tyre, and so I checked his petrol, and found it was ours too. Well, naturally, after that I drove him and his vehicle round to the Gendarmerie. Lieutenant Vroons said it was impounded pending enquiries, and I persuaded him to give it to us.'

'To lend it,' said Cuthbert. 'How can he give it?'

'Well, as good as give it. Of course, Vroons had to hand the owner a receipt for it, so I had to give the Lieutenant another in exchange.'

'You wrote him out a receipt for this car?' I said.

'Only to declare we'd taken it over to investigate the tyres and petrol. And then I got Vroons to give me a chit saying the car was detained by him.'

'That makes a third chit.'

'Don't you see why? So that we can show it to any of our people if they ask us how we got the car. We can tell them we have it on personal loan from the Belgium Gendarmerie.'

'What about the owner?' said Gordon.

'The ex-owner? Well, apart from the fact that he's a notorious smuggler, all we have to do is send him to and fro between this office and the Gendarmerie till we move somewhere else, whereupon we drive off in this Buick out of his life forever.'

'Do you think you could keep it that long?' Walter said. 'It's a shaky deal, in my opinion.'

'Vroons assures me there'll be no difficulty whatever. And if we want to make doubly sure, all we have to do is go and see his Commandant at the provincial capital and explain the circumstances, and he'll certainly let us have the car indefinitely. If we let Vroons know we're going there, he'll telephone the Commandant and put him in the picture.'

'But what about this receipt you gave Vroons?'

'That's purely a matter between him and us. It remains in his archives, and is there to prove he hasn't kept the car himself.'

'Why didn't he keep it himself?'

'That might have been difficult, Gordon, because the owner could take the matter to Brussels.'

'Suppose he takes it to Corps?' I said.

'Then we show them Vroons's chit or, better still, the Commandant's, when we've got it. Don't you see, it's difficult for the Belgians to keep it themselves, but easy for them to give it to us. I think it's very nice of them.'

Dennis walked about massaging the back of his head. Walter examined the Buick's engine. 'What are you going to do with it?' he said.

'Do with it? Paint it grey, put the regimental signs on it and make a Christmas present of it to the Captain.'

'Why, Dennis?' said Gordon. 'It should be worth a lot of money.'

'We're not going to do anything like that,' I said.

'No? Why offer it to him? Why not take it in to Brussels?'

'This is disgusting,' cried Cuthbert.

'The Captain's in the office, Dennis,' I said to him.

Dennis was away for about ten minutes while the rest of us argued round the car which, the more we looked at it, seemed to be our own. Then the Captain came out with an intent look, and by the glint in Dennis's eye, I could see he'd been seduced. The Captain looked the car over, then turned to Dennis and said, 'All right, get it painted, and you'd better have that Peugeot of yours done at the same time.'

'Certainly, Sir.'

'I'll use this car myself, and I won't want anyone else to,' he said, frowning at us all. 'Is that clear?'

This frown may have been to disguise his own scruples, and to show we mustn't think that if he disobeyed the rules, it entitled us to take any liberties.

'Well Dennis,' Walter said, as the Captain went off, 'you've got away with it again, but sooner or later they'll turn up your number and then—clang! I for one will be highly delighted to see you polishing buckets in the detention barracks.'

'With your beer-sodden regular pals standing by swinging their coshes.'

'Just so, Dennis, just so.'

'If you could forget all the square-bashing they taught you, Walter, and learn a bit more about efficient civilian methods, you'd have more of a right to express an opinion.'

'You shouldn't have spoken about it to the officer at all,' Gordon said. 'It's wasted on him.' 'All I can say is,' Cuthbert told us, 'if the Captain thinks he can allow this sort of thing and keep proper discipline, he's greatly mistaken.'

The first of the local officials to arrive for the evening meeting was the Resistance leader. I found him in the kitchen eating a high tea which his sister-in-law, our cook, had made ready. He was a small, sharp-faced man, who looked as if he would be difficult to persuade and, once his mind was made up, as difficult to budge.

'Oh, oh,' he said. 'So they want us back again. Then why were they in such a hurry to disband us?'

'I suppose when they got here, our people thought they were going straight on into Germany.'

'Straight into Germany! They disband the citizen army for

political reasons, and now the Germans come straight back into Belgium. Well, I don't know. All our men have returned to work, they will not be enthusiastic. And they have been made to surrender their arms.'

'You'd have arms again.'

'Oh, I suppose so. You would not expect us to patrol the roads for you at night without arms. What else shall we have?'

'Rations and uniforms.'

'And proper pay?'

'No—they don't offer that.'

'Don't they; but if our men are to do the work of soldiers, they should be paid like soldiers.'

'Pay's not offered.'

'Isn't it. Well, I shall ask them. Give me a day or two and I shall ask them. I expect they will do it, but I don't know.'

He emphasised these points with his knife and fork.

'You used to have your headquarters in this house, didn't you?' I said to him.

'We? No, in the Town Hall. In this house, it was the Partisans. Ours was the bigger organisation—there were not many Partisans up here, this is a very Catholic region.'

'Did you work together?'

'Oh yes, during the occupation we did, from time to time. They were young fellows, hotheads, with different ideas from ours. They did wild things. They arrested many people it was not necessary to arrest.'

'Who, for instance?'

'Various people.'

'Who in particular?'

'Among others, the Lieutenant of Gendarmerie here.'

'I didn't know Vroons had been arrested.'

'Oh yes, he was in prison for some weeks.' He seemed reluctant to go on. 'Well, he was sent to the provincial capital and there was talk of a trial, but when our military authorities got there, they ordered him to be released. Quite right. There was no need to arrest him.'

He took a great gulp of tea and stood up.

'The war is not over yet, you know,' he said. 'Myself, being a reservist, I am waiting to be recalled to our army and I shall be glad to be in uniform again. The trouble is, your people underestimate the Germans.'

'We do?'

'Certainly. Look at how your soldiers go round unarmed with the Germans now attacking in the south and here waiting just across the river. Do not go unarmed when you get into Germany, that is all I say.'

'No, no,' his sister-in-law chimed in. 'It was because my husband was unarmed when they came, that they were able to take him away.'

The Resistance leader nodded. 'I warned him, but he was foolhardy. When he heard your troops had crossed the frontier, he began to insult the Germans openly. His death was the result.'

They were both silent until the woman got her handbag off a hook, and took out and gave me a coloured photograph of her dead husband, which she said had been taken ten years ago. He was dressed in the uniform of a Belgian soldier with helmet and greatcoat, and the photographer had placed him in a defiant, martial pose, so that he looked out at the camera with this aggressive air, but also with a fragment of a grin in the dropping away of his lower jaw, and a natural, unposed firmness in his half-clenched fists and in the posture of his feet on the ground.

'It is all we have left to remind us of him now,' the wife said, looking over my shoulder. And when I handed the photograph back, she wiped it holding her sleeve over her wrist, as if not so much to make the faded snapshot clearer as to revive her own inner picture of him. And from the way they both still stared at it before she put it away, I thought I saw another regret: their feeling that the Resistance was already passing into a legend, which so many knew only from hearsay, which others would belittle and which they alone could remember as a part of their daily lives.

Norman came in to tell me the Burgomaster had arrived. 'Ah-ha, our worthy Burgomaster,' the Resistance leader said.

The Burgomaster had stooping shoulders and a pointed nose set in the middle of a white, circular face. He held his hand out in front of him, as if to be ready either to shake mine, or ward off a blow. Then he stood blinking with diffidence at finding himself in our office at all: 'Don't take any notice of me,' he seemed to say. 'I'm only an insignificant civilian.'

'Well? Well?' he said out loud. 'What is one to think? The Germans will be repulsed, in your opinion?'

I told him yes.

'Of course. But if not, you must find a place for me in one of your motor-cars, do not forget it.' He put one finger on my chest and prodded me as he spoke, nodding as if half with pathetic humour, half with timorous gravity. 'You are young, and do not know how terrible they are. I am an old public servant, trying to do his duty in difficult times. If ever they returned, what would become of those who have helped you?' He looked round the room, as if calling on its greater understanding. 'Well, I hope you are comfortable here,' he went on. 'You like it in the town? We are very anxious you should like it here.'

The Resistance leader came in wiping his mouth, and shook hands with the Burgomaster in a perfunctory way.

'And is the Town Major to be present this evening?' the Burgomaster asked. 'Such a good man.'

'He'll be along later.'

'He takes all the best houses and leaves me to make peace with the townspeople, still, what else is one to do?'

'Has he taken your house yet?' the Resistance leader said.

The Burgomaster turned slowly towards him. 'No, not yet,' he said. 'Isn't the Burgomaster to be left with his own house?' The Resistance leader gave him a cynical smile.

I went up to the Captain's room to tell him they were there, and on the way down met Lieutenant Vroons, who was taking off his cape in the hall. 'You are pleased about the car?' he said, adjusting his regalia. 'Go and see my Commandant, he will give you a paper to keep it. But do not waste time, or that smuggler will be there before you.'

'All right, we'll do that.'

'Now, perhaps you could give me some tins of petrol from time to time, for my own cars? And there is another small service I would ask. This afternoon, I seized British military stores from a civilian truck crossing over the bridge. Could you give me a receipt for these?'

'You want to hand them over to us?'

He smiled. 'I wish to distribute them among my men,' he said. 'Your receipt will enable me to do so.'

During the meeting about the patrols which followed, the Captain listened patiently to the visitors' objections, then overrode them by ignoring the difficulties they put forward and insisting on his own point of view. Afterwards we all went into the dining-room, where some of the other guests Dennis had invited were assembled.

The Regimental-Sergeant-Major was there, and he'd brought with him the Major who had objected to the degrading dance. This officer wore a battledress with pressed lapels, and his huge eyes protruded alarmingly from a mottled face. He was gloomy and agitated to begin with (shifting his feet and saying, 'Y'h, y'h), and I wondered why he'd come to the party at all.

The Captain offered him a drink with the right mixture of deference and impersonal friendliness. When they'd warmed up a bit, the Sergeant-Major said to the Captain, 'Now, I think the Major's got something to ask you. Isn't that so, Sir?'

The Major blinked, looked suddenly angry and said, 'Yes, well, I'm billetted with a solicitor, a decent sort of chap, but apparently he collaborated, and the Belgians have confined him to this town, but he wants to go to Brussels, and I really don't see why you shouldn't oblige him with a permit.' He barked this out as though the Captain had already refused.

The Captain stood with his mouth open as if doing his best to understand what was being asked. They watched him with the challenging air of men used to enforcing regulations themselves, and to interpreting them also, when asked to do so by a colleague.

'Well,' the Captain said at length, 'there are all sorts of rules laid down about civilian movement, but just what particular way was the individual you mention thinking of travelling?'

The Major frowned harder and said, 'I thought of arranging a lift for him in one of the Service Corps trucks.'

'Yes, I see. Well, what I could certainly do is issue the driver with a permit to carry a civilian passenger. It wouldn't be necessary to say who. Would that cover it?'

They all nodded their heads in favour of this military solution.

Dennis came over and said, 'The Seminary Director wants to meet you. He's offered to lend you some books.'

I'd noticed this tall, thick-set man in black, who'd been standing in one corner holding a half-drunk glass of gin, throwing courteous, guarded glances round the room. Dennis introduced us, and the Director gave me one half of his hand to shake, inclining an ear above the growing din. 'You were kindly going to lend me a book?' I said to him.

'Yes, with pleasure. Most of my books will be of small

interest to you, but you are welcome to those I have confiscated from older pupils of the school that is also attached to our institution.'

I thanked him.

'At present my school is occupied by your soldiers, but I have persuaded the Colonel to give me back two classrooms at least. It is months now since the children had any lessons, and they are beginning to act wildly.'

'Schools are one of the first places to be requisitioned, unfortunately.'

'So it was also with the Germans. You often make for identical places,' he said, with a slight smile. 'For instance, this house, too, was formerly a rendezvous of German soldiers.'

'They told us the same thing in Holland.'

'No doubt. It is in a sense to be regretted, as the population grow to dislike a building for its associations. But that, of course, is not of your choosing.'

He put his glass on the mantelpiece and stared at me. I began to feel that something else was coming. Sure enough, he dropped his voice and said, 'I have a message for you from our Dutch friends,' And he mentioned the name of the doctor whose assistants Dennis had arrested earlier on.

'They've been down this way again?'

'Yes, on a visit this morning. They regret they had not time to visit you personally, but say they will do so later, and meanwhile one of them has left a message for you.' I waited to hear what it was. 'No, a written message,' the Director explained. 'Perhaps you will come and fetch it at my office this evening? Also the books. I shall have them ready for you.'

I said I would.

'Well then, now I shall say good-bye to your Captain and these others.'

The Director shook hands with the tips of his fingers again, then went up to each group in turn, standing waiting for the conversation to subside, as it invariably did, and saying good-night in a way that suggested he didn't want to spoil their pleasures by his further presence, nor quite want them to forget how idle those pleasures were.

Cornelis, who'd been handing round drinks on a tray, came up and told us more bottles were needed. 'Quartermaster!' Dennis called out to Gordon. 'You're slipping.'

Gordon left the group round the Sergeant-Major, and handed Cornelis a key. 'I've kept some of the whisky back for the Town Major,' he told us. 'He wants a couple of extra bottles for when he goes on leave. I asked him about the place next door, too. He said as far as he's concerned, we could have any house in the town.'

This was confirmed by the Town Major himself when he arrived flanked by his sinister Belgian Lieutenant.

'Hullo, hullo, hullo,' the Town Major cried, as he came into the room. 'I waited till Holy Joe had gone before dropping in, I hope you don't mind. But I haven't avoided Slippery Sam, I see. Ah, my old pal the Burgomaster,' he said, going up and wringing his hands violently.

The Belgian Lieutenant gazed coldly at the civilian guests, and came over and joined us. 'You must look more closely into the Universal Hotel,' he said. 'There is a strange woman staying there. I have seen her in the bar, and do not like her appearance.'

'What don't you like about her appearance, Lieutenant?'

'That she sits writing letters, and glances curiously round about. Also that the Manager of the hotel is often seen whispering in conversation with her. Look into it, I say. You may find bad things going on . . . espionage, who knows?' He stared round at each of us in turn, jerking his head abruptly, like a bird.

When the civilians had left, the German attack was discussed more freely. The Major from the Armoured Division said his Unit had been ordered south, and the Town Major reported a rumour that an American Army was to come under British command on the northern flank of the bulge. While these confidences were being exchanged, the party transformed itself rapidly into the habitual pattern of a military booze-up.

These evenings of military drinking resembled one another, whoever happened to be present: the dirty songs, sung raucously out of tune, with the solo vocalist trailing out the final notes and not knowing all the words; the raconteurs with the circle round them listening to the stories not for their sense, but for the mental drug they provided, adding to the effect of the alcohol by making it needless to think any more; and the moment when glasses broke of their own accord, and lighted fag-butts fell like dew on table tops and carpets, in hazy forgetfulness. What was pleasant about these parties was their atmosphere of easy. uncritical amity, for though the quality of such friendships was a low one, they grew quickly; and there were many men who knew that their paths might not cross a second time. But what was lacking, and gave these gatherings their hard, sterile quality, was the presence of women. The company of men among themselves is delightful, but only when there are women in the next room, or in the next day. Those the soldiers had at home were too far off, and those they had in bars and borrowed flats were not often loved; so that each glass of spirits they poured down their throats was a measure of longing and regret.

The Seminary was on the other side of the square from the Universal Hotel. A porter showed me along dim, well-mopped passages, and into a large study, barely furnished with a minimum of necessities, like a waiting-room in the voyage of life.

When the Director came in, he asked me if I'd have a cigar. He went to a safe in the corner, unlocked it and took out a box, looking sheepish as he did so. 'In these times, nothing is secure, even here,' he explained. 'We have all developed bad habits during the war.'

He lit the cigar for me, and went and rummaged in a bottom drawer of his bookcase.

'Here are the confiscated books,' he said, holding up several yellow-backed novels. 'For my pupils, unsuitable reading, but for yourself . . .' He handed them to me as if pleased to think they wouldn't be wasted. Then he took two envelopes from the table and held one of them up in the air. 'This one will explain the other,' he said, giving it to me.

It was a letter from the fair young Dutchman who'd introduced me to his sister as I was leaving the doctor's house. Opening it, I read:

> My sister asks that you kindly take a letter for Maarten, the student she is engaged to, and my friend. That is to say, she asks you to carry it with you when you go to Germany, knowing the unlikeliness of your getting knowledge of him, but in the hope of it. Please excuse the trouble, it is a consolation to my sister to think she has not neglected any possibility of getting news to him. P.S. Please post it back to the present address if the war is ended and you have heard nothing.

I looked up. The Director, sad and slightly embarrassed,

handed me the second letter without saying anything. It was addressed to Maarten in a tilted hand. I put both letters in my pocket.

'Yes, well, a glass of Burgundy, perhaps,' the Director said.

While he was warming it, he told me that the organisation they all belonged to had helped Allied airmen and escaped prisoners from the Low Countries to reach Lisbon and Gibraltar. 'Such persons were brought here to me usually for a week or so,' he said, 'and then other helpers took them further on towards France.'

'How many have you hidden here during the occupation?'

'Here? Eleven . . . I think it would be eleven. But I was not the only local man who did this work. There must have been others, but who they all were I do not know, nor tried to discover.'

'How did the organisation get in touch with you in the first place?'

'It was through a parishioner. He brought an airman here one day without warning me, and as soon as they entered the room, he simply declared he was leaving this airman with me. So what was there to do but to agree? Yet I was very alarmed about it, for this parishioner was extraordinarily indiscreet—he boasted of what he had done all over the town.'

'And no one denounced him?'

'Apparently not. Or perhaps they thought he was so untruthful, that they did not bother. Besides, denouncing was a dangerous matter. Not only would such a one become an enemy of the Resistance, but if an informer went to the Germans to tell something, that would not be the end of it for him. They would give him other tasks, and make use of him. Therefore even many of those who were not favourable to the Allies kept away from the Gestapo.'

The Director poured out a glass, and excused himself from joining me. 'And it was through this parishioner that you got to know Maarten and the other students?' I asked him.

'Yes. It was often they who brought the airmen here. And it was while doing so that Maarten and the other were arrested. Not long before your troops set foot in France, it occurred. Here near the frontier—a great misfortune. Now they are in Germany . . .' He put his hands on his knees and looked at me.

I asked him how he'd got on when the Germans had been billeted in his school.

'That was in 1940, before the secret work began. Except that my school was closed, they did not much trouble me, I saw little of them, only what was necessary. When first they arrived, two of their Almoners visited me, priests from the Rhineland, they said. However, we did not find that we had much to talk about. They spoke of their resistance to the Nazis, but I confess I was not greatly interested in hearing of it . . . our conversation was mostly of a general nature. And then, of course, they all came back here a few months ago. But not for long, this time.'

The Director now rose to his feet and said, 'Well, excuse me, I have things to do, but you would perhaps wish to hear some music? Our seminarists have a machine that will certainly interest you, since they built it themselves. Come with me, please, and bring the bottle.'

He led the way to another room where two young men in cassocks were sitting writing among festoons of electric wire. 'A soldier to hear your apparatus,' the Director called to them from the door.

The apparatus was a home-made radiogram with its works showing, and I noticed that the devotional statuettes in the room were picked out in neon lights. While the smaller of the two seminarists was getting the records ready, the other came up and planted himself in front of me with his hands in the sash of his cassock. 'Well,' he said aggressively, 'they are at it again. Invading our Ardennes and dropping V-weapons on my old father's house.'

'You think this offensive of theirs is really dangerous, then?'

'You should tell me!' he cried, in an overpowering voice. 'No, in my opinion, no. It is a last gasp, a death-rattle! But not nice for us, to see them here again. And do you know what will happen when you have driven them back? You will fling yourselves into their arms, as you did after the last war.'

'What should we do, exterminate them?'

He looked abashed, then clapped his hand down on my shoulder and, laughing from the stomach, said, 'Yes, that's it, exterminate them.'

The smaller cleric stood with the needle poised, waiting for us to be quiet. We sat down, and he began to play a long choral work, during which he said nothing, only getting up to change the records. If the large man and I spoke at all during these intervals, he glanced at us without a frown, but with a look that hinted he'd make one if he weren't so self-controlled.

When the music was over, and we were sharing the remains of the Burgundy, the smaller cleric asked me, with a respectful air that kept you at a distance, whether I'd enjoyed it. I said I thought it was wonderful. 'And it was German music,' I said to the large one.

'Agreed, but of the 18th century.'

'The singers are of the 20th century,' said the small one.

'Well, they all know how to sing beautifully,' I said. 'Even their prisoners sing beautifully.'

'And their beautiful marching songs, we heard them too,' the large cleric said. '*Wir fahren gegen England*, for instance.'

'They have great gifts, great gifts misused,' the small one suddenly cried, clasping his hands and shooting a guilty glance at me, as one heretic might to another.

'A cuckoo has a pleasant note in the woods, but not when it sits inside your nest,' the large one told him. 'But how can you teach sense about them to an Englishman? They are half Germans themselves, the English,' he said, smacking me again benevolently on the shoulder.

'Well, we are and we aren't.'

The small cleric said, 'Then my colleague is right in thinking you English see qualities in the Germans?'

They sat looking at me, the large one judiciously, the small one invitingly. I wondered whether it was worth it, then emptied my glass and said, 'When I was interrogating German prisoners in Normandy, I used to look at their faces and then look at our men guarding them, and wonder if I could always have told the difference if they'd been dressed alike. But though the features were often similar, it seemed our men usually looked gentler and more reflective, and the Germans wilder and more intense. You could see the difference in the eyes sometimes, if eyes tell you anything. Our people looked as if they'd forgotten something the Germans remembered, or learned something the Germans hadn't learned. They're an older people than we are or rather, they've remained young longer, and their ways are older.'

'A profounder people?' said the small cleric.

'I don't mean profounder, I mean they have something pure and unspoiled, or unimproved, if you like. They seem to have a natural force, as if they were closer to the earth. But it's a nature of the forest more than of the fields they're close to.'

'Very attractive,' the large one said.

'It is what attracts me about them—this innocence and purity of instinct they have. They're not self-critical like some other peoples, and even at their most violent and cunning, they don't really know what they're doing. They're single-minded and extreme, and always capable of the maximum.'

'But the maximum of what?'

'Despair or ecstasy. The maximum in any direction.'

'And their purity and innocence? What of the things they have been doing in the war and before it?'

'I mean that the instinct itself is pure, the force of it is pure, and the unconsciousness of what they're doing is innocent. I don't mean that the acts that result are pure or innocent. On the contrary, their instinct can drive them in terrible directions. But what is remarkable is its force. They're such great givers. That's why when they gave themselves to Hitler, they gave themselves completely.'

'To Hitler!'

'To what was mindless and destructive. He told the men to become warriors again and the women to become guardians of the hearth, and they did that. And they started to build their dream, their horrible dream, which has brought them and everyone else so much misery.'

The large cleric stared at me charitably, shaking his head. 'It is not the only dream they could have had,' his companion said.

From the conversations he'd had the night before, two ideas were uppermost in the Captain's mind: that we were to raid the Universal Hotel in the evening to find if there was anything in the stories about the strange woman, and that he'd have to go at once to the provincial capital to ask Vroons's Commandant about the Buick. He also planned to visit an Army doctor while he was there, for his strained wrist had swollen badly during the night, and he was already having to support it in a sling.

The Captain asked me to drive him down, and he sat giving directions with a map spread out on his knees, glancing anxiously at the way I handled his car and wincing for the springs. The road was crowded for miles with vehicles and armour of the fighting Units hurrying south to stop the Germans, and among them, we saw those of the Armoured Division. We dodged in and out of these convoys in our brown civilian car, intent on our different mission.

'Easy, easy,' said the Captain. 'Turn off here to the right.'

'Down that brick track?'

'It's a short cut, you'll see. We can by-pass all this heavy stuff'.

I sighed out loud, but the Captain ignored this and we set off across a sandy moor along a road that soon became so humped that we had to drive at a sharp angle. It wound about in wide crescents through an unwelcoming landscape of planted conifers, in which high wooden towers for fire-spotting rose up from time to time. Occasionally it was crossed by long, sandy lanes whose endings were invisible, and the further we advanced, the stronger grew the impression that the track we were on led nowhere in particular. When the red bricks of its surface became broken up and mingled with the sand, we had to drive slowly along the gorse beside it.

'Gently, gently,' the Captain said.

'Could I see that map, Sir?' I asked, pulling up.

He handed it to me crossly, with his finger pointing to the road we were on.

'It's a dotted line that peters out,' I said.

'Granted. But it meets this other dotted line which turns into a surfaced road.'

'There's a quarter of an inch between the dots. That's where we are now.'

We looked at the flat emptiness. 'What about turning back?' I said. 'If we get stuck here, there'll be nobody to drag us out.'

'Carry on, Sergeant,' the Captain said.

We slid and danced over the sand for more than a mile, till we saw a farmhouse standing alone among some trees. The Captain, who had been peering ahead like a pilot in search of land, relaxed and lit a cigarette. 'It's a bit more stable here,' he said. 'Let's get out and stretch our legs.'

He walked round the car, bending to examine its axles. Looking back down the road, I was startled to see one of those jeeps with checkers on it, and with a large, red lamp that flashes on and off to announce the approach of a notability. A staff-car came bouncing along the road behind it. In the jeep were two Redcaps, and on the staff-car were a General's stars.

'It looks like the Corps Commander,' I said.

The Redcaps stared at us, as if they'd like to stop and ask why we were standing by a Buick in this remote prairie. The General looked out of the window with mild curiosity. The Captain, standing beside me with his heels together and in his neatly creased trousers that were rather too short over the shoes, saluted. The General lifted his hand automatically and turned away his eyes. They jolted out of sight.

'He must be taking a short cut too,' the Captain said. 'That proves it is one.'

When we got back onto a solid road, we turned west and met with much less traffic. In this region, there were surprising sharp hills, and narrow valleys which fell suddenly away from the habitual flatness. Nearing the provincial capital, we were held up by a double Bailey bridge across a river, and waiting to get across, we looked at the signboard the Engineers had left there. It said what Company they were, how long it had taken them to build and the quantities of material they'd used. A concrete tablet commemorated the soldier after whom the bridge was named.

In the provincial capital, there was the different atmosphere of a rear area, with soldiers wearing polished boots and vehicles only muddy round the wheels. We were kept waiting a while at the Gendarmerie headquarters before being shown into a smooth office in which a short man was standing behind a wide table, free of papers. His uniform was tailor-made and his shirt was fresh that morning. This was Lieutenant Vroons's Commandant. He shook hands with a bright stare in his wet eyes, and asked us to be seated.

The Captain, not quite sure of his ground despite Vroons's assurances, had prepared a speech which, judging by the look on the Commandant's face, was quite superfluous. It seemed all the Captain had to say was, 'Can I keep the car, and could I perhaps have that in writing?' But with an instinct to find good reasons for his desires, he embarked on a rigmarole to which the Commandant listened with his thick lips motionless, until the Captain had absolutely nothing left to say. Then the Commandant rang a bell and dictated a word to his secretary.

This readiness to comply made the Captain uneasy; a surface moralist is suspicious of anyone who acts without stating some principle or other. But the Commandant knew that the man with powers to apply the law can be that law; so he signed a chit and handed it to the Captain as if giving him something of little consequence. 'And Vroons,' he asked, 'how is he? You are pleased with him?' The Captain said Lieutenant Vroons was an excellent man. The Commandant nodded evenly.

When we got back to the car, the Captain seemed restive, perhaps because of this anti-climax, and perhaps because his wrist was giving him pain. 'Now we'll take this arm of mine to the hospital,' he said, and we drove across the town in search of if. Half an hour later, he came out with a long face. 'They tell me I've got to go to bed in there tomorrow.'

'That's no good. You know if they get you into hospital, you may never come back to us?'

'Why not? It won't be for long, they say.'

'Once you're in the medical machinery, they strike you off the strength of the Detachment. When you come out, you'll have to go to the Depôt for a re-posting. Corps will have to find another officer in the meantime, and they may not be able to get you back here at all.'

'Is that how it is? I'll have to have a word with Major Bane.'

We both meditated on this prospect during the return journey. I was certain all the Sergeants would want him to stay. Since his arrival, a shifting equilibrium of ranks and personalities had come into being, in which the position of each one was determined by the demands of all the others, by the instinct for compromise and by the growth of personal affection and dislike. The Captain's conviction that it was natural he should be in charge, was a force that made him the centre of gravity of the Detachment; and the way he accepted each man for what he was, made it possible for us to obey most of his orders without too much reluctance. Above all, he had in common with us that he was a civilian: a soldier who, however long he may serve, never ceases to be astonished by the Army, and fundamentally hostile to it.

As soon as we got back, I told Dennis of this possible disaster. He pondered deeply, then said, 'There's only one thing to do. Send someone to the hospital every day to find when he's coming out, and as soon as they post him off to the Depôt, simply collect him and bring him back here and leave Major Bane to straighten out the paper-work.'

'Would Major Bane play, do you think?'

'Undoubtedly. He thinks the world of the Captain, and wouldn't want to lose him when we go into the Reich.'

So we put this proposition to the Captain who listened carefully, but received it enigmatically, evidently flattered by our insistence, but anxious not to agree too openly to a plot. 'Well, we'll have to see,' he told us.

After supper, the moment had arrived for the raid on the Universal Hotel, for which the Captain had drawn up elaborate plans and enlisted the help of a squad of Vroons's men. The idea, which he detailed to them in his merciless French, was that all exits were to be sealed, that no one was to be allowed to leave the building, and that the upstairs rooms were to be examined, particularly those of the Manager and the blonde. During these explanations, Lieutenant Vroons, who had by now made up his mind that we were amateurs, stood listening with a patronising smile, nodding apologetically to his men from behind the Captain's back. After asking for any questions, and getting the usual idiotic one, the Captain led us resolutely across the square towards the hotel.

When we'd posted sentries at the points the Captain had selected and made our way into the café, it took us some time to persuade the Manager, the staff and the numerous clients, that a raid was in fact in progress. The soldiers there, in particular, absolutely refused to believe it, and being in many cases flushed with drink, tried to undermine our position by loudly facetious comments. The Manager expressed all the injured dignity of a Banker accused of coining; until shrugging his shoulders, he led us up to an office-bedroom on the first floor, furnished in gangster style. With Vroons looking interestedly on, in the manner of a neutral observer, Walter and some of the others began fossicking about in the furniture. While the Manager, who stood with his arms folded and a martyred expression on his round and calculating face, watched them out of the corner of his eye as he answered the questions the Captain put him about the blonde.

'But Captain,' he said, slowly smoothing down his brilliantined hair. 'If you wanted to know about her, why did you not come and ask me? There are no secrets. Why did you find it necessary to compromise my reputation in this way?'

The Captain ignored this, and insisted on knowing who she was.

'It is quite simple. She is the mistress of a certain young Count.'

Lieutenant Vroons pricked up his ears. 'Of the château nearby?'

'Yes, that one.'

'Why has she suddenly come here?'

'Because the Count has arrived from Brussels to stay with his widowed mother, and naturally he would not take her there, or at least, I suppose so.'

'Who is this Count?' the Captain asked Vroons. 'Is he all right?'

'He is a rather elderly gilded youth,' the Lieutenant explained.

'Go along and get her story,' the Captain told Dennis.

I caught Walter's eye. With an expression of triumph, he was holding up a small plated revolver. 'What about this?' he said.

Everyone looked round.

'Have you a permit for that thing?' the Captain asked.

'No,' said the Manager simply. 'I have not.'

The Captain handed the pistol to Vroons who said in English, 'I would prefer you to keep it, Captain. If I take it, I shall have to arrest this man, since it is an offence for civilians to have weapons.'

The Captain looked at him, trying to fathom the logic of his remark. But he said nothing, and handed the pistol back to Walter. 'You'd better hang on to it,' he said.

Norman and Gordon now came in, Norman laden with some half-dozen new Army jerkins, and Gordon carrying a pile of cartons of English cigarettes.

'We found these in the room over the way,' said Norman, laying the jerkins neatly on the bed, and glancing at the Manager more in sorrow than in disapproval.

'I do not like that you search other rooms without my being present,' said the Manager.

'Where did these come from?' the Captain asked him.

'They were gifts from the officers who had their mess here until recently.'

'Gifts?'

'I repeat: gifts.'

'There are about a hundred American torches in one of the cupboards,' Gordon said.

'Were they also gifts?'

'No. I am looking after them for a friend.'

'Which friend?'

'One of my customers whose name I do not know and who is at present on a visit to Antwerp.'

The Manager said all this imperturbably, with a great air of 'This is my story and I'm sticking to it, and the next move is up to you.'

At this point, Dennis's face appeared at the door, and he signalled to me to come out into the corridor.

'What do you know?' he said delightedly. 'We found the Town Major in one of the rooms with a popsy. He told us to get to hell, and we apologised and bowed ourselves out. This must be his abode of sin.'

'But it was his Lieutenant who tipped us off to come here.'

'So it was. Do you think he knew? I'll bet he did. The dirty dog.'

'What about this blonde woman?'

'I couldn't do much with her, she only speaks French. But she's full of life and liquor. I wanted you to have a go at her.'

She looked up eagerly as we came in, and I saw she was of the kind who likes nothing better than to be asked intimate questions. She was swollen and rather re-conditioned, but with the still useful remains of a lively figure, and she was sitting on the bed in her stockinged feet.

'You wish to see my papers?' she said, handing me a half-open, greasy handbag.

'No thanks. Just tell us what you're doing here.'

She was delighted to be taken for a spy, and as she told us the story of her affair with the Count, I began to suspect she was eager for any publicity that might ensue from our visit, so that the Count would be forced into the open.

'I don't think there's anything wrong with her,' I said to Dennis, after about ten minutes of these confidences.

'Except that she could do with a wash and brush-up, I agree with you. We ought to go up and see this Count, though.'

'What, tonight?'

'Certainly. Before she's had a chance to warn him.'

Our raid had begun to peter out, and when we got downstairs to the café, we found that some of the men whom we'd put to guard the exits had accepted free drinks from the Manager. But

Cuthbert had remained true to his post by the kitchen door. 'You can fall out now, Cuthbert,' I said.

'Thank you. I'm glad it's over, I don't really like this bursting into other people's houses.'

Walter came up, holding the pistol lovingly. He had already discovered how to take it to pieces and re-assemble it. 'I must try to get some more ammunition for this,' he said. 'Why didn't Vroons arrest him for having it?'

'I expect they're pals,' said Dennis. 'Old Vroons knows he's got to go on living here after we've gone.'

I found the Captain, and told him about the blonde woman and Dennis's plan of visiting the château.

'Yes, do that,' he said. 'And you can distribute those leather jerkins to the Resistance people.'

'What about the cigarettes?'

'That individual had the sauce to ask me for them back. You'd better put them away in our stores.'

'Are you going to do anything about the Manager?'

'No. If Vroons isn't interested, stolen property's no concern of mine.'

While I was waiting for Dennis, who was still prowling about in the other ground floor rooms, a young man left a group at a table and came up to me. He said he was one of the leaders of the Partisans.

'I thought perhaps you had come to arrest us,' he said with an ironical smile, 'when I saw you come in with the good Lieutenant Vroons.'

'Was it you who arrested him?'

'Yes, I did. He was a friend of collaborators and now, it seems, a good friend to yourselves. Those who have no principles are always on the side of the victors. And now tell me. I hear you have given back arms to the others. But I don't suppose you will be offering them to us. Your Generals are opposed to us, are they not?'

'Yes. They won't be giving you arms.'

'Yet why not? They sent us arms during the occupation. And we are just as ready to use them now against the Nazis. Well, you may defeat the German army with weapons, but you will need right principles to eliminate Nazi ideas. You cannot do that with weapons alone. What matters, is the ideas you hold. If they are correct, your conduct is correct also.'

Dennis joined us, and I asked the Partisan to show us the way to the château. When he pointed it out on a moonlit rise a quarter of a mile way, Dennis and I decided to walk there across the fields. As we got nearer through the snow, we could see that it was of the 19th century castellated kind.

'That's the sort of place we should have for a billet,' said Dennis. 'A real *Schloss*, like they've got in Germany.'

'Do you imagine we're going to live in places like that when we get over there?'

'Naturally. Only the best will do.'

'We'll probably be in a tent in a field, or in some ruin.'

'Nonsense, my boy. We're going to live off the fat of the land.'

'What fat?'

'Well, whatever fat there is. Believe your uncle Dennis. Once we're in Germany, we'll be on velvet.'

We stopped to help each other through a barbed wire fence.

'Isn't it going to be dangerous over there?' I said. 'What about the Gestapo and the werewolves?'

'Werewolves! They'll eat out of our hands, you'll see.'

'What makes you so sure?'

'I know the Germans, I tell you. Strong in victory, mild in defeat. Just the opposite of the dear old British.'

The snow was so deep that we had to oblique off to the right. 'What are we going to say to this Count?' I said.

'Scare the life out of him and ask him for a drink.'

'Then why are we troubling to visit him at all?'

'Well, it's an opportunity of seeing rare social specimens and of prying into their private lives.'

We were approaching the principal façade, and the light from three large windows was cast onto the snow. But the entrance was at the back, and we made a détour round to the gravel drive on the further side. When we reached a large door, we rang and hammered on it. The light of a torch appeared at the side of the house, and the crunching footsteps of the person carrying it came closer.

'What is it?' said a high male voice.

'Are you the Count?' Dennis shouted.

'Yes.'

'We've come to see you about the lady at the Universal.'

'Nothing has happened to her?'

'Not yet.'

'Oh. Come with me, if you please.'

He went ahead of us to a side porch, holding the torch behind him so as to light our footsteps. He let us in by a small glass door, and we stumbled along a corridor. When we'd turned a corner in it, he switched on the light. He was a meagrely built man with a brush of black hair on a head too big for its body.

His face had the look of one who is promiscuously friendly.

'Please tell me what it is before we go in to see my mother,' he said.

'We don't need to see your mother.'

'Oh, you must. She would be most dissatisfied if you did not, and besides, it is the only heated room in the house.'

When he had listened to our questions, he said, 'Yes, it is indeed exactly as the young woman says, but of course, you will want proof of this. What proof can I offer you, I wonder?'

He stood reflecting, with his hands in the side pockets of the Sherlock Holmes dressing-gown jacket he had on. 'Would it reassure you if I mentioned that my uncle is a member of an English Royal Yacht Club?' he enquired.

'That puts you definitely in the clear,' said Dennis, patting him rather disgustedly on the shoulder. 'Let's go in to the only heated room.'

'Yes, at once. But what will you give as the motive of your visit? I hope it is not necessary to tell her the real one?'

'We could say we saw your black-out is defective, which it is.'

'Oh, I am sorry. Please come with me.'

We set off down some more corridors.

'Either he's simple-minded, or he's trying to pull our legs,' Dennis whispered. 'Luckily for him, I think it's the former.'

The Count flung open a tall double door, and we found ourselves in an enormous main room that must have been opulent and fashionable in the 1900s. The walls, which were lined with tattered striped brocade, were covered with rows of pictures, as in an old-fashioned museum. Near the tall windows, to which the Count was now hurrying to adjust the curtains, there was an unfinished picture on an easel. And one large corner of the room was given over entirely to an indoor greenhouse of huge pot-plants, some of which rose shakily to the ceiling. In the middle of all this, an elderly and still coldly handsome woman was sitting playing a game of patience. She had an air of uncompromising hauteur, and she fixed us both in turn with two sharp, hostile eyes.

'Mother,' said the Count, 'here are two English friends of mine.'

She gave us a ring-covered hand and looked at us sceptically. 'And where did you meet these friends?' she said.

'Oh, in Brussels, at the time of the liberation, when I was able to do them one or two little services. And imagine, they are now in the town and have kindly come to warn us about our defective black-out.'

She received this in a way that suggested she was used to his lying to her, and had given up pretending about it.

'Show them the pictures,' she said.

'Yes, Mother, I shall show them the pictures, but first of all, being Englishmen, they would certainly like a strong drink.'

The Count asked Dennis to go to the pantry with him, and the mother drew my attention to the pictures, not getting up from her seat, but pointing at them from a distance, so that it was difficult to tell which one she was describing. They seemed to be of the same period and quality as the furnishings, though she kept assuring me that they were rare and valuable.

When I reached the unfinished work on the easel, she said, 'Do you admire it?'

'It's a view of the town, isn't it?'

'Yes. Painted by my son. What is your opinion?'

This seemed to be some sort of a test question. 'It's not bad, is it?' I said.

At this she gave one short, loud laugh—'Ha!'—and then remarked, 'It may interest you to know that, at the time your Army was marching up from Brussels, this house was for a week the headquarters of a German General. In this room he held his conferences, and stuck up maps which seriously damaged the walls.'

'Did they let you stay here?'

'Oh, yes. Fortunately the General was not of the S.S., and he allowed me to remain in two rooms. Nevertheless, at one point, he threatened to shoot me.'

'Why was that?'

'Noticing that they were eating the preserved fruits from my larder, I caused them all to be emptied from their jars onto the flower beds. They told me this was sabotage, to which I replied that I had seen them driven out in 1918, and was delighted to see them departing once again.'

'Good for you. Was your son here then?'

'Oh, no. He was in Brussels, living on our capital, of which little now remains. He was for the Allies, of course, but he lived well. He represents an average of mankind.'

She said this in matter-of-fact, bitter tones, and I was not altogether surprised when she suddenly cried, 'And how is that disgusting creature? The one who has eaten what was left of our fortune?'

She didn't seem to expect me to reply, but I was relieved that the Count came in again with Dennis.

'Well?' said the Count, noticing I was standing by the easel. 'Your judgement, please.'

He wasn't interested in having it, though, but coming over and taking the picture up between both hands, he gave me his own about this and other works of his that were stacked against the wall.

'You should come here during the day,' he assured me, 'so that you could recognise how truthful my art is to reality.'

'If only he would settle down and develop his talent,' the mother said sarcastically. 'But my son is very capricious in his interests.'

'It is the rolling stone that never gathers the moss,' the Count said gaily in English, and handing Dennis and me two tumblers full of gin, he cried, 'Chin-chin, Mamma,' and tossed back his own in one gulp.

During the weeks the Captain was away in hospital, we settled down in the town and became almost a part of its familiar landscape. Norman stuck pins in the map to show the supposed development of the Ardennes battle, and often climbed up on the roof to see if untoward activity could be detected on the high-road to Maas. By night the patrols left regularly on their tours of the area. The method was for our Sergeants on duty to issue the volunteers with weapons, permits to carry them, and the evening's rations. Then the volunteers got into the trucks supplied by the Area Commander and drove out into the dark, while the Sergeants sat up by the central heating drinking tea against their return. The patrols never caught anyone, and on several occasions were mistaken for Germans, and detained by orthodox sentries.

We got into trouble of this kind, too, for when we went about the countryside, following up rumours of the presence of German parachutists, we were sometimes taken for parachutists ourselves. One evening, I was kept in conversation by a farmer who secretly sent his son round to the local Infantry Unit to tell them a German was in the village. And a Sergeant-Major, using the technique laid down for these occasions, which was that of asking trick-questions about Army procedure in rapid, colloquial English ('Don't they salute a Sarn't-Major, then, cock, where you come from?' etc.), at last decided I was probably not one, but sent me back to be identified by the Town Major, escorted by a still suspicious Corporal. The Town Major humourously pretended he'd never seen me before, and called me loudly to attention in defective German, 'to see if he springs to it automatically,' as he explained to the Corporal, who was holding his Sten gun at the ready.

Dennis spent much of his time with the Americans at the Signals Unit. There was a fashion among them just then for wearing our battledress blouses, and he used to go and trade these with them for coffee. At least, that was his ostensible object in visiting their camp, but it may also have been because of the great attraction which any powerful, organised body exercised over his mind. He used to bring American Sergeants back with him to drink at our mess. These men were immensely sociable, though their natural friendliness had a slightly menacing quality—they seemed to be holding it like a pistol, demanding you to deliver up your own in return. If you did, they were generous and uncritical, and talked to you in a steady stream as if they'd learned what they were going to say by heart. They seemed to be liking, in you, some personality you hardly recognised, and this gave you a feeling of happy irresponsibility in their company.

Gordon, meanwhile, without using methods as spectacular as Dennis's, was very efficient at providing us with more of everything than we were entitled to. He regarded the Army as a vast department store, and military forms as a substitute currency. Sitting at his table with an extinguished fag hanging out of the corner of his mouth, he would read carefully through the circulars we received from the Supply formations, and mark with a red pencil passages which seemed to indicate a new channel of provision, or a loophole in an existing one. And if news reached him of a distribution of whisky or captured *Wehrmacht* cigars at a distant supply point, or of a limited issue to first-comers of some rare garment, he'd put on his blanket-jacket and drive off with Cornelis to get them. Perhaps these activities were an outlet for frustrated energy, a business-man's determination to keep his hand in. Gordon seemed to feel that fortune owed him a debt, and that the war must give him back what it had taken.

Cornelis had now come into his own, for he showed rare talent as a contáct-man. He got to know all the neighbours, and was constantly to be seen stepping across the road carrying tinned food and bringing back iced cakes, coming out of front doors laughing and shaking hands, and deep in conversation with cronies in the cafés. The most diverse people seemed to like him—he was so small, so energetic, so cheerful and ready to oblige, that they treated him like a household pet. So friendly too—or so entirely uncensorious. As he gave you his beaming smile, he made you feel that whatever you were, or did, was just what was to be expected. It was more than astute slyness—it was a waif-like acceptance of a hostile world that he had to fight against single-handed, and make use of as best he could.

Gordon was firm and patient with him, and treated him like a nephew who may inherit the business one day. He made Cornelis all sorts of gifts in kind from the stores, and though these delighted Cornelis, he never gave the impression of being greedy or grateful. Gifts flowed to him naturally, it seemed.

And when Gordon took a leaf out of the smugglers' book, and began to organise civilian deals, Cornelis always went with him. They were often to be seen setting out together in the stores truck, Gordon at the wheel, Cornelis sitting beside him like a boy on an outing. 'A pretty night, Sir,' Cornelis would say, as you came up. And Gordon, leaning out of the window, would answer your enquiry with, 'Confidentially, we're going over the border to deliver a consignment of glassware. Glass is plentiful in Belgium, but in Holland, it's in short supply. So until normal trading is resumed, we're helping both countries out by buying up glasses here and selling them over there at a small profit. Trade follows the flag, chummy, remember that.'

The two young Dutchmen never visited us after all, and I heard from the Seminary Director that this was because their organisation had transferred them to the north, where they were serving as couriers through our own and the enemy's lines into the occupied provinces of Holland. But as they'd promised, they sent some of the other local men who'd belonged to their escape route, to see us. Four of these farmers gathered in our office one afternoon, accepted drinks and cigarettes, but weren't much help. They mostly sat in silence looking at us quizzically, evidently thinking that working for their own organisation was one thing, but giving us information, quite another. In any case, they pooh-poohed the idea of there being German agents in the area. They seemed to have some instinct which told them there was no real danger of this.

But that was not the opinion of Major Benedict-Bane, who also visited us regularly throughout these weeks. He'd tacitly agreed to the plan for getting the Captain back, and hoping this would be soon, had decided not to send us a temporary officer. He'd arrive in the Buick, which the Captain had lent him for safe-keeping, and would stand in the office sipping coffee, and examining our files.

Major Bane was very curious to read the accounts, most of them probably unreliable, which we had collected about supposed enemy parachutists in the area; but he was even more curious about the circumstantial reports on people who were said to be ready to hide and help such parachutists, even though nobody knew for certain whether they would do so if the opportunity arose. For in common with a great many of those engaged in Intelligence work, he easily became interested in confidential information for its own sake: not so much because of the use that could be made of it, as because it had been gathered with great labour, was about personalities, and above all, because it was secret.

In this, Major Bane resembled the true Intelligence experts who were excited above all by any details that could be discovered about the personnel and past activities of the Intelligence organisations of the enemy; and who would spend most of their time and energy not so much in discovering items of immediate use to the Army, as in compiling dossiers of information about the names and movements of their opposite numbers on the other side.

Their own work and that of their German rivals might thus be likened to that of two competing publicity agencies. Neither produced anything, but if either can persuade a client that his help is indispensable, then any rival of this client must employ a rival of the agency, so as to counteract the temporary advantage he may suppose his competitor to have gained. And once this process starts, there is no end to it. Each new German agent calls for another Allied agent to find out about him, the total effect being an enormous expenditure of ingenuity to discover not what the rival nation is doing, but what its agents are doing.

This mental climate encourages, in the experts themselves, a very empirical attitude towards all principles and human beings, and eventually leads to their becoming devoted more to the activities of their organisations, than to the causes these organisations are supposed to serve. The Intelligence expert grows to believe that all men have interesting secrets, of varying value to himself, which it is his right and business, when the occasion arises, to extract from them. So that whatever the motive from which his victim may act, be it noble or base, it will not be the motive which interests him, but the secret.

Major Bane was still a relative dilettante, and had not yet evolved to the state of complete conviction about what he was doing, so that the futility of much of it, by comparison with any serious activity, may still sometimes have struck him. He was at the stage in which, although he would have laughed at the picture of the secret agent that is presented in fiction, he did in fact model himself on such a pattern, while pretending not to do so. The deeper and almost mystical reverence for Intelligence work—an attitude common to all those (except cynics) who engage on highly secret and unproductive activities—was yet to come. But if ever he reached this condition, he could reassure any doubts he might have as to the use he was making of his life by reflecting that no civilised society can survive without organisations of this kind.

Our own experience was widening too. One day Lieutenant Vroons sent word he wanted to show us two suspects. A call for help from Vroons was unusual unless there was a hidden motive, and I drove round to the Gendarmerie with a double curiosity.

Standing on the bare boards of the guardroom were two men with the devalued, shop-soiled look that settles even on the honest—even on the respectable—after spending a few hours in a police office. According to Vroons, these two had been arrested at the canal bridge 'on suspicion.' When I asked of what, he made a face that allowed for a variety of crimes and said, 'Smuggling, at any rate, for certain.'

'That's a matter for you to deal with, isn't it?'

'I thought perhaps there might be more: things of interest to yourselves. They have no papers—are illegally in the forbidden zone—refuse to give a logical explanation of their movements.'

I looked at them. They stared back in an exaggeratedly injured way, and shot sharp glances at each other to decide whether their attitude should be meek or else aggressive. 'I'll take them round to our place and talk to them,' I said.

'No, Sergeant, what I would suggest is that you question them further here with me. Let us get to the bottom of this together.'

It seemed he wanted a military stooge in the room to help scare them into talking about the smuggling. 'I'll take them with me,' I told him.

'Well, as you wish. I will give you an escort.'

'That's not necessary, just tell them to get in the car.'

Back at the billet, I brought them one by one into the mess, and asked them what they'd been doing.

Most of the remarks men make, and the expressions on their faces that go with them, suggest different, underlying meanings to a wary observer; and you often feel that two or three forbidden questions would quickly bring you to the edge of secrets whose outward traces you detect in dubious statements, and see imprinted on guarded eyes. Because of our position, and even when mere curiosity was really the motive, the habit of asking these questions was growing on us. And we had learned that even when a man came into the office on some innocuous errand, a few deft, irrelevant feelers would often start a hare that could be pursued to the visitor's discomfort. But the perfect opportunity was the set interrogation of a suspect.

In simple cases, provided the interrogator is patient and asks sufficient questions over a period of time, it is always possible for him to discover whether the suspected person is telling the truth or not. Truth is so powerful a force, it needs such effort and ingenuity to try to suppress it, that it is impossible to tell a long story of supposed events without contradictions, particularly if the interrogator asks you to repeat your tale a day or so after you have first told it, and if he has made notes of what you said at earlier hearings. For if it is hard enough to lie convincingly, it is harder still to remember the lies you told.

Of course, most persons, on being subjected to an interrogation, will be sensible enough to offer a story that is largely made up of truth. But as he listens to your tale the interrogator, paying attention to how you tell it as much as to what you say, will become aware of certain passages in which the story no longer flows naturally; and he will conclude that here are the parts of it in which the facts have been altered or suppressed.

Yet when the participants in the duel have reached the point at which the one has detected these areas of untruth and the other knows they have been detected, that is only the beginning. To discover a lie is not the same thing as discovering what really happened. And at first the interrogator may pursue the suspect up a blind alley, since a reluctance to reveal the facts may not mean that a person has performed the actual deeds of which he is suspected. For instance, if these men didn't want to say what they were doing between 9 and 9.30 on the evening before last, that might not mean they were German agents, which was what interested us, but perhaps that they were looters, or were working a black-market deal. So that the labours of the interrogator may lead to the discovery of discreditable facts which are of little interest to him.

Equally, the interrogator may encourage the suspect, by pointing out the absurdities in his story, to tell another one, just as untrue, which has also gradually to be discredited; and when this has been done, the suspect may invent another tale, and then another, while the ultimate truth recedes even further away. Or in other cases, a stupid person, or one who can pretend to be stupid (which is very difficult), will repeat the same story again and again in slightly varying forms, even when it has been clearly exposed as incredible; or else, after giving two or three quite different versions, he may obstinately return to his original story from afar, and deliver it up as if it were now a new one.

To break the deadlock, an experienced interrogator can make use of two sorts of technique: violence to the mind and violence to the body, or a combination in varying proportions of the two. His choice will depend on the personality and physique of the suspect, also on whether the particular interrogation concerns a matter of opinion, or one of fact. On whether, for example, a suspect is pro-German, or has sabotaged a bridge. Acts and ideas are involved in each other, but an interrogation will usually aim principally at detecting the one more than the other.

Interrogations on matters of opinion are by far the more complex, because the total personality of the suspect is in question, and also, if he is to discover anything, the total personality of the interrogator too. Mind must speak to mind if facts about the mind are to be known. In this case, the interrogator will not be so likely to use physical violence, though demoralising doses of petty cruelty will be a help. Physical force might get an immediate, crude avowal; but as coherent statements may have to be secured from subtle men, and since it may be desirable for the suspect to repeat his admissions to the interrogator's superiors, and even to repeat them in public, the more intensive and durable technique of mental violence will be preferred. What the interrogator will aim at is to undermine the suspect's inner confidence in his own beliefs, whatever these may happen to be.

These psychological methods (as they are called) seem extraordinarily effective in the majority of cases if applied with relentless persistence. By these means it may be possible to make most men admit to any opinion in the long run; that is, not only to admit what they themselves believe, or think they do, but even to admit what the interrogator wants them to say they believe. One reason for this may be that few men have beliefs that are entirely their own, reached by personal endeavour and held not blindly, but with free conviction. And where a man has clung to his ideas fanatically, it may be this very fact that leads to his collapse in the total solitude of the interrogator's room. There he may find that it was the will to faith, not the faith itself, which he was living by; so that the interrogator's own rival faith may now seem equally desirable. Or if the ideas which the suspect has long held involved the denial of other truths once clear to him, the painful weight of suppressing these truths will fall from him when he is invited to confess. It may be so even when his confession is compounded of half-truths he believes in less.

This is the moment at which the interrogator makes use of

his enormous tactical advantages. All interrogators, however temporarily, have power, all suspects are alone and weak—their names (so easily reversible) describe their relative positions in a given context. It does not matter that the interrogator may be inwardly guilty of the same heresy as the suspect, nor that he be one who, potentially, is in a similar psychological condition. However spurious his claim may be, he must try to cow the suspect with the moral and physical force invested in him by circumstance. He must be diety, father, tyrant, and force the suspect to his knees as sinner, child and slave. He must abuse the deep-seated urge to confession that seems to exist in many men, and which in some arises from fear, in others, from humility. For men often have a prescience of some ultimate interrogation, of which this is the fraudulent parody.

So it would be revealing to compare the interrogator's report on the suspect with all that has been said and thought (if one could know it) in the concrete room where they have been alone together. If they are both persons of a certain degree of psychological complexity, a peculiar relationship may sometimes establish itself between them in which their minds, locked battling together, seem to desert their personalities and achieve a promiscuous intimacy like that of two bodies which have come together in lust. The further they advance into this mental forest, the more the questions begin to contain other questions, and the answers, other answers. Till sometimes the initial object of the inquiry may partly be forgotten; and since the interrogator must necessarily reveal much about himself (as any question is always, in a sense, a statement), the answers of the suspect may themselves become questions, which fly back into the interrogator's soul and challenge him on points of human conduct far removed from the ones which were at first to be established. For everyone in the world has secrets he does not wish to reveal, and almost everyone has unworthy secrets. So that the interrogation, though it begins as an attack and may often result in the suspect's confession, can also become a defence on the attacker's part, or possibly even end in a mutual, unspoken confession of the kind with which priests and psychiatrists, as well as political inquisitors, must be familiar.

But in fact, however much the interrogator may himself have disclosed during the struggle, his report to his superiors will confine itself to the admissions of the suspect. An interrogator can never afford to be interested in the total truth—even as he sees it. For him, truth is a raw material, and the confession he extracts from it, his commodity. He does not see that it is impossible to tell truth to a man who is himself untruthful; or that only in the case of two entirely honest men, would truth and the confession ever be the same. And yet, what is striking about political inquisitions is how haunted they are by the presence of truth, how vehemently those who conduct them affirm, from out of their distortions, that they have found it. As if they knew that darkness cannot exist of itself, but only because of the absence of light which must at all costs be hidden.

This preoccupation with discovering truth by means that must destroy it, with mechanisms for extracting confessions by pseudo-scientific psychological tricks, by truth-drugs, by lie-detectors, by inflicting mental and physical wounds—all points to an immense fatigue with the mask men's mouths draw over their minds. And hints at a sick longing for simplicity, and even at a hidden wish for the relief that would come from the awful clarity of direct, wordless communication of thought.

In the present instance, my interrogation of the two men Vroons had caught, was getting nowhere; perhaps because in this 'matter of fact' I was not using 'violence to the body.' But I had never dared do that, and therefore didn't know what physical force would make a man disclose. I guessed that in most cases, if you went far enough, you could get him to admit any particular act he'd done, or that you wanted to pin on him. But this was conjecture.

So I gave up for a while, and went in to tea. Dennis was there, and I told him about them. When he said he'd soon get at the facts, I let him go in there without me.

After a while, I heard him walking with them down the corridor to the garden, and suddenly ashamed, I ran out and found he'd put them face to a wall, and taken out his pistol.

'Put that away!' I shouted.

'Don't interfere!' he screamed.

'What the hell do you think you're doing? Put that bloody weapon away.'

His eyes had a killer gleam, animal, not vicious. 'Do you want to get results, or don't you?' he cried out.

'Not that way.'

'Not that way! Do be realistic. You ask for my help and then come piddling out here to stop me.' The men moved away from the wall and stood looking curiously at us. 'If all our troops had your mentality, they'd drop their rifles and apologise to the Germans.'

'That's different, and you know it. Shooting at an armed soldier isn't shooting an unarmed prisoner.'

'What do you take me for? I was only trying to scare them.' The gleam was fading, and his eyes showed irritated exasperation only. 'Do you suppose if the Gestapo got hold of you they'd share your point of view?'

'No, I don't. Do you want to model yourself on the Gestapo?'

'Well, do you imagine if our people caught Himmler they'd just take down what he said on a typewriter?'

'No, they'd probably hit him.'

'Well, then.'

'They'd know who they were dealing with. What do you know about these two?'

'That's just it. They won't talk, so I'm treating them rough.'

We took the men indoors, bustled them through to the mess, and went on with the argument in the corridor.

'Look here,' said Dennis. 'I'm not brutal by nature, but what you mild-mannered people don't realise is that most men aren't as scared of getting hit as you are. There are certain cases where a good, straight bashing will get at the facts without damaging a man all you think. It all depends on the man, and it's all a matter of degree.'

'Of degree. Where do you stop?'

'That's a question of using your sense of proportion.'

'A sense of proportion changes.'

'Let's get this straight. Are you against violence because you're against it, or because you're afraid of it?'

I had no answer.

'You can't do this job with kid gloves on, you know. You can't soldier on in this nice cushy Unit and leave others to do the dirty work that has to be done. If those were your views, you should have joined the Medical Corps, or got yourself into a reserved occupation. But not once you're in the Army. An Infantryman can't stop to think of his principles when he squeezes the trigger. He's looking after us, and it's up to us to look after him in our department, even when it involves doing what you disapprove of.'

'I agree to all that as far as I'm concerned personally. But I tell you, I'm going on the same way and, as far as I can, I'm going to prevent you doing any more of that.'

'Well, good luck to you, but I think you'll find I'll go my sweet way too.'

There was a loud rat-tat on the outer door. We both shook ourselves slightly, then opened it. Lieutenant Adeane was standing there. 'I've come to collect the coal,' he said.

We stared at him.

'The coal we left in the cellar here, Sergeant, when you took over. The mess at that refugee camp is horribly chilly, and as I was coming down this way in the truck, Major Parsons suggested I drop by and recuperate it. May I come inside?'

'Yes, come in, Sir, come in,' Dennis said. 'But you know the coal belongs to us now? "Incoming Unit takes over fuel from outgoing" is the drill.'

'Now really, Sergeant, I've never known a Unit like yours for unnecessary awkwardness.'

'Well, I expect we could oblige you, Sir. Will you have a cup of tea in the office while we get some of it loaded on your truck? Cornelis!'

While this was being done, Dennis came up to me and said, 'About those two persons in the mess, the subject of our little difference of opinion. What about making a present of them to Lieutenant Adeane?'

'You mean as suspects?'

'No, no, no. We'll tell him they're destitute refugees.'

'But they're not even Dutch.'

'Will he know the difference? Not till he gets them back to his camp, anyway. Then he can issue them with Red Cross comforts and evacuate them to some peaceful region. It'll be a compensation to them for this afternoon's drama.'

All this time, we'd been going down every few days to the hospital to keep in contact with the Captain. And when Dennis and I walked into the ward one afternoon, carrying a baked turkey and two dozen eggs, we found him sitting up in bed wearing spectacles and with a contented expression on his pointed face. 'All things being equal,' he told us, 'I'll be back among you in a few days' time.'

'You're going to short-circuit the official channels then, Sir?' Dennis asked him in a histrionic whisper.

'I'd put it this way. The Administrative Officer here, a reasonable chap, says he'll post me off in the general direction of Brussels, but what happens to me after that is no concern of his.'

We all glanced round the ward at the Majors and Colonels lying comfortably, or suffering, in bed.

'I'll get your Buick back from Major Bane, Sir,' Dennis told him. 'We'll come down and fetch you, and lay on a gala reception for your homecoming.'

The Captain asked us how we were getting on.

'Well, now that the Ardennes offensive's petered out, thank goodness, the locals don't take our patrols quite as seriously as they did.'

'The Germans only hold ten miles between our armies now, don't they? But it's probably delayed our own offensive quite a bit.'

'That may be,' said the Captain. 'But according to various buzzes I've heard here in the hospital, we're getting ready for our own offensive now. We're going into the Reichswald opposite Nijmegen, and the Americans are coming north from the Aachen area. The idea is for the two armies to meet and clear the enemy from the west bank of the Rhine.'

'Then we'll be going over the Maas?'

'In due course, I expect so.'

'Into the Holy German Reich!' cried Dennis, slapping the trussed-up turkey on the bed table.

On the journey home, Dennis said, 'We'll have to get back to normal a bit when the eye of authority is among us once again. Had that occurred to you at all?'

'You'll have to keep clear of the Universal Hotel.'

'You're referring to my association with the Count's *femme fatale*?'

Dennis had become involved in a triangular relationship with the two of them. He visited the blonde woman at the hotel and sometimes stayed the night, but apparently remained on good terms with the Count, for the three of them were to be seen having supper there together.

'She's by way of being your own *femme fatale* now, isn't she?'

'Well, the position's as follows, if you're interested. She yielded to my pressure at first so as to make the Count jealous, but now she finds she can't do without me. As for the Count, he tells me in confidence he quite understands, and that as he wants to get rid of her anyway, he'll pretend not to notice, and meanwhile I'm very welcome to her.'

'So you've got her by the Count's kind permission.'

'Not a bit of it. If he'd have objected, that would have made no difference to me. And besides, the truth of the matter is he's still very drawn to her, and he'd rather wait his turn till I'm gone than risk losing her altogether by making a scene. Then if later on she reproaches him for not introducing her to mother, he can shoot her down in flames by reminding her of her familiarity with your uncle Dennis.'

'He must dislike you quite a lot.'

'I don't think so. He's a very nice man, quite gentlemanly and ready to forgive.'

'I thought you didn't admire the blonde.'

'Well, she's no Cleopatra, I admit, but after all, that village isn't Cairo. And what about you, my boy? Aren't you every bit as friendly with the little seamstress?'

She was a dark girl with closely-curled hair worn down her back, teeth lined with gold, and a figure that moved with harmony. I'd met her first when our cook, whose niece she was, had invited me to supper at their house across the road. She'd stared at me curiously in an impersonal way, and had only expressed any emotion at the sound of my Flemish, which sent her into fits of uncontrollable giggling.

It wasn't till her aunt had secured her the job of laundress and mender to the Detachment, that I'd got to know her better. She made a point of finding out which man each garment belonged to, and she used to deliver the bundles to all of our rooms in turn. I followed her up one day, and watched her laying underclothes tenderly on the bed, dropping her eyes, but with an occasional chuckle.

We talked about Belgium. 'The Belgian woman,' she told me, 'is very faithful, and very jealous.'

That evening, I looked out for her coming across the road to fetch her aunt. I went and waited in the lane beside the house, and scared her out of her wits. 'You stood there like a thief,' she cried. 'Like a thief,' she said, lingering.

Through pompous discretion, I didn't like to take her in to the billet, and I was jealous of the others, too. She came with me into the garage, but she wouldn't stand for necking in a car. 'In such a place? Oh, no. Oh, no.' When the house seemed emptier, we went upstairs.

There she examined me limb by limb. She picked up an arm and looked at it, as though deciding how to roast it. Then she gave a little laugh, half of apology, half of derision. 'Yes, you are tall,' she said, 'but lean. One can see you have not worked in the country.' Gazing into my eyes, she told me, 'You have a mistrustful face. Why?' then ran a finger over each feature. 'Now you look optimistic. But soon you will be serious again.'

'Put ye old footy down, Colonel, or we'll never get there,' cried Dennis. 'I'm dining with the blonde at 8.15.'

'Give her my love,' I said, accelerating.

'I will, but she doesn't exactly approve of you, you know. Do you know what she says about you? She says you have a tortuous mentality. "At first I found him relatively sympathetic, but later I became aware that he has a tortuous mentality." Those were her very words.'

'Thanks for letting me know.'

'Still, women are women, the whole world over, you can't do without them. Look at old Gordon, too, seducing the resistance of the Resistance.'

Gordon's girl was the large-boned, hearty daughter of one of the Resistance volunteers, and she was often to be found in the kitchen holding a basket laden with stores he'd just given her. Gordon used to go round to her house on the evenings her father was out on the patrols, and when their affair was discovered, Gordon told us that the father had denounced his conduct as 'not correct.' This choice of adjective struck him and Dennis as very comical; but correct or not, he'd gone on visiting her.

'And what about young Norman's valiant attempt in a similar direction, thwarted by me in the nick of time?' Dennis said.

'It didn't need much thwarting. She slung him out on his ear.'

One day Norman had found in our letter-box an anonymous denunciation, written by a female hand, that accused the daughter of the man who'd been Burgomaster during the occupation, of having fraternised with German soldiers, and of preparing now to receive them back with open arms. Norman, on his own initiative, had summoned this girl round to the office for questioning, and had tried to get fresh with her. At any rate, Dennis had surprised them as the girl was trying to punch Norman's face. Both gave different versions, but Dennis had come down on the girl's side, and had given Norman a severe talking to.

'Yes,' Dennis now said, 'the only virtuous man among us is old Walter.'

Walter, when he'd nothing else to do, was often to be found writing home, and there was sometimes a letter a day of his in the censorship tray. Like so many soldiers, he carried a wallet of photographs of his wife and children, and to him this was a sort of ikon. He used to produce them and tell his listeners about each one in turn. 'Yes, faithful to the core, that's me,' he'd say. 'Mind you, I may weaken, but until temptation comes my way, I'm not going out to look for it.'

'And Cuthbert?' I said to Dennis. 'He's virtuous enough, isn't he?'

'That's not virtue, it's total abstinence.'

'Loose-living,' as Cuthbert called it, seemed genuinely abhorrent and even inexplicable to him.

We were drawing near our town.

'Ah, lust, lust,' cried Dennis, stretching his arms up to the car roof. 'The lust of the soldier in an alien land.'

But it was loneliness just as much, and the longing for love.

THE FRONTIER

AS WINTER DREW TO AN END, THE NEWS CAME THROUGH THAT THE British and American armies, fighting between the Maas and the Rhine, would be making contact. Our Corps now shifted position, and we had word from Major Bane to move back to Holland, and wait there ready for the advance into Germany. He told us to go to a small town near the border. And as we knew it was full of troops, we sent Dennis and Gordon on ahead to do their best about billets, and Cuthbert with them to drive back and guide the rest of us in.

Cuthbert returned next morning in an American jeep. 'Everything's arranged,' he said. 'The Town Major laughed in our faces, but Dennis managed to fix everything up without him.'

'What's this jeep?'

'Oh, it's absolutely all right.'

'Come on, Cuthbert.'

'Well, you see, we've taken over a garage for the transport, and the people told us some Yanks left it there a week ago and never came back to claim it.'

'And you notified the American Provost Marshal?'

'We should have, in theory, I admit. But there it was, obviously abandoned, and the most sensible thing seemed for one of us to take it over.'

'Why you?'

'Well, Gordon has his truck, and Dennis his Peugeot and he says jeeps are too dangerous, anyway. Besides, it's got a wire-cutter. For cutting wires stretched across roads, you know. They'll be doing a lot of that in Germany.'

'So it's going to Germany with you. Isn't that against your principles?'

'In a sense it is, and I'm not altogether happy about it. But having taken charge of it and painted it over, I can't very well hand it back, can I.'

Norman and I were waiting to move off, but the others weren't ready yet, so we asked Cuthbert how to find the billet.

'It's billets—separate houses for each of us. But you'll probably find Dennis in the tailor's shop next to the garage I spoke of, he's got that for an office. Oh, the tailor has no business—no cloth at all. It's quite suitable.'

Travelling up the road to Holland, we noticed the changes that had taken place since the success of the operations across the river. The anxious atmosphere there'd been when we'd come down to Belgium had given place to an air of expectation. The road we were on had been chosen as one of the supply routes for the German campaign, and groups of Engineers and civilian labourers were re-surfacing it. Everywhere we saw that farms and villages once occupied by troops, had been vacated. The civilians were coming into their own again, and it was striking how quickly the military occupation seemed forgotten.

While the Army had been there in strength, the civilians seemed submerged; but now, except for Bailey bridges and bits of gear left lying about, the traces of the Army were rapidly disappearing.

We reached the pleasant and quite undamaged Dutch town, whose roads and canals ran in circles round its old central core. We made our way through heavy traffic to the tailor's shop, and were welcomed by Dennis, who was sitting behind the counter drinking coffee among life-sized dummies with highly coloured faces and glass eyes.

'The billets?' he said. 'I simply called at houses in the fashionable quarter, such as it is. The rooms are spread out a bit, I admit, but we can all meet down here and at the mess.'

'And where's the mess?'

'It's in the convent.'

Dennis rubbed his hands.

'It seemed rather a brilliant idea on my part. I hunted high and low without finding anywhere big enough for us to eat together, and then I heard about the convent which, funnily enough, belongs to a German Order. So I went along just now and saw the Mother Superior who was most obliging. She says if we give her the rations, she'll have our meals cooked in the convent kitchen with the greatest of pleasure, starting from this evening. Now let me show you the billets. Norman, you can stay here and make friends with the tailor.'

Dennis had allotted us to the houses in accordance with their degree of comfort and his rating of our importance. He'd put the Captain in two large rooms near the centre of the town, himself and Gordon in the grain merchant's florid villa on an outer avenue, myself with Walter in the pork dealer's next door, and the rest in humbler dwellings.

The pork dealer was a sad-faced man who told us his pigs had all been requisitioned by the Germans, so that he'd been forced to live on his capital for some time. 'It is not the financial misfortune, but also the lack of useful activity that oppress me,' he told us. His wife, who said she'd learned her English at Tunbridge Wells, was a rather resplendent person, and she soon confided to us that this small town gave her little scope. 'I am from Amsterdam, you see. And here, for me, is little better than an exile.'

When Dennis had helped get my kit into the room they'd given me upstairs, he raised the question of Cornelis's future.

'Have you thought about him at all? I've spoken to Gordon, and he agrees with me Cornelis will be even more useful in Germany, supervising the *Herrenvolk*, than he has been here among the Allies.'

'Does he want to come with us?'

'Yes, I've asked him, and he says he'd like to make his fortune over there. We could easily rig him up in full marching order, and everybody will take him for an accredited Dutch ally.'

'Is the Captain going to agree?'

'You must use your eloquence on him.'

We went back to the office where we found Norman arguing with the tailor, a quavering man with a butterfly collar, as to what should be done with the glass-eyed dummies. 'Do explain to this old chap,' Norman said to us, 'we can't possibly have things of this description in a military office. It would quite detract from our dignity.'

We persuaded the tailor to let us move them to another room, but while Dennis and I were easing one of them gingerly up the stairs, the head fell off and broke into fragments. The tailor, who was following close behind, broke into lamentations.

'I shall never get another like it,' he cried. 'They come from Germany, they are the only people in the world who know how to make them.'

'Never mind, never mind,' said Dennis, patting him on the arm. 'We'll bring you back a new one just as good.'

'You will? You promise that? From Germany?' the tailor asked him, also taking Dennis's arm, so that they stood holding each other in the narrow stairway among the débris.

Norman called out to us from below to say a visitor had arrived for Dennis. And when we went down, I saw a Sergeant of the Military Police who was standing listening to Norman in a deliberate way, as if prepared to go on listening all his life.

'Do you know who this is?' cried Dennis, hurrying over. 'It's my old pal Sergeant Thackeray, the cream of the cream, who I collaborated with in cleaning up the vice in various French towns.'

The Sergeant shook hands with him and smiled slightly. He had a burly body and expressive, intelligent eyes. 'Well, I wouldn't quite remember about that,' he said.

'And what's this I see—the Corps flash on your shoulder? Don't tell me they've transferred you here to us.'

'They have, you know, Dennis, they have.'

'What, for the campaign? They've dug you out of your hidey-hole in France? The heartless sods.'

Sergeant Thackeray glanced all round with another slight smile. 'Yes,' he said, 'that's about how it is. The old Corps is packing up down there and taking over in Holland from your mob. And they seemed to think some of us might be a bit more useful over in Gerry-land, and posted us to you.'

'Our gain is Germany's loss,' said Dennis. 'I pity the poor enemy from the bottom of my heart. Come round with me to the billet immediately, you'll find Gordon there, and we'll introduce you to our grain merchant and his four huge marriageable daughters.' He propelled the policeman by the shoulder to the door.

Dennis picked me up at the pork dealer's that evening, and we went round for the first meal at the convent. 'Do you know what happened when I dropped in there this afternoon?' he said. 'I found there was a military clergyman on the premises. Somehow or other he'd got wind of our presence, and he had the cheek to say it was contrary to international law and we'd have to move out. He asked to see the Mother Superior, and I thought it best not to interfere, and left it to the professionals. She tells me she dealt with him quite effectively, apparently she knew the theological answers. Of course, she being a German, and not altogether popular in the town, it makes her very glad to have us as guests.'

Dennis led me into a quadrangle, where controlledly aloof nuns were hurrying silently about. 'I'll take you in to meet her,' he said. 'You'll find she's a person of great character.'

The Mother Superior was a short woman with a severe, pale face, and eyes that glinted behind rimless glasses. She received us standing in a vestibule, and when Dennis had introduced me and paid court to her, she said, 'Yes, yes.' Then she said, 'It is thus. Here we are short of everything, but nearby in Belgium is another convent of my Order. Could I not go there with you to collect necessary things that I am told our Belgian Sisters have still got?'

'What sort of things?'

'Such as needles, cloth, chocolate, exercise-books for the

schoolchildren and so forth. I have asked the Dutch Militia for permission for this journey, but they say that, in present circumstances, they refuse it to me.'

'Excuse me just a minute,' Dennis said, 'if I say a word to my friend in English. It's going to be a bit awkward, isn't it, smuggling her over? Suppose she got picked up over there and slung inside? It wouldn't be very dignified, would it, and we couldn't very well disguise her . . .'

She had been watching us with her sharp eyes, which seemed magnified and duplicated on the outside of her lenses. 'Wouldn't it be better,' Dennis said to her, 'if one of us went down there and got whatever it is you need?'

'Yes. Thank you. That would be an alternative.'

'Then will you make out a list of all you want?'

She had thought of that, and sent an assistant to fetch it from her office.

'Which part are you from yourself?' I asked her, as we stood waiting.

'From nearby Aachen.'

'Have you any news from there?'

'I know nothing personally, but the local papers gave the report that my village is now non-existent.' She said it in a way that seemed to invite neither blame nor commiseration.

'We'll get young Cuthbert to nip back there in that jeep of his,' Dennis said, as we walked up some cold, stone stairs. Then pausing at a landing, from which a small room opened off, he said, 'This is for Cornelis to eat in. They've asked us not to let him in the kitchen, by the way, but to hand the rations over at the door.'

We went up another flight, and into a long, high-ceilinged refectory that was painted dark green and hung with pious photographs. Some of the others had arrived, and seeming oppressed by their surroundings, had gathered near the windows round Cuthbert's portable radio, in a slightly protesting group.

We explained to Cuthbert about the Mother Superior's list. He heard us in silence, then said, 'All right, I'll do it for you, though why we should be tender-hearted to a person of that description, I'm sure I don't understand.'

Punctually at the hour, the food was brought in by white-robed nuns who laid it out with an air of friendly detachment. And just before the meal began, the Mother Superior herself came in to bid us welcome. She walked half way up the room, clasped her hands over her stomach, smiled an ambigious smile, nodded her head several times and wished us a Good Appetite. We all said, 'Thank you.' This chorus seemed to satisfy her, and after a word or two to the nuns, she went away.

I took the opportunity during the meal of saying to the Captain that I supposed Cornelis would be coming with us to Germany.

'Oh, no. He stays here.'

'I think he might be very useful. Conditions may be primitive over there, and according to this new Non-fraternisation order, we won't be able to have German civilians working for us.' The Captain watched me. 'Of course, I suppose we won't have to apply the Non-fraternisation order to the letter.'

'If it's laid down that German civilians can't be employed as domestics,' the Captain said sharply, 'then as far as this Detachment's concerned, that rule will be obeyed.'

This was overheard by some of the others, and a short silence followed.

'Well, in that case, Sir, isn't there all the more reason for taking Cornelis?'

'Cornelis is a Dutch citizen, and we've no right whatever to take him into Germany. We've brought him back to Holland where he came from, so please arrange to pay him off here.'

'He's quite willing to come.'

'Now, Sergeant, just do as I say, and don't argue the toss.'

The Captain's attitude came in for severe criticism by some of those who stayed on after he'd left. 'I expect it's because we'll be campaigning again that he's decided to have a bash at tightening up the discipline,' Walter said.

'Well,' Dennis told me, 'you'll have to go round later on to his billet, and tackle him again when he's in a mellower mood. But surely the Captain's not going to take this nonsensical Non-fraternisation order seriously. Four million virtuous soldiers among sixty million untouchables. How long do they think they're going to keep that up?'

'You're wrong, Dennis,' Cuthbert said. 'It's the best way we have of showing them their conduct puts them right outside the pale.'

'Oh, you think so? According to that ridiculous document, when we requisition a house we have to push the Germans out and surround ourselves with barbed wire, so as to protect our bodies from contamination, I suppose. Well, let me tell you. In the first place, will the Germans understand what it's all about? Of course they won't. It'll be a complete mystery to them.'

'They'll realise it shows we think they're guilty.'

'My dear Cuthbert, they don't think they're guilty. When they find us cutting ourselves off from all normal social relations, they'll merely wonder why we're making ourselves so uncomfortable.'

'But Dennis,' Walter said. 'We've got to make their war guilt clear to them in every possible way.'

'Hark to this old soldier talking of war guilt! Listen, Walter. Fraternisation's got nothing to do with what you think about war guilt. The point is that soldiers have a perfect right to quarter themselves on civilians, enemy or otherwise. It's a long-standing military custom, and it doesn't mean that you approve or disapprove of them, but simply that you're both going to behave like human beings.'

'That's not good enough, Dennis. If someone does the dirty on me, and I fight him for it, I don't shake his hand until I see a change of heart.'

'So you're going to make the Germans change their hearts.'

'We're going to re-educate them,' said Cuthbert.

'Re-educate—listen to him. How are you going to do that if you cut off all contact with them? By correspondence through the barbed wire?' Dennis glared round at us. 'Well, all I can say is that they tried Non-fraternisation after the last war, and it was an utter failure. And you can take it from me that if the British soldier wants to fraternise with a German girl he'll do it, ban or no ban, you'll see.'

'Of course, Dennis, you would think of the ban in terms of women.'

'In making that remark, little man, you've let the cat out of the bag. Because the real reason for this ban is a so-called moral one. It's just another form of those horrible booklets they issue you with, where they recommend you to leave the women alone and play a lot of football. But if that's the real object, why don't they admit it?'

'Well, you know them better than I do,' said Walter, 'but

all I can say is that I resent what they've done and I'm going to let them see it.'

'My own view,' Cuthbert told us, 'is that until we see signs of improvement, we must be firm and distant, though correct.'

Dennis snorted and got up.

'Don't you see?' he cried. 'You can do anything with a people if you establish a flesh and blood relationship with them. But there's one thing they won't stand for, and that's British fairness. Non-fraternisation! Even the word's ridiculous. Love, hate—yes; but Non-fraternisation!'

Gordon reminded Dennis that Thackeray was waiting for him at the Sergeants' Club. Cuthbert turned the radio on for the news, got the German programme for British troops playing 'There's no place like home,' and switched the set off again.

'Let's hear what old Mac thinks,' Walter said. 'He's had less to say than usual.'

'I think by the time you've been there a month or two, Walter, your dream will be to command a platoon of S.S. men, converted and loyal to the core.'

'Oh? What makes you think I'll want to do that?'

'Because you're like a lot of those who say they're going to tear the Germans apart. Once you get over there, you'll fall for their smart turn-out, un-foreign appearance and perfect knowledge of English.'

'Cock and nonsense.'

'And your colonial instinct will make you feel that nothing could be nicer for them, once disarmed, than to be governed and protected by yourself.'

'Go on.'

'You secretly admire their strength, and think they must be a wonderful people to have scared an even more wonderful people like us as much as they did. And when you've beaten them, as I suppose we shall, your pity will be aroused by the sight of them lying at your feet for the time being.'

'Listen. I don't like them, get that, but you're not denying they have qualities, are you? That they're clean, hard-working and good fighters?'

'No. I'm saying that it's not their real qualities you'll admire, but their efficiency, obedience and instinct to flatter you if you can get on top of them.'

'What makes you think I'm going to admire them at all?'

'A lot of Englishmen do. They think the Germans are a people who've made a good try at being English, haven't quite succeeded, but deserve a pat on the back for the effort. It's a race feeling some of us seem to have for them. One they haven't got for us, incidentally.'

'Well, they are a bit like us, aren't they?'

'They couldn't be more unlike. Both in what's best about them, and in what's worst.'

'Mac, as we've often seen,' said Cuthbert, 'likes to lay down the law and be wiser than everybody else.'

'As for you, Cuthbert, the self-indulgence of judging without understanding what it is you're judging, and without being equipped to judge anything anyhow, will be irresistible. You'll go round forgiving them sins they're unaware of, and teaching them lessons for which they won't give a damn. The Germans will take advantage of it, and I don't blame them.'

'All this comes oddly from you, I must say. I always thought you were a bit pro-German yourself.'

'What does that mean, "pro-German"? Once we get there, you'll be calling me "anti-German." All I'm telling you is that a great many, of which you're one, will miss what's remarkable in them, admire what's inferior and won't see how their qualities are related to their defects. And that very soon, your sentimental hatred will turn to sentimental adoration.'

'Personally, I'm not sentimental, and I don't hate them. I merely condemn them.'

'Cuthbert, you're a man of principle with a great gift for self-deception. If you had a particle of imagination, your moral pretention would be unbearable.'

'And you, Mac, if I may say so, are a bit of an awkward know-all.'

I found the Captain at his billet in shirt sleeves, writing a letter. He looked up, took off his spectacles and said, 'Hullo. Have a noggin.' I could see he knew what I'd come about. And after beating about the bush, and when the whisky made me talkative again, I put the case for Cornelis even more plausibly.

'No, Sergeant Mac,' he said. 'I've said No, and it's No.'

'But do you mean, Sir, that if we can't employ Germans or

take a Dutchman, the men will have to do the cooking and sweeping over there?'

'The men can rough it a bit like everybody else. It won't do them any harm.'

This was like the officers in England who used to tell you, when a complaint of any kind was made, that you'd have to put up with worse if you were in the Desert. I saw I had only one tactic left, the non-commissioned officer's trump card. 'Well, I'm sorry about that,' I said. 'I think the men will feel rather strongly about it.'

The Captain sipped his drink in silence.

'After all, Sir, this Unit's never been given the Army cook it's entitled to. And it'd be a bit awkward detailing Sergeants to do a Private's job.'

He looked at me and said, 'It's very irregular . . .'

'If Cornelis gets in the way, we could always send him back to Holland.'

He flicked the rim of his glass several times. 'Then that's what we'd better do,' he said, and I took this to mean that he agreed.

He poured out some more, and we clinked glasses. 'Do you know who I saw at Major Bane's office on the way over?' the Captain said. 'My predecessor in the Detachment.'

'Is he posted back to this Corps?'

'No, he was just passing through.'

'And how was he?'

'All right.'

'He didn't give you a good account of some of us, did he, before you came?'

'Oh, I wouldn't say that, you know.'

I went on to the Sergeants' Club to tell Dennis about Cornelis, and found him drinking beer there with his old pal Thackeray. The policeman was sitting back with one arm resting on a chair, relating some story with measured relish. Dennis's sharp nose sniffed at what he was being told, and his mouth was shaped as if he was about to gobble something up. As I came closer, his shoulders shook and he laughed at the back of his throat in spasms.

'What do you think of that?' he cried, catching sight of me. 'He's been telling me about his dealings with deserters.'

Sergeant Thackeray frowned slightly, and kicked a chair

aside for me to sit down. 'And how do you treat deserters?' I asked him.

'Well, you see, with them it all depends. If they're obviously shaken, and we see they've had too much of it, we handle them more or less with care. But if, like these birds I was telling Dennis about just now, we think they're hard cases who've decided life would be more to their liking in Brussels, we push them round a bit, as is only right.'

'And relieve them of their surplus possessions,' said Dennis. 'Still, they've got something to desert from, judging by what you hear of the fighting across the river.'

'True,' said Sergeant Thackeray, 'and it's not deserters we'll be having on our hands from now on, so much as Gerry prisoners, I expect.'

'Are we taking many now?'

'Yes, there's a cage-full not far from here I've been down to have a look at. As for that lot, I've no pity on them.'

'Why's that?'

'Why's that?' the policeman said, turning slowly to me. 'Because of how they've treated our lads, our prisoners. In days gone by, remember, when Gerry had more of ours than we had of his, he wasn't over nice to them. Now it's our turn.'

'Make them pay for how they treated ours.'

Sergeant Thackeray stared at me. 'That's right,' he said. 'And when it comes to pulling in Gerry civilians proper, well, I shan't exhaust myself, but I'm going all out. There's several hundred thousands due for arresting, and I'll try to see to it they're not less than three to a cell.'

'Sling them all in.'

'Listen. You're not trying to get at me in any way by any chance, are you?'

'The Colonel here,' Dennis explained, 'has unorthodox notions about prisoners. It's best to keep him off the subject, if possible.'

'And just what are you proposing to do yourself over there?' Sergeant Thackeray said, looking at me with uninterested curiosity, 'Turn them all loose and kiss their arses?'

'That's it. Let them all go. There are too many prisons, too many men in them and too many bloody policemen.'

The Sergeant smiled. 'If that's the principle you're going to work on,' he said, 'I look forward to seeing the consequences.

Meanwhile I suggest this conversation's getting a bit subversive, and we'd better have three more pints to help keep some of us quiet.'

On the way back through the streets to the billets, Dennis said, 'You know, you're wrong to expound your theories in public and aggravate a man like Thackeray. What you must realise is that he regards you as doing the same job as himself, and looks to you for support. Of course, I understand your point of view, but all the same, it seems to me you don't appreciate policemen at their full value.'

'What is their value?'

'Suppressing crime, my boy. Admittedly, they're crooks themselves, but they keep the bigger crooks at bay. That's what you've got to remember.'

'All right, I'll remember.'

'A policeman's job, you see, isn't always a pleasant one, in fact, don't quote me to old Thackeray, it's even a dirty one at times. But it's a dirty world, as you and I well know. Do away with the dirt, and you'll do away with coppers. But not until.'

We stayed on in this small town doing nothing at all, and waiting for the word to go forward. As the days grew longer and warmer and the troops began to leave, we saw unusual sights on the highway: veteran Divisions that had come up from Italy and Africa to join in the battle; boats, nearly fifty feet long, groaning by on trailers which chipped large chunks off the houses at street corners; convoys of jeeps with guns mounted, that slithered across the dewy roads like performers in an ice ballet; and strings of huge vehicles driven by Negro soldiers, all signalled on their way by the Traffic Policeman outside our office, who waved his hand over his head in a sweeping gesture that ended pointing towards Germany.

When Walter and I were drinking tea there one afternoon, Harry rode up full of news. 'We've joined with the Yanks near Geldern,' he told us. 'There's no Germans now left west of the Rhine except for a small bridgehead in the north.'

'What's happening to us, do you know?'

'I've got your marching orders here. Corps headquarters are moving up to Germany already, and you've got to get over there tomorrow. I'm on my way after them now.'

'Well, you're not in such a hurry that you can't stop for a cup of tea.'

We noticed he was wearing a bit of orange ribbon over one breast pocket, and Walter said, 'What's that in aid of, Harry? Did your girl give it to you?'

'Yes, it's the Dutch colours. She says it'll bring me luck. As a matter of fact, as soon as I heard we were leaving, I went over and said what about getting wed, and she gave it to me then.'

'I'm very glad to hear it,' Walter told him. 'And all I can say is, you shouldn't have dilly-dallied as long as you did. You'll have to wait till after it's over now, before you can get paired off, won't you?'

'Yes, as soon as I get back, it'll be.'

We went out with him to his bike, which was heavily loaded with kit. 'Take care of yourself, if only for her sake,' said Walter. 'Nice girls like that aren't two a penny these days, I can tell you.'

'Don't worry, I know when I'm fortunate. Well, be seeing you up there in Germany.'

When the Captain came in, I handed him the envelope Harry had brought, and after putting on his spectacles and reading it, he said, 'Get everyone round to the mess in half an hour.' As soon as the men had all gathered in the refectory, the Captain put down his tea-spoon noisily, and looked along the table with his eyebrows raised till there was silence.

'Well,' he began, with the fondness speakers have on solemn occasions for first saying something everyone knows already, 'Well, this is the last meal we'll be having on Allied territory, apart from breakfast tomorrow.'

The Captain looked at several faces, then continued.

'According to Major Benedict-Bane,' he said, consulting the letter and picking up his map-case, 'Corps headquarters are going to a small place mid-way between the German frontier and the Rhine. And we have to go on beyond that and find ourselves a billet somewhere on this road I see marked here that runs parallel to the river just west of it. What we then have to do, is lay on patrols and examine people moving up and down the road by night and day. In fact, it's much the same job as we were doing in Belgium except, of course, that there won't be any Allies to help us.'

There was a silence. 'By night and day?' someone asked.

The Captain didn't answer, but nodded.

'Now what I want you all to remember,' he went on, 'is that you'll be operating where nobody will be your friend, and closer to the front line than we've been before. So there'll be the German army, the *Volkssturm* and the werewolves, not to mention the Gestapo, *Sicherheitsdienst* and all the Nazi fanatics up against you and fighting for their lives. In fact, the whole bag of tricks. So remember that quite apart from the Non-fraternisation order, it's in your own interest not to trust anyone. Are there any questions?'

There were none, so the Captain told us to start packing and be ready to move off next day at nine.

Some of us walked to the billets together. 'You appear considerably excited,' Walter said to Dennis, who was prancing along the pavement. 'I look forward to seeing those werewolves getting their fangs into you.'

'Farewell to the Liberation Army,' cried Dennis. 'Roll on the victory, the armistice and the peace.'

'There are still Allies there to liberate.'

'Yes, and a lot of the Germans too, I shouldn't doubt,' said Walter. 'Well, I shan't be sorry to leave this country, it's been too rural for my taste. Though it has been peaceful, and that's something.'

We reached the pork dealer's. 'Do you want a hand loading up your truck, Walter?' Dennis asked him.

'Oh, no. I never really unload, you know. I'm always ready to move on.'

'Will you unload when we get to Berlin?'

'No, only when I get my discharge.'

'Aren't you going to soldier on, then, when the war's over?'

'No. My time's expired already, and I'm going to say goodbye to the Army, come the peace.'

I went through the kitchen to collect washing from the line, and found the pork dealer having a snack there with his wife. 'So tomorrow you go,' he said, very nicely, but sounding pleased.

'Who told you that?'

'Well, everybody goes,' his wife remarked, 'and we see you take in washing while it is still wet.'

'Try to get my pigs back from the Germans,' her husband said, as I sat down to have a cup of coffee with them.

2

Behind the Advance

THE RHINE VILLAGES

THE SUN WAS WELL UP WHEN OUR FILE OF TRUCKS, MOTOR-bicycles and civilian cars drove off from the tailor's shop. The Captain set so brisk a pace in front that the convoy soon fell apart, and the drivers lost one another. But as everyone had a map-reference of our destination, they had only to follow the familiar Corps signs which they'd seen nailed up on trees and walls the whole way up from the beaches.

Dennis, who had chosen to ride with me in the utility, was in high spirits. The piled-up kit behind him tickled his neck, and he pushed it back energetically. 'No more of those miserable dumps we've been in,' he cried. 'From now on, we're going to live in the best hotels and *Schloss*es. So step on it, Colonel, or we'll lose our place in the vanguard.'

'If you were in such a hurry, why didn't you go in your Peugeot?'

'The Peugeot? It's a thing of the past as far as I'm concerned. I'm going to find myself a Horch, or a Mercedes. The ripe fruits of victory, all waiting for the plucking.'

In the early spring light, the flat country looked more cheerful than we'd seen it hitherto. We joined the stream of traffic which was heading towards Venlo, and crossed the Maas on a pontoon bridge that rose and fell like a W. The dynamited girders of the old bridge protruded awkwardly from the water nearby.

The newly liberated town on the further side was hung with orange bunting. As we drove through it, an enemy 'plane came over and several guns went off. 'There's life in the old dog yet,' said Dennis, looking skyward. 'Crossing the Maas is one thing, but getting over the Rhine will be another.'

At first the roads outside the town were little more than churned-up earth, and we were reminded of Normandy, where country lanes that had become military highways overnight had been quickly broken to pieces. As we neared the German frontier, we met with more armour and with vehicles driven in the tougher, busier way of front-line traffic. Soon we came to a deserted Dutch customs-post, and then to the German one, of which only a wall remained. Beside it we saw a large notice, painted in the unmistakable Army lettering, which warned us against fraternising and told us to remember Coventry. Dennis made a great gesture of pitying despair as we drove by.

'Let's stop and celebrate our entry into the Reich,' he said, as soon as we'd crossed over, 'by getting out at the first *Gasthof* and drinking their healths.'

But as we drove for miles through the fields and past ruined farmhouses, we saw what we had never seen before: an area that was absolutely abandoned, not only by human beings, but even by animals. These farms in which there were neither pig, horse nor cow, gave a stronger impression of desolate emptiness than did even the sight of a ruined city.

Dennis, impressed, had fallen silent. 'Never live near a frontier,' he said gloomily. 'You get the first onslaught, whether you deserve it or not.'

We reached a village in which our troops were quartered. Here we saw another new sight, which was that the houses had been taken over without any regard whatever for the civilians. Hitherto, though they'd been made to move out or make room, their belongings had been respected more or less. But now the Army was in complete possession.

'Let's halt a moment and set foot on German soil,' said Dennis.

We walked round the streets looking through the gutted windows into rooms where military kit and broken household goods were jumbled up together. We reached a row of shops, all deserted. The first was an ironmonger's, which still had some stock on view behind the jagged remains of a plate-glass window. After hesitating, we pushed open the door and went inside.

We were struck at once by the tremendous physical energy of the looters. Furniture was upended and flung about in heaps in a way that made movement from room to room as difficult as rock-climbing. Anything of glass was smashed, walls had their paper torn from them or were splashed with ink, wood was gouged out of cupboards and tables, upholstery had been sliced open on the seats and arms of chairs and sofas, and curtains were ripped to tatters. It seemed that all this expressed a hatred of organised life, and a yearning for primitive chaos on as large a scale as possible.

Dennis tried to climb past a cascade of furniture on the stairs, but gave up; and clambering back to the door, he turned and faced the mess indignantly. 'That's not looting,' he cried. 'It's fouling your own nest to no purpose.'

On the way back to the car, a group of soldiers passed us, wearing black top hats. 'Well, boys will be boys, I suppose,' he said sadly.

When we reached the next smashed village, blackened, coated with red dust and bathed in sunlight, we saw our first Germans moving slowly about in it. We stared curiously at them, for 'the Germans' had become, with all the years of the war, an increasingly abstract idea unrelated to an image of actual people. These villagers ignored us, seeming thoroughly preoccupied with their own troubles.

'Isn't that Cuthbert?' I said, when we saw a jeep coming towards us.

'The Captain's stuck in a ditch about a mile up,' he told us, drawing alongside. 'He got ordered to the edge of the road by a Colonel for trying to overtake his convoy, and then he backed his car into this ditch. The Colonel told him he was a road-hog.'

We found the Captain smoking a cigarette and examining a rear wheel which was sunk up to the axle. We all got out and looked. 'An interfering busybody was the cause of this,' he muttered. 'Let's stop and have some lunch here, anyway. Afterwards you can try pulling me out.'

We sat by the roadside eating sandwiches the convent had prepared, and watching the vehicles go by. Till Cuthbert, who had been walking about on the roadway holding a map and gazing at the pill-boxes in the fields, said impressively, 'Do you realise where we are? You're having your lunch in the middle of the Siegfried Line.'

'You speak as though you'd captured it single-handed,' Dennis told him.

We got the Captain out, and set off again in the warm afternoon. The signs told us we were nearing the place which Corps had taken for its headquarters, and when we arrived we saw that by the hazard which flattens one village and spares the next, this one was almost intact. Here we found the rest of our convoy, and the Captain went in search of Major Bane.

I walked into the perimeter, where a tented camp was being laid out. A group of German civilians were digging ditches dismally, while two sentries looked casully on. A truck drove in with a German boy sitting beside the driver. A Sergeant-Major, seeing this, strode over and pulled the lad down from the cab. The boy looked surprised and the driver very offended.

The Captain said, 'We'll leave the rest of them here, and shoot on ahead to that road of ours to find a suitable billet.'

'What had Major Bane got to say?'

'Nothing very much. Apparently we sit down in front of the Rhine until they're ready to cross it.'

'Doing our patrol.'

'That's right. Although we may have to help out with refugees once again. It seems there's a lot of them milling about the area, getting in everybody's way, and they're being collected together at a village not far from here. Major Bane has sent over some of his staff, and he may have to borrow some bodies from us as well.'

'To work with the Military Government?'

'Yes, with the Military Government, as we must now call them. Their team was in there with Major Bane just now. One of them was that theoretical Lieutenant we met in Belgium—Adeane, wasn't it? The other's a Major Parsons, who kept calling me laddie. Well, there it is. Mil. Gov.! Mil. Gov.! The name just about suits them.'

We travelled over undulating country until we reached a village about three miles from the Rhine. Here we drove south along the road we were to patrol. It ran between a high cliff and fields stretching over to the river. We went along it searching for empty farms, but the Units were very thick on the ground and we began to have doubts about finding a good place. Till nearing another village, we saw a large farm on the Rhine side of the road and turned in to have a look at it. We noticed Army food boxes littered about as we drove into the farmyard. 'If there's not a Unit here, there has been,' the Captain said.

A young lad came out of the house, looked at us, and ran quickly in again. The Captain slammed the car door, adjusted his beret, put his map-case under his arm and marched up to the rustic portico. He went in without knocking, and we found ourselves in a kitchen full of people, all standing up. There was an elderly farmer, a golden-haired woman perhaps in her forties, the lad we'd seen outside and one or two others.

'Who is the house-owner?' the Captain demanded.

'I am he,' said the farmer.

'This house is requisitioned for fifteen men,' the Captain told him. The farmer bowed his head, the woman looked startled and said, 'Again!' The lad seemed pleased.

'Show me the premises,' the Captain ordered.

The farmer opened the door to let us through, and ushered us into a bright room looking onto an orchard. He pointed out the various fittings, naming them one after the other as though we were going to buy them. Then he took us into the bedrooms one by one.

'What is in there?' the Captain asked, pointing to another door. The farmer opened it onto pitch blackness. 'The cheeses,' he said. 'And here?' said the Captain, crossing a corridor. He opened that door too. The room was stacked to the ceiling with furniture. 'The property of various refugees,' the farmer explained. 'And upstairs?' the Captain continued. The farmer led the way to the loft, which was filled with vegetables and hung with tobacco leaves. He crossed the boards and opened the door of a dormitory that was built into it. 'Here the East-workers lived,' he told us, 'but they have now gone away.'

'What East-workers?'

'Girls from Poland and such places.'

'And where have they gone to?'

'Your officers are making camps for them, I hear, from which they are later to be sent home.'

When we went downstairs again, the Captain asked him if there were cellars.

'Yes, certainly.'

'What is in them?'

'There we live. I and my family.'

It was almost as though he'd been expecting us. But the Captain drew himself up and said, 'It is forbidden for a German family to remain in a house that is requisitioned by British troops.'

The German looked at us with his mouth open. 'But we remained here with the others,' he said.

'What others?'

'The Canadians. They were here several days. See what they did.'

Before the Captain could stop him, he shuffled out into the

front yard. We followed him as he walked across to a wall and leaned over. Lying in a ditch were two headless peacocks.

The Captain looked at these in disgust, then changed his map-case from one arm to the other and said, 'You will have twenty-four hours in which to move with your family elsewhere.' He turned aside and led the way back to the living-room. The farmer shook his head and walked slowly into the kitchen.

The Captain opened the door of the bedroom facing the orchard and said, 'I'll have this one. You wait here while I drive back to fetch the others. Stick up the Detachment sign on the main road, and make sure no one else gets in. And see these people start moving.'

As we walked out to the car, I said, 'It seems a pity to turf them out.'

'It may be, but there it is.'

'What about their livestock? What happens to it?'

'They'll have to move that too.'

'And who's going to cook for us if they leave?'

'Cornelis can cook for us. That's why you wanted to bring him, wasn't it?'

'Yes, that's right.'

'Very well, then. I'll be back in a couple of hours.'

I drove with him as far as the main road. 'You might stake out our claim to this place at Corps,' I said.

'I'd thought of that. See you later.'

I stuck the sign in a tree and walked up the drive to the farmhouse. I started sorting out my kit in the bedroom, then left it and went over to the kitchen. A consultation had evidently been going on, and they were all looking very grave. But the old farmer hadn't lost heart, and he got to work on me at once. I asked the woman to make some tea, and sat down and listened to him. He told me he had not left his farm, not even during the battle. He didn't mind what happened to him, he said, so long as he stayed to the last in the place where he was born.

It seemed to me the Captain wouldn't keep it up, so I said, 'The officer has given you twenty-four hours. Why not wait and see what he decides when he comes back again?'

When he was partly reassured, the farmer asked me to come and look at his pigs and cattle. The chickens, he said, had mostly been eaten by the Canadians. We went out into the fields to see another farm nearby which belonged to his brother. He told me both farms were well known in the district, and that they used to have agricultural students working there.

'And now?'

'That stopped with the war. The young men left, and later they sent me foreign girls, whom I did not ask for.'

'I don't suppose they asked to come either.'

'They were better off here than in their homes.'

'Did they say so?'

'They were better fed. Conditions in their own lands were catastrophic.'

'And they left you when we came here?'

'They suffer from homesickness, no doubt.'

'And who works the farm now?'

'I, some relatives, and my young son.'

'The boy in there?'

'Yes. He is the son of my second wife.'

'The lady?'

'Yes. My elder son is dead, he fell in Russia.'

When the rest of the men arrived in the evening, they spread themselves out in the farmer's rooms, and everyone took it so much for granted the family would be staying, that the matter wasn't referred to again. The Captain said the patrolling of the road would begin at once, and that we should have a guard-post in the village, so as to be able to call on one of the Units there if we needed help with prisoners.

'What are the civilians on the road supposed not to do?' I asked him.

'There's to be no movement whatever by night. Question anybody you find there, and if you're doubtful of them, whip them in.'

Some of us set off to the village in Cuthbert's jeep. Dennis said the Post Office would be the obvious place for our headquarters, 'because it will be full of stamps.'

The Post Office was a small house with a front porch laden with hanging flowers. Very much knocking brought a deaf, timid man to the door. Dennis marched in and turned on him savagely. 'Give me the keys,' he shouted. They were yielded tremblingly up. Dennis fumbled with several locks, then handed them back. 'Make everything open,' he ordered.

The man did so. The drawers were empty.

'Where are the stamps?' Dennis cried.

The German made a gesture as of a bird flying away, and said, 'All gone.'

'You lie!'

'The soldiers have already taken them, good Sir.'

'Those bloody Canadians!'

We went upstairs and found a room, and brought up bedding from the jeep.

'You're a nice one, Dennis,' said Cuthbert. 'Shouting at that old fellow and trying to steal his stamps. You're worse than a Nazi yourself.'

'Do unto others as they would to you. You're a biblical scholar, you should know that.'

'Is that what you want people to do to you?'

'It's what they have done, isn't it?'

'Not to you.'

'Listen, Cuthbert, I know the Germans. There's only one way to treat them—authority. They respect it. Well, what now, Colonel? Let's have some action.'

We left Cuthbert with the Postmaster, and drove down the road in the jeep, picking up Walter as we passed the farm. Our lights were dimmed, and we went all the more slowly because a ground mist had arisen. Before long we saw a horse, then another, then a cart filled with furniture. Three women were sitting on top of it, and three men were trudging at the horses' heads.

'Halt!' Dennis cried.

They halted. Dennis got down.

'Who are you?' he said, striding up and poking a torch in their faces. 'Don't you know movement on this road is strongly forbidden?'

A German answered in a dialect difficult to understand, and this exasperated Dennis.

'Show me your papers,' he said. He examined them by the light of the torch. I saw the women's eyes looking down at us from the cart. The men gathered round Dennis in a circle.

'What is your name?' he asked one of them.

'Trieps.'

This seemed to tally with the papers.

'And where are you going?'

'We do not know for sure. To Goch, perhaps, or Kleve.'

'Why?'

'Why? Our house is destroyed. We have relatives in Kleve.'

'And why do you not wait till it is day?'

'An English officer told us to leave our farm immediately. It is by the Rhine.'

Dennis flashed his torch around. 'What goods have you got on that cart?' he demanded.

'Come on, Dennis,' I said, 'they're farmers. They don't look like S.S., do they?'

'But they haven't accounted for themselves.'

'Let's speed them on their way,' said Walter. 'If they keep on for a mile or two, they'll be out of our area, and someone else's worry.'

Dennis climbed onto the uncomfortable rear seat of the jeep, the farmers started up again, we overtook them and went on. 'You're vexed, Dennis,' said Walter. 'You wanted to see what was in the cart, didn't you.'

'Of course I did. Why not? It might have been full of grenades.'

'Or valuables of some kind.'

'Well, you two know best,' Dennis muttered, gathering a ground-sheet round his shoulders, 'but next time, let me handle it my own way.'

We pulled up with a jerk, almost running down a solitary civilian who stood blinking in front of the headlights with his arms outstretched.

'This time we're taking no chances,' said Dennis, leaping onto the road and hustling the stranger up on the back seat beside him. 'Home, Walter,' he cried.

We passed the farmers on the way back, and brought our prisoner in to the Post Office. Up in the guardroom, Walter made tea, while Dennis strode up and down shouting questions at the stranger. He had a bald head and tortoiseshell spectacles, and he wore white tennis shoes and a polo jersey. He reflected carefully before answering Dennis's questions.

'What do you think of this?' said Dennis, slamming an identity card down on the table. 'It says he's a Dutchman.'

'Perhaps he is.'

'But he speaks German.'

'You questioned him in German. See if he speaks Dutch.'

'I don't know Dutch. I thought we'd left that horrible language behind.'

Cuthbert talked to him, and said his Dutch seemed satisfactory.

'And what would a Dutchman be doing in Germany?' Dennis demanded.

'There must be thousands of Dutchmen in Germany. Prisoners of war, deported workers, Dutch fascists . . .'

'There you are!' cried Dennis.

Walter and I went out again while Dennis and Cuthbert continued the examination. When we got back, Dennis was sleeping and the Dutchman was sitting drinking tea.

We asked Cuthbert what he'd discovered. Speaking cautiously, he said he thought this man had come over from Holland to see if he could steal a horse.

'Why has he come this far?'

'Because all the livestock near the frontier have already been driven over into Holland.'

'He doesn't look like a horse-dealer to me.'

'He isn't. He's a commercial traveller in agricultural accessories.'

'What are we going to do with him?'

'Turn him loose before Dennis wakes up,' said Walter.

'We might take him back to Corps.'

'Who might?'

'We'll get one of the others to run him up there in the morning. Can you get something down in writing about him, Cuthbert?'

The Dutchman seemed pleased to be causing us this trouble. 'So you send me back to Holland,' he said. 'I live in Venlo.'

'We don't care where you live. They'll put you over the frontier, and you can find your own way home.'

'Perhaps I shall return again.'

'Don't return our way.'

Cuthbert put on his spectacles and sat down in front of the portable typewriter. Dennis lay looking innocent asleep. Walter and I got ready to follow his example.

One day, after we had been a week or so on the farm, the

Captain said we ought to get to know the Staff of the local Division. 'But first of all,' he added, 'I think we might drive down to the Rhine and have a look at it.' So we took a turning east in the village, but before long, were stopped at a road block.

'Have you got the Blue Pass, Sir?' the sentry said.

The Captain showed him his other passes, but the sentry was adamant, so the Captain asked to see his Guard Commander. After argument and telephoning, he let us through with one of his men to see that we reported to 'the Major.' This Major said yes, we could go on to the river, but firstly he admonished us as follows: 'Since you're billeted in the area, there's one thing I'd like to say. Please don't kill any more chickens. It's pure selfishness to do so, since it deprives the rest of us of eggs.'

When we had driven on two miles, we were halted once again and told to park our car behind a rise. A Lieutenant took us up towards the bank, and advised us to keep our heads down. We looked cautiously over the top. The river was wide and swollen, the water flowed steadily by. The German army must have been on the other side, but we could see no signs of it.

'Well, there you are,' the Lieutenant said.

'How are we going to get over that?'

'Oh, I expect they've got it all worked out. Bombing from the air to soften them up, heavy stuff from the Artillery, then paratroops and gliders and landing-craft and all the usual paraphernalia.'

'It'll be D-day all over again.'

'Yes, you might say so, on a rather smaller scale.'

'You'll be getting a bit of a pounding here yourself, won't you?' the Captain said.

'Oh, definitely. We're digging in.'

The Captain and I thought about this as we drove back. 'Would our farm be within range of their guns?' I said at last.

'Sure to be.'

'What should we do about it?'

'I'll have a chat with Major Bane some time,' the Captain said, after a short silence.

We turned back onto our road, and then set off through the hilly ground beyond it to the Divisional headquarters. When we had driven some way inland from the river, we came to a railway embankment that crossed the road on top of an arched bridge. Looking up, we saw Army vehicles bumping along the embankment overhead. The Captain stopped the car and stared at them. 'That's ingenious,' he said. 'The Engineers must have pulled up the tracks to make an extra road.'

We drove under the arch, but were halted on the further side by great droves of cattle. Soldiers were shooing them through a gate beside the railway and into a field already filled with hundreds of horses and lowing cows. While the Captain advanced at a snail's pace, I got out and asked a soldier what was happening.

'It's Operation Round-up, Sarge.' And he explained that livestock left behind in the empty farms had begun to wander about the roads and get in the way of the convoys, until someone at Division had thought of collecting them up from all over the area.

'And who looks after them?'

'Well, we've got some Gerry farmers working for us, though as regards the cows, it's awkward when it comes to milking them all. But most of our lads are learning how, and some of them are making a packet out of it.'

'Selling the milk?'

'Oh, no. They've been loading calves on their trucks and flogging them back in Belgium. They're getting quite a bit for them, I'm told. I wish I had charge of some transport myself.'

The Divisional headquarters was in a real *Schloss* of the kind Dennis talked about. Its park was full of tents and transport, and paths and buildings had already been signed with Army notices. We made our way to the Intelligence officer's room, and there we found that Major Bane was also paying a visit. 'Hullo, old boy. Good morning, Sergeant,' he said, introducing the officers.

The Captain described our visit to the Rhine. 'You know,' he said, 'we're always looking at the German army over rivers.'

'It'll be the last,' the Divisional officer told him. 'Once we get over this one, the others won't hold us up.'

'And when does the big attack begin?' the Captain asked.

'Oh, they don't tell me things of that sort.'

'I hear they're studying Caesar's "Gallic Wars" for inspiration,' said Major Bane.

'They'd do better to study the Americans. They seem to have got over down by this place Remagen.'

'Yes, but the Germans left a bridge behind for them, and they're not up against von Rundstedt.'

'Well, anyway,' said Major Bane, 'there won't be much for us until we do get over. Everybody that's anybody from our point of view, seems to have skipped across the river with their army.'

When the Divisional officer had gone to order extra lunches, the Captain turned to Major Bane and said, 'Do you want us to stick down on that highway when the balloon goes up?'

'I suppose so. Why?'

'Our billet's near a cross-road, you know. We're probably somebody's target.'

'That's bad, isn't it.'

'No, all I meant was, once it starts, no civilians will be using that road we're patrolling anyway.'

Major Bane glanced at me, eyed the Captain and said, 'Well, as a matter of fact, old boy, I'm trying to arrange with the Division here to take over that patrol of yours, so as I can use your people down at the village I spoke of where Mil. Gov. are sorting out refugees. So perhaps you'd hang on a bit longer at that cross-road you speak of, till I give you the wire about the patrol.'

The Divisional officer took me into the room next door to meet his Sergeant, and asked him to fix me up at their mess. This Sergeant told me the *Schloss* used to be a German headquarters before we'd arrived. 'They left all their maps on the walls,' he said. 'Take a look at these.'

It was curious to see maps that had been marked by someone with the opposite point of view. One of them gave prominence to the Ardennes offensive, and the German advances were shown in thick, convex lines with the dates entered neatly beside them. I saw that the unknown soldier, who was probably drawing lines on new maps somewhere across the river, had hopefully put his army over the Meuse at several points; and also, that he had not marked in the retreat which followed after.

'And what do you think of this?' the Sergeant said. 'They must have known we'd come here, and they left one or two messages for us.'

He pointed to a wall, on which was written, 'Hullo, Tommy. If you catch up with me, you can——my——.'

'Well, it's ridiculous to call us Tommies,' the Sergeant said. 'That word went out long ago.'

When we got back to the farm, we found Sergeant Thackeray and some of his Redcaps there. They'd been re-signing roads in preparation for the Rhine crossing, and had called in to see us as they were passing by.

'Well, it looks as if we'll have to turn the old farmer out after all,' Dennis said to the Captain.

'Yes, Sir,' Sergeant Thackeray explained, 'there's a new order been posted, and as from tomorrow All, repeat All civilians living between the road and the river are to be evacuated. So as I was saying, it might be best to tell your Gerries about it now, and save us the trouble of slinging them out at short notice.'

'They're only just this side of the road.'

'It's an operational order, you know, Sir. And quite apart from the fact that if I may say so they shouldn't be here at all if you are, we can't let them stay once this order comes into effect.'

'Must you apply the law to the letter, Sergeant?'

'Speaking personally, Sir, it's all one to me, as you can imagine. But the Assistant Provost Marshal has been seen riding around on horseback checking up on this and that, and knowing him, I'd strongly advise you to comply.'

'You said on horseback?'

'Yes, he's abandoned his jeep for the moment, and reverted to a horse he's found himself. It seems he prefers travelling that way.'

'Well, it's highly inconvenient, but I suppose there's nothing for it,' the Captain said, going off for his siesta.

'Have they turned out all the civilians up at Corps?' I asked Thackeray.

'Oh yes, they've applied the regulations to the letter, and our instructions are to come down on any cases of fraternising we discover like a ton of bricks.'

'And you do?'

'Well, I might say we do and we don't. We have to protect ourselves, of course, and pull in anyone who's dozy enough to do it openly. But what goes on off the beaten track, particularly in the evenings, we don't bother to enquire into too closely.'

'So it's becoming an underground movement,' said Dennis, shaking his wrists.

'Yes, you might say so, and that seems to give it an additional attraction to some. As far as I can see, though, it's only the fanatics among the officers who bother about it greatly, and in the fighting Units, I'm told they just ignore it. Still, it's best to be careful. Up at Corps two days ago, they stripped a Sergeant down to Private for waving to a Gerry girl which, in my opinion, was overdoing it.'

'And what about people who have to come in contact with civilians in the line of duty?'

'People like yourselves, you mean? Well, we've got a pretty good alibi, it seems to me. For instance, there's one of my Corporals was called along to a house about a robbery, and he seems to go over there to take statements from the daughter a bit more than is really necessary. But in our case, what can they prove?'

We decided to tell the farmer immediately, but when we went to see him, it took some time for him to understand. 'You have let me stay,' he said. 'Why do you now try to make me go?'

Dennis reminded him of the second battle that would soon be starting, and said he and his livestock would be better out of it anyway.

'Let there be another battle,' the farmer cried. 'If I am to end my life, let me end it here.'

His wife came in at that moment, and when she heard the news she literally wrung her hands, and kept repeating a monosyllable of lament.

'Well,' I said, 'you'll be turned out anyway, so why not leave while you've still got plenty of time?'

'How can I leave? Where am I to take my cattle?'

'Haven't you friends somewhere across the road?' Dennis asked. 'There's no need to go further than the village.'

'There are many bad people that would steal our animals,' the woman said.

'Hundreds of farmers are having to leave with less notice than you're getting,' I said to him.

He sat looking old and dejected. I was exasperated at his taking it so much for granted that we sympathised with his predicament, and at his lack of gratitude for our advice.

'Come along now,' Dennis said to him. 'If you get started this afternoon, we'll give you a hand to move your beasts across the road through the traffic. And if you don't go too far, we'll see to it you're still allowed to slip across during the day to keep an eye on your property and cook our meals.'

We left them debating together, and went back to the mess to gather volunteers. Walter and Gordon were out on the patrol, so we tried the others.

'But what would I have to do?' said Norman.

'What? Good Heavens!' Dennis cried. 'Just give them a hand. Ride on a horse, if you like.'

'No,' he said, 'no. I don't care for animals, and I've some filing to catch up on.'

'I suppose that means you're going to ask me,' said Cuthbert. 'Well, considering his decent behaviour, I've no real objection.'

When we went back to the kitchen later on, we found that the farmer had taken heart, for he had collected together some neighbours, and was striding up and down in front of them, telling each one what his task would be. From time to time he looked round at us as if to say, 'There, I'm doing my best for you. Where there's a will, there's a way.'

When the neighbours (some of whom seemed pleased that this misfortune should have overtaken their prosperous friend) filed out of the kitchen, the farmer asked if I'd shoot a cow. 'It is sick, it cannot walk, it is too old to move,' he told me.

He led me to a barn, followed by some of the neighbours and their children. The cow was sitting awkwardly on the grass, and it rolled its eyes back without turning its head as we came up. I asked the farmer where to fire the shots, and he showed me the spot with his forefinger; then he backed away, snatching aside a little boy. This was the first time I'd used the pistol, so I took careful aim. After three shots, they told me the cow was dead, though it didn't look as if it was.

As the group was dispersing, the farmer's son came up, leading a horse. 'Sergeant,' he said. 'Can we take that cart yonder?'

'Of course, why not?'

'The Canadians put it there as a barricade.'

'Well, take it.'

I watched him harnessing the horse. 'They nearly made me a soldier, did you know that?' he told me, grinning. 'They tried to put me in the *Volkssturm*. What a comedy! There were not even weapons.'

'So what are you going to join now? The werewolves?'

'The werewolves!' he said scornfully. But then he looked at me guardedly, as if he suddenly felt doubly guilty—towards his own people for his disparagement of the werewolves, and towards ourselves because they were to have been used against us. 'No, I am no werewolf,' he said at last. 'But I shall be a soldier one day, just the same.'

'Do you think there will be a German army after all this?'

'Of course there will be a German army.' He smiled in a friendly way.

'What do you want to be a soldier for? It's an idiot's life.'

'Are you not one?'

'You'd be better off as a farmer.'

'Oh, I am not going to be a farmer, in any case. I'm going to be a salesman.'

'What will you sell?'

'Whatever there is. Anyway, I shall not be a farmer. That's an idiot's life.'

During the afternoon, the cavalcade of laden carts and heavy-footed, reluctant cows moved across the road to a farm five hundred yards away. At critical moments, Dennis halted the traffic, and Cuthbert darted about in his jeep like a mechanised sheep dog.

While we were resting in the almost deserted farmhouse, drinking tea Cornelis had made us, we had another visit. This was from a Major of the Artillery, who came in followed by his Sergeant. 'Good afternoon to you,' he said to the Captain. 'I'd just like to have a bit of a look round.'

'Oh? How so?' the Captain said, rising.

'Tomorrow you'll have a Battery here to keep you company. An advance party with a gun or two will be joining you tonight.'

He told us that Batteries were moving up all over the area to prepare for the preliminary bombardment. Their locations, he said pointedly, had been allotted on the map at a higher level than that of our Corps. 'Mind you, you've very welcome to stay,' he continued, 'so long as you don't mind squeezing up a bit. The windows will fly out with the blast, of course, and we'll probably lose a good deal of the roof.'

He went into the orchard with his Sergeant, to look for sites for the guns. From the comments we heard through the window, it seemed they found the ground rather softer than they liked.

'First the Germans, and then us,' said the Captain crossly, staring out at them.

'With all this big stuff coming up, we might try for something on the far side of the road ourselves,' I said.

'What chance will we have of getting our Germans across to look after us with a Battery swarming all over the kitchen and the best bedrooms?' said Dennis. 'We'll have to move, Sir.'

'Well, I'm sick and tired of being badgered about like this,' the Captain told us. 'I'm going in tomorrow to see Major Bane, and I'm going to tell him that as soon as he calls off the patrol, we're coming to live with him at that village of his, and the sooner the better. Meanwhile, perhaps it'd be only polite to ask those Gunners if they'd care for a cup of tea.'

'Big dog eats little dog, Sir,' Dennis said. 'And perhaps they are more use to the war effort here than us.'

The Major had wandered off to the bottom of the orchard, and the Sergeant was standing by himself, gazing towards the river with his eyes half closed, as if looking into his memory.

'Yes, I don't mind,' he said, when I asked him about the tea. 'And I expect the Major would like a drop as well.'

'Are those big guns you've got?'

'They're the biggest there are, lad. They do quite a lot of damage. Were you up by Goch way at all? We used them there last. The destruction's terrible, you ought to see it. I've never known anything like it, it's shocking.'

His face wore a tranquil, ruminative expression. He spoke in a soft, insensitive voice and didn't take his eyes off the horizon.

Dennis called out to me from the barn we were using as a garage, and I found him there with Gordon and Walter, who'd come in from the patrol. They were standing round all the gear that had been unloaded from the stores trucks onto the straw.

'Look here,' said Dennis. 'I've told them about our impending move, and if we're going to have to keep shifting about like this, it's high time we ditched fifty per cent of this stuff.'

'Why ditch good kit?' said Walter.

'Because everybody's sick and tired of loading and unloading it and cluttering up the trucks with useless rubbish.'

'And what in particular do you consider useless, Dennis?'

'This,' he said, kicking a field cooking oven. 'Do you imagine we'll ever use such a thing? And these,' he went on, stamping on the heavy tents that the Depôt had issued out to us so grudgingly.

'We've been all right so far,' I said, 'but how do you know we won't need these later on?'

'Later on! Later on! Haven't you realised yet that once we're over the Rhine we'll be in clover? So for pity's sake, dump them, flog them, or give them away as gifts.'

'What about my signature for them in the books at Brussels?'

'Brussels! How will they ever know what happens to us back there? We'll write them off as "Lost by enemy action." All you do is get Norman to put it down in your returns.'

'Dennis is right, they're no use to us,' said Gordon. 'But what we could do, is trade them for something useful with this Battery.'

'Well,' said Walter, 'it's a shame to waste good stores, but so long as the Battery takes them over . . .'

'We'll divide it all up into two piles,' Dennis said, 'and simply ride off and leave the surplus stuff behind.'

We did this, then joined in helping to move the last of the animals. When none was left, the farmer's wife cooked our supper and her own family's farewell meal. We went into the kitchen to say good-bye to them; and when the farmer had filled his pipe with our tobacco, which he blended with his own, he questioned us as to the future with a serious air.

'And what will happen to us when you have crossed the Rhine?' he asked.

'You think we'll get across?'

'Assuredly.'

'Well, then things will settle down, and you'll be ruled by the Military Government,' I suggested.

'Shall we have occupation troops?'

'Yes, certainly.'

'That will be a misfortune.' He paused. Then, as if we were holding a peace conference, 'Perhaps this region will be given to Holland.'

'Oh, I shouldn't think so.'

'So long as we are not given to Belgium. We had Belgian troops here after the last war.'

He looked at us sagely, reflecting. 'The road outside was built by Napoleon,' he said. 'At one time, the Rhineland belonged to France. We also have the same religion as the French, for we, too, are Catholics. The Catholics here have never been for the Nazis. You should have seen how we treated our *Ortsgruppenleiter*.'

This may have been true, but I didn't like him to be so virtuous about it.

'Don't worry,' Dennis said to him. 'They'll always be needing you. After the war, everyone will be hungry.'

This thought comforted him, and he puffed more happily at his pipe. I was reminded of farmers we'd met in the Allied countries, who also seemed to regard themselves and their land as the only permanent reality.

'Come I will show you something,' the farmer said suddenly; and rising to his feet, he led us downstairs into the cellar. It was packed with wooden beds from which the bedding had now been removed, and it was horribly stuffy. The farmer stood nodding on the threshold and waved his arm. 'Here we all sat when the first battle was in progress,' he told us. 'And while the shells fell all about, I worked at my paintings.'

He picked up from the table a crude, expressive picture painted on a three-ply board. It showed a wolf-hound attacking a deer, with a thick row of trees in the background.

'For you,' he said, handing it to us collectively, like a prize. 'Since you have helped me, you may have it.'

When we'd thanked him, I said, 'Do you do a lot of these?'

'Yes. Now that I grow older. Ever since my son died, I do them.'

'Well, you've still got the other lad,' Dennis said to him.

'Oh, yes.' He looked at us seriously and rather defiantly and said, 'And perhaps I shall yet have another.'

We helped him and his family gather up the rest of their crockery, and pile it into one of the trucks. They got in too, and as we were driving them across the road, the advance party of the Battery arrived, and began to unlimber its guns.

The Captain came back from Corps next morning, and masking his cheerfulness, said, 'Here's the drill. The patrols are definitely off, and I've fixed up we all move in with Corps. Major Bane wants two men down at Mil. Gov.'s village every day, and they've got to stop the night there. So some of you swan off now, two to get a billet and two to invigorate Mil. Gov.'

When four of us reached Corps headquarters, Dennis said, 'The only way to get a decent place in this overcrowded spot, is to see the new German Burgomaster and make him surrender a house in the ghetto the locals have been herded into.'

Dennis persuaded the Burgomaster to part with a villa that had been intended as a Food Office. 'It belongs to a dentist,' Dennis explained to us, 'but it's nice and empty. He being a *Stürmbannführer*, I expect he's departed across the river with his family.'

We found that the villa was of fairly recent construction, for a swastika motif had been embodied in its brickwork. 'Well now, he'll have trouble conforming with Mil. Gov. edicts about forbidden signs,' said Walter, fingering a large swastika let in to the side of the porch.

Going inside, we saw that it hadn't yet been looted, though the instruments in the surgery were scattered all over the floor, and the portraits of Nazi personalities had been smashed. Upstairs in a cupboard, we found the *Stürmbannführer's* uniforms on coat-hangers, still neatly pressed. And opening an unlocked drawer in the study, we discovered his political testament. It was enclosed in two sealed envelopes, and the inner one was marked, 'To be opened in the case of my death.' The testament itself gave a confidential account of the *Stürmbannführer's* subordinates, with recommendations for promotions and dismissals. Another envelope, also sealed, contained Dutch and American banknotes.

'He must have left in a hurry,' Gordon said, as we distributed these. 'Fancy Major Bane not having inspected this place. He must be slipping.'

Walter and I left them making the usual arrangements, and drove on across the sandy roads to the other village. There they told us Mil. Gov. had set up its headquarters in the Town Hall. Walter waited by the cars, and I walked over to the building.

The crowds of refugees outside were kept at bay by notices in two languages warning them that admission was forbidden, and by several respectable-looking German civilians at the door, rather of the type of a Park Attendant, who wore white armbands with black lettering which said, also bi-lingually, that they were Military Government Police. These made as if to ask me my business, but I glanced sharply at them, and went on. In the hall there were some more of them, and they guided me towards a door marked, 'Interpreter: All Enquiries Here.'

'I want to see the Military Governor. Where is he?'

'Certainly, certainly. But will you not first pass through the office of the Interpreter?'

They showed me into a room in which a neatly-brushed German was sitting behind a desk. He looked up at me with an interrogative frown and said in English, 'What is it I may do for you?'

I waited for him to stand up, then snapped back in German, 'Which is the officers' room?'

'Through here, Sir. But my orders are all visitors should first address themselves to me.'

I knocked and went into the next room. Lieutenant Adeane was on one side of the table, and on the other a heavily attractive blonde woman was taking down a letter which Major Parsons, leaning over her with one arm on the back of her chair, was slowly dictating. As I came in, she glanced up at him for the next words with a look of alluring and impatient expectancy.

'Well, well, Sarge,' the Major said. 'So it's you they've sent us. Righty-oh, Miss Fleck, thanks, that'll be all for just now.'

The Secretary gathered up her papers rapidly, and gave us a look suggesting no serious business would be done while she wasn't there. Major Parsons sat down in her chair.

'Well now,' he said, 'you've arrived a bit late in the day, but there'll be plenty for you to do. We've got a big job on. These refugees keep moving in from Heaven knows where, and the art of it is to spread them out evenly among the locals so as we don't get swamped.'

'It's in moments like these, when the first shock is brought home to them, that we can show them what decent treatment means,' the Lieutenant added.

'I don't know about that,' the Major said. 'But we've got to make sure they get a fair minimum of food and clothing, to preserve public order. Now what I'd suggest is, Lieutenant, that you take the Sergeant along to the military clerks' room, so as he can muck in with them and catch up on what's been happening.'

On the way through the Interpreter's office, the Secretary gave us a bright look which Lieutenant Adeane ignored.

'Between ourselves, I don't much care for that pair,' he said, when he'd closed the door. 'They're really quite the wrong type. The trouble is, you know, the Major hasn't the gift for picking suitable Germans to work with us. He's taken in by sycophantic people.'

In the clerk's room, where he left me, I found Harry, who told me he'd been working there ever since the collecting-point had been set up.

'Major Bane asked me if I'd like to come, and I jumped at it,' he said. 'I've got myself a snip job—clothing king. I go round all the houses and issue the families that need them with the suits and dresses they've requisitioned from the local people.'

When he took me into his private office, I asked him how he got on with the Major and the Lieutenant. 'Well,' he said, 'they're learning as they go along, aren't they? Of course, it's a pity Major Parsons doesn't speak German, because when he gives orders through that Interpreter and Secretary of his, they're apt to interpret his meaning too, as far as I can see. At any rate, a sentence of his in English takes ten minutes to tell the refugees, plus a lot of pushing around. I've had to step in and tell them to stop shouting more than once. And now that Secretary's so well in with the old Major, she seems to be trying to play him off against the Lieutenant.'

'Adeane speaks German, doesn't he?'

'Oh yes, he does. And he's got a lot of ideas, which is more than the Major has, but some of them are a bit unpractical. He's got a mania for helping anti-Nazis, and he goes round looking for them everywhere.'

'That's right, isn't it?'

'Of course it is. But you see, the Lieutenant's idea of an anti-Nazi is someone like himself—nicely brought up and well-spoken. There may be some like that, but I've got to know a good deal of the families here these last weeks, and there are plenty of real anti-Nazis among them. They don't all come from these parts, a lot of them were evacuated here before we came. But I don't think Lieutenant Adeane would recognise an anti-Nazi without a collar and tie on if he saw one.'

'And the Major's interested in what he calls keeping order.'

'Well, that's right so long as there's fighting, but once it stops, you've got to hold the people down, or else work with some of them. And if you haven't a clear notion which, you'll chose the wrong ones, or just those you happen to like personally. If you had a definite policy, it wouldn't matter if you spoke German or not, because there'd be men you could trust to help you out. But Major Parsons picks that girl as Secretary, who all the locals tell me is a Nazi. The Interpreter too, though he's a smaller one, they say.'

'Official policy is that no known Nazis are to be engaged other than temporarily.'

'Temporarily. Well, there aren't many signs of applying that policy yet. And when Mil. Gov. gets over the river, they'll have to rule in the big towns there. How are they going to find the people then? And yet, it shouldn't be all that difficult. You've got lists of categories who've got to be arrested, haven't you? Why haven't they made lists of the kinds of men who are to be supported? Men who worked against the Nazis? If it was me, I'd go straight to the concentration camps for them. They're the men I'd back. Anyone who could show he'd been active against the Nazis.'

'Even if they started working against us?'

'You've got to take a chance on that, haven't you? Anyway, sooner or later all Germans are going to work against us, more or less. It's their country, and it's they who'll have to begin again and have another try. Either we hold them down forever, or take a risk. And whatever you do is better than letting the Nazis in again by the back door . . . Still, there's one thing I'll say for the Major and the Lieutenant, they both seem quite sure they know how to do the job. They're full of confidence.'

Harry came out with me and showed Walter where to park the cars, and then took us over to the clerks' mess for tea. It was brought to us by women refugees. 'It means they get eats,' he told us. 'Strictly speaking, they shouldn't get Army rations, but the Major says nothing, and we see to it they do.'

'And when you visit these families you speak of,' Walter asked him, 'can you make yourself understood?'

'Oh, yes. I can speak as good bad German as you can, now.'

'Let's hear you perform.'

'*Hier ist für Sie und hier ist für Sie*, and *Willst Du mit* me *spazieren*?'

'I didn't get that latter part of it.'

'*Mit spazieren*? Go for a walk with me.'

'And who do you say that to?'

'Well, there's a girl here from East Prussia I've got to know.'

'East Prussia? She's a long way from home, isn't she?'

'Yes, her father and mother are dead, and she came here on farm work, she says.'

'And you've been seeing her?'

'Yes, I've been round there off and on.'

Walter drained his cup beyond the dregs, then fixed Harry with his most penetrating stare. 'I hope you're not forgetting your *mejuffrouw* in the middle of all this,' he said.

'Oh no, it's just for company.'

'Company. Oh. Well.'

There was something of a pause, till Harry said to me, 'You remember about the brother of that girl of mine in Holland? I haven't heard any news of Dutch prisoners yet, have you?'

'No. I expect any that were here will have been evacuated over the Rhine.'

'We'll have to wait till we cross it too, then.'

'Well now, Harry,' Walter said, 'where is it you're fixing us up for a billet?'

'Do you mind if I get the Corporal to show you? I've got to go back on duty myself. If you could lend me your utility a moment, it'd be a help.'

'How long's a moment?'

'About an hour. I've got some clothes I said I'd deliver tonight if I could, and the trucks'll be off the road by now. I'll bring the car back to your billet before it's dark.'

The Corporal took us to a former tobacconist's, and gave us two rooms on the first floor with furniture upholstered in green plush with tassles. 'You won't mind if you see me round the house from time to time, will you?' he said. 'I come along here evenings, to do my bit of fratting. But it means they'll look after you well, because I've promised them they won't have any refugees billeted, and I bring them stacks to eat.'

Walter frowned at this, but only because the Corporal was a Corporal. Then, catching sight of some framed photographs on the wall, he strode over and examined them. They were of soldiers of the previous war, and one of the groups was posed against a painted background of a cannonade.

'Do you want me to take them down, Sarge?' the Corporal said.

'What, these? Why?'

'There's a Mil. Gov. edict out about such things, you know. Any pictorial examples of the glorification of war are to be eliminated, it says.'

'What, regimental photos stuck up in the best bedroom? Don't be daft. Won't Mil. Gov. be glad of a snap of themselves dressed up as soldiers in twenty years' time?'

'It's what we're fighting to prevent, according to that edict.'

'I tell you, boy, I'd rather have the lads in these photos with me in a tight corner than I would Mil. Gov. If anyone tried to destroy my souvenirs, I'd certainly resent it.'

'Then we'll leave them be, Sarge, and if you're ready for your meal, I think it's just about ready for you.'

'He's a forward bugger for a Corporal,' said Walter, as we went down to the tobacconist's kitchen. 'Some of these clerks and such are rising a bit above themselves, with all the power they're getting. Because they control some fancy forms you can pick up off any desk in Blighty, or stores and rations they know these Gerries are badly in need of, they start acting as if they were Captain Quartermasters.'

'They're probably just as efficient.'

'Just as crooked, you mean. Still, there's no doubt the British soldier has initiative, once he's given his head. He knows how to use the power he gets, even if he does look after himself in the process. And he does use his influence to help the locals to a certain extent, even if it costs him nothing.'

When we'd finished the meal, we went out to immobilise the trucks, and found that the utility wasn't back. We walked over to the clerks' mess, and the Corporal there said, 'Harry? You'll find him out at his farm, I should say. Do you know how to get there?'

'We'll leave it, Walter. He'll be back.'

'No, I don't think we'll leave it. In the first place, he hasn't returned a vehicle he said he would, and in the second, I'd like to check up on his activities a bit. I don't want to see him running into trouble.'

'I've had enough of checking up on activities.'

'I thought you cared for that lad. If so, shouldn't you keep a friendly eye on him?'

'If you want to try and stop him spending his evenings with a German girl, it's up to you.'

'Spendings his evenings. It depends how, and at what. Don't forget he's engaged to be married.'

'I'll be seeing you, then. Tell him to bring my truck back.'

Walter drove off with a set expression. I walked back to the tobacconist's, and found Harry and the utility outside. 'You're overdue, aren't you?' I said.

'Yes. Sorry.'

'An hour's an hour, you know.'

'Yes, sorry. I was out for a ride.'

He was sitting on the mudguard with his arms folded and his thoughts elsewhere, caressing a sensual memory. His body was heavily easy, and his face wore a relaxed, mindless look.

'All right, thanks for bringing the car, I'll see you tomorrow.'

'Yes. Well, there it is. I've gone and fallen for this girl. She's different from anything I've ever met.'

'It's always different.'

'You think so? Not this time. I've never known anyone behave like her to me. She frightens me a bit, sometimes. She's so deep in her feelings, I know she'd go a hundred miles and wait ten years for me. The way she acts, you can see she's afraid of nothing. She'd murder me if she knew I was friendly with another girl, but when she saw I liked her, she didn't care what anybody else thought, she didn't hide her feelings.'

'It's sudden, isn't it? It took you longer to make up your mind in Holland.'

'Yes, it did . . . and I'm fond of her too, believe it or not. The girl in Holland is like the girls at home a bit, loving and good hearted. But this now is something special. I never knew it could happen to me.'

'You're in love with them both, then.'

'I don't know.'

Walter drove up in his truck. 'So there you are, my lad,' he said. 'I just missed you.'

'Missed me where?'

'Up at that farm of yours.'

'You went up there? Why?'

'You seem to forget you kept that vehicle rather longer than you said.'

'Is that what you went there for? You weren't spying on me, were you?'

'What's that word you used?'

'Spying.'

Walter got down, slammed the car door and slapped his gloves together. 'Are you going to listen to me,' he said, 'without getting hasty?'

'If you've anything worth saying.'

'Calm yourself down and hearken. Why fool about with some Gerry girl when you've given your promise?'

'Do I have to answer your questions?'

'Not unless you want to, but you might try listening to them. I've been married myself seven years now, and I know what I'm talking about. Apart from your wife, you meet half-a-dozen women later on you could have gone for. By and large, I tell you, women are much the same. But you can't have them all, and when you've found one you care for, and you've taken time to make up your mind about her like you did, then you've got to stick to her and forget about the others, or you'll just cause yourself more misery.'

'All right, Sergeant, I know you mean it well. But I don't like inteference, see? And you shouldn't have followed me there.'

'I'm not interfering, lad. I'm telling you this for your own good. So think it over, that's all I'm asking. Don't get tangled up. Be careful.'

Walter hit him across the shoulder with his gloves, a friendly blow but hard, and went in to the billet. Harry cleared his throat, didn't spit, and swallowed.

'Careful? I don't know what he means. The way I feel, I can't be careful or not careful.'

'Well, be careful about the Non-fraternisation order.'

'That's no worry. I drive with her out in the fields, it's the only place where I can get her alone. But they're so used to seeing me with civvy passengers in the trucks they don't interfere. And even if they did, how can I help it? You can't sit drinking cups of tea among twenty other people with a girl like that. She's one out of a book, I tell you. And yet, you know, she's said to me she doesn't think she's beautiful.'

'You'll have to sort it out.'

'I know I will. I'm torn two ways, really. I've given my word back there, and there's her brother I've said I'd look out for . . . But if I hadn't met the girl in Holland, I'd have done something permanent about this one.'

'How could you do anything permanent? They're not going to let us marry German girls.'

'Not now, but the war's going to end one day, isn't it? They won't be able to keep that up forever. Well, sorry I was late getting back. Tell old Walter not to worry himself.'

Up in the green plush bedroom, Walter was cleaning his pistol. 'You may think I spoke out of turn,' he said, 'but do you know what the old woman up at that farm told me? He's told this girl he'll marry her.'

'How does the old woman know that?'

'She's seen a ring with his initials on the girl's finger.'

'That doesn't prove he's promised anything.'

'No. But he never gave that ring to the lass he spoke to first.'

'What's she like, this girl?'

'A fairly typical Gerry type, I'd say, with certainly a smashing figure built up in the right places, and silky hair all over her eyes. She sat there like in a trance when Harry's name was mentioned—you know? Looking beyond and all round you. She's certainly far gone herself, he must be her childhood's dream.'

'What did the Germans there think of it?'

'The old lady's scared in case of trouble. This girl being an orphan, she considers herself responsible for her. When I went up there, it was all I could do to get inside, they were so suspicious. There were dozens of them crowded in the kitchen, looking hard at this girl as if she'd committed some deadly sin. But they seemed sorry for her, too. She was standing there beside the stove when I came in, cooking. I couldn't see her all that clearly, there was only an oil lamp, but enough to see she was a snakey-looking man-eating type. Still, a lovely bint. I wouldn't mind going after one like her myself, if I was free and Harry's age.'

Arriving back at our new billet in the morning, I saw three or four men climbing about on the roof and Dennis shouting instructions at them from the ground below. 'I'm having it re-tiled,' he told me. 'And when they've finished, they're going to re-glaze the windows too. We must keep out the wind and the rain.'

'How did you get hold of these people?'

'I went round the village and collected up a working-party.'

He glanced upwards with satisfaction. 'Well, when we take over their houses, we certainly do all we can to put them in good repair.'

He'd also got hold of some staff. There was a middle-aged cook, two sisters to help in the kitchen, some housemaids and a mechanic to look after our transport. Gordon told me all this in the office, where he was boxing up some dental equipment to send to Belgium.

'You're going to help the Allies get back what the Nazis took?' I said to him.

He looked up. 'Nazi or no Nazi is much the same to me, chummy,' he said. 'I've got nothing against the Germans personally, but I'm going to see to it they help me start up again after the war. If you're taking their stuff, you might as well take plenty and turn it into cash. I suppose you disapprove?'

'Do you mind if I do?'

'Not a bit.'

Cornelis, who was helping him, was wearing an ornate ring. 'That's new, Cornelis, isn't it?' I asked him. 'Where did you get it?'

He opened wide his heavily-lidded eyes, and smiled with all his white teeth. 'From a refugee.'

'Did you take it?'

'Oh, no, no, no, Sir. I bought it with some cigarettes.'

'How many did you give for it?'

'Thirty. He asked for more and even threatened me, but I laughed at him and gave him thirty.'

'He must have wanted a smoke.'

'Oh yes, he did.' Cornelis put on an expression of grief, and shook his head as if to say, 'Poor world.'

While I was arranging with Norman which two men would go down to Mil. Gov., Dennis came in and told me a dinner was to be held that evening in honour of Major Benedict-Bane. 'It's an opportunity to show our appreciation of him,' he said, 'and to do it properly, we must kill the fatted calf and create an oasis of plenty.' What this amounted to was that he wanted someone to go out to the farms and get fresh food. Walter said he'd come with me, and Norman handed over his office, to make one of his rare excursions into the outer air.

When we went round to the car park we found the mechanic there tinkering with the transport, and he held us in conversation for a while. He told us he'd been wounded in Russia and discharged, and went on to say that our motor-cycles were all right, but our trucks, no good at all. 'Equipment,' he said. 'War is a question of equipment.' And he went on to discuss the war as if it was an event that could already be considered in retrospect. 'The English airplanes are good,' he told us, watching some that came flying overhead. 'But the *Luftwaffe* machines—what about them? Say what you like, they were high-class material, and our pilots, prime fighters.'

We took two trucks, because I was going on to the other village again to invite the Mil. Gov. officers to the dinner. We travelled through fertile country, among farms that were quite unscathed, until we stopped at one surrounded by a high wall. In the yard, cackling geese escaped from under the wheels of our cars. 'A couple of those would do nicely,' Walter said.

The men were in the fields, and a massive woman came shuffling out in slippers to meet us as we walked in through the back door. She showed us into a main room with a wide brick fireplace covered with iron-work of the kind usually found in a museum. She treated us like large boys, who could be prevented from doing anything foolish if they were handled properly. And when she had offered us some bean-coffee, she sat watching us with a look on her enormous features like that of a motherly murderess.

We told her we wanted milk, eggs, butter and two geese. She nodded solemnly at first, but threw up her hands and let them fall on her huge knees when she heard us speak of geese. 'My man would never allow it,' she said.

We offered her chocolate, soap, tobacco and some petrol. She agreed at last to the geese, and came out to the truck to take what she wanted from the ration box. She chose the tins carefully, seeming to know exactly what she was entitled to. We watched her, and she us, like wary natives of two tribes on a desert island, far away from it all.

'Will you take them alive?' she said, pointing at the geese. We hesitated; and seeing Walter fingering his pistol, she roared with laughter in a great bellow and waddled into the yard, calling to the geese in their language till she cornered one of them against the wall. What she did exactly we couldn't see, but one moment she was holding a flapping goose to her body in a loving hug, and the next she'd dropped it writhing on the ground and was cooing menacingly at another.

'A robust old girl,' said Walter, as we carried them out to the cars.

'You're far too pleasant to these Gerries,' Norman told us. 'Why don't you take what you want and give them their due without all this tiresome negotiation?'

Walter and Norman drove back to the dentist's, and I went on to Mil. Gov.'s Town Hall. Lieutenant Adeane declined rather testily, but Major Parsons said he was 'all for an orgy.'

'It's a pity the Lieutenant couldn't come along,' he said, as we drove over the country in the late afternoon. 'But one of us has to be on the spot, and I expect he's happier, really, hob-nobbing with his peculiar pals.'

'What's peculiar about them?'

'I may be prejudiced, Sarge, but he goes for a slimy, obstreperous type I can't abide. Give me the German who keeps his mouth shut and isn't ashamed of the fight they put up. That's the type I prefer.'

When we got back to our house, I found that the rest of the guests hadn't arrived yet, so I took Major Parsons up to the Captain's room for a preliminary drink. Down in the dentist's sitting-room, the Sergeants had gathered for the same purpose. Norman, holding a gin and orange, was having a conversation with Cuthbert in a corner.

'Well, personally,' Norman was saying, 'I don't feel strongly about them one way or another. All I long for is the day I see the last of them.'

'I'd like to like them, I suppose,' Cuthbert said, 'but they make it very difficult to. They're not straightforward. You don't know where you are with them.'

'I see what you mean, but in what particular way?'

'Well now, for instance, what do they think of us? We've been told they hate us, and no doubt they've reasons for that from their point of view, and yet it's very rare to find one who isn't talkative and polite.'

'That's just to win us over.'

'No, it can't be diplomacy,' said Cuthbert, 'because they go out of their way to be pleasant, even when there's no advantage in it. I believe they admire us.'

'I don't think they admire us, I think they admire the winners,' said Norman. 'That's why they used to admire themselves so much. The trouble is, Cuthbert, you're too determined to be fair. Why, they never think of our troubles, do they? My house was bombed, for instance. Now, the people here whose English I can understand all tell me about their disasters, but none of them has ever enquired about what happened to me.'

'That's asking too much, isn't it?'

'Oh, I don't want their sympathy, but why do they expect mine? What I object to, is that they take if for granted they'll be liked. They're just the same as children in that respect.'

'Their own children are very delightful,' said Cuthbert. 'They'll do anything for you.'

'So will all children.'

'Oh no, they won't. You try getting English kids to clean a car.'

'Well, that only shows they like to do what they're told from early youth. Anyway, the adults are just the same. If you want to get them to do anything, you have to butter them up and threaten them at the same time. If you do that, they'll follow you as if you were the Pied Piper.'

'He was a German too, of course.'

'Personally, I think they're stupid,' said Norman. 'Have you seen how easily our squaddies can handle them? Any ordinary squaddy knows how to handle them as if it came naturally to him.'

'I admit they're stupid in one sense,' said Cuthbert, 'and that is, in the way they often assume you're stupid yourself, when they talk to you.'

'They're clever and stupid, a very bad combination. Just like the papers have always said. And what proves it, is that they don't pack it in while there's still time.'

'They couldn't do that.'

'Why not? It's never too late to stop. You can always cut your losses.'

'Well, Hitler said they'd go on until twelve-fifteen.'

'Oh, that.'

'Old Mac here maintains that if they can't win, then they want to sacrifice themselves. They're rash and uncalculating, according to him.'

'They're always calculating,' said Norman. 'Look how they started this war.'

The rest of the party had by now arrived. There were several

Staff officers from Corps in addition to the guest of honour, Major Benedict-Bane, one or two Mil. Gov. colleagues of Major Parsons, an Ordnance Captain who had given Gordon a jar of rum intended for troops in the firing line in return for two beds and mattresses out of the attic, Sergeant Thackeray and ourselves; a cross-section of the rulers of the land.

As Cornelis went round serving drinks, dressed in one of the dentist's white coats, we heard about the imminent attack down by the Rhine.

'Strictly between ourselves,' Major Bane explained, dropping his voice with gin-primed gravity, 'it's due for the day-after-tomorrow. The British Second will be on the left, the American Ninth on the right, and we're going over somewhere between Rheinberg and Rees—Wesel's the crossing-place, I believe. After the artillery barrage, which is to begin in the evening, the Commandos will go across the river in ducks, and the Paratroops should be overhead some time in the small hours. I hear they're flying them in from as far away as Paris and back home. It's going to be the biggest amphibious operation since the beaches.'

About twenty-five of us sat down to dinner to a meal composed partly of the produce of the farm, partly of Army rations and partly of the wines and bottled fruits from the shelves in the dentist's cellar. During the serving of the geese, a 'plane flew over low and there was a loud explosion. Everyone ducked, and the newly-glazed windows were blown out again. After a few seconds of silence, there were roars of laughter.

With Major Benedict-Bane on his right, the Captain was in a surprisingly formal mood. He gave us the toast of the King, and then made a speech about our loyalty to the Major and the Corps, and even went on to refer to the part we would be playing in the forthcoming advance to victory over the north-German plain.

Afterwards, the party followed the pattern already described, though with novel variations. Some played cards, some the gramophone, some drank too much too fast and broke the glasses, the records and the views of the Black Forest hanging on the walls. Soon the officers and the other-ranks split into separate groups. The officers seemed more restive, their clipped voices rose to a higher key, their jokes grew more bitter and their laughter more unhappy. They began to play games. The

Stürmbannführer's political testament was read out aloud with the names of Corps personalities substituted for those of the Nazi officials he had wanted to degrade. Grotesque operations were performed in the surgery on Majors held struggling in the dentist's chair. A group put on the *Stürmbannführer's* uniforms and sang *Wir fahren gegen England* at the tops of their voices; then poured gin down a cat's throat. As the fun reached its climax, their friendly physical violence grew more violent. The other-ranks, sunk into easy chairs and crude, sentimental good-fellowship at the end of the room where they had gathered, stared back at all this with sodden disfavour, thinking it boyish to get rough if you weren't going to be serious about it.

I went out into the kitchen, where the cook and the two girls were washing up, and stayed and talked to them facetiously.

One of these girls was dark and reserved, though perfectly easy in her manner. She gave the impression of modesty, which is so attractive in anyone who is beautiful as well. Her replies to my stupid remarks were unaffectedly polite. She kept herself free, and me in my place, without being silent or aloof.

I went out into the garden, and walked up and down on a pebbled path under some climbing roses. Half drunk, I thought of Schubert.

The girl came out to empty the slops, and I asked her to stay a while. She sat on a bench beside me and I took her hand.

I got the impression she wanted me to kiss her if I had been somebody else. She told me she had a friend in the German army, of whom she had no news.

I asked if I could see her home, but others had thought of this too, and we were quite a party going down the street by torchlight, each man trying to make his 'Good-night' sound different from the rest.

THE NORTH–GERMAN PLAIN

I WAS LEFT BEHIND WHEN THE DETACHMENT SET OFF IN THE WAKE of the fighting troops who had been pouring over the Rhine for days in pursuit of the Germans. Our men were suddenly ordered away while I was out at the refugee village with another young Sergeant, and it was evening before we got their message to catch up. So when we'd disentangled ourself from Mil. Gov., we packed up ready to start after them the following morning.

It was a hot, fresh day as we took the road back to the farm by the river where we'd been at first. The camps in the villages had gone, and the road to the Rhine, where vehicles were lining up in a queue to get across, no longer seemed the dangerous, lonely place it had been before. The young Sergeant got ahead of me on his bike and disappeared as I joined the waiting cars which turned slowly in to the muddy track to the pontoon bridge. It was a lovely sight to see it resting on the boats, and the trucks passing steadily over in the morning sun.

On the further side was a newly ruined town which the road by-passed to the left. On the west bank we had seen only villagers, but now I noticed people who'd been evacuated across the river and who'd been unable to retreat any more, or had decided it would no longer be worth while: officials in uniforms and men in city suits, looking incongruous among the ruins with their felt hats and satchels. On the fields outside were traces of the battle—smashed gliders, bits of airplanes, abandoned guns and burnt-out metal.

Except for what I'd heard on the radio, I didn't know how far ahead the Corps had gone, though it seemed they'd by now be well beyond the Ruhr. I followed the signs which, sure enough, appeared at vantage points as the miles passed by. But I had to keep a close watch out for them, as they marked a capricious route which often forked off down secondary roads and across improbable fields, to make a way round German demolitions on the highways.

After I'd driven several hours, I began to meet parties of civilians moving in the opposite direction to the Army. Some were in small groups on foot, and others in larger bands with belongings heaped on farm carts. It was some time before I realised they were our Allies—the freed prisoners-of-war and deported workers who were beginning their homeward trek. At first I'd taken them for Germans, and it wasn't so much their dress as the delighted and rather solemn expression I began to notice on their faces, that made me realise who they were. They went steadily on as if nothing on earth would stop them.

Then I began to overtake parties of Easterners moving along in the same direction as ourselves, in bodies that were even larger, often riding in a chain of waggons pulled by a tractor which carried a red flag. In some of the villages I passed, they seemed to have taken possession, and I saw whole communities camped in barns by the roadside, cooking themselves meals. I wondered what was happening to the farmers.

These three streams of traffic grew thicker and thicker: our lorries going north-east along the road, the eastern Allies pushing on beside us along the grass verge and the Westerners moving back in the opposite direction. It was as though a day of judgment had come, with the Germans fleeing hopelessly, and the victims rising up and setting out for separate paradises beyond the frontiers. And yet, among the thousands of people I saw, who were only a part of the immense migration, there did not seem to be much outward joy. The imprisonment had been too long and terrible, and their one overpowering instinct was to get away. And though all these processions were on the roads because of the same event, there seemed to be little exchange between them. The Army hurried on, and the Allies of the east and west passed one another by.

I reached a big town whose débris lay all fresh and repellent in the sun. The desolation here was the most striking I'd ever seen, because the town was smashed beyond the point at which it had any recognisable shape. There wasn't even enough left of the buildings to see what had been ruined. Jagged bits of wall stuck out of avalanches of rubble in a landscape like a gigantic ash pit. As I drove up the main road, which had been uncovered by bulldozers, it was impossible to see where side streets had once turned off. Broken trees, and great areas where there was just nothing, completed the picture.

'This is a nice mess you're living in,' I said to an Engineer who gave me some petrol.

'——ing terrible, isn't it. Kesselring told them to resist, so our General gave the order to bash the place to bits. That stopped them.'

'Is Kesselring in charge now?'

'Yes, von Rundstedt's been demoted. It means it's nearing the end, you don't change your Generals when you're winning, do you. The Ruhr's cut off now, too, we've joined up with the Yanks this side of it, and we're taking ten thousand prisoners a day, they tell me.'

I asked him if he knew where our Corps had advanced to.

'They passed through here a few days ago, but ——ed if I know where they are now. Well, I'll be glad to get out of this place. All they can do with it now is write it off.'

After I'd left the town I made a wrong turning somewhere, and found myself riding along an empty road among hilly pasturage and orchards, with low-lying mountains in gentle waves on the horizon. As I'd also driven off my maps, I was glad to see a motor-cyclist coming up the hill towards me. I waved him to a halt and, as he came nearer, I saw the Corps flash on his mudguard. It was one of Sergeant Thackeray's Redcaps.

He leant his bike against one leg with the other resting across the saddle, and pushed his crash-helmet on the back of his head. 'Hot enough for you?' he said.

'I've lost myself. How do I get to Corps?'

He showed me on his map. They were still thirty miles ahead.

'One of your lads has blown himself up, did you know?'

'Who?'

'I don't know his name. The little fair-haired kiddy.'

'How bad is it?'

'Oh, nobody's dead, I don't suppose. His vehicle ran into a mine.'

I hurried on under the lee of some mountains which followed along on the skyline about five miles to the right. As evening fell, I reached a village where I found the Corps headquarters. Norman was in there getting the mail. 'What's gone wrong?' I said.

'Yes, it's Cuthbert. His jeep's a total loss.'

'But Cuthbert, Norman!'

'Oh, there's nothing much the matter with him.'

According to Norman, on the previous night the Detachment had stopped at a big country house that had been occupied before them by a German Unit. Cuthbert, looking for a good parking place, was driving down an avenue covered with pine needles, when he was suddenly seen to fly into the air as a mine exploded underneath him. Walter, running up along the bank beside the track, had found Cuthbert dazed but uninjured.

'Walter and Dennis rushed him off to the nearest First Aid Post, but the doctors probed him and said all he needed was a good night's sleep.'

'And he's quite all right?'

'Absolutely. Dennis gave him a lift in his Opel coming up here today. He told Cuthbert it was a judgment on him for pinching that jeep.'

'Has Dennis got an Opel now?'

'Almost everybody has. Even Cuthbert. He's found one this morning in the town we're at now. Come along, I'll show you.'

Norman told me they were living beneath the mountains a few miles back on another road, and he led me there on his motor-bike. We crossed a river by a bridge with gaping holes in its surface, and rode beneath the hills to a fairy-tale town of red brick, the first of any size I'd seen that was quite undamaged. Neat white flags were hanging out of the windows, as they had done in other towns and villages I'd passed; and Norman said, as we halted a moment at the market place in the fading light, that he'd been told they were always there, however early our troops had arrived. They must have been hung out spontaneously at a mysterious communal signal, as soon as the citizens had seen their army go, and even before our soldiers had come in.

I followed Norman again up a steep road to the prosperous quarter where big, ugly villas were grouped among trees at the foot of the mountain. We drove into a dank front garden, parked our vehicles there and walked up to a multi-balconied house. It was clearly the most imposing we'd yet been in.

As I met the men in the Detachment, I realised that big changes had taken place since they'd crossed over to the east bank of the Rhine. To begin with, there was a prodigious accumulation of loot, on a scale quite different from that we'd got by our earlier, tentative efforts.

As Norman had said, most men had found themselves civilian cars. Even the worst drivers had one. The stores had been transferred to these vehicles from the trucks, which now carried only motor-cycles, like travelling garages.

Excited beyond his usual reticence, and in the manner of one who is going to initiate you, Gordon took me into his bedroom and showed me silverware, table-cloths and cases of bottles. When I asked him about the box of pistols and ammunition, he told me they'd ordered all the arms at the village near the country house to be surrendered. As most Nazi Party members owned a pistol as part of their uniform, the collection had been a large one. After making a selection, they'd dropped the rest in a lake.

'The trouble about some of these things,' he said, 'is that they're too bulky to carry, particularly as we'll be picking up more stuff as we go along. But what I plan to do, if possible, is to salt them away in various places and come back and dispose of them later on.'

Norman led me into his office with a similar air of one who's going to surprise you, and showed me new typewriters which had come from a factory where they'd stopped for lunch. He hunted about in one of his chests and brought out four pairs of binoculars, which he held by the straps for me to look at, saying, 'Here you are. I kept one of these for you.'

Dennis was in his element. He showed me round the billet as if he'd built it himself, and its splendour vindicated his prediction that in Germany, we'd ride on the crest of the wave. Before, I had doubted these tales, but now I began to wonder whether he wasn't a reincarnation of one of the redcoats who had fought in this very town. Well aware of the power the changed circumstances had given him, the note of menace preponderated in the kindly toleration of his voice. And in a curious way, the instability of the conditions around him, with their atmosphere so like that of his own temperament, gave him an unexpected equilibrium and calm.

The things the others had stolen varied with each man's nature. Some had chosen useless souvenirs (decorated daggers were a favourite), others things of value. Cornelis had got some watches, Walter had Lugers and sporting guns. Cuthbert, who seemed to have recovered fully from his shock, said, 'I've only helped myself to things of general use—nothing personal. The Opel, you see, and these radios to replace my own that was defective.'

Looting is irresistible to anyone who has not a real indifference to possessions or a rare sense of duty. The opportunities are enormous, and there is no risk during the first few days of the fall of a town, when the old authority is overthrown and the new one not yet established. Even for those who are not thieves by nature, the attraction of what seems at first a delightful game, is overwhelming. As time goes on, the playful looters either see that the game isn't one, and stop, or else go on till it becomes a habit, and their characters change. Sometimes they carry this habit back into their civilian lives, unless they have the valuable national gift, noticeable also in times of peace, for sinning energetically abroad, and becoming pillars of rectitude when once again at home.

The Captain, whom I found on the verandah sipping wine under a mauve satin lampshade that must have been three feet wide, seemed unperturbed; he took whatever happened, however unusual, for granted. This faculty, which might seem a consequence of English phlegm, and sometimes is, was more probably due in his case to having one of the English forms of imagination: the well of originality and invention that lies hidden, often evaporates in day-dreams, but abundantly overflows when its owner finds himself living the improbable.

He was also helped by a powerful dose of our native talent for practical hypocrisy: not the odious hypocrisy that is ignorant of itself—but that of the man who does one thing, says another, and knows it. This can be the precarious cement of otherwise impossible relationships; and how could the Captain have kept some sort of control from now on without it?

Of some of our dishonesties, he knew nothing; but when he shared them, he took full responsibility. If he forbade any project that he knew of, then it was either abandoned, or else done surreptitiously, at the individual's own risk. When he found out what we were doing and didn't ban it, but didn't take part in it himself, he pretended not to see what everyone knew he did see, and this convention was generally accepted.

To this compact of agreed duplicity and mutual blackmail, the men contributed their part: knowing the Captain would protect them as far as could reasonably be expected, they were determined to protect him in return. If any had been lacking in this particular sense of loyalty, the structure would have rapidly collapsed.

So now the campaign appeared to us in a new and fascinating light. We thought we would have what we liked and live where we liked, and we looked forward to travelling on forever, skimming the cream of goods and sensations from all the places that awaited us.

An elderly woman and her young companion lived in the

house, but the husband, who was a deputy *Kreisleiter*, had disappeared. The woman herself had withdrawn to two rooms on the top floor, and she greeted us on accidental meetings in a chilly and terrified silence. The companion acted as her ambassador.

We had breakfast next day in the enormous dining-room. Two maids served, supervised by Cornelis in his new rôle as butler, and by the companion, who also supervised Cornelis.

'As far as I can see,' the Captain said, 'we bash on now towards the northern ports, but first of all they'll have to get a bridgehead over the Weser. I'm going over to Corps this morning to collect the latest news, so sit tight and, above all, don't go up in the hills. They say there's S.S. still milling about up there.'

I went down into the town and wandered about. There were not many people in the streets, and those that passed me hurried by with averted eyes. As I passed a white hotel facing onto the square, I saw that a Military Government team had arrived, and was unloading its trucks. Going closer, I found it was the one from the refugee village.

I walked on down into the lower part of the town, where the houses stood among gardens by the river. I heard the sound of singing coming from a big villa, and I went in and climbed up to the first floor. Going into houses without knocking was becoming second nature.

I found myself in a huge dormitory. About forty men and women, most of them young, were walking about or sitting on piles of bedding. They gathered round me and called out to their friends to come and look.

They were Easterners from Baltic countries, and we spoke to one another in broken German. They told me they'd been brought there to work in the forest, and said they'd been short of food for days. I wondered why they hadn't helped themselves. They showed me all over the building, which was crowded and in a great mess. One moment they were solemn, and the next they all burst out laughing. I got the impression of there being some joke I wouldn't have seen the point of, supposing I'd known what it was. It may have been myself.

At this moment, a large German woman arrived. They seemed to be in some awe of her, or rather, their attitude was a mixture of respect and mockery. This woman explained she was the caterer, engaged by the municipality to look after them.

'They say they haven't enough to eat,' I told her.

'Oh, I know they say that. But where is the food to come from? I cannot produce it from nowhere, and for a week now there is little organisation in the town.'

'They say they've never had enough.'

'Oh yes, well, what is one to reply to that? I cooked them all I was given, and have never robbed them—they will tell you so. Is that not so?' she said, wheeling on the throng that hemmed us in.

Nobody expressed disagreement, but they all watched us both with interest.

'They call me "Mother," all of them,' she said. 'Don't you call me "Mother"?' she demanded.

Nobody denied that either, though they glanced at her slyly, I thought.

She took me to see her kitchen, still followed by the crowd. 'Look!' she said. 'How could I cook properly for all of them in so small a place?'

'Did you ask for a bigger one?'

'Of course I did. But what is the use of asking?'

I realised they all expected me to do something. If that wasn't my intention, why had I come? I asked who at the Town Hall was responsible for the place, and said I'd see if anything could be done.

Two of them came back to the billet with me, and I gave them tins out of Gordon's stores. They were very polite about it, but it was clear they found what I offered them quite inadequate.

When the Captain came back for lunch, I told him about these Allied civilians and the arrival of the Mil. Gov. team.

'Well, I don't know that it's anything to do with us,' he said. 'I told Major Bane we'd ordered the arms to be handed in, but he says not to make any more changes till the permanent Detachment that's coming here to live, arrives. However, as we're staying a day or two, apparently, and they haven't got here yet, I don't think it'd do any harm to contact Mil. Gov. and go and show the flag with them at the Town Hall.'

We found Parsons and Adeane still having lunch among the disorder that follows an unloading, and the Captain laid his proposition before them.

'Well, Captain,' the Major said, 'we're rather in the same position as yourselves. It's true we've been transferred from Displaced Persons to Civil Administration, but this isn't our town, you see, we're only lodging here. The static team's expected any time—two of them, in fact: one for Civil Admin., and a special one for Courts. This is to be a provincial centre for Courts.'

'We mustn't queer somebody else's pitch by interfering prematurely,' the Lieutenant told us. 'The proper people would be most annoyed if they found we'd butted in.'

'Well, I don't know,' said the Captain. 'But several days have gone by, and I think a Mil. Gov. rep. ought to put in an official appearance.'

'Oh well,' the Major said, after pondering. 'I don't mind coming along with you for a bit of a chat with the Burger-bloke. There can't be any harm in that.'

Leaving the Lieutenant shaking his head, we drove to the Town Hall. We found it filled with people who fell aside as we went in, and anyone with a peaked cap saluted. We were shown into a room on the first floor overlooking the market place. It was panelled in oak, and had a damp patch on the ceiling from which water was dripping into two pails.

'What's gone wrong here?' asked Major Parsons, pointing upwards.

A small, plump man, who had risen from a boardroom table, bowed slightly, and said, 'It is a consequence of the fire.'

'And what's the fire a consequence of?'

'Some English soldiers entered the room in which the arms collected up according to your orders, were kept. There was an accident, and one, they say, is now dead.'

'What happened to them?'

'Their comrades took them away in a lorry immediately. This occurred late last evening.'

'The arms were properly guarded?' the Captain asked.

'Yes. The soldiers ordered the guards placed there to stand aside.'

'Bad show,' said Major Parsons. 'It's this passion the lads have for souvenirs.'

The officers sat down, and so did the Burgomaster, after having been invited to do so. The Captain raised the matter of the Allied workers, and asked what was being done for them.

'Do you permit me to call for the official in charge of this branch?' the Burgomaster asked.

The Captain said yes, and soon an energetic woman was among us, explaining the situation. 'Despite the difficulties caused by present events, we are continuing to assure the identical ration as previously,' she told us.

'Then they're getting something to eat?'

Certainly. But they are not now giving any work at all.' She eyed us with a severe, pitying look.

'My Sergeant tells me they're half starving,' the Captain said.

She turned to me with disdain. 'You must not believe all they say to you. What interests them is much food and little work.'

'What interests them is to go back where they were taken from.'

'If that is decided, well and good. But if they remain and do not work, then soon there will be an even greater disorder.'

'So you've no objection to their remaining?'

'Not if they remember to be well-behaved,' she said primly.

Major Parsons was staring at her legs, and the Captain seemed more impressed by her answers than by my sarcasm. But just then we heard a commotion outside the door, and after a loud knock, it opened to reveal a tall man carrying a shining satchel. The Burgomaster vacated his chair, and standing between the stranger and the Captain, said, 'Since here is the provincial *Oberregierungsrat*, you would wish to address your observations to him?'

'No,' said the Captain. 'Go away,' he said to the newcomer, who hesitated, then withdrew.

'You are responsible for the welfare of all the Allied civilians,' the Captain said. 'You are to see that they have proper food until we arrange for their evacuation.'

The Burgomaster nodded, made notes on a pad, and told the woman to go. Then he put several practical questions, on which the officers weren't prepared to commit themselves. So the Captain cut him short and said, 'These matters will be dealt with by officials who will visit you shortly.'

But the Major raised one other point. 'Have you a good lock-up in this town?' he asked the Burgomaster.

'I beg your pardon?'

'A good jail?'

'Oh yes, we have a very good jail.'

'That'll come in handy,' the Major said. 'No prison, no Courts.'

The Captain was disgruntled when we sat drinking gin that evening. 'These static Detachments are far too slow in arriving,' he said. 'The Burgomaster ought to have been arrested long ago, and that *Oberregierungsrat* too—they're both in the Automatic Categories. As for Mil. Gov., whatever branch they belong to, they should sail right in and sort things out at once. That's what I'd do if I had their opportunities.'

But he didn't mention this when they came round to supper, and while white wines were served to them after the meal on the paved terrace, a discussion on the problems of government arose.

'You know,' Major Parsons said, puffing a cigar, 'our own little team will be setting up local courts somewhere too, and I'm looking forward to seeing myself on the bench. I've always fancied myself in the judge's robes.'

'I must say,' said Lieutenant Adeane, 'that the powers we'll have almost frighten me at times. I've been reading through the military laws, and some of them are terribly vague and comprehensive.'

'Oh, don't get the wrong idea,' the Major told him. 'I won't come down hard on them all, and I might even let some of them off, you never know. But I reckon an old bobby will be able to pick out the hard cases all right.'

'What worries me a bit,' said the Lieutenant, 'is that we've invented the laws we're going to apply.'

'Well, that's natural, isn't it? Thanks, Captain, I don't mind another glass. You know, I liked that woman over at the Town Hall this morning, didn't you? I'm almost sorry we're not staying here, she'd have been just right for the job of Secretary. Quick-witted, practical and speaks nearly perfect English.'

'From what you told me, she sounds most unsuitable,' the Lieutenant said.

'Oh? And why so, may I ask?'

'Because she's an obvious Nazi.'

'Oh-ho! A Nazi. But so long as she's not in an Arrestable Category, that wouldn't matter.'

'It's people of that kind we have to de-Nazify.'

'Do what to?' said the Captain.

'As part of the de-Nazification policy. Even if a person's not actually in an Arrest Category, we should pass them by and try to encourage genuine anti-Nazi elements.'

'And do they exist, these anti-Nazi elements?'

'Of course they do, and it's our business to discover them. The trouble is, a great many of them are still in prisons east of the Weser.'

'And you're saying I should have an old lag as my Secretary?'

'But these people have been put in prison on political grounds.'

'Maybe, maybe. But I'm always a bit suspicious myself of anyone who's done time in the nick. It does something to you.'

'Now really, Major, I must say, that's a very discreditable point of view, and quite contrary to official policy.'

'I care more for common sense than I do for books of rules. Of course, if a German's been a big Nazi, our Intelligence friends here will see he's put inside. But that doesn't mean we shouldn't use practical men and women with administrative experience, and a lot of them are bound to have been Nazis.'

The Lieutenant bit his lip.

'You know, Lieutenant,' the Major said, 'the trouble with you, as I've pointed out before, is that you're a bit too pro-German.'

'That's exactly what I'd say of you.'

'Oh, is it?'

'Yes. Your attitude is that everything in Germany's all right, so long as you make a few changes at the top.'

'And your attitude, Lieutenant, is that the Germans are very nice people who were deluded by the Nazi Party. I think they're all Nazis, and if we put the biggest ones away, they'll follow us instead.'

'On the contrary. What is wanted is to encourage the genuinely democratic elements. To revive the Germany of liberal and internationalist traditions. The Germany of the great musicians.'

The Major smiled. 'What's wanted is men who know their job and can get on with it.'

'Then I warn you, Major, if you make use of supposedly

converted Nazis, you'll find they'll bide their time and make use of you.'

'Time will show, laddie. But Heaven preserve us from your musical friends. Once you let them start playing, you'll find it'll be subversive elements who beat the big drum. And before you know where you are, you'll have lost your job as the conductor.'

The Captain sat listening with the judicious air of one who doesn't believe anything in particular, and as the discussion developed, the Sergeants disappeared one by one.

When I went out and crossed the dark hall by torchlight, I was startled to see a *Wehrmacht* officer coming down the stairs. He paused, stared at me, and went quickly up again, disappearing into a bedroom. I was wondering what to do when Dennis, who was drunk, came out of another door. 'Yes, that's the son of the house,' he said. 'The little companion's told me.'

'What's he doing here?'

'He got separated from his regiment, so he says, and he thought the best thing to do was to come back to mother.'

'He's a prisoner-of-war now, isn't he? We can't let him wander about our billet.'

'What else do you want us to do? Mount guard over him all night? He won't do any harm, and they'll pick him up later on. Well, excuse me for now, I'm having a drink with the companion.'

'She didn't look all that friendly to me.'

'She wasn't at first. It's the price she's paying for my silence about the son.'

'You're a nice bastard, aren't you.'

Dennis leered at me. 'Are you envious?' he said. 'Well, I'm a sinner, if that's what you mean.'

A few days later, after our Corps had crossed the Weser, some of us set off for a town marked 'Health Resort' on the maps. After driving twenty miles beyond the river, we came to a cluster of large hotels round a park in a valley, with hills not too high for invalids rising gently up all round.

We noticed a peculiar flag hanging from the hotel windows, and on enquiry, were told the town had become a national evacuation centre for persons with infectious diseases. We'd parked our trucks beside the bandstand, and we stood gazing at these dismally flapping flags in a divided state of mind.

'Well, we can't stay here,' I said. 'These hotels will be full of invalids, anyway.'

'Don't you believe it,' said Dennis. 'That's camouflage to keep us out.'

After an argument, it was decided to go looking for something in the neighbourhood, and we drove into a forest whose narrow roads were cut in lines that met at right angles from time to time. We explored several of these without seeing anything, going gingerly because of the thought of mines, until we met a solitary man in a bright green uniform. He told us there was a big house nearby, and gave us vague directions. 'Well, jump in and show us the way, *Herr Forstmeister*,' Dennis said, bustling him into the Opel.

He led us to a large place, half farm, half country house, which stood in a clearing, and was built round a courtyard in the form of a U. The owner, a huge-limbed man wearing civilian clothes as if they were a uniform, showed us round. He was disparaging about his property, and pointed out its disadvantages as a billet. It seemed all right to me, but Dennis moved from room to room with increasing disapproval.

'No good at all,' he said. 'Useless. Far too rustic and too small. And look at the furniture and stuff. It's primitive. We'd stand a better chance back at the health resort, like I said.'

'Are you going to evacuate a hospital?'

'Now, don't exaggerate. But I tell you—some of those hotels are empty.'

The owner had listened with growing approval, and seeing we'd decided to go, he offered us a cup of bean-coffee, which was served to us by a younger woman in the kitchen. 'Yes,' he said. 'I can understand you take the best you can. In war time, only the best is good enough for a soldier.'

'You served yourself?' I asked him.

'Oh yes, in the last war. I rose to be Colonel, but was gassed. In this one I served at first, but my health could not stand up to it.'

'So you went back to farming?'

'Precisely.'

'And this is your farm?'

He glanced at the woman and said, 'Not exactly. It is the property of this lady.'

The woman said nothing.

'You're her manager, are you?'

'Not exactly. A friend—I am staying here.'

'Just staying here.'

The woman, sensing danger, said, 'It is my husband's property, but he is away in Italy. This gentleman is taking care of things.'

'And you were properly discharged from the *Wehrmacht*?'

'Of course. I have papers.'

'Made out by yourself?'

He had turned red, and didn't answer. Dennis plucked at my sleeve and said, 'Oh come along, come along, do stop trying out your skill. Of course he's a deserter living in sin, but what interest has that to us?'

The deserting Colonel, as if drawn despite himself, came out with us to the cars.

'With my ill-health, I have not much of a future,' he said. And glancing back at the house, he dropped his voice and added, 'What I would like to do, when things become more normal, is to go to South America. They always need able men in South America.'

'You think you'll be able to get there?'

'Oh, there will be difficulties. But no doubt there will be ways and means.'

Back at the town, we found that Dennis's guess had been correct. Going into a large hotel with hospital flags hanging from the windows, we saw nobody about at all until, on the first floor, we came to a locked door covered by a Japanese screen with damp towels over it. After we'd knocked loudly, a thin, unshaven man stepped out and stood in front of us in the corridor. He said he was the Manager.

'Why aren't you downstairs at your desk? Where is your staff?' cried Dennis.

He explained the hotel had been requisitioned for German medical officers until a few days ago, and that when they'd left, his staff had all gone too, 'so that now I am alone with my wife who is ill.'

'Your wife?' said Dennis. 'Is she in there?'

'Yes.'

'What's she got? Anything infectious?'

'Heavens, no. It is heart trouble. And I myself am little better.'

'This bird's a broken reed,' said Dennis. 'We'll have to go into hotel business ourselves.'

So we walked down the empty corridors, picking ourselves rooms. 'What extraordinary counterpanes like bolsters,' said Norman. 'They'll stifle us to death.' I looked out over the bandstand and watched Dennis and Gordon stepping across the gravel in search of the Burgomaster, their pistols swinging by their sides.

I climbed up the hilly track behind the hotel. It was one of those walks that are arranged, in Germany, with such taste and ingenuity, so as to give you a maximum number of favourable vistas. I came out onto a terrace, with a seat overlooking a perspective of the town. Nearby was a cairn on a rocky rise, commemorating something. I watched the convoys rattling on in the direction of the Baltic. All I could hear of their engines was a faint whine.

Coming up the track, I saw what I took to be a Russian officer, wearing a grey astrakhan cap. He was accompanied by a girl, and they both sat down on another bench a little way off.

After a while, I walked over to them. He looked at me with a frown as I came up, but as soon as I gave him a half-wave, half-salute, he grinned, rose to his feet and shook hands. Then he moved up on the bench, and I sat down. After fumbling a bit, we spoke to each other in the language of our common enemy.

'You're from Moscow?'

'Yes. Are you from London?'

'That's right.'

'London is a big city—the biggest in the world.'

'Not so beautiful as Moscow.'

He smiled, accepted the flattery, and we exchanged cigarettes. He was short and muscular, had a small, pointed nose, dark wavy hair and eyes that were bright and mobile. He sat on the bench in a free-and-easy posture, with one long arm hanging over the back, and the other round the girl, who watched me suspiciously.

'How did you land up here?' I asked him. 'Were you taken prisoner?'

His face darkened, and he said yes. I got the impression that while our men might regard this as a misfortune, he looked on it as a disgrace.

'It's almost over,' I said. 'Your people are just outside Berlin.'

'That's right, Germany *kaput*. Now at last we shall go home.'

'And all have a bit of peace for a change.'

'Yes, now we shall all have peace.'

We smiled with slight embarrassment to see a doubt in each other's eyes.

'You're a *Feldwebel?*' he said.

'That's it.'

'I am a Lieutenant. This is not really a part of my uniform (pointing to the astrakhan cap). I got it after I was taken prisoner.' He opened his jacket and took out a wallet. 'My usual uniform,' he said, showing me a brown photograph.

The girl, who hadn't said a word, leaned over and looked at it too. The Lieutenant took my sleeve and felt the material. 'Also a good uniform,' he said. 'And that is a German pistol?'

'No, English.'

'You have a German pistol?'

'We have got some, yes.'

'You will give me one?'

'I don't know about that.'

'You give me one,' he repeated pleadingly, but as if certain of his right to it.

I asked him if they'd both come down and have lunch with us, but the girl made a negative face when he spoke to her. He countered with an offer of schnapps at his billet later on, and pointed it out in the valley below. 'And bring the pistol,' he said, waving good-bye and turning to wrap himself round the girl.

Back at the hotel, I found the kitchen and restaurant had been staffed and opened up, but Dennis said lunch would be late as they'd taken all morning to fire the boiler. I asked him if there was water for baths, and he said, 'Yes, I've already partaken one, and I'll get Cornelis to run in another for you on the residential floor.'

When I came along the corridor, I heard sounds of laughter and slapping. Cornelis was sitting on the edge of the bath, stirring it with one hand and with the other round a muscular girl who was writhing and squealing spread out on his bony lap.

He got up, the girl gave me a 'Don't you wish it was you' look, and ran into the corridor. Cornelis assumed a dutiful, vacant expression, poured in a little more cold, flicked the water off his hands, then stood back with a sudden smile.

'Who's she?' I said. 'One of the new helpers?'

'Yes, Sir. From the kitchen. The girl to look after this floor is sweeping rooms. It was because she was occupied, that I had the kitchen girl up to clean things.'

'You'd better go and join her. She seems to like you.'

'Oh, she is an idiot,' he said, and a smile of contempt came over his olive face. 'A slow-headed country girl, wishing to be bright.'

'She seems bright enough.'

'Yes. Too big for me, really.'

'She's quite a size.'

Cornelis was eyeing me with a look of calculation. I got his drift, and our minds spoke quickly without words. Then he said, 'Shall I tell her you would like to see her?'

A glaze had come over his almond eyes, and he watched me with his mouth falling open. I shot him back a glance that didn't refuse, but said. 'I don't want to see her.'

'If you wish it, I could tell her.'

He clasped his hands and turned sideways, not avoiding my eyes particularly, and waiting for me to go on. He seemed very small and helpless, but confident and serene because his attitude was consistent and unashamed.

'You'd better get along, Cornelis,' I said abruptly.

He nodded, gave a respectful wave, and went out.

The Russian Lieutenant's billet was in a house that released Eastern prisoners had taken over. The stairs and corridors were crowded with people, and the atmosphere was casual and disorderly. I was shown into a small room with several beds, on one of which the Lieutenant was lying full length. The girl was sitting beside him with her arms across his chest.

The Lieutenant poured out schnapps, and introduced me to a young Tank officer. This man's immensely powerful frame was bursting out of his clothes, and he turned on and off a smile that he didn't seem to approve of himself, if you could judge by the defensive stare in his narrow eyes. He seemed to grudge even a rigid gesture, and you interrupted him glancing sideways at the room, as though he wanted to clear it all up and get away somewhere to orderly action.

He examined my uniform surreptitiously, and when the Lieutenant had given us some further glasses, I asked the Tank officer for his impressions of our Army. He praised the weapons but hinted politely the bearing of some of our soldiers was slovenly.

When he'd left us, the Lieutenant told me this officer had escaped once before. A year ago, knowing only Russian and German, he'd got as far as the Pyrenees in an attempt to reach home via Gibraltar. He'd been arrested in Spain, and sent back again to Germany, 'since when they have tried to kill him by starvation.'

The Lieutenant poured out more schnapps, picked up my beret and tried it on, wearing it high on the forehead and drooping down behind. Then he took Russian banknotes from his wallet, read out what was printed on them, wrote his address across one of them, and gave it to me as a souvenir. The best I could find for him was a Mil. Gov. hundred franc note, and I drew him a picture of Peter the Great in Deptford High Street, and put my address underneath too. We said we would visit each other, and believed this idea. All the time, the girl had been staring out of the window.

Now half-a-dozen men came rushing in and spoke excitedly to the Lieutenant, who sprang up and cried, '*Feldwebel*! The Germans have murdered two Poles!'

'Where?'

'Listen to this Polish boy.'

A lad was pushed forward who told me frantically that the farmers had killed two of his comrades in a labour camp a few miles off.

'You're sure of that?'

He made a gesture of anger and impatience.

'You've come from there yourself?'

'Yes, yes.'

'We'd better go down and have a look.'

We all hurried over to the hotel to get a car, and seeing Walter in the hall, I called out to him to join us. First eyeing the group superciliously, he grew interested, and we piled into the utility.

'*Feldwebel*,' said the Lieutenant, 'you have got the pistol?'

'We have pistols.'

'But for us.'

'We've got two. Two is enough.'

The young Pole directed us over country tracks to the south of the town, and when we reached his village, he led us to a hutted camp outside it. We all got out and crowded into one of the buildings. It was full of Polish men and women. They gathered round us, and the Lieutenant strode among them in an energetic, reassuring way.

'Ask them where the bodies are,' said Walter.

'Where are the bodies?' I said to them.

Nobody answered, and I got the impression the question was somehow the wrong one. But they told us even more vehemently that two of their comrades had been taken away by German farmers and killed.

'If they can't produce the bodies, they can't prove there's been a murder,' said Walter.

'Who are these German farmers?' I asked.

They pointed out of the window, and we all set off down the road in a procession of groups. We reached a farmhouse and they banged on the door, but no one appeared. Then somebody shouted, and a farmer could be seen coming up from the fields. They all rushed ahead and surrounded him, dealing him blows. A woman's wail came out of the shuttered house as Walter and I ran after them.

'All right, that's enough of that,' said Walter, pulling the German on one side and standing in front of him. The farmer lowered his hands from his face. He wasn't hurt, but was intensely indignant.

'Where are the Poles who have been killed?' I shouted at him.

'No Poles have been killed.'

'Well, they have disappeared. Where are they?'

'Listen, soldiers. Two of their people stole our bicycles. Some of our men went and took them back. That is all. Nobody was killed.'

'Did you fight?'

'They resisted, but so did we. We were in our right.'

'Well, where are they?'

'I do not know. Why should I know? I have no control over them now.'

The Lieutenant came forward and threatened the farmer, but he stood his ground and stuck to his story. After a lot of shouting and jostling, we told him to go home and saw him indoors. The crowd waited outside, then gradually dispersed.

The Lieutenant made it quite plain what he thought of us. 'You do not know how to treat them,' he said. 'You have not seen what we have.'

'Nobody has found the bodies. How do you know they were killed?'

'We know it. We have seen it often before.'

He was nice about it, but we could see he thought us weak and easily deceived.

We went back to the Polish hut, and they seemed to lose interest in the matter or, at any rate, not to bear us a grudge. They treated us to home-brewed liquor of which the Lieutenant took a great many glassfuls. He lay among the Polish women who made much of him, and we couldn't get him away.

'We'd best leave him here a while,' said Walter, 'and pick him up again when he's had his issue.'

We drove down into the village to look around. As we passed the farmhouse, we saw the farmer tending his vegetables. He gave us an angry look.

A string of tanks was passing through, and we stopped to watch them. A small German in city clothes who was watching too came up, raised his hat and said, 'Excuse me. Is it permitted for a British soldier to take a civilian's watch?'

'Why?'

'One of your soldiers has just done so. Is that permitted?'

'No, it isn't.'

This admission seemed all he wanted, and glancing at us reproachfully, he moved off to the opposite pavement.

When we heard our Corps had reached the Aller, we sent off an advance party one morning, even though we hadn't yet had orders to leave the health resort. It was now considered necessary to find a bigger and more eccentric billet in each new town, and to forestall competitors, we had to keep as close as was prudent on the heels of the fighting troops.

Gordon and Dennis were in their civilian cars, I was still in the utility, and Norman, who hadn't got a car of his own because he'd refused to learn to drive, accompanied us on his motor-bike. He alternately overtook us and fell behind, like a destroyer convoying merchantmen; and when he hadn't appeared for some time, we all slowed down and waited. There wasn't a sign of him. We turned our cars round for about a mile, and found him sitting on the verge with a gash in his forehead and a bloodless face. His bike was lying on its side. He had skidded.

We asked him if he'd like to be taken back, but he said he felt all right, and the cut didn't seem a bad one. 'Help me get his bike on my truck, Dennis,' I said.

'I don't think you'll find it'll fit, with all those stores you've got.'

'Yes it will, come on.'

'Why don't you leave it and pick it up later on?'

'You don't imagine it'll still be here, do you?'

'What does that matter?' said Gordon. 'We've got enough of these useless things, haven't we? Park it on the roadside and forget about it.'

'But it's my bike,' Norman cried. 'I'm responsible for it.'

'We've still got several cluttering up the trucks for you to chose from.'

'But I've ridden this one all the way from the beaches.'

Norman was at last persuaded. Dennis took out the tools and carburettor, raised the bike on its stand, and we left it there and set off again. Dennis and Gordon, in their faster cars, were soon out of sight, and Norman sat silently beside me, nursing his physical and moral wounds.

'It's terribly flat up here,' he said at last, surveying the slightly undulating country with disfavour. 'I thought Germany was full of mountains.'

'We've left them behind now. This is the north-German plain.'

'Is it? Well, its flatness is altogether too monotonous.'

As we drove on, we noticed a new element that had come to join the streams of Allies moving east and west. These were German soldiers, who tramped along the verge, sometimes in ranks, and sometimes as stragglers. Prisoners were being taken in such numbers now, that once they'd been disarmed, they were told to find their own way to the nearest assembly-point.

Perhaps most of them did this, but in the smaller groups there must have been men who, like the refugees and freed prisoners, were trying to make their own way home.

'You've got a puncture,' said Norman.

'I believe we have. And the spare wheel's flat, too.'

'These things should be foreseen. You won't mind if I'm not much use to you on account of my head?'

While I was jacking up the car, a young German soldier came trudging up. His shirt was open at the neck, his socks were turned down over his boots, and he had a flower in his cap.

'Puncture?' he said.

'That's right.'

He lowered the rucksack with a heave of his shoulder, came over unbidden and started to unscrew the spare wheel.

'That one's got a split. I'm going to take this off and mend it.'

He asked where the tool-kit was. 'There beside the gerry-cans,' I said.

'Aha. The Gerry-cans. Why not the Tommy-cans? That was no compliment, to name your tins after us.'

'It was to copy your tins.'

'That is so. Were you there in Africa?'

'No. You were?'

'Yes. Also in Crete. A wonderful campaign.'

'You're a paratrooper?'

'That is so. Or was, I must say. Now I shall have to try my hand at being a civilian.'

He had a frank, thoughtless face, and he said it laconically, with a strong undertone of regret. And as he told us about the African battles, I couldn't help feeling reluctant sympathy for someone who'd enjoyed campaigning so much, and looked as if he'd have been so good at it.

'Now what about a lift?' he said, when the wheel was on.

'He'll have to go in the back,' said Norman.

'Jump in.'

He threw on his kit and we started off.

'Where else were you?' I asked him.

'In France a while, in '40.'

'You liked that?'

'Oh, I love France. You know the Loire? We made excursions on it by canoe, with comrades in our truck carrying provisions along the road and taking it in turns to paddle on the river. Such scenery—a smiling country. More beautiful, in my understanding, than anything here of ours.'

'How did you get on with the people?'

'Well, that depended. Occupation is not always pleasant, naturally. But we had it good and were happy. Ah, the *châteaux de Tourraine*!' he cried ecstatically.

'What's he on about?' said Norman.

'He's praising France.'

'France? I never thought much of France myself.'

'Well, it is over now,' the German said, after a silence. 'We've held out against the entire world, but it is over.'

'We like to think we did something of that sort, at one time.'

'You? You always had the Americans.'

'Didn't you have the Japanese?'

'Oh, the Japanese! They're Asiatics. We should never have been allied with Asiatics. We should have chosen allies among Germanic peoples, like yourselves, for instance.'

'He's not saying we're Asiatics now, is he?' Norman asked.

'No, he's saying we're a Germanic people.'

'Us? Germanic? Even if we were, what's that got to do with him?'

Arriving at the new town, we stopped to drop our passenger among its ruined suburbs. In the centre, the old timbered houses were still standing, and there was a foolish castle on a miniature hill with a circular park beneath it, in which Allied workers were strolling. We asked the way to the Town Hall where Gordon and Dennis had said they'd wait for us, and as we drove into the cobbled square behind it, we saw Gordon there taking cases out of his car.

'Hullo,' he said. 'We haven't fixed all the houses yet, but the mess is here in the Town Hall. Down in the basement, you'll see.'

The Town Hall itself seemed old, but the cellar-restaurant was decorated in fake medieval style. 'Here's where we eat,' said Gordon, throwing open the door of a dimly lit room with coats of arms on its stained-glass windows. Girls wearing aprons, who were standing about chattering and polishing glasses, stopped and stared at us. 'The waitresses,' Gordon said. 'Now you'd better see the Manageress.'

He led the way into a small office, where Dennis was sitting between two women, examining a ledger and grasping a hock bottle. 'Meet Frau Dieckhoff,' he said, swinging round on his chair. 'And this is her touch-typist, Miss Käthe.'

The Manageress was a gauntly handsome woman in the late thirties. The girl had dark fluffy hair, and a cross expression that made her even more pretty.

'Well, first of all, we must show you the holy of holies,' Dennis said. 'The key, please, Frau Dieckhoff.'

But she kept hold of it herself when she preceded us up a low, dark room with wooden seats built in round the walls. She opened a door at the far end, and we looked into the gloom. 'The wine store,' said Dennis exultantly, flashing a torch. There were shelves of bottles up to the ceiling.

'You will remember what you have promised?' the Manageress said.

'Certainly, certainly. Just give us a dozen for now.'

When she'd gone, I asked him what this meant.

'I promised to let her get the wine for us herself. She won't mind how much we take, provided it's her who issues it. But if we were simply to help ourselves, she wouldn't approve. Let me fill your glass.'

'You're not usually so considerate, are you?'

'I mean she wouldn't be so useful to us. Treat her right, and she'll do all we want. Rub her up the wrong way, and the organisation will break down. Cheerio. She's an exceptionally talented woman. Her husband's in their navy, and drinks like a fish. She's run this place all through the war.'

'Has she?'

'Yes, she has. And a few days ago, she had a very unpleasant experience. Some pimply-faced Lieutenant who billeted himself on her tried to rape her. That sort of thing disgusts me, it's so unnecessary.'

'Has she told you this already?'

'Yes, she's confided in me. It all came out in a flood of tears when I was overcoming her objections to having us here. What made things more difficult is that the Lieutenant succeeded, thanks to threatening her with a pistol. It's turned her very anti-British.'

'Congratulations on winning her over.'

'Now, don't misunderstand me. My relations with her are

purely business. Besides, it's the young waitress I have my eye on.'

'Which one?'

He pointed with his glass at a sour-faced, sporting-looking girl with a superb figure, like a long distance swimmer's.

'You'd better pick yourself a companion, too. The little touch-typist's the nicest. Too nice for me, unfortunately. Innocence embarasses me, you know, and I prefer a woman to be more mature.'

There were heavy feet on the cellar steps, and an elderly man appeared, carrying a long parcel wrapped in brown paper. He had yellow, watery eyes and a long jacket hung down over his bandy knees. He paused at the entrance with a look of total disaster.

'Yes?' Gordon said.

He held out the package in our direction. 'I have handed in my arms, as it has been decreed,' he told us, drawing himself up.

We unwrapped the paper and found two curved dress swords, with silver work and gold tassels.

'He's a literal-minded sod,' said Gordon. 'He can't blow Mil. Gov. up with these useless relics.'

'The old boy must have worn them in the Hundred Years' War, and taken them down from their hooks over the fire-place,' Dennis said.

'Well, they'll do for souvenirs,' said Gordon. 'All right, you can go.'

He looked at the swords a moment, then past us as if the sight of us hurt him, turned, and went painfully up the steps.

Dennis said he'd got me a room at the Pastor's house across the square where we'd parked our cars. It seemed as if he'd been waiting behind the door, for when I rang, it opened immediately on a middle-aged man with a rather too finely lined face and blond-grey hair. He ushered me up to the first floor with the extreme politeness reserved for dangerous inferiors.

'Which might you prefer?' he said, showing me two adjoining rooms. I chose the one near the staircase. 'Is this satisfactory?' he said.

'Fine. Thanks very much.'

'If there is anything else, then you will ring the bell.'

'Yes.'

'We hope you will be comfortable.' He retreated to the door, then turned and stood there with his feet together and his hands clasped, as if he was holding an egg. 'May I enquire if you expect to be here long?' he said.

'I shouldn't think so. A few days, perhaps.'

'Then you go forward?'

'That's the idea.'

He sighed.

'And how are things with you?' I said.

'Please?'

'How are conditions here with you?'

He seemed to have so much in his heart, that he could only say, 'Terrible.' He hesitated, and then, as if I'd pressed it out of him, said, 'You have yet to establish the order that existed formerly.'

'Oh, yes.'

'Our children run wild with no school, everywhere our people are homeless and in misery, the forest huts are full of refugees, they camp out in the open too, poor folk. Some flee from the east, some from the west.' He looked at me as if to say, 'And there's no need for me to tell you who's the cause of that.'

I nodded.

'And then,' he continued, 'many bad things have happened. Pillage; wanton violence—and worse. In this house, for instance, is a young woman who . . . one of your soldiers . . .' he paused significantly '. . . it is a terrible thing.'

I mumbled something.

'But perhaps exceptional. And the majority are no doubt not to be blamed for the minority.'

'Let's hope so.'

Warming up, he began to address me in a pulpit voice.

'Now that we are defeated, everyone wishes to teach us,' he said. 'Even a high English bishop, I hear, is rebuking us severely now. But should he not be preaching rather to those still strong and powerful, whose souls are in greater danger?'

He paused, I went on looking at him.

'There are those who dare to rebuke a child, because it is weak, for the same faults they would not dare to rebuke in a grown man. Such persons should first seek in their own hearts for wickedness.' So saying, he raised one finger and let his hand fall till it pointed to the floor. 'Each man has his own personal misfortune,' he went on, in more normal tones. 'And it is bitter for us, you will forgive me, to see you here.'

He nodded slowly, and went out; then reappeared and said, 'Do you wish for a key?'

'Yes, you'd better give me one.'

'We lock all after dark, on account of East-workers.'

'What do they do?'

'They come marauding.'

'Have many come yet?'

'Not yet, but we expect them. I will fetch the key for you.'

As I walked round the room, looking at the objects in it, I noticed on the wall what we were seeing in so many houses—a photograph of a young soldier, surrounded by a wreath of evergreens.

Crossing to the cellar, I saw a car outside with Harry, Major Bane and a man with a War Correspondent's badges, getting out. 'We spotted your sign,' said Major Bane. 'Can you give us some light refreshments?'

I brought them down to the café, and while Cornelis was getting them drinks, I went over to the restaurant to order lunch and silence the screams and giggles of the waitresses. When the meal was ready, Harry said he didn't want anything, and that he'd wait outside in the car.

'I expect it's the place we've just been to that's put him off,' said Major Bane, and when they'd sat down, he told us of their visit to Belsen-Bergen that morning. He was subdued, and spoke with a gravity we weren't used to, glancing at us to see if we believed him, as though he hardly expected us to. 'You should go out there and see for yourselves,' he said. 'You really ought to go and see for yourselves.'

We asked him questions but were soon silenced, because it was clear the questions we could think of fell short of grasping what he had to tell. We noticed that he and the War Correspondent didn't eat very much either, though they both went on drinking. The Correspondent confirmed the Major's account, but his description seemed less real because it was mixed with vituperation. Perhaps he had been telling tales of horror so long from hearsay that when he met it, his emotions were too stale to realise what he'd seen. And as he cried out for vengeance, for forty thousand other corpses, he spoke as though the outrage had been done to himself alone.

Soon nobody had much to say, though the subject still filled our minds. Trying to move away from it, we asked Major Bane for news of the campaign. He turned politely to the War Correspondent, who said, 'Brunswick's fallen, and we're on the Elbe beyond it and at Harburg, further north. It shouldn't be long before we link up with the Russians. The only thing left to them—and it may cause us some trouble—is to try to make a last stand in their Alpine Redoubt.'

He made us feel that discretion prevented him from telling us more, and that the reality of these operations depended on their appearing in print in his paper. But when we asked him which this was, he seemed offended. Evidently we should have known that from his name.

Major Bane got up, brushed himself, and eager to plunge back into the present, took Dennis on one side and asked him where he could get hold of liquor. 'We're practically cleaned out here, Sir,' Dennis told him, 'but if you and the Correspondent care to come with me, I'll show you some prominent local wine stores.' When they'd left, Harry changed his mind about eating, and afterwards we went out for a walk down by the river. We crossed over the Bailey bridge, and looked back at the red houses lining a wide bend, nestling into their own reflections. Parties of soldiers were rowing clumsily up and down, and even sailing.

'What about it, Harry?' I said. 'Is this place as bad as they say?'

'It's ghastly.'

When he went on to tell me what he had seen, I still found it difficult not so much to believe it, as to realise its scale. His account was more dreadful, because he spoke as though he was somehow involved in what had happened.

'What are you to think?' he said. 'Did they all know that was going on? Why did they allow it, then? I don't believe they could have known—not all of them.'

We had reached an empty garden café with a boathouse by the river, and we sat down at a table there. He looked over the water, threw his cigarette into it, and went on:

'I don't care what they say. I've told that Gerry girl I'll

come back and fetch her when it's over, and I'm going to, in spite of the other promise I made, and that concentration camp and what the lads are saying. The people here aren't all like that, they can't be, it's impossible.'

We were interrupted by the owner of the place, who came up, pointed across the water and said, 'Soon all my boats will be sunk or stolen.'

I tried to hustle him away, but he persisted, so I said, 'You'll collect them up in time.'

'You think so! They will drift down to the weir, and that will be the end of them.'

We went further upstream, through meadows full of browsing cows.

'Were there Allies in there?' I said. 'Did you find out anything about that at all?'

'I didn't even try. How could you find anything in a shambles like that? There are thousands of them, thousands, dead, half dead and dying. You'd have to wait a while before you could find out anything there.'

'Didn't they keep lists?'

'Lists?' He shook his head vaguely.

We had reached a footbridge and hung over it, staring at the stream. Soldiers were bathing nearby. One of them was floating on his back and whistling.

'You remember I told you my Dad was a conchy? He was right about one thing, and that's in what he said about a war. Whatever good it does it makes everything worse. Look what's happened to the Germans, and look what's happening to our lads, they're getting to like it quite a bit, some of them. And those poor bloody prisoners . . .

'You start with a fair fight, but a camp like that's where it leads to in the end. Fighting's not what's wrong. But when it gets to the size of a war, it is. You soon lose control over how the fighting goes. So what can you do? It's no use staying away. That's just keeping your hands clean at work, and putting yourself out of action. And it never stops anything. No. What you should do, is fight it.'

'Fight war?'

'Yes, go to war on it yourself. We'll have to find out how. They say we'll always follow when the war begins. But isn't it better to use the life you've got in a fight that's really your own?'

Some of us met for drinks before supper in Frau Dieckhoff's office. Sergeant Thackeray, whom Dennis had met while out with Major Bane, was telling us, amid shouts of laughter, how he'd signed one of the wrong roads on the way up. 'Well, you may laugh, but it can happen very easily, let me tell you.'

'No wonder. Look who does it.'

'You may say that; but would you do better, do you suppose? See what happens. The forward troops bash on regardless, and no one knows quite which way they've gone. I go along to the Map Room, and they show me what they think their general direction is. Right. I gather up my party and a jeep full of signs, and off we go.' He paused to throw back a glass. 'Off we go, into the wilderness. We follow the roads they've told us of, and what do we frequently find? That there aren't any bridges, or the roads lead the wrong way.'

'Then you go home for tea.'

'Far from it. Then we discover the best road all by ourselves. But to err is human, and sometimes we make a bit of a balls-up of it.'

'And lead the unsuspecting vehicles into a minefield.'

'Oh, nothing as bad as that, I shouldn't think. But we certainly did get muddled on the way here. The road we chose was all right as far as it went, but it just didn't go anywhere. After we'd signed several miles of it, it petered out. Nobody was as surprised and vexed as we were, I can tell you.'

He smiled at Frau Dieckhoff (who hadn't understood a word) with a sexually-loaded ogle. She stood watching us as one who knows how to deal with men provided they're a nuisance in the right sort of way. The typist sat behind her, drinking nothing, looking as if she'd rather have been at home.

One of the waitresses came rushing in. 'The store, Frau Dieckhoff,' she cried. 'They have broken into your store.'

An expression of bitter rage came over the Manageress's face. 'Oh, help me,' she shouted, shaking her fist.

'Which store?' said Dennis, starting up.

'The goods I have in the basement of a nearby street.'

'You didn't tell me about those. Who's broken in there?'

'The East-workers,' she and the waitress cried in shrill chorus.

We went up into the street, headed by Sergeant Thackeray

who resumed his professional gait. The women stopped at the corner and pointed. Outside a shop, two middle-aged civilians, wearing 'Mil. Gov. Police' armbands, were talking agitatedly to each other and to the onlookers.

'Where?' said Thackeray, thrusting his way through.

'In here, Sir,' said one of them, leading us up to a broken glass door.

We climbed in. Two men came along the dark corridor, carrying bundles. Thackeray pointed at the floor and after hesitating, they dropped the bundles there. 'Tell them to show us where the others are, Dennis,' Thackeray said. They led us further along the corridor and down some steps, up which a light was shining. Four more men were swarming over piles of goods. Two were Easterners, and two soldiers.

'This is nice,' said Sergeant Thackeray.

The Easterners smiled winningly, letting parcels gently go. The soldiers looked defiant.

'Airborne troops, too,' said Thackeray,' who ought to know better. Well, you might have thought of stopping these aliens.'

'Why?' said one of the airborne men. 'These people are entitled to get what they can, same as we are. They've been plundered enough, haven't they? Now it's their turn.'

'A fine mentality. We've got to stop the Allies making free with everything sooner or later, haven't we?'

'I don't see any cause to stop them,' the other soldier said. 'The Gerries brought them here. Now they've got to learn to suffer.'

'Well,' said Thackeray, 'that'll be all for now. Take what you've got and go.' The soldiers gathered up what they could carry and made off. 'We'll take these four enthusiasts along with us,' the Sergeant said. 'Tell them to pick up their loot, it'll be needed as evidence. Dennis, slip round and get a truck, will you?'

We went up to the street again. The Mil. Gov. policeman hurried forward. 'Soldiers also have emerged, bringing stolen articles,' they said.

Sergeant Thackeray wheeled on them. 'Never you mind about soldiers. Have this place sealed and put a guard on. You're abetting crime, leaving a shop unlocked.'

'A guard? How can we guard if we are not allowed to carry weapons?'

'A good policeman doesn't need them, as any London bobby will tell you.'

But they didn't understand. 'Persons like these should be dealt with the hard way,' a Mil. Gov. policeman said, looking vengefully at the Easterners.

Dennis drove up, and we got into the truck. Two blocks away, Sergeant Thackeray told him to stop. 'Vamoose,' he said to the Easterners. 'I don't get promotion charging waifs and strays. Hi, there!' he shouted, when he saw them trying to take their bundles off the truck.

They smiled hopefully, then looked at each other and went slowly off.

'We'll run this stuff round to your billet later on, Dennis,' Thackeray said.

'Agreed. Meanwhile, I'm going to give Frau Dieckhoff a good bollocking. Fancy her holding out on me about that store.'

'I could scare her a bit, if you like, by saying why hasn't she declared her stocks to Mil. Gov. as decreed.'

'And then offer to hush it up for her?'

'Something of that sort. I've rather fallen for that woman. I could go for her in a big way.'

'Don't forget what I told you about her resentment at rough treatment she's had from soldiers.'

'Oh, that? Well, you know, what they call rape is as often as not reluctant consent.'

The rest of the Detachment had arrived while we were away, and Gordon had been out showing them their billets. We sat waiting for them, drinking gin with the waitresses. When the Captain came in, the girls got up and made half-hearted efforts at decorum. We all went in to dinner. It lasted a long while, and we drank a lot more.

'Sorry,' Gordon said to me, 'but I've had to put the Captain in with you at the Pastor's. Hadn't time to fix anything else. Sorry, and all that.'

I was passing into the state of drunkenness in which the faculties become sharp in focus at the expense of a general deterioration. 'In the room with the evergreens?' I said.

'How's that?'

I got up from the table and went into the office. The typist was dressing up to go. 'Can I see you home?' I said.

'No thank you, it is not necessary.'

'You might get into trouble, by yourself.'

'That is unlikely, I do not think so.'

She had a grave, sensual face, and her expression had something childlike.

'Who's the photograph of?'

'It is my brother.'

'Are you sure it's your brother?'

'Yes, it is my brother.'

'How many brothers have you got?'

'Only one. Good evening,' and she walked past me up the steps into the road.

I followed her and watched her going down the street. I hesitated to go after her till she was out of sight in the dark.

My mind, floating in fumes, turned mathematical, and it said, 'To have infinity, you must look for one. If you look for an infinite number, you will not find even one.'

Grasping a pilaster of the doorway, I tried to think what this discovery, clear a second ago, meant.

'It means,' said another track in my mind, 'that all the girls in the world are in one girl. Love decreases in proportion to the number you have without love.'

Yet another track said, 'To have more and more without love does irretrievable damage to your heart. To find the one needs an entire heart.'

'I thought this girl I followed now might be the one.'

'If so, you didn't impress her by the way you went about it.'

A different track now said, 'Then go downstairs. To see the light is the first step to rejecting it.'

These notions, passing with a rapidity greater than that of speech, were interrupted by Dennis, who came up with Sergeant Thackeray and the Manageress.

'Say good-night to Frau Dieckhoff,' Dennis said. 'The Sergeant's kindly giving her a lift back to her flat.'

'We must see she's not molested by the patrols.'

'No fear of that now for her,' said Dennis. 'This is your city. Good-bye, my son, and if you can't be good, etcetera.'

I went down again with Dennis, and spent half an hour listening to the Captain, who sipped a liqueur throughout that time. As soon as he'd left, and then such men as Cuthbert and Norman, we all started on the hock again.

When the waitresses gathered round us, and we fooled about with them, I thought how it was a parody of the first days of the liberations, when we'd sat drinking too with girls who'd welcomed us. But then it was not only the wine and their presence which had animated us . . .

I thought how on the roads and in the towns we'd passed through now, the parody had been the same. The Allies welcoming their freedom and not us, the Germans greeting not us, but the coming peace . . . There had been the agitation and relief of the liberation, but none of its joy . . .

I gazed at the girls in the cellar and wondered what would have happened if the Germans had come to England in 1940. I asked Dennis.

'*Was*?'

I asked him again.

'If the German army had come to England in 1940, my lad, they'd have had a bloody good time.'

'That's a dirty libel, Dennis,' Walter said. 'Why ask such questions, anyway?'

'Well, here and there they would have. And the real question I want to know is, who's going home with who?'

The women themselves had decided this, and each of them had chosen one of us—or one of all of us but Walter, who got up unsteadily and stalked off.

A girl with fair hair and peculiarly pink lips sat beside me in one of the alcoves. She smiled with the grimace of a comic mask, and we sat staring at each other without any sensible or kindly feeling.

When I turned her head round, I saw that the irises of her eyes glinted as much as the pupils, and that they merged into the whites, so that the whole of each eye looked at me. This look seemed to come from a long way off.

'I can't take you to my house,' I said, remembering the Captain, if not the Pastor.

'Come with me,' she said, taking my hand.

We went up the steps to the square and got into the car together. She directed me to a suburb of the town, and I parked the car in a yard. I looked up and down the road for a patrol, then we went up to the door of a middle-class house.

'You live here?'

'I am billeted here by the Town. I have my room in the attic.'

She opened the door with a latchkey, and we walked up a carpeted stair, hand in hand in the darkness. I trembled a little, and we saw a light coming down the corridor. It was held by a woman with a sad, ugly face, and with her hair down over a dressing-gown. She looked at us pitifully, and the girl looked back at her with defiance and quite a bit of venom.

'I ask you please to leave,' the woman said to me.

I'd stopped, but didn't say anything.

'My son is killed in the air raids, he is lying in a nearby room.'

The girl dragged at my hand, and we went up two flights and crossed a loft hung with plants. She opened the door of the attic room, shut and locked it, and mixed up together by the door she whispered, 'They have treated me like dirt here, ever since I came.'

One morning a day or two later, when the Captain had got back from Corps, he took me on one side and said, 'According to Major Bane, a certain *Hauptstürmführer* Brachvogel lives at number 3 of the Lindenallee.'

Nobody else was about but Norman, so I drove round with him to the address. It was in a road with a brook running beside it, and we crossed a little bridge to get to the house. The door was opened by a pale woman with a helpless, dignified face.

'Mr. Brachvogel?' I said.

'What is it for, please?' We walked in past her. 'To speak with him.'

She called down the passage. A man with tucks in the sides of his cheeks came out of a room and nodded us into it. He said, 'I have been expecting you.'

'Why?'

'On account of my political activity.'

'Well, show us your pistol.'

'I have no weapon,' he said, holding out his arms.

'Your papers.' It seemed to be him all right. 'You must come with us.'

'Is it permitted to say good-bye?'

'In our presence, yes. You must not come in close contact with anyone.'

He called the woman in. She'd been standing outside the door.

'Ah! Ah!' she cried, throwing herself into his arms. He looked at us across her shoulder, as if to say he wasn't responsible for her conduct. She patted him all over to fix his shape in her memory, and gazed at him as if drinking his image up. She began to ask him questions really addressed to us.

'Where are they taking you?' she cried.

'To imprisonment.'

'For how long?'

'That we cannot know for certain.'

He took a bunch of keys from his pocket and held it out to Norman, saying, 'Is it allowed to give her these?'

Norman handed her the keys, and as we set off down the passage she came as far as the steps outside and stood bending forward, her hands two feet apart with the fingers opened. He didn't look round at her, and when we reached the car, stepped aside for Norman to get in first.

We stopped at the cellar to get one of the forms that enabled you to arrest someone. When we drove on, the prisoner asked if he might smoke. He took out a packet, looked carefully at how many he had left before lighting up, and then, taking a deep breath, said, 'May I ask: the cellar-restaurant is now your headquarters?'

'Yes.'

'It was formerly a place much frequented by our people.'

We took him to a collecting-point for prisoners outside the town, and handed him over to a Provost Corporal who wrote down particulars in an exercise-book.

'You've looked him over for arms?'

'He says he hasn't got any.'

The Corporal eyed me, and patted the German all over. He moved his arms again to help.

'He's clean so far as I can see,' the Corporal said. 'Has he got a watch?'

'I haven't looked.'

The Corporal eyed me some more, said nothing and began writing out a receipt. Just then a truck drove in, with more civilian prisoners standing in the back. Among them was an elderly man wearing a rucksack. As soon as our prisoner caught sight of him, he bowed and said respectfully, 'Good morning, *Herr Staatsrat*.' The elderly man bowed back at him from the truck.

'You know,' said Norman, on the way home, 'that's the first time I've arrested anybody.'

'It won't be the last.'

'No. Walter was telling me his score's seven to date, but being in the office, I don't get much of a chance. I wish this had been something better, though. He didn't look much of a *Hauptstürmführer*, did he?'

'I expect he did in his uniform.'

'He wasn't in his uniform. Oh, I see what you mean. Did you notice he behaved as if it was all quite natural?'

'He's probably watched that scene before in a different capacity.'

As we were nearing the billet, I noticed some French soldiers outside a building, and saw that they had rifles and seemed to be doing some sort of sentry duty. I pulled up and got into conversation with them.

They said there was a dump of *Wehrmacht* stores inside, and that a British Colonel, being short of troops of his own, had issued them with arms and asked them to guard it. 'Against the Germans, of course,' they said. 'If there is anything you would like, go in and help yourself, by all means.'

These Frenchmen, who looked tired and underfed, all spoke in the matter-of-fact way they have; but they couldn't hide their relief and amazement that it was over, and there was a gentleness in their voices I hadn't heard before.

One of them came up and asked where our General Headquarters were. He was a small, ginger-haired man wearing a linen suit and a blue, white and red armband. 'I really don't know,' I told him.

'Nobody can give me that information.' He had limpid blue eyes, and a mild, persistent manner. 'I am the delegate of a group of deported workers, and we wish to return to France.'

'Of course. But most of them seem to be setting off under their own steam.'

'We are a big party, with women and some sick among us, and I thought that, as official arrangements were bound to be made, we had better take advantage of them.'

'Well, I don't know. Have you tried the Military Government?'

'I have been to their office, but could not manage to enter.'

'Couldn't you? Jump in the car.'

Driving along, he told me he was really a prisoner-of-war, but that he'd been attached to a civilian labour camp as interpreter.

'And how long have you been in Germany?' I asked him.

'Almost five years. I was taken prisoner at the *débâcle*, like so many. Tell me, please, did you pass through Rouen? Is it true that Rouen is destroyed?'

'It's badly damaged. Are you from there?'

'Yes. I was a Controller of Taxes in that place,' he said, with a mixture of modest pride and distaste.

We dropped Norman off at the cellar and went on in search of Mil. Gov. Thinking how I could best impress them in his favour, I asked the Frenchman if he was an officer.

'Oh no, I am a private soldier. This armband (looking at it apologetically) is nothing. My comrades asked me to speak for them, and I put it on in the hope of gaining attention.'

The Mil. Gov. office had proclamations pasted on its front fence, which most people glanced at and passed by; but one or two older Germans had stopped to make notes from them in a furtive way. I led the Frenchman past the guards, and once in the office, we came face to face with Parsons and Adeane. 'Well, what is it this time?' the Major said.

I told him the Frenchman's problem, and though he nodded with hollow approval, I wasn't surprised that he broke in and said, 'Not up our alley, Sarge. Not a Mil. Gov. matter. These people must realise there's a bit of a scrap in progress.'

'Aren't there arrangements for evacuating them, then?'

'Not so far as I know, lad. Why are you so interested in these Frenchmen, anyway?'

'This man asked me, and I said I'd find out.'

Shaking his head amusedly, the Major went into the next room and came back carrying a painted wooden castle, with beautifully carved animals and figures that represented what might have been its medieval population. 'What about this?' he said. 'Isn't it a beaut?'

Lieutenant Adeane turned impatiently away. The rest of us gathered round and looked at it as the Major adjusted the peasants and oxen, and set out the soldiers on the battlements to greater advantage.

'It's a gift from an old boy here I was able to do a little favour to,' he said. 'I look forward to seeing the wife's delight when I get it home. Well, what do you think?'

The Frenchman examined it politely and incredulously. 'You'll have to get some policemen made for it,' I said.

'Now, now, don't be sarky,' the Major said, pointing a pikeman at me and grinning unpleasantly.

When we'd admired it sufficiently, I took the Frenchman into the clerks' room and typed out a note about him on one of the sheets of paper impressed with the Detachment stamp of which I carried a supply. I suggested he take this to the Service Corps, whose trucks drove back to Belgium empty. He seemed pleased to have this document, and folding it carefully, thanked me and went away.

Lieutenant Adeane called me back to the inner office. 'Have you seen these things, Sergeant?' he said, handing me a large printed form. 'It's a *Fragebogen*.'

'What's that?'

'A Fraggybogen, Sarge, as you should already know,' the Major said, 'is a Personal Questionnaire to be filled in by Germans who'll be applying to us for jobs, or who we want to find out about in some connection.'

I read the *Fragebogen* through. It was a sort of mammoth *curriculum vitae* and auto-confession on personal, political and financial matters. It was so designed that anyone with a compromising past, if he completed it accurately, would put a pair of handcuffs round his wrists.

'And if they fill them up incorrectly?' I said.

'Then if we catch them, they do a year or two in the cooler. Look, the warning's there at the foot of the page in black and white.'

'How many of these things are going to be issued?'

'Oh, hundreds of thousands. And it'll be up to you Intelligence people to see they're filled in properly.'

'Will a big Nazi put down all he's done?'

'Old Gerry'll fill it in right, you'll see. He knows a form's a form.'

'Besides, you must look at it from another point of view,' the Lieutenant explained. 'With these questionnaires, we'll be able to pick out reliable anti-Nazis.'

'There he is, he's at it again,' said the Major.

'When we re-open the schools, for example,' the Lieutenant persisted. 'Suppose we want to find which schoolteachers weren't Nazis, and are therefore suitable for employment, we get every one of them to fill in his form.'

At this point the Interpreter, who'd been listening discreetly, said, 'Excuse me, *Herr Leutnant*.'

'Yes, Mr. Kirchenpauer?'

'In this town, for instance, I should warn you there are about four hundred schoolteachers of which I think at most a dozen were not Party members.'

'Oh.'

'Of course, the majority were not enthusiasts, and only joined in 1937, when this became practically imperative.'

'Yes, well I see, thank you. At any rate, these *Fragebogen* will be a good basis for deciding which of all the others were real Nazis or not.'

During lunch, I had seen the pink-lipped girl watching me. I'd avoided her the last two days, and she had resented this. But now, when we were left alone, she beckoned me over with a frown to a seat in the corner. 'I must see my child,' she said.

'What child?'

'My baby,' she said, pulling me down beside her.

'You've got a baby?'

'Yes. I keep it at a village nearby. I have to see it—a week has passed now since I went there.'

I asked her how far this village was, and she said about ten kilometers. We put some rations in the car and set off north through a forest towards the distant sound of shells. She sat beside me with her eyes half closed not saying much. I was curious to know who the father was, but didn't like to ask.

'Why did you leave him at the village?' I said, after a long silence.

'It is her. To get more food, better milk. Also there was bombing on the town.'

'Where is it she's living?'

'With a farmer. I pay half my wages to them. I get nothing from any other . . .'

'You mean from her father?'

'Yes, her father.' She looked round at me, but with her

thoughts away. 'I do not know . . . ' she said, her eyes looking inwards and her lips falling open, disclosing her teeth, 'I do not know where he is.'

'Is he with the army?'

'Yes, but I do not know where'.

We reached the village and had to detour over a ford, as the bridge was gone. We passed by an Infantry Unit and drove off down a track she pointed out. A sentry stopped us.

'Where to, Sarge?'

'Over to that farm.'

'And who's she?'

'She's a friend of mine.'

'A friend of yours?' He looked all round. 'Well, keep her out of sight, will you?'

She had a lot to say to the people at the farm, and gave them the food we'd brought. She fondled the baby and chattered to it on the lawn outside the house.

While I was talking to the farmer, I saw a Second Lieutenant coming over, with a different sentry this time. 'What Unit are you from, Sergeant?' he asked. I told him. 'Can you identify yourself?' I showed him some papers. 'And who is this person?'

'She's a hospital nurse, Sir.'

'Oh, really? Are you bringing her here on official business?'

'She's come out to see her child.'

'Has she? Well, I hope your Officer Commanding knows all about it. Didn't he give you a chitty of some sort?' He went over to the girl and her baby. '*Guten Tag*,' he said. 'Baby?'

She jerked it up and down and tried to get it to smile at the Second Lieutenant.

'*Sehr schön*,' he said. 'Look in at the guard-post on the way out, will you, Sergeant?'

She stayed on for an hour or more before I could get her to leave. I took a different track round to the main road and accelerated back through the woods. The gunfire had that far off, muffled sound, more reassuring even than silence.

The girl was miles away, and hadn't answered more than a few words when I'd spoken. But when I changed gears once, she took my hand and held it. I stopped the car and kissed her. Then told her, 'I need that hand to drive with.' She put her arms round me and said, 'Why did you not return?'

'I don't know.'

'You don't know. What do you know?'

'It's getting dark. We must get back.'

She rested her head against mine a moment, then took away her arms and sat with her teeth over her lip. We drove on. 'Such things happen to me,' she said, as though to herself.

Back at the cellar, I found the Frenchman waiting for me. He said he'd managed to arrange transport, and had come to say good-bye. He stopped on for a drink, and as we toasted his homecoming, I asked him to tell me how he'd been taken prisoner in 1940. 'Entirely through my own stupidity,' he said. Apparently, when his Unit had found itself cut off behind the German advance, they'd been disarmed and told to drive in their lorries to the nearest town, with only their own non-commissioned officers in charge to see they surrendered there. When they'd stopped at a farm for water, the farmer, an old soldier, had offered to hide the Frenchman for the night and give him civilian clothes to get away in. But he'd hesitated too long, and once they had reached the town they were put under guard, and the chance had not returned.

'It seems to me incredible now that I refused,' he said. 'It would have been quite easy, no one would have missed me, or if so, would have said nothing. And the Germans had other things to do at that time than look for deserters. But I let the opportunity slip by. We were terribly depressed, and it seemed a dishonest thing to desert. But when an army disintegrates, that is clearly the intelligent thing to do. I should have found my way home and got false papers, and would have lived my own life for five years.'

He shook his head resignedly, and helped himself to more hock.

'How were you treated here?' I asked him.

'Myself personally, not badly, since I was a soldier, not a deported civilian, and because I have a certain understanding of the Germans, I think, and an art in treating with them. But of many brutalities I have witnessed, I prefer not to speak.'

'Did you see anything of the Allied political prisoners?'

'Little. They were kept away from us, of course.'

'You didn't see any Dutch politicals at all?'

'Dutch? No. Well, perhaps. Some weeks ago, lorries of Allied prisoners evacuated from further west passed through the town.

Perhaps there were Dutch among them. There were certainly French. But most political prisoners were at the concentration camp nearby. You have been there?'

'I went out yesterday, but they wouldn't let me in. It's closed to sightseers now, they said. I saw some of the sick being evacuated, though. Did you know about it before we arrived?'

'We knew by rumour there was such a camp in the district. But frankly, we scarcely dared to think of it. When your fate is already bad, you close your mind to those whose lot is worse. You fear to become them, and cling to the lesser misery.'

'Did the Germans know about the camp?'

'I cannot say. Not to know what is dangerous is a general human instinct, and it is one the Germans have to a supreme degree.'

Warmed by the wine, he went on, 'I do not know what is to be done about this people. Sometimes I have thought that the best for them and for us is for the Germans to come out of Germany, away from the forces here that intoxicate their minds. One thing is certain, however. So long as there are still nations, there will always be, for us and for them, a German problem.'

He got up to leave, and I went and found him six bottles of the hock. 'Would you allow me to ask for your address?' he said, as we were wrapping them up. 'I should like to send you a post card so that you will know of our arrival.'

I saw him to the door and watched his small, compact, self-confident figure as he walked off down the road with his bundle.

When word came through that we were to move up close to the Elbe, Dennis and I started out early one morning from the cellar. The town we were heading for had been attacked only the day before, and the route up hadn't yet been fully signed; so that we'd hardly gone a few miles before there was a confusing choice of roads. Wishing to take those clear of enemy troops, we thought it best to follow a convoy; but growing tired of this, we overtook them and hurried on, stopping to drink Frau Dieckhoff's bottles from time to time. We travelled miles without seeing anybody much till, in a valley, we met a lonely Signals Unit, and asked if the road ahead was clear.

'I think it is, chum. Some vehicles passed this way, and they haven't come back.'

At a hilltop further on we met two stationary trucks, and an officer signalled us to stop. 'Have you people any idea where you're going?' he said.

'We hope we're heading for the Elbe.'

'Let me see your map a minute.' The officer compared it with his own. 'These two maps tell very different tales. Still, I expect you've got the right idea'.

After this we found it simplest to ask the farmers, who gave accurate directions for short distances. Then we began to meet traffic again, and on the outskirts of the new city, we were halted by a lot of vehicles at a cross-road. Dennis jumped out of his car and came striding back. 'Look at that,' he cried, pointing to a camp by the roadside, where a lot of our soldiers were standing together. 'They're British prisoners-of-war.'

We went over, and were told they'd been a liberated a few hours before. The prisoners were gathered round our men and their trucks. Some groups were animated, but those in others were talking in what seemed a casual way.

On the further side of the road, there was a platoon of German Infantrymen with one of our freed prisoners beside them. He was wearing a tattered battledress and a forage cap of the type that had long gone out of use, and he was clutching a German rifle as if it was the material proof of his freedom. He was so tremendously pleased, that he could only look at the Germans with a vacant, almost friendly delight.

'Hullo, soldier,' said Dennis, going up and putting his hand on his shoulder. 'Where did they get hold of you?'

'It was Dunkirk time,' he said, eagerly but half diffidently.

'And what are you going to do with this lot?'

'I dunno, Sarge. I rounded them up, but now I've got the buggers, I'm ——ed if I know what to do with them.'

Dennis turned to the Germans. 'Which is the senior man among you?' he shouted.

A Sergeant stepped forward. 'That I am.'

'And what are you doing here?'

'Tell us where we are to go. We wish to surrender. We have nothing to eat, no quarters.'

'Fall your men in,' Dennis ordered. 'There you are,' he said to the prisoner. 'March them up to the barracks and put them in there. That's the thing to do.'

We drove into the town, and looked round for hotels. The

first that we found was picturesquely perched above a mill-dam, but on the other side of the stream there was a factory. This outlook, and the modesty of the reception rooms, made Dennis ask fiercely of the proprietor, 'Haven't you anything here like the Adlon?'

'Oh, this is not Berlin. This is a provincial city.'

'Why did you build your hotel opposite a factory?'

'Ah no, Sir. It was the factory that was built later. It is the most modern paper factory in Europe.'

We drove on into the central square, lined with ancient brick houses, tall and narrow. In two of these joined together there was a hotel called the Pfeufer. It was bigger than it looked from outside, for it rambled over both buildings and into a large, modern annexe. Dennis thought it old-fashioned but, as we'd have about eight rooms each, satisfactory. The show piece was the main suite overlooking the square. One room was decorated to imitate, for anyone living in the oval triple-bed, a panorama of the heavens by starlight; and the one next door was lavishly upholstered in dirty gilt and plush, in the style of some very late King Louis.

The owner, an old, hook-nosed man, seemed pleased to have us. Perhaps he thought we'd be some sort of protection till better times came.

'And the guests at present here,' he said. 'They may remain?'

'Who are they?'

'Oh, not many people. I could show you the register.'

Dennis said he needn't bother. 'It's nice to have some civvies about,' he told me in the bar. 'They provide variety. Still, this ancient place has one disadvantage I expect you noticed, the lack of decent garages. Hold the fort a moment while I step out and get one.'

There were two civilians in the bar, a plump man with oiled grey hair, and a lean-limbed woman nearing thirty. They'd been murmuring together and glancing furtively at us, and when Dennis left, the man came smiling across to the counter. He said the woman was English, and wanted to speak to me.

'And who are you?'

'An inventor, Sir, from Hungary.'

'A friend of the lady's?'

'By no means. A fellow hotel guest.'

I left him at the bar and went over to the woman. She was

good-looking in a raw-boned way, and as I came up she stared at me with a look that was haughty, nervous and appealing in about equal parts.

'I'm sorry to be a nuisance to you,' she said in a drawling voice, 'but I wanted to ask you if you know what's happening up at Hamburg.' In contrast to the rest of her words, she pronounced the name of the city with an exaggeratedly German accent.

I sat down and handed her a cigarette. 'It's not taken yet.'

'No, that's what I thought.'

She dragged on the cigarette and puffed out the smoke in a greedy, masculine way. She was eyeing me evenly, but when she spoke again, her voice was painfully calm, with unexpected treble jumps.

'I just wondered, I've got relatives up that way, you see,' she said, smiling and showing her teeth.

'Have you been long over here?'

'Oh, quite a while. I was in England last in '38.'

'You married here, I expect.'

'Yes. My husband's dead, though. He was in their air force.'

She tapped the ash off her cigarette and went on tapping it when there was no ash left.

'What do you plan to do now?' I said. 'Will you be going back to England?'

'No, I don't think so. Perhaps on a visit if I can, but I'd do best to stay on, I think. I've my boy here, you see, and besides,' she said quickly, 'I'm naturally rather out of touch with connections at home.'

I asked her if there was anything she wanted doing.

'No. No thanks. I just wanted to exchange a word with you . . . When it's over in Hamburg, I'll be going on there.' I got up to say good-bye, and as she shook hands she said, 'Well, thanks so much for talking so nicely to a German woman.'

'There's no need to say a thing like that, is there.'

'Then you're not one of those who think it's a mistake to have married a German who was in the *Luftwaffe* bombing our cities before he crashed?' It poured out as if she'd often rehearsed it.

'Don't think about that now.'

'No. No, it's not much use, is it. I'm a bit jittery about the attitude of you people, though.'

'We're your people,' I said, not altogether feeling it.

'Yes, I suppose so,' she answered, looking at me absently. 'But you can't imagine what it's been like. You can't imagine what it's been like all these years.'

Dennis hadn't returned, so I walked down the square looking for garages. There was one a few doors away, and when I went in, I saw German mechanics working on some cars. One of these caught my attention immediately. It was a very large Mercedes, painted silver.

'It's ours,' said Dennis, coming out of a built-in office. He was followed by a man saying, 'But will you not at least give me a certificate? Otherwise, do you not see, I shall be in difficulties.'

'I told this garage owner I've requisitioned it,' Dennis said to me. 'But he's shaky because of this scrap of paper.'

He flipped away a sheet stuck under the windscreen wiper, and handed it to me. It warned all comers that the car was reserved, on authority of Corps Staff, for a War Correspondent. The signature was that of our visitor at the last town.

I handed it back, and Dennis, crumpling it up and shaking it under the garage owner's nose, said, 'I've told you this person has no military status. When was he here?'

'Early this morning. He said he would return in the afternoon to fetch it.'

'We'll have to work fast.' Dennis climbed into the driver's seat. 'Just make him out some sort of a chit for it.'

The garage owner beckoned me insistently into his office, where I wrote out an evasive document. 'Send two men with grey paint to the Hotel Pfeufer immediately.' Dennis told him. We drove round to the back entrance and put the car in the hotel courtyard.

As we were walking in through the lobby, we saw a tall, elegant officer strolling about in the empty restaurant as if he was selecting a table. He looked like the hero's confidant in a light comedy, and he was examining everything in an interested, critical way.

Dennis eyed him suspiciously, then putting on an engaging manner, walked briskly up and said, 'Good morning to you Sir. Can we do anything for you?'

'Oh, hullo,' the officer said. 'Are you the people who're settling in here?'

Dennis gave him the grim smile of the first-class passenger who confirms that the corner seat is indeed engaged.

'Well, it's a nice place, Sergeant, and I think I'll come and join you in it. You see, I'm Town Major here. I've just arrived.'

'Oh, well in that case, you'll be wanting a drink.' Dennis strode to the door and called out. 'We'll be delighted to have you, Sir, and we'll do all we can to make you and your clerks comfortable.'

The Town Major went to tell his small convoy to drive in. Dennis rubbed his hands. 'It's like having the Lord Mayor under your thumb. We'll be able to organise this town properly, before all the other vultures arrive.'

I got ready now to drive back to the cellar to show the Detachment the way over. I was held up in the square by a string of our lorries, carrying German soldiers. A knot of civilians standing on the street corner waved to them and cheered forlornly.

I thought I'd go another way home that seemed shorter, but after driving eight miles, reached a blown bridge. I tried to find where I was on the map, but losing patience, wandered on all over the country, taking whatever roads seemed to lead in the right direction. I met no traffic until I overtook a repair truck, travelling by itself. The driver blew blasts on his horn, so I drew up and waited. The truck came alongside and the driver asked where I was going.

'Then will you take three passengers? They're Raf bods, escaped prisoners, we picked them up some miles back. You'd get them there long before I can.'

They were men from bomber crews who'd got away from a transit camp that morning. Not knowing how close the Army was, they had hidden in a wood, until a farmer they'd met had advised them to make for a main road. The truck I'd just taken them from was the first they'd seen of their own people. They were tremendously friendly and impatient to get near the airplane that would take them home. I was clearly no person at all, but a figure in a vision, sent for the purpose of driving them at top speed to an airfield.

To begin with they all talked at once, telling me of experiences in different camps, jumping from one theme to another. Then the man next to me asked about England, and was vaguely surprised when I told him I'd left it long before he had. 'Nigel's the only man among us who's been grounded here since before your invasion started,' he said, turning and looking over his shoulder at one of the men on the bucket-seats.

'Yes, and he got away once, but the goons caught up with him,' said the man by his side.

'Where was it they caught you?' I asked this Nigel, without turning round. And as I was saying it, the thought came into my mind that it was he whom the Dutchman Maarten had tried to help over the Belgian frontier to freedom.

But it wasn't.

'It was down near Hanover somewhere,' the voice behind me said. 'I didn't get far, but I was out eight days. They didn't catch me, either. It was hunger and cold that did that.'

'Did you ever meet men in the camps who'd got as far as Holland and Belgium?'

'Well, you heard tales. But those that knew of these escape routes didn't talk much unless you were in on a scheme with them.'

He said nothing more, and I thought, 'Of course, how can they be interested in escaping now? That's all over.' Then I began to sense that there was another reason for their silence—a slight suspicion at my having asked about escape routes at all. This growing silence became embarrassed, as if they were saying to themselves, after months of caution among enemy soldiers, 'Why is he asking that? Could it be this man isn't really one of ours?' I realised this only afterwards, for now I too had begun to feel, perhaps because their mistrust had infected me, a sudden doubt of my own. And glancing at them, it struck me that their faces and bodies, dressed in fragments of Air Force battledress, looked German; and as we drove in the deserted landscape, the thought came into my mind that they were last-ditch saboteurs, hurriedly disguised in British uniforms. I looked at their features again, all of which now seemed so German, though so English.

But this must have been a result of habitual suspicion and of the excitement of the past days. For when we came up with an Army Unit, camping in the sun, a hundred familiar sights made them break into nervous smiles. The tenseness in the car relaxed, and a dreamy look came over their faces.

'Soldiers. They haven't changed,' one of them said.

But they were still silent, and sat glancing at the speedometer, lighting cigarettes and putting them out and shifting around in their seats.

'So you think something's laid on to fly us home,' one of them said at last.

'Sure to be. We'll run you out to the airfield as soon as you've had a meal.'

'Oh, we don't need a meal.'

But when we arrived at the cellar, Gordon gave them plates of ham and eggs which they looked at in astonishment, laughing unnaturally before wolfing them. Then he drove them away; and when he came back, we all set out for the Hotel Pfeufer.

A few days later, Harry arrived at breakfast with the news. The Americans had met the Russians south of Berlin, and our own troops had got into Bremen. It seemed an attack would soon be launched over the Elbe to drive right through to the Baltic. 'So roll on the peace. They're very optimistic up at Corps.'

'There's still the Japanese, don't forget,' said Walter. 'But I agree it looks like ending over here. That'll mean wedding bells for you, won't it, Harry?'

Walter looked at him probingly. Harry said nothing. I opened the letter he'd brought from Major Bane.

> 1. Herewith list personnel *Sicherheitsdienst* office this town, from captured documents. Ascertain whereabouts and detain.
>
> 2. Current interrogation Dutch informant SNOUCKAERT should disclose names Gestapo officials this area. Further information follows.
>
> 3. Area Commander wishes conduct house-search for enemy deserters and asks co-operation. Send representatives his office 10.00 hours this morning.

I showed it to Walter. 'You and Dennis can go after the *Sicherheitsdienst*.'

'Dennis? He left this morning at daybreak. Where to? Of course he didn't say.'

'Well, take Cuthbert. And give this letter to the Captain,

tell him it's after nine, and that I'll wait and go round to the Area Commander's with him.'

'About this Snouckaert,' said Harry, when Walter had gone out. 'You remember telling me you'd heard Allied prisoners were driven through that last town? Well, I got in a word with Snouckaert up at the office, and he says the same, and there were Dutch among them. They shouted to him from the lorries as they went through here. They shouted out the name of that Dutch town my girl lived in, too.'

'You were thinking her brother might have been among them?'

'It's just possible, isn't it? But he said a lot of them looked like they were dying on their feet.'

'I'd like to see this Snouckaert.'

'You'll be seeing him. As soon as Major Bane's got the dope out of him, he'll be sending him down to you to show where the people he's been denouncing live. They're still grilling him now.'

'Grilling? Didn't he volunteer the information?'

'Yes, but they think he knows too much about the Gestapo not to have been mixed up in it himself.'

As I went out with him to the street, I said, 'You'll be writing to the girl in Holland about those prisoners passing through, won't you?'

'Yes, I've written to her. I still write to her. And I'll try to find out about her brother, even if it's the only promise I keep.'

'Have you told her anything else? That things have changed?'

'No. No, not by letter. I'll have to wait till I can see her.'

'You're certain about it now?'

'Yes. I could never go back to her after the other.'

'And the German girl, Harry. You realise you may lose track of her altogether? What if they evacuate her somewhere else, or try to send her home?'

'I won't lose track of her. She's given me addresses. And I write to her, too.'

'How? There's no mail in Germany.'

'No. I get the drivers in the Service Corps to drop a letter off at the village as they're passing through. At least, they promise to. Whether she gets them or not, I don't know for sure . . .'

He got on his bike. 'Do you know what two people stopped me to ask the way as I was coming down this morning?'

'No . . . Parsons and Adeane?'

'Right first time. They're going to that hotel down by the mill. This is their permanent town, they told me. They're settling here for good.'

'Let's hope it's for good.'

'They'll cancel each other out, I should say. Well, so long.'

The Area Commander had his headquarters in the barracks near the former prison camp for British soldiers. We waited in the Adjutant's room, from which the patriotic mottoes in Gothic lettering and framed photographs of German Generals had not been removed. When the Adjutant showed us into the adjoining office, we saw a stout Colonel with greying hair and protruding eyes that looked at us sideways; he seemed reluctant to turn their full glare on us in case we should shrivel up, or perhaps detect a slightly lunatic glint in them. He wore boots laced up his calves, and his red hands dangled on either side of a swivel chair. But his voice was mild. 'Come in, come in.'

We sat down.

'Well now,' he began, 'as you may know, this town is full of enemy troops, and a great many of them, instead of giving themselves up, have preferred to disappear into private houses and make themselves comfortable there. That I don't approve of.' His eyes looked straight at us a moment, then flew back to an oblique position. 'So what I propose to do, as my troops are rather idle till this attack over the Elbe begins, is to go round this evening after curfew and drag them all out.' He gave us a terrific smile, and paused. 'As a matter of fact,' he then went on, 'a night raid should have a good effect. I'd like the civilians here to realise it's not only their *Wehrmacht* we disapprove of.'

I could see the Captain wasn't enthusiastic, though when the Colonel called for maps, the interest of planning an operation grew on him. The Colonel, rubbing his hands, egged him and the Adjutant on as they fixed up the details. It was decided we should all meet there at nine in the evening.

When we went out to the car, I saw Sergeant Thackeray driving up. 'Been seeing the Beast?' he said.

'The Colonel in there?'

'They call him the Beast of Belsen, I'm told. I understand he's taking us housebreaking tonight.'

'You're in on it too?'

'Reluctantly. As if I hadn't my own business to attend to.'

Driving back to the hotel, the Captain said, 'A bit of a fanatic, if you ask me. Of course, there's no harm in showing a firm hand, but after all, some of us will have to live with these people when it's over, and I don't know if that's the way to begin.'

'You're not thinking of staying on yourself, are you?'

'Me? Not a moment longer than I have to. Though mind you, at one time I did consider stopping and becoming an administrator. But from what I've seen, I don't think there'll be much in it in the long run, despite indirect advantages. It's like a lot of places where you could make a living if you had to—the trouble is, the people.'

Up in the starlit room at the hotel, I found Cuthbert sitting opposite two women perched on chairs. 'A couple of *Sicherheitsdienst* secretaries,' he said. 'They were all we could find.'

'Have they told you anything?'

'Anything! As far as I can see, I'll be taking down notes all day. They've given me names of scores of arrestable persons. And look at these documents we've collected.'

He pointed to some loaded waste-paper baskets. I picked up a directory listing Allied personalities who were to have been arrested when their countries were overrun. 'Do you want help sorting these out?' I said.

'Oh no, Norman will do it. Gordon was here just now, but he was only interested in the women. I told him I could manage, and he said he'd relieve me later on.'

'Is Dennis in yet?'

'Yes, I just saw him. He's been all the way back to the cellar, he says, to pick up some kit he left behind there.'

Dennis lived in the modern annexe at the back of the hotel, and when I knocked, the door opened a few inches to reveal a strip of his cautiously peering face. 'Oh, it's you,' he said. 'Come on in.'

Sitting at the table, combing her hair, was the athletic girl he'd been with at the last town. She nodded and went on combing.

'There she is, all complete,' said Dennis. 'I promised not to desert her, so I drove back there and collected her up.'

'What happens to her when we move on again?'

'I'll leave her here, and return for her once more as soon as convenient.'

'You're going to settle down with her eventually?'

'Who can tell, my boy? A man must cleave to a woman, you know. Though mind you, on the way up this morning, I nearly stopped and slung her out of the car once or twice. She would keep interrupting my thoughts to point out the beauties of the German landscape.'

As we went down to lunch, Dennis stopped at the kitchen and ordered a tray to be sent upstairs. In the restaurant, while the Captain was inviting the Town Major to join in the house-search, Norman came up to say that the War Correspondent was outside with his Escorting Officer.

'It'll be about that new Mercedes I got for you, Sir,' Dennis told the Captain.

'Just a minute,' said the Town Major. 'How many people have you promised that car to? I thought I was going to have it.'

Dennis stuttered and rolled his eyes about. 'Don't you see, Sir, the Captain hadn't seen it when I spoke to you, and naturally, he has first choice.'

'You've worked a flanker on me, that's what you've done,' the Town Major told him with a taut smile.

The Captain listened, and said, 'You'd better step out by the back door and get it off the premises while I see these people.'

The Correspondent wanted to settle the matter in a friendly fashion, but his Escorting Officer was irritated, and not to be mollified by offers of drink. 'The German at the garage maintains your men removed it a couple of days ago,' he said.

'How does he know my men?'

'He says they drove to this hotel.'

'Naturally, we have a number of requisitioned vehicles, but I can't say I recollect where they all came from originally.'

'Might I ask if one of your men wrote this?'

The officer handed him our receipt. The Captain took it as if it was soiled, read it carefully and said, 'This document is meaningless and the signature illegible.'

'I thought you might recognise the writing.'

'Sorry. No—sorry.'

'Looks like a Mil. Gov. job to me,' the Town Major said. 'They're the boys to try. They've a car for each day of the week.'

'Now it's like this, Captain,' said the Correspondent. 'Surely there's plenty of enemy transport for everybody. One car more or less can't mean all that to you, but for me, they're not easy to come by.'

'If it's a car you want, I could possibly fix you up.'

The Escorting Officer said, 'What I am speaking of, is a large, silver Mercédes.'

'I can't help you there, you know,' the Captain told him. 'But if you're hard put for transport, I could probably let you have something or other.'

Half an hour later, he took them to the yard and gave them the Buick he'd set out with from Belgium.

I was lying in my room after lunch, reading a well-worn copy of the Correspondent's newspaper, when there was a knock on the door and in came one of the servants of the hotel, a fair girl of about nineteen. She closed the door and said, 'Cornelis has sent me. They have arrested him.'

'Who has?'

'The English police have put him in prison. He told me to come at once and fetch you.'

She said she'd taken Cornelis to see some friends of hers who had a gold cigarette-case to sell. After an argument over the price, which Cornelis had wanted to settle in cash and the owners wanted paid in kind, Cornelis had tried to force the issue by putting the money down and running off with the case. They had grabbed him, taken him round to the Military Police, and accused him of robbery. The Redcaps were holding him as a suspect until he could explain who he was, and how he'd got hold of the money.

'And where did he get the money?'

'Oh, that I do not know. But please, come now and release him. It is my fault, I should not have told him about these people. But I thought they were to be trusted.'

As we drove round to Sergeant Thackeray's hotel, the girl sat with her hands between her knees looking scared and worried. I had noticed her accent, and when I asked her where she came from, she said she was a Belgian from West Flanders. Her fiancé had volunteered for the German army, and later on she'd got a job herself in Germany so as to be near him. But when she'd reached the town where he had been training, she found he'd already left for the front. She had moved from place to place in different jobs and hadn't had any news of him for more than a year.

She asked me what I thought would happen to her, and when I said she'd probably be sent back to Belgium, it seemed that the thought of seeing her mother, of whom she spoke fearfully, was worrying her more than the prospect of official punishment.

'And what should I say to them when I reach the frontier?' she asked.

'You'd better tell them you came here because you loved him.'

'Well, I did love him.'

'Stick to that. Say nothing else.'

'Cornelis has promised to give me Belgian money.'

'Make sure he does give it to you, then.'

She nodded, looked into space and said, 'It has not been a happy life for me in this war.'

I hoped to find Sergeant Thackeray at the Military Police hotel, but the place was in the charge of a dry-skinned Lance-Corporal. I began to plead to him for Cornelis's freedom. He listened with a blank surface to his face, and having the ace in his hand, demanded heavy tribute of deference. I laid it on thick.

At last he said, 'It's a pity I've entered it all up in the Book—that's going to make letting him out to please you a bit awkward to explain to my officer, isn't it?'

He looked at me. I kissed his toe a bit harder.

'Well,' he said, 'I'll be keeping that cigarette-case pending enquiries, meanwhile you might as well have him against a receipt. If I'd known he was a nark of yours, I'd have pulled in the Germans that brought him here.'

He went and got Cornelis and, shouting at him as a matter of principle, handed him over. The Corporal tried to keep us in conversation as part of the price, for a policeman is often lonely, and hankers after the love of the outside world. But I cut him short, and hurried the culprits out.

The girl cheered up when we were in the car; she became pert and bright and put her hand through Cornelis's arm. Cornelis was subdued and apologetic. He said these friends of the girl's had stolen the case themselves, and that he'd tried to talk them into giving it up at a lower figure. But they'd become violent, and Cornelis was now rather frightened. 'One must be careful with these Germans, I can see,' he said. 'They can be dangerous people.'

'And what about this money, Cornelis? Where did you get it from?'

He told me Dennis had given it to him.

'Well, mind you give her that Belgian money you promised.'

'Oh, her? Yes, of course.' He dropped his voice. 'But there is another girl, really, in the hotel, whom I did not find when we first arrived. This one can be for anybody, it is the other one I now prefer. Could you not perhaps give her some money, Sir?'

I met Dennis in the bar before the Area Commander's raid, and asked him about the money Cornelis had.

'Oh, that. Yes, I didn't tell you about it before, but now we've got a bag-full of *Reichsmarks*, and I've been distributing them out to those that need them, including Cornelis.'

'Do you mean a bag?'

'Yes, it's a fair-sized bag.' He put his hand in his hip pocket and pulled out a wad. 'Here's your ration,' he said. 'You're not going to draw pay while you're in Germany, are you?'

'Where did they come from?'

'Money is always money, my boy, wherever it comes from. Here you are, you're very welcome.'

He poured out another drink.

'What about the Mercedes?' I said. 'Have you squared that with the Town Major?'

'Yes, more or less. We had another visit from that Escorting Officer, you know, to try and get a second car for himself. But the Captain sat there like the respectable director of a fraudulent company, and he didn't get a sausage out of him.'

'But what about the Town Major?'

'He's a bit irritated, I think, but I've promised to get him another just as good. Either I'll succeed, or else we'll have left before he can take reprisals, and that'll be the end of that.'

'We may meet him again in some other place.'

'No, no, he's staying here. This is his town for keeps.'

A merry company assembled in the restaurant for supper. All the Sergeants were going on the raid except Cuthbert, who was still interrogating the *Sicherheitsdienst* secretaries, and

Norman, who was to guard the office files. Thackeray was there, and the Town Major, and the Area Commander's Adjutant, who had come to make final arrangements with the Captain.

When we arrived at the barracks, we found the raiding party assembled in a dining-hall. The soldiers, as often on 'schemes' of this sort, looked bored and a bit sheepish. The Sergeants were in a dignified group apart, and the officers strode up and down, awaiting the arrival of the Beast. Everyone stood up when he came in, carrying a fly-whisk and accompanied by brother officers of other Units who'd come to join in the fun. He stood with his arms akimbo, gazing all round at his men with sardonic appraisal.

'He's a bit of a ——t and he's a bit of a bastard,' said a Sergeant standing next to me. 'But when it comes to action, he certainly knows his stuff.'

We were divided up into small parties of an officer, a German speaker, a non-commissioned officer or two, and about a dozen men. I went with that led by the Town Major, and he paced ahead of us to the trucks with a gay, mock-valiant step. As we drove along, sarcastic comments arose from the invisible faces of the men.

We reached a block of flats in the moonlight, and clumped into the front hall through an unlocked door. We waited, amid shuffling feet and banging of rifle butts, for the Town Major to tell us what to do.

'Well now,' he said. 'Which should we try first? Let's go up to the next floor to begin with.'

We thumped on the door of a flat. It was opened by a woman in a dressing-gown. There were whistles of approval from the soldiers. The Town Major, in a German phrase he'd learned by heart, said, 'Have you flags, weapons or deserters?'

She gaped in alarm without replying, and the Town Major edged his way past her. We went from room to room, while the woman stood holding herself by the dressing-gown. In the bedroom, there was a man wearing a grey coat over his pyjamas.

'Your husband?' said the Town Major.

She said no, it was her fiancé.

'A fiancé!' said the Town Major in a dirty voice. 'Well, I'll leave a couple of men with you while you question them,

Sergeant. And I'll go upstairs myself and see what else I can find'.

I took the man into the dining-room. He was most indignant, and said yes, certainly he was a soldier. 'What should one do?' he cried. 'I went to the assembly-point, and they told me it was full up, and I must come back later.'

One of the soldiers called me to another room, and handed me a pistol. 'What about this?' he said. 'It was in the drawer there. He can get shot for having it, can't he?'

I asked the German about it.

'It belongs to the lady's brother, but he is away. She feared to hand it in, lest they ask for news of him.'

'Is he a Party official?'

'No, he is a naval man, an officer. But he was on submarine duty, and she fears reprisals.'

Word came that the Town Major wanted me upstairs. I pocketed the revolver, and we climbed to the next floor. There, in another flat, the Town Major was examining an album of photographs of Adolf Hitler, with a buxom woman and a lad of about fifteen looking on. The woman was helping him turn over the pages. The lad was very angry.

'What do you think of this?' the Town Major said. "A propaganda book. I'm going to confiscate it.'

The woman told me her son had won the book as a prize when he was a leader in the *Hitlerjugend.* She looked at him with pride as she spoke, but shaking her head as if to say what a pity all his efforts would now be wasted.

'He is a clever lad,' she said, 'and you will see, he will do well in any field of action.'

All this was in German, but the Town Major, cocking an ear, caught the word *Hitlerjugend.* 'Ah, he's a Hitler youth,' he cried triumphantly.

'You won't find many lads who weren't.'

I tried to talk to the boy, but he was too furious to speak in other than monosyllables. Standing stiffly by the table, he looked like a figure in a patriotic poster. He was still wearing his uniform, from which only the badges had been removed, and his blue eyes stared at us from a face white with rage—so pale that his snow white hair grew out of his skin without noticeable change of colour. All this time his mother watched him with solicitude, looking at us as if to say, 'See how wonderful he is. He may have been wrong in his ideas, no doubt, but what a boy.'

We visited a few more flats with diminishing enthusiasm, and in one of them a sly, obliging man suggested we should go to the ground floor and see the *Blockleiter*, 'the Party representative in charge of the purity of the residents' opinions.'

When we knocked there, we heard a woman's shriek of fear. At last the woman, clutching a child in her arms, came to the door. The *Blockleiter* was lurking behind her. Her terror was so great that it began to cause the soldiers acute embarrassment. The Town Major, perhaps to hide his own, pointed to a stock-whip hanging on the wall and demanded whether it was used for beating democrats.

'No, no, no,' said the *Blockleiter*. 'I am a cart-driver.'

'A likely tale. I'd better confiscate it.'

As we were going down again to the trucks, the woman came rushing out, still clutching her child, and cried, 'My money! Your soldiers have stolen my money from the chest of drawers!'

When this was translated, the Town Major glanced from the woman to the indignant soldiers, on whose faces could be read, 'I haven't taken her ——ing money, and if I have, what of it?'

'Yes, yes,' she cried. 'The little-one saw him take it. Tell the gentleman you saw Uncle take the money,' she prompted the child.

'We can't very well search everybody, can we,' the Town Major muttered. 'You'd better tell her she's mistaken, and if she comes round to my office in the morning, I'll see what I can do.'

By now the Town Major decided he'd had enough, and he asked the drivers to drop us off at the hotel.

The Sergeants had gathered in the bar to exchange anecdotes.

'Here's the man who's been purifying the city,' said Dennis, waving his glass at Sergeant Thackeray. 'We got tired of house-searching, and went round to the brothel, see? When they saw his red hat, they thought he was a General.'

'What were they like?'

"Quite friendly, rather terrible, you know. It's a small sort of a place. The directress was very taken by old Thackeray, though. Do you know what he told her? That they're all out of bounds except to us, and they'll have to be examined at once as a matter of routine.'

Everyone was convulsed with laughter.

'You mustn't give away these state secrets, Dennis,' Sergeant Thackeray said. 'Our friends here will be thinking we do these things for ulterior motives. Well, of course, we do, but it's also liad down in the book of rules that we have to supervise the vice.'

'If it comes to that, they're turning the whole country into a brothel, with their Non-fraternisation ban,' someone said. 'That's the effect it's having.'

'Have you heard it's out in Orders that the ban's extended to cover Allied women as well?' said someone else. 'That shows what it's always meant.'

'It'll checkmate more than one crafty sod who thought he'd found a loophole.'

'There's a rumour they're going to let us fraternise with Gerry children.'

'What are children?'

'Anything that's too young.'

'So you can talk to the little girl by kind permission of the Army, and get busted if you speak to her elder sister?'

'Perhaps the elder sister won't feel like letting you talk to the kid either, if that's our attitude.'

'Give me the Non-frat. order, rather than that. At least you know where you are.'

A toast was drunk to the Area Commander, and soon the conversation turned on the real Beast of Belsen, and what would be his fate. Thackeray, it seemed, had a knowledge of hanging. 'I've studied the matter a bit,' he said, 'and it's all a question of the knot. You must get that right in relation to the weight. As a matter of fact, we've made a few experiments, though I don't suppose our services will be needed in that connection.' As he developed this theme, a hush fell on his audience.

Walter created a diversion by saying, 'Well personally, I don't approve of hanging, unless it's done in public.'

'Now, you're mistaken there,' Thackeray told him. 'That would create undesirable mob interest.'

'I say if you're going to do it, everybody should be there, the judge and jury and the members of Parliament. It shouldn't be done behind locked doors.'

Sergeant Thackeray shook his head. 'Only the lowest of the low would turn up to see. It's much better to have it done discreetly by experts, in the proper way.'

I went up to the office, where Cuthbert was still sitting typing. He rubbed his eyes and said, 'Thank goodness that's nearly finished. And if Gordon thinks he can get anything more out of those secretaries than I have, I'm sure he's mistaken.'

'They've gone, haven't they?'

'Oh, I should think so, by now. Gordon came up an hour or so ago and suggested he should see if he could find out something further. He let one of them go, and took the other off to question her.'

'Took her where?'

'Where? I don't know. I didn't want him disturbing me here.'

I went through to the annexe to Gordon's room. There was a light under the door. I listened a minute, heard nothing, then mentally shrugged my shoulders and went out into the yard and over to the servants' dormitory.

The Belgian girl was mending stockings, and sitting on another bed I saw Cornelis, with his arm round a lean girl. He greeted me with his usual politeness, and when half an hour had gone by, said, 'Good night, Sir,' and turned off a light that plunged his end of the room into near-darkness. The Belgian girl frowned, and shaking her head and tut-tutting, she turned out the other light as well.

Another message reached us from Major Bane next morning:

> Dutch informant SNOUCKAERT states HOERNER, high Gestapo official, may be hiding at one of three addresses known to him. SNOUCKAERT will be brought to your office to indicate these addresses and identify HOERNER.
>
> Though interrogation not yet pressed home, it would appear SNOUCKAERT was himself in service of Gestapo. Consequently, after capture of HOERNER or otherwise, arrest SNOUCKAERT.

'You'd better do this,' the Captain said.

'I've got a lot on today.'

'Well, it seems important, and I think you'd better see this person.'

'I'd rather get one of the others to do it, if you don't mind.'

The Captain looked at me. 'I'd prefer you to do it, you know. I leave it to you who you take with you, of course.'

As it happened, only Gordon was available, and when Snouckaert had been brought round from Corps, we saw him together in the office. He was a devious, voluble man. He seemed so used to invention that he could no longer divide fact from fiction, and he seemed aware of this himself. Yet he was positive about the Gestapo official Hoerner, and very anxious for us to believe him.

'How did you come to know him?' Gordon said.

'I gave him information, you understand.'

'What sort of information?'

'Unimportant things.'

'Such as what?'

The Dutchman dropped his voice, and looking over his shoulder, said, 'I also know where there is a treasure hidden.'

'A treasure? What sort of a treasure?'

'Things brought from Jewish homes in Holland.'

'And where is it?'

'You will see. First we will catch Hoerner, then I shall show you.'

Following the Dutchman's directions, we drove south for twenty miles until we reached a fair-sized town in ruins. He showed us to a hotel near the central cross-roads. 'That was the headquarters of the Gestapo,' he said. 'Hoerner also lived there.'

'He won't be here any longer. Didn't he have any other address?'

'Yes, but I am not sure of it.'

'I thought you knew all the places where he could be found.'

'Oh, it is the address of the treasure that I know—not all the secret addessses of Hoerner. But here we can see the hotel Manager, he will surely tell us.'

'Was the Manager working for the Gestapo.'

'No, no, they took rooms from him only. But he would know such things, perhaps.'

We found a military canteen had already been started on the ground floor, and the Dutchman led us up to a large room where steel filing-cabinets were piled in a pyramid on the linoleum. 'This was their office,' he said. 'Evidently now deserted.'

We were told the Manager had moved to an outbuilding at the far end of the courtyard. The door there was opened by a wiry man whose face was lined and weather-worn. He apologised for being in slippers, and invited us into the dining-room. We asked him where Hoerner had gone.

'That I cannot say. If I knew, I would surely tell you, as I do not like those people.' He looked pointedly at the Dutchman, who returned him a self-satisfied leer. 'They all left some days ago, though I expect they are still in the neighbourhood. Don't you know where your friend Hoerner is?'

'I have explained to these gentlemen I do not know all the different places.'

The Manager shrugged his shoulders wearily. 'Have you enquired in the Notification Office at the Town Hall?' he said.

'Hoerner wouldn't have left his address there, would he?'

'One never knows. It is, after all, a regulation that all residents, whatever their occupation, must register their address. Why do you not enquire?'

He came with us as far as the door.

'You have seen the state of the city?' he said. 'A pretty sight. For that we have to thank the S.S. General. He ordered a fanatical resistance. A fanatical resistance! The S.S., when they retreated here, behaved as if in enemy country—shooting, looting and so on and so forth. Elite behaviour!'

At the Notification Office, a clerk told us Mr. Hoerner lived at the hotel we'd just left. 'What about the other address?' Gordon said. 'The second one,' he added sharply.

The clerk handed him a card without answering. On the foot of it, under the word 'Private,' another address was typed. It was that of a house in the road down which we'd driven into the town.

We left the Dutchman trying to hide himself in the back of the car, and knocked at the door. A middle-aged woman opened it, and we walked in and asked for Hoerner.

'There is no Mr. Hoerner here.'

We pushed past her up the stairs and opened the doors of several rooms. In one of them a man's clothing was lying about, and there were two half-packed suitcases. We started looking for papers in drawers and cupboards.

'What are you doing?' said a voice, and we turned to see another, younger woman in the doorway. She had a hard, passionate face and her voice, though she spoke with great emphasis, had no exactly definable emotion.

'Who might you be?' Gordon said.

'I am who I am. What do you seek?'

Gordon went over, stood in front of her and said, 'Where is he?'

'I live here alone.'

'With these clothes?'

'Well, he is already gone,' she said, after a slight pause.

The older woman had come up on the landing and interrupted in a hurried voice, 'No, it is not true, he is at the market garden.'

'Ah, Frau Rümelin, Frau Rümelin,' the younger woman burst out.

'I cannot help it. He is at the market garden, engaged as a labourer, I cannot help it—I must guard myself also against trouble.'

We asked where the market garden was, and hurried down to the car.

'Do we leave her here?' I said.

'Why not? She won't have time to warn him. The old lady can look after herself. And if we don't find Hoerner, we'll pick the young one up later on.'

'You think she was in on it too?'

'Whether she was or wasn't, if we hold her, it'll make him give himself up if we don't find him now.'

The market garden was on a rise overlooking the town. We went into an office surrounded by greenhouses. A very old man said he'd no one called Hoerner working for him.

'Have you taken on anyone in the last week? This man would be about forty-five.'

'Oh yes, I have engaged several, but I do not know the ages.'

'Take us to see these men.'

'Can you not see them after their work? They are busy now in the fields. Why does this man interest you?'

'Don't be nosey. Come with us at once.'

We set off with the Dutchman some distance behind. After we'd crossed a road, we came into another field where men were hoeing in the distance by a railway line.

'There!' the Dutchman said.

'Which one?'

'See! Over by himself, on the left.'

Snouckaert halted, and we started off in a wide circle so as to get between Hoerner and the railway. As we came nearer, one or two of the hoers looked up, but went on working. When we got close to him, he raised his head. He had a pale, clever face without any expression at all.

Gordon sidled up and patted him all over. 'Hoerner?' he said. The man nodded. 'Then come with us.'

He dropped his hoe and walked between us without looking back. The market gardener hurried up.

'Where are you taking him?' he cried angrily. 'If you take away my men, how can I grow vegetables for the town?'

When we reached the Dutchman, he looked malevolently at Hoerner, who glanced at him without recognition. 'Congratulations,' the Dutchman said.

We drove back to the house to get his kit. Gordon stayed with Hoerner in the car while I went up to the first floor again. The landlady was nowhere to be seen. The younger woman had been collecting his clothes together in one of the suitcases.

'You have him?' she said. 'What will happen to him?'

'He will be imprisoned.'

'I want to go with him,' she said coldly and formally, with a desperate note in her voice. 'I demand that you also arrest me. We cannot be separated.'

'Even if you came, you would be separated.'

'Then I can come?'

'No.'

She sighed, and looked at me intently. 'Can I see him?'

'No, it is better not.'

She said nothing, and I took the suitcase and went out.

'We'll park him somewhere while we look for this treasure the Dutchman talks about,' said Gordon.

'Let's get back.'

'What's the hurry? There may be something in it. We'll find a Unit with a guardroom, and put Hoerner in there an hour.'

First we drove to the hotel again to get Hoerner to say in which filing-cabinets the important documents were kept. He told us in a serviceable way, neither with reluctance nor zeal.

I stayed at the hotel to look through the papers while Gordon took him off in search of a guardroom. I read some of the confidential reports. They had all the meanness, the self-satisfaction of the author, the determination to fit the crime to the man, and the smell of relative inaccuracy as to fact and total inaccuracy as to the spirit, common to secret police reports the world over.

The hotel Manager came strolling in, still in his slippers. 'So you got him?' he said. 'Good riddance. These people have corrupted us all.'

He picked up a file of reports, and thumped it down on a cabinet. It slid onto the floor, scattering its sheets.

'Our leaders,' he said, emphasising the word disgustedly, 'have plunged our people light-heartedly into catastrophe. And they, who thought they could rule a nation—not one of them is fit, as I was, to be captain of a ship. See! Even at this late hour, they could still save half the destruction going on! But they lack all sense of responsibility. They have taught us Germans that no one is responsible for anything. Obey! Obey! Nothing else. In a ship we also obey. But we know why we do so.'

When Gordon came back with the Dutchman, he led us down different streets, seeming to forget their names, till we grew certain that the treasure was an invention. But he must have been whetting our appetites, for at last he cried triumphantly, 'I remember!' and directed us to a warehouse near the hotel. 'In there,' he said. 'Ask for the chests brought from Holland.'

We went into the office, and when the clerks there seemed doubtful, we said we meant the chests left by Hoerner. Without further demur, a foreman took us out to a courtyard where a dozen big packing-cases were stacked beneath an overhanging roof. We said we wanted to see inside them.

'In all of them?'

'Open this first,' said Gordon, and we gathered round. Someone fetched a chisel, and as the lid was prised up, we saw a strange collection of articles inside, all carefully packed. It was as though someone had gone round a rich country house, taking his pick of the best things in it. There were jodhpurs, sporting guns, porcelain dinner services, flannel and linen suits, small carpets and oil paintings, among other things.

Gordon nodded slightly as each object came into view. 'We'll come back here with one of the trucks.' he said.

'We ought to declare this stuff.'

He looked at me and said, 'Why?'

'It's Dutch, isn't it?'

'How do you know it is?'

'The Dutchman says so, and there are the markings on the cases.'

Gordon smiled, showing both rows of teeth. 'Do you really imagine these things will ever find their way back to the owners? If you report them, you'll be making a present of them to whoever you tell.'

'That's not the point.'

'Well, what is the point? If you don't want some of this stuff, the rest of us do. And even you may be glad of a bit of it, I should imagine.'

'I'm going to declare it now.'

'To who?'

'To Mil. Gov.'

'Mil. Gov.! This is the end. Won't you be good enough to wait twenty-four hours and consult Dennis and the others first?'

'No. Take what you want, and then we'll go round to Mil. Gov.'

He off-loaded some of the things into the car, had the case sealed again and gave the foreman instructions I couldn't hear.

On our way round to the Mil. Gov. office, he said, 'There's really no need for you to report anything but the guns.'

'I'm going to report the lot.'

The German policeman at the Mil. Gov. office showed me to the Interpreter's room, and she turned out to be an elderly lady. The argument as to whether 'a visitor's business must first be stated' was arising, when a red-faced Major came in.

'More trouble, Mrs. Krumsel? Never mind, I'll deal with him. What is it, Sergeant?'

'I want to report some arms and other things that have been found.'

'Arms are a Provost matter. Take it to them, will you?'

'I thought the Public Safety Officer might be interested in the arms.'

'We've no P.S.O., as it happens, so do as I say, will you? And while you're here, there's something you can do for me. You see those people sitting on that bench? Just keep an eye on them for me, will you, while I send my policeman round to the mess.'

'Sorry, Sir. I'm on duty just now.'

'We're all on duty. But first things first. Do as I tell you, now.'

'I've a prisoner waiting downstairs I'm escorting to Corps Staff.'

'Have you? Well, in that case, you'd better be on your way. I suppose I'll manage somehow.'

As I got into the car, Gordon said, 'Well, did you tell them all about it?'

'They weren't interested.'

'You mean you didn't tell them?'

'No. They say the guns are a Provost matter.'

'So they are. All right, we'll inform Sergeant Thackeray.'

We returned in silence to pick up the prisoner. We found him sitting in the guardroom with his boots off, being examined by officers and soldiers who had come to see a Gestapo official. I drove on the way home, with Gordon and the Dutchman in the back among the loot, and Hoerner sitting beside me. He gazed steadily ahead with his hands resting on his knees, and didn't open his mouth till we were nearing the outskirts of our town. Then he said, 'May I speak?'

'Go on.'

'I wish to offer my services to the new authority,' he said, without pleading and without diffidence.

'There's no question of that.'

'But to whom do I make this application?'

'It won't be any use making such an application.'

He ran his tongue over his lips and said nothing.

When we got back to the Pfeufer, Gordon drove Hoerner off to Major Bane, and I went up to the office with the Dutchman. He was pleased with his day's work, and sat on the edge of a chair like a dog that expects to be patted. But when I asked him for personal details and began writing them on a form, he realised something had gone wrong.

'Why do you ask me these things?' he said suspiciously.

'You also have to be detained.'

'But why?'

'Because of your work for the Gestapo.'

I could see he felt he had been betrayed.

'But why? But why? I came to you freely, I enabled you to capture this valuable man and told you about the treasure . . . Also of your Dutch friends, and I have other informations, important informations . . .'

When I drove him round to the city jail, his buoyancy had left him, and he looked at me less with hatred than with wounded astonishment and fear.

THE BALTIC CITY

WHEN THE CORPS SECURED A BRIDGEHEAD OVER THE ELBE, AN Armoured Division broke out and started racing towards the sea to link up with the Russians and cut off the German armies up by Denmark. As soon as we heard of the capture of a big town on the Baltic, we started out. It wasn't necessary to travel by night, but we were urged on, like everybody else, by an instinct to quicken the pace in the last lap of the journey.

We reached the bridge over the Elbe at a point where it passed between steep banks. Gordon hurried across, but Walter and I were held up among the vehicles waiting on the cliff. We got out of the car and stood looking down on the river.

A motor-cyclist came over the bridge against the traffic, and as he accelerated up the hill towards us, picking his way among the trucks, we saw it was Harry. Walter hailed him and he rode up. He told us he'd gone ahead with the despatch riders to check the road for the headquarters convoy. Then he said, 'This is the last time you'll be seeing me, I expect. Do you know what they've done? As soon as the Corps gets to that town, they're posting a draft of us despatch riders back to the Regiment, and then out to Burma.'

'Burma? You poor sod,' said Walter. 'That's a bit of bad.'

'I'm unlucky, all right. The dirty bastards, they've picked me on purpose.'

'What do you mean, "on purpose," lad? They've drawn your number out of the hat. It might happen to any of us.'

'It's happened to me, that's all I know. And I say it's because they've found I've been going with a Gerry girl.'

Walter gazed at him unblinkingly, mildly but severely. 'You should have stuck to the one and only back in Holland.'

'Maybe I should. But that's no reason for high-jacking me out to Burma.'

'You're making a mistake, Harry. If you were an officer they might have done that to you, but for people like us, they just shut their eyes and stab.' Walter reflected. 'I'll tell you what you should do, though. You should put in at once for retention here on compassionate grounds.'

'Which?'

'That you're getting wed to the *mejuffrouw*.'

'I couldn't do that.'

'Why not? Because they'd think you were dodging the column? Don't be daft.'

'No. I couldn't because of the other woman.'

'Can you be all that serious? She's not as important to you as all that, is she, this Gerry girl? It's your whole life you've got to consider, not just a passing fancy.'

'This wasn't a fancy.'

'Park your bike, Harry, we haven't got that much time. Listen to me. If you give up one woman you're pledged to for another, you'll give up the second as well before long, and then you'll have two big worries. Go with other women if you find you have to, by all means. But don't try to marry them all.'

The traffic clattered by on the bridge below. 'I've made up my mind,' said Harry. 'It's her or nothing.'

Walter shook his head. For the first time, I saw him really worried.

'Well, Harry, in that case, there's no more to be said, is there. But just a minute. You want to stay here in Europe anyway, don't you? Why not take Major Bane into your confidence, tell him the real reasons, and get him to back up an application for retention?'

'Take Major Bane into my confidence? You know the Major. Still, it's an idea. But the order's from high up, way above Corps level.'

'Try, Harry, all the same.'

'All right, I will. The trouble is, I've always been pestering the Major for a transfer back to the Regiment. But I'll have a bash at it.'

'That's the spirit. Stake all your luck. You've nothing to lose.'

The trucks began to move down the hill.

'Well, look after yourself, Harry, and keep in touch,' said Walter. 'Let us know what happens.'

'Thanks, Walter, I will. And whatever they do, I'll be back. They can't keep me out in Burma forever.'

'Of course they can't,' Walter shouted, as we started over to the car. And then, as we drove across the river, he said, 'A thoroughly decent kiddy. It's hard on these lads, you know. There's five years of his youth gone soldiering, away from the proper influences. He's tried to make something of his life, too, but what a pity his falling in love with a bit of frat.'

'Have you been in love, Walter?'

'Me? As a matter of fact, I've never known for sure. I'm not sure I know what they call falling in love, really means.'

We caught up with Gordon, and night fell as we drove on. Convoys took different roads and some turned off over tracks across the fields. Lurching along in the twilight, we saw trembling lamps all over the country. No one thought about air attack or mines any more.

By two o'clock we'd grown so tired we stopped at a farm-house. It was packed to the ceilings with refugees. We exchanged food with them for the best bedroom. The convoys rolled by all through the night.

In the morning we joined the traffic, struggled over cart tracks, and reached a macadam road that ran beside a lake. Soon we could smell the sea, and we drove into a big city.

Civilians were removing road-blocks that had been put up to defend it. Others gathered round notice-boards, reading messages that separated families had pinned there. Easterners and freed prisoners were wandering diagonally all over the streets, many carrying arms. Shops were broken open, and one or two fires had been started. A lad ran up and pushed a Luger through the car window. 'For you,' he cried, with a face of delight. 'I have myself disarmed a German soldier.'

Standing at a street corner, watching the scene, was a man in a grey Homburg hat. We beckoned him over. 'Do you know this town?' I said.

'I am not of it, since I am from Stockholm. But I know it well enough.'

'Will you show us where the big Nazis live?'

He smiled, and getting in beside me, he directed us over bridges that spanned narrow arms of the sea. We reached a quarter with wide roads and big houses set back in their own gardens. He waved his hand at several. 'Here might be suitable,' he said. 'That one is the *Oberbürgermeister's*.'

We didn't care for it, and preferred a gabled building next door. As we were getting out, an important looking man came out of the Burgomaster's house and walked down the pavement towards us. After hesitating, he came over. The Swede raised his hat.

'Excuse me,' said the *Oberbürgermeister*, if such he was. 'May I ask a question? Who will occupy our town? Will it be your good selves—or the Russians?'

'The Russians, I expect.'

'Oh, Heaven preserve us.'

'Would you prefer the stupid English?'

His eyes narrowed, he sketched a smile. 'Stupid? Oh, no. Stupid? No one says that.'

We went into the gabled house through an open terrace door. A large man was standing there with his hands behind his back, gazing through the windows at a view of the towers of the city. He turned round with fussy alarm when we told him fourteen men would be coming to live with him. 'Impossible!' he cried. 'My wife is nervous, apart from all else.'

'We won't disturb your wife. Will you show us over?'

'No really, this is unheard of. There are other houses. This is a small house.'

'This is a colossal house.'

'Why do you choose me? Are there not others?'

'Are you a Party member?'

He looked at us as if we'd dealt him an unfair blow. 'Does that matter—my being a National Socialist? Is that why you come here?'

Later on, he sought me out and said his wife would like to meet me. 'I have explained you are a respectable person,' he said. She was a tired, anxious woman, and a lanky girl of fifteen stood beside her, holding her hand. 'My husband was wrong to make difficulties,' she said. 'I hope you will be comfortable, but we have little food.'

'We bring our own.'

'And the war is over?'

'Not yet, but soon now. They say the Generals are arranging an armistice.'

'And Hamburg—Hamburg has fallen?' said the husband. He shifted from one foot to another. 'We are maritime cities here,' he said. 'We have always had close relations with England.'

I went out for a walk in the town. It was the biggest we'd been in yet, with towered gateways and red brick houses backing onto estuaries of the sea. Though parts were destroyed, there was enough left to give the feeling of being in a living city again.

As I was passing some modern villas, I noticed a hand-made American flag hanging from a nautical arrangement of lines and pulleys above a porch. I went over and knocked, and getting no reply, walked round to the back of the house. In a garden there I saw three people sitting in deck-chairs at the top of a rise sloping down to the water.

A woman caught sight of me, and she nudged the two men, who got up. One was tall, with a high-domed forehead, and the other had a coy, mincing manner. 'Good afternoon,' I said. They bowed interrogatively. I asked about the flag.

'Oh,' said the tall man, 'though a native of this city, I am, as it happens, also an American citizen, having lived in the States many years. This lady is my wife, this gentleman a colleague.'

'How do you do?' she said. 'It is only my husband who is the American, not I.'

'As for me,' said the colleague, 'to be an American is beyond my modest ambition.'

The tall man explained that he was a bookseller. 'I have specialised in seafaring works,' he said, 'and in my lists you will not find much that is controversial. This question interests me, though, for I imagine certain books will be forbidden?'

I said I thought they would.

'Works of a National Socialist tendency, of course, and no doubt historical books of a patriotic nature? Books on Bismarck, no doubt, perhaps?'

'But how far back is one to go in such a process?' the mincing colleague asked. 'A work relating to the conquest of England by our joint forefathers, would that be considered objectionable?'

I said I wasn't so sure about that.

'I am in some perplexity,' the bookseller went on. 'I was looking through what volumes are left to me only yesterday, and I said to myself: "These few may be confiscated, these will be secure—but what of this and that?" And I decided the best would be to put the doubtful works aside a while, till passions grow calmer.'

The mincing man, who had listened with a fixed smile, said, 'Forgive the question: why did the Royal Air Force bomb this city which has clearly a cultural rather than a strategic importance? What is the purpose of such terror-raids?'

I said it was a matter of an eye for an eye.

'You imply we did also such things in England?' They looked at one another. 'If that is so, we have not heard of it,' the bookseller said.

They asked me for news of English firms I knew nothing about, and the bookseller invited me to see his collection of rare editions. He offered me a volume of woodcuts, given away by his firm as a New Year gift, which showed the beauties of a hundred German cities. 'And how many of these now remain for our children to love as we have done?' he said.

Gordon sat at the lunch table, reading in the last copy of the local paper the news of Adolf Hitler's death. Walter said to me, 'When you've finished, what about going and having a look at the Russians?'

'They'll still be a long way off.'

'Come on. I want to see what they're like.'

We had great difficulty finding a way out of the city. The streets were littered with burned-out vehicles and the crowds of refugees grew denser.

'And still they come,' said Walter. 'Well, there's one thing you can say for the Gerries—they've got guts. If only they had a bit more sense and were better led, they'd be all right.'

We turned east through a wood, and drove along parallel to the Baltic until we met an Artillery team manning a gun that pointed down the road ahead of us. Walter got out and talked to them, then came back looking puzzled.

'They don't know what they're here for,' he said. 'The road ahead's supposed to be clear now, It wouldn't be on account of the Ruskis, would it?'

'Well, we might as well go on.'

We passed caravans of people, now all heading east. At a hill too steep for the loaded trucks, they had got out to push. We overtook struggling and shouting parties until, nearing a village, we saw another gun, this time pointing towards us. We drove up very slowly and found it was manned by American para-troops. 'It's a bit of a mystery,' said Walter, 'unless we've been going through enemy-held territory.'

We asked an officer. 'Yes,' he said, 'there's still some Germans holed up between the road and the ocean.'

'We didn't see any. Is the road clear from now on?'

'You got me, Sergeant.'

'How far are the Russians from here, do you know?'

'Not sure. You'd better ask a British outfit, there's one up the road beyond here, east.'

We went on again. 'A typical military balls-up,' said Walter.

We coasted along a flat patch for several miles, until we saw the sea again and came into a small town. The houses were shuttered, and there weren't any civilians about. Our own tanks were moving about in the streets, and we stopped an armoured car and asked an officer where the Russians were. He seemed suspicious, and waved us vaguely on.

A few miles outside the town, there was a barrier across the road. Some soldiers of ours were standing next to the Russians by the side of it. We stopped and walked over. One of our men was comparing medal ribbons with a Russian. Otherwise each small group was keeping to itself.

'Do you see much of them?' we asked a Corporal.

'Only up here.'

'Don't they come down into the town at all?'

'Oh, no. Nothing like that.'

'Do our people go over their side?'

'No, it's not allowed.'

A truck came up laden with Easterners. The barrier was raised and they drove over the hilltop into the Russian zone.

3

The Occupation Begins

THE GENERAL

THE DAY AFTER OUR ARRIVAL IN THIS BALTIC CITY, THE CAPTAIN went to see Major Bane, and came back rather dissatisfied. 'All very vague,' he told us. 'I know the name of our next town, it's about twenty-five miles further north, in fact it's the one we'll be settling in to occupy. But Major Bane seemed to think some sort of an armistice is being negotiated, and until he hears about that, we ought to stay put down here.' But we persuaded the Captain to let the usual advance party leave that evening, and Dennis and Gordon went off ahead with two of the others.

The rest of us left next morning, and after travelling fifteen miles, we reached a road-block manned by a Tank Regiment. When they said we weren't allowed through, the Captain got impatiently out of his Mercedes and made out to the sentries that we'd been ordered up by Corps. 'Then will you see the officer, Sir? Our instructions are nobody.'

We walked across to the farmhouse. The Captain showed his papers and asked the Major there for permission to go on.

'Not unless you've got a signed permit from the Corps Commander, I'm much afraid.'

'That's unusual, isn't it?'

'Theirs not to reason why, old boy. My orders say absolutely not anyone.'

'Couldn't you ring through to Corps?'

'You can, if you like. You'll find it's as I say, though.'

The Captain tried for twenty minutes, but couldn't get on to Major Bane.

'Well, you can go ahead if you really want to,' the Tank Major said at last. 'But it's on your responsibility and without my permission, in fact I don't think I've seen you.'

We returned to the check-point, the barrier was raised and we went on. After we'd driven several miles, we began to realise something was wrong. We met no British troops whatever, and as we passed through the villages we saw the German army intact, with its transport, Unit headquarters and guards mounted armed. The countryside was packed with soldiers, as if a gigantic force, used to free movement in big spaces, had suddenly been confined into a small area. Our convoy attracted great attention. It was frequently saluted, and enemy vehicles drew aside to let it pass.

The Captain halted beside a lake. 'The war is over, isn't it?' he said. 'But look at that body of men there. They still seem warlike, don't they?' He pointed to an Artillery Unit camped by the lake. 'Let's go over and see them.'

'We can't very well ask them what's happening, can we?'

'No, but perhaps they'll tell us.'

We left our convoy and drove through the camp. The men there stopped in what they were doing and watched us. We reached a chalet, surrounded by pines, that was perched above the water's edge. We walked past the guard up to the front verandah, where a group of officers and women personnel were sitting gazing at the water. They all rose and stared at us curiously, nobody saying anything. Some of the women melted out of sight, and a Lieutenant came up to within a few feet of us, waiting for us to speak first.

The Captain said Good-morning, and asked if we were on the right road for the town we were going to. The Lieutenant didn't know, and glanced round at his companions, who looked at one another till someone said, yes, he thought so.

'We are not from these parts, we have just arrived here,' the Lieutenant said. 'We moved up over the armistice-line last night.'

'The armistice-line,' said the Captain.

'Yes, we are certainly well within it, are we not?'

'Oh, I should say so.'

There was a pause.

'You would wish to see the Colonel?' the Lieutenant asked.

The Captain said that wouldn't be necessary, and we walked back together to the car. 'I didn't like to ask him about that armistice-line,' he said, 'but it seems there is one, and we're on the wrong side of it.'

'Should we go on?'

'Yes, I think so, now we're here.'

As we drove back to the main road, he looked over his shoulder at the chalet. 'That might do as a week-end villa, once these people are demobilised,' he said. 'We could come down here swimming when it gets hotter. Remind me to send someone to book it later on.'

We started again towards the town. As we drove into it, the crowds in the streets gathered round our cars, and we had to slow down to a walking pace. Their attitude seemed one of intense curiosity, and there was a great air of expectation. We pulled up outside the Town Hall.

A platoon of armed policemen came marching down the road towards us. This surprised Walter so much that he called them to a halt in parade-ground tones. They stopped in the middle of the crowd, and a stocky Captain, who looked like a wrestler, hurried forward.

'Why are these men carrying arms and marching?' our Captain demanded.

'We have the General's permission, the General's permission,' the police Captain said.

'What General?'

'The English General who came through here. Till your own troops arrive.'

'Are there no English troops here?'

'Yes, on the airfield, some air personnel have landed. Also there are four British soldiers at the Gessler villa. Otherwise none. That is why we keep order till they arrive.'

'Those four got here last night?'

'Even so. Please: come with me into the office.'

We made our way up the steps through the onlookers. The police Captain led us into a guardroom, and a number of persons gathered there spun round. Some threw up *Heil Hitler* salutes.

'Who is the senior officer?' said our Captain.

'Colonel Kritzler, one moment,' the police Captain said, and he knocked at a door. A bald man with a large belly and small, weak eyes, came out. With him was a civilian in an expensive overcoat.

'Police Colonel Kritzler, the English officer, the Burgomaster, the English officer,' said the police Captain.

Everyone looked at everyone else.

'They have arrived, then?' the Colonel said.

'Only about ten of these gentlemen.'

'And what are your orders?' the Colonel asked our Captain.

The Captain told them about gathering in the arms, cameras

and binoculars, and the Colonel nodded as though he considered this reasonable. The Burgomaster came forward and asked the Captain what should be done about the stocks of food, the electricity works and whether officials should remain at their posts. The Captain made some vague recommendations; then said, 'Why are there no white flags?'

They looked at one another as do those reproached for neglecting a duty they are unaware of. 'White flags?' someone said.

'Yes. White flags should be hung from all houses.'

'What size of flag?' the Burgomaster asked.

'At least one metre square.'

'And from private dwellings as well as public buildings?'

'Especially from public buildings.'

The door was flung open and a burly man, wearing a belted mackintosh, stood poised in the entrance. He took a sharp pace forward towards the Captain, as if to receive a decoration, and cried, 'Horser.' The Captain stared at him. The officials looked embarrassed, and some frowned. Horser held out his hand. The Captain didn't take it. 'Who is this?' he said.

'The former *Kreisleiter*,' said the Burgomaster, after a general silence.

'I have come to render account to the British authorities,' said Horser.

'Yes; well, later on,' the Captain said.

'The archives are at your disposal. As the new authority, I place myself at your service.'

'We don't want you just now.'

'Whatever the future may be, continuity in affairs will have to be assured.'

'You may leave now. We shall inform you.'

As one intent to show he's not rebuffed by lack of understanding, Horser inclined his large body and went out.

The Captain told the officials that would be all for the moment, and asked them to show us to the Gessler villa where our men were. Only the Burgomaster gave a Nazi salute this time. The Captain glanced at him. 'Do tell that man not to do that,' he said to me.

An even larger crowd had gathered outside, with many Allied prisoners-of-war among them. A policeman got on the running-board of the leading car, and directed us through the town.

'Can that *Kreisleiter* really imagine he has any future?'

the Captain said. 'He'll be for the high jump, as soon as we can get some guards.'

'What about the others?'

'The Colonel's honorary S.S.—yes. The Burgomaster's an Automatic Arrest. Perhaps the police Captain will be all right.'

'Did you notice Horser's name?'

'What about it?'

'You remember Hengist and Horsa?'

'What about them?'

'They came from this part of the world, didn't they?'

The Captain was not interested in this idea.

Rivulets and small canals meandered round the town, and the villa, a big, new building in the style of a farmhouse adapted for town use, was set on an artificial island. We had to cross a bridge to reach it, and two *Wehrmacht* sentries standing at the entrance-gates, stepped back and presented arms. We went down a narrow, winding drive. Beyond the house, we could see a factory about a hundred yards off.

A very tall German, in a discreetly smart suit, was standing at the doorstep as we arrived. His hands were in his jacket pockets, and he looked at us out of mild, cautious eyes. 'Good morning,' he said, bowing slightly.

'Where are our people?' I asked him.

'Inside. They await you.'

'You are Gessler?' He partly bowed again.

We went through a hall into a light dining-room, with wide windows overlooking melancholy vistas of the island park. The furnishing was in the sort of taste that is rather tasteless, though expensive.

'Well, how do you like the billet?' Dennis asked. 'The smartest house in town.'

'What does the owner do?'

'Rudolf Gessler? He's a local magnate. He runs the cutlery works.'

Gordon rang for lunch.

'Well, in the first place,' the Captain said, as we all sat down, 'it looks as if we shouldn't be here at all.'

This was received with self-satisfied laughter, which subsided when the Captain didn't join in.

'I'll have to get in touch somehow with Major Bane before this evening, and ask him what the form is. Meanwhile, since we've got here, we might as well get dug in, but I shouldn't advise doing anything energetic till I've heard from him.'

'The German army were certainly surprised to see us,' said Dennis. 'They sent round an armed guard last night to protect us.'

'I noticed that. Against what are they protecting you, exactly?'

'They said they were responsible for our safety.'

'Is there anybody else in the town at all?'

'Only the Raf. We've contacted them.'

'And what do they say?'

'They've orders to stay on the airfield.'

I went out on the lawn after lunch, and walked round the park. In the middle of it there was an ornamental lake. Under some trees, sitting at wicker tables, I saw Rudolf Gessler and with him a grey, pink-faced woman as tall as himself, whom I took to be his wife. There were also two enormous girls. When they saw me, the ladies gave a stiff bow and Gessler got up and came slowly across the lawn, as one accustomed to show he is not in a hurry.

'Your comrades have said you will also need an office in the factory,' he told me. 'Would you wish to visit it?'

'All right, thank you.'

He led the way across the park. Beyond the lake was a late nineteenth century villa, painted white. 'My father's house,' he said.

'He lives there?'

'Oh no, he is no more. His own father built it.'

'Who's in it now?'

'Bombed-out relatives of ours, also some refugees.'

'And you built the new house?'

'Yes. You admire it?' I nodded. 'At all events, we Germans can be proud of our house-culture,' he said, with an interrogative frown. 'That much, I think, must be allowed.'

We had reached the office buildings beside the factory at the far end of the park. We went up the steps, and he opened the glass door with a latchkey.

'Normally, there is a door-keeper,' he explained, 'but at present, the factory is closed. There is little coal, you see, and the workers have dispersed. Besides, we await new orders to begin.'

'I should think there will be plenty of work.'

'Yes? Why, if I may ask?'

'Cutlery will always be needed.'

'Of course. Well, if we can get raw materials.'

He opened the door of an office with his name painted on it. There were leather chairs and a lot of carpet space. Behind the desk, there was the framed photograph surrounded by the wreath. He saw me looking at this, but said nothing.

'Was it a relative?'

'My son. He fell in Russia.'

'I'm sorry. Have you other children?'

'Another son, and my two daughters.'

'Where is he?'

'We do not know. He left us two months ago and we fear it was for the east. He was barely seventeen.'

He took me upstairs and showed me rooms that might do for an office. I told him I'd speak to the Captain about it.

'Excuse me, may I put a question? The Captain is your leader?'

'Yes.'

'And who comes next?'

'I do.'

'I see. But how does one tell that from your uniform?'

'By this crown here.'

He examined it and seemed to be making a mental note.

'Then you are the superior of those who came last night?' He paused, then went on confidentially, 'Well, they have made certain arrangements in the house . . .'

'If there's anything you don't like, you can always mention it. But you ought to know they could have put you out altogether. The regulation is civilians and soldiers mustn't live in the same place.'

He meditated on this, and sighed. The expression on his face, if I read it rightly, said, 'Perhaps it is not your fault personally that you bring these troubles on me, but you cannot know what sorrows I have to bear.'

I thought it would be a good idea to look round the town

before evening, so I drove back to the Town Hall to pick up a guide. Another British car was standing outside, hemmed in by a big crowd. I went over and found it belonged to a War Correspondent—not the one from whom we'd re-stolen the car.

'Oh Sergeant, are you living here?' this Correspondent said.

'I think we're going to.'

'Well, I've been interviewing these fellows, these Frenchmen and Belgians. Apparently they've got nothing to eat. Hasn't anything been laid on?'

'There are only a dozen of us, we've just arrived, and we're not sure if we should be here.'

'I was a bit surprised to see you, I admit. I thought it was one of the arrangements of the cease-fire that no British troops were to come over the imaginary line yet awhile.'

'What is this imaginary line?'

'The road here crosses it at a check-point about ten miles back. You must have passed it coming up. This side of it, the Germans are still in charge, pro. tem.'

'How long is the pro. tem. going to last?'

'Oh, it'll only be a matter of days, I expect. It doesn't mean a thing. Well, I must be on my way to Copenhagen, if I can get there.'

'I'd like to go with you.'

'Come on.'

'No, no such luck.'

'So long, then. I know it's not my business, but see what you can do about food for these people, won't you. They told you about the prison, I suppose?'

'What prison?'

'They all say there's a prison here full of Allies.'

I questioned the Frenchmen and Belgians about this as soon as he had left. They insisted that it was so, and that these men should be let out at once. I said I'd go and see.

The police Captain allotted me an elderly constable, who seemed to welcome the prospect of an outing. 'What do you wish to look at?' he said, rubbing his hands with a scraping sound.

'Everything. The airfield, the barracks, the labour camps, the prison. All the big places.'

The policeman explained, as we drove along, that he wasn't really a policeman, but a reservist. 'I am a grocer,' he said, with satisfaction. 'Soon I shall be able to go back to my shop.'

Going down a bumpy road, we saw a lad in a blue cloth suit running up towards us. He came on full tilt at the car, and as I swerved to miss him, he jumped onto the foot-rest, and looked through at us with an expression of torment. 'Come! Come!' he cried.

'What is it?'

'To our camp! Come! Come! The *Lagerführer* . . . you will see . . . . come!'

This was all he seemed able to say, so I told him to get in and show us the way. As he pointed out the road, he patted my back and grabbed hold of my arm. The policeman looked on tolerantly. 'It will be the Polish camp,' he said.

When we arrived, the young Pole seized my hand and pulled me along, looking ahead, then looking back at us, until we came out into a field surrounded by huts. Outside one of these, men and women were moving about in groups, and on the threshold, facing them, there was a man wearing a black suit. The young Pole shouted to them, and they gathered round us.

'Who is in charge here?' I said. They pointed to the man in the black suit, who approached till he stood on the outskirts of the crowd. 'The *Lagerführer*,' they cried.

'Which is your own head man?'

A Pole wearing breeches and leggings stepped forward. The others fell back slightly. 'I am,' he said.

'Well, tell me what it is.'

'The comrades wish to hoist the Polish flag, but the *Lagerführer* has forbidden it.'

'That's all right. Hoist your flag.'

They shouted, and ran over to the flagpole, leaving the *Lagerführer* standing alone. I went over to him, followed closely by the spokesman in the breeches.

'Why did you refuse them?' I said. He was a severe man with grey, unshaven cheeks. 'It is my duty to refuse them,' he answered.

'Why?'

'I am in charge. Until I receive new orders, I must enforce those that have been given me.'

A home-made flag had reached the top of the mast. The crowd gazed at it with rapture.

'And what do I do now?' the German said. 'You have stripped away my authority.'

'Stay here and see to the organisation of the camp until you get further instructions.'

'And discipline?' He looked at me coldly. I turned to the man in the breeches. 'Tell your people that they must stay quiet till we make new arrangements.'

'And do they have to obey the *Lagerführer*?'

'He remains in charge of administration.'

'Administration? That will be difficult without control. However, we shall do for the best.'

Three or four men who had detached themselves from the group round the flag, were trying to attract my attention. I went up to them. Their faces wore a serious, reproachful look. 'What is it?' I said.

One of them shook his head and said, 'A bad man.'

'Who?'

He pointed to the spokesman in the breeches, who was walking back to the hut with the *Lagerführer*. 'A traitor,' a second man said. They looked at one another, lowered their voices, and the first man whispered, 'A bad Pole. The Germans appointed him camp leader. But he is not our leader.'

'Who is, then?'

They said that they were.

'I can't do anything about it now. You'll have to wait for a day or two. Then new arrangements will be made.'

'We cannot obey this man any longer,' they insisted. And their eyes said, 'If you do not accept responsibility, it is understood we shall assume it.'

The man in the breeches came up again, and the others turned away. 'Everything will be as you say,' he told me in a loud voice. 'I shall carry out your instructions for these people.'

I went back to the car. Two girls ran up and gave me a bunch of tattered flowers. As I carried these along, the policeman walked flat-footedly beside me, humming a tune to himself. 'Difficult, difficult . . .' he said. 'One tries to do one's best in such cases . . .' He saw my look, and added cheerfully, 'Now I will show you the barracks.'

'What regiments are there?'

'Oh, something of everything, a real Macedonia. There has been great confusion.'

We drove down a newly tarred road with a big, modern

barracks built along one side of it. The barrack square was thronged with soldiers. 'Poor fellows,' said the policeman.

A young soldier came up and leaned against the window. 'English?' he said. 'We are glad you have come. We have been waiting for you.' He stared at me, clutching the car door. It was difficult to tell whether he meant it, or in what way he meant it.

We drove past the barrack blocks, all crowded with men. The policeman sat at attention, as though being driven in a review. As we reached the further side of the square, an officer came running out of one of the blocks and over to the car. 'The Adjutant would like to see you,' he said.

'What about?'

'Please. Come to see the Adjutant.'

I hesitated, then got out and followed him to the first floor through corridors filled with soldiers waiting outside offices. He knocked, a ringing voice answered, he opened the door, stood aside, and I went in.

An athletic looking officer, covered with ribbons, was standing behind a kitchen table with both hands on it. 'Ah, good day,' he said. 'Ah, you are . . .?'

'You asked to see me?'

'Yes—yes. May I ask: who are you?'

'I'm from a Unit that's just arrived in town.'

'And you are an officer?'

'I'm a Sergeant.'

'Ah. Well: the General would like to see you.'

He tapped on a communicating door, and bending his body forward, said something to the person inside. Then he raised his eyebrows at me, and held out one hand in the direction of the inner room.

The General was an elderly man with a red stripe down his trousers. I took him to be a veteran of earlier wars and, as Garrison Commander of this small town, not a very significant General. His voice was shrill, and his manner precise and rather pedantic. He came round from his roll-top desk, took my hand, pressed it, let it go and offered me a cigarette. 'Please be seated,' he said. The Adjutant shut the door and stood behind me.

'So,' said the General. 'I asked for you to come up, since there are many questions, as you will understand. To whom am I speaking, if I may ask?'

'This Underofficer is of a Unit that has just arrived in the town,' the Adjutant said over my shoulder.

'Which, if I may ask, is your function?'

'We're here to look for billets.'

'For billets. Well, we have other fine barracks here, besides these ones. And you have an officer?'

'Oh, yes.'

'Naturally. Well, since you are now present, perhaps I can speak to you. You see: there are a quantity of questions. I should be interested in your opinion.'

'I'm not entitled to give any opinion.'

'Yes, yes, I understand. Well, a personal opinion.'

'On what?'

'Kindly read this,' he said, taking up a letter from the table. It was a peremptory note, signed by a General officer of the Allied Staff, and it told General von Wallwitz that, until the arrival of the British troops, he was responsible for order and public safety in this area. I handed it back to him.

'Well?' he said. 'In your view, what is my exact position?'

'I've already said I can't express an opinion.'

'Please,' he insisted, spreading out the letter on the table, then putting both hands in his side pockets.

I gave up trying to behave myself. 'You appear to have full powers for the moment,' I said.

'Ah! You think so?'

'Well, doesn't it say that?'

He took up the letter. 'Powers over the civil administration?'

'That letter doesn't mention the civil administration.'

'That is so. Well,'—he hesitated—'should I issue a proclamation?'

'Certainly. It would seem so. Why not?'

'A proclamation saying . . .' he paused, as if coaching me in a lesson.

'Repeating what's in the letter,' I suggested. 'That you are responsible for public safety in this area until the arrival of the British troops.'

The General looked over my head and nodded emphatically at the Adjutant. 'And what of the Hungarian Regiment?' he then asked.

'What about it?'

'The Commander refuses to obey my orders.'

'Show him this letter, then. Your authority isn't open to doubt.'

He appeared very satisfied, then sat down, fiddled with some papers and lost interest in me. 'Well, thank you,' he said. 'We must do for the best in these altered circumstances. Is not that so? Good-bye, my dear Sir. My best wishes . . .'

He gave me a toothy smile, nodded quickly several times and became engrossed in the papers. The Adjutant saw me out. 'You have been very helpful,' he said. 'The General is most pleased.'

I went down to the car, deciding that the less I said about this visit back at the billet, the better. The policeman interrupted my thoughts. 'You wanted to see the prison,' he reminded me. 'And after that, if you will permit me, I shall go home to my supper, as my wife will be getting anxious.'

Evening had set in by now, and I turned up the sidelights. We crossed the town again, and driving up an avenue overhung with trees, we stopped in front of an imitation medieval tower. It had a heavy wooden door studded with nails.

The policeman got out, rang a bell, and spoke to someone through a grille. One half of the door was opened, and I drove into a courtyard. Round it were high, brick buildings, with narrow windows. Beyond the courtyard the roofs of other blocks could be seen sticking out at angles. In the distance there was a high wall surmounted by battlements and spikes.

A warder came up to the car door. 'I want to see the Commandant,' I said.

'He is at home, at his evening meal.'

'Well, whoever is in charge.'

'Please come with me.'

He led me up to the main block, opened a small door at the side of it, and preceded me into a smaller courtyard. Walking up and down in the gloom, with his hands behind his back, was an extremely tall man in civilian clothes.

'Mr. Rose,' the warder called. The man turned quickly round. 'This gentlemen wishes to speak with you.'

As I got closer to this civilian, I saw he had wide-open eyes, a nose you could see up, thick, pale lips and wavy hair brushed to hide a bald patch.

'What is it?' he asked.

'How many prisoners have you here?'

'How many? Who asks, if you please?'

'I ask. How many have you?'

He hesitated. 'The English General has told us to wait till the special Commission arrives.'

'Yes. How many prisoners have you?'

'Fourteen hundred, perhaps.'

'Who are they?'

'Please?'

'What kind of prisoners?'

'Criminal, also political prisoners.'

'Are there Allies of ours among them?'

'There are German political and criminal prisoners, also foreign political and criminal prisoners.'

'How many political prisoners?'

'I do not know the exact number.'

'Yes, about how many?'

'Perhaps one half.'

He followed me back to the car, suspicious, apologetic and scared. 'As soon as the English Commission arrives, these things will be seen to,' he said.

I dropped the policeman off at his home and hurried back to the billet. I parked the car in the factory yard, and as I was going through the garden gate, a man wearing a leather suit, who had been parleying with the *Wehrmacht* sentries, came running over. 'It is of the utmost importance that I see at once an officer of the British technical Staff,' he said.

'I'm busy now.'

'Excuse me: are you a technical officer? A chemist, for instance.'

'No, I'm not. What's it about?'

'That I cannot explain to you fully. But briefly, it stands thus: Nearby the Aller, is a secret deposit of a particular war material. It would be highly dangerous if carelessly handled, not only to yourselves, but also to the civilian population.'

He went on to say he was one of a team of specialists who'd been making this war material. When the German army had fallen back across the river, his team had been evacuated with it. Seeing that everything was over, his conscience, he said, demanded that the British be informed at once.

I took him to the billet. The Captain was having high tea prior to setting off to Corps, and after listening to the chemist's story, he decided to take him along there too. I told the chemist to wait in the hall, and drew up a chair beside the Captain. 'I've got something on my mind,' I said.

'Have you?' He munched an egg. 'Let's hear all about it.'

I told him of my afternoon's excursion, with omissions, and of the need of getting food and transport for the prisoners-of-war and released workers. Then I came to the question of the prison, and said, 'That's the most important.'

'Why?'

'Well, think of it. Hundreds of Allied civilians, political prisoners, crowded in there without enough to eat. They must know the war's over, and be wondering why we're not getting them out.'

'What can we do until some troops arrive? And don't forget we shouldn't even be here.'

'We ought at least to go and see them and find out if we can do something.' The Captain was silent. 'There are certain to be men in there who've done dangerous work for us.'

'You think so?'

'Of course I think so. That's what I'm saying.'

'The job's too big for us, isn't it? We'd only stir up trouble, and they might try to break out.'

'What the hell does it matter if they do? They shouldn't be in there.'

He looked at me judiciously, still saying nothing. Inspired, I said, 'There may be Englishmen there.'

That did it.

'Well,' the Captain said, 'as soon as I get back from seeing Major Bane, I'll go round and have a look.'

'When will that be?'

'Not till tomorrow. I shall be stopping over at Corps tonight.'

'Well, tell Major Bane about it, will you? Get him interested and get his authority to do something?'

'I'll try. But I'm not sure what sort of reception he's going to give me. Anyway, I'll try. But remember, until I get back, don't put up the Detachment sign, don't see any visitors, don't go out any more than you need, in fact don't *do* anything.'

I saw the Captain off with the chemist, and when I came into the house again, and was going by the rooms which Gordon had allotted to its owners, I noticed Gessler through an open door. He was hanging a picture on the wall, and standing back to admire the effect. Catching sight of me as I moved off, he called out, 'Now, I bring them up from the cellar. Come through and tell me, please—do you like this one?'

'Not very much.'

'You do not appreciate the colouring, the vivid pattern? It is by a well-known Munich painter. My father was a great collector of his work, and also of older masterpieces, which I have kept for safety in our country villa. Later, I shall go and fetch them back. Here,' he went on, showing me a black picture, 'is the work of a celebrated old Dutch artist, purchased by my father when on business in Amsterdam.' We stared at it together. 'Well, after all, these races, Englishmen, Dutchmen and we Germans, are nevertheless cousins. I have visited those countries, and the deep affinities were clearly apparent to me.' He nodded persuasively, but doubtfully. 'My father was not merely a connoisseur, he was also an excellent businessman. And so was his father.'

'Then it's an old business.'

'For four generations we have made cutlery in this town. If my son returns, it will be five. That is,' lowering his voice, 'if the British authority gives us permission to continue. Come, since you are interested, I shall show you something that is the proof of what I say.'

He led me through a sliding door onto the verandah. Set into the wall of the house was a bas-relief showing a labourer and a man with a frock coat, shaking hands.

'My grandfather's idea. I had it removed from the old house to this one when I built it.' I gazed at the stone. 'Do you not see? The unity of work and intelligence, always the characteristic of our firm. It is perhaps an ideal conception, but then I have always found it practically wise to have ideals.'

He glanced at me, smiled cautiously, then pressed me to sit down and gave me a cigar. 'What the future will be, I do not know,' he said. 'I am very pessimistic. It will be a long occupation this time, of that I am certain.'

'I'm afraid so.'

'You say that?'

'Well, it's we who will have to make the occupation. Your soldiers will be demobilised sooner than ours.'

'Ah, that is a bitter jest,' he cried, 'for our fate is much harder. After so terrible a defeat, Germany will not rise again for perhaps a hundred years.'

'Hitler said that, in such a case, it would be a thousand.'

'Ah, Hitler! He was a fiend, a fiend.' He said this so earnestly that I asked him if it had always been his opinion.

'It was thus. At first I was not his supporter, but then he seemed to bring many things we needed, things that were indispensable to us.'

'And you joined the Party?'

'Not till 1937, like so many. To refuse to join the Party by that time would have meant losing control of my factory. For the sake of my family, how could I do that? Picture yourself in my position—what, I beg leave to ask you, would you yourself have done?'

'And when did you begin to change your mind?'

'When I saw that in the end we were being brought to nothing but disaster. Yes, we have been lied to and betrayed.' His face expressed real grief, as though he felt himself abandoned. 'Yes, surely,' he continued, 'it is a year ago now that we should have put an end to this war.'

'Or not have begun it.'

He looked at me blankly, then said, 'Yes, or perhaps have never begun.'

We sat in silence for a while, gazing out at the dark gardens. 'Do you supply the prison?' I said.

'Prison?'

'Do you supply the prison here with cutlery?'

'We? I cannot say. In a prison, wooden utensils are used, are they not? We, in any case, are wholesalers. I could enquire... Forgive me, why do you ask?'

'Have you ever been in there?'

'Been in? I? Oh! As a vistior! No, no. My club-colleague, the prison Commandant, knows it well, of course. I know nothing of it, Heaven be praised. You are interested? He could take you there.'

'I expect I'll be meeting him. Well, thanks for the cigar.'

But Gessler held me gently by the arm. 'I hear that white flags are to be hung out,' he said. 'Before doing so, I thought it best to enquire: Is this also necessary for us?'

'Yes.'

'But here are your headquarters.'

'That makes no difference. It's a general order.'

'But will there then be a white flag beside the Union Jack we are making for you?'

I asked him what he meant. He told me that Dennis, on his arrival the night before, had asked him where in the town he could get one made, and Gessler had recommended a tailor of his acquaintance, who was already sewing it together. 'It will be ready for you tomorrow. My associate has promised to bring it to your office in the morning.'

I was digesting this, when the door half opened and Frau Gessler came in, but seeing me there, she hurriedly withdrew.

'Do excuse my wife if she is nervous,' he said. 'Things have been done which distress her. I say no more of that—and above all, she is anxious about our young son.'

I asked where he'd been mobilised, and said I'd try to find out from the Adjutant at the barracks where he'd been posted to. Gessler thanked me, and escorted me to the edge of the military section of the house.

The Sergeants were sitting round the dining-room table drinking, and I asked Dennis about the flag.

'Well, yes,' he said. 'It struck me that now we're in permanent residence, we ought to have one on view. Besides, there's a regulation out that all headquarters must display one.'

'Couldn't you wait till we get one on issue? Why ask them to make it here?'

'My dear fellow, you've got the wrong idea. The tailor had no objection whatever. It's all in the day's work to him. We're not asking him to fly it himself. Here, have some of this hock. These bottles are just samples, but I've got an option on what's left in the town.'

Gordon twisted the coloured stem of his glass, and said, 'We could send off down to the Rhineland later on, and build up a really decent cellar. We might arrange to crate some of it and send it home.'

'Gordon's idea,' said Dennis, 'is that when Hamburg's throughly occupied, our ships will move in and he'll be able to get friendly with some skipper who'll help him get merchandise across the channel. Failing that, we could even try the Navy.'

'There's a lot of stuff here, too, that might as well leave when we do,' Gordon said, glancing round the room. 'These carpets, for instance.'

'Now, now,' said Dennis. 'Charity begins at home. No robbing the till.'

'Oh, I said when we go. But look at the scale this place is furnished on. It's a disgrace, when you think of the shortages at home.'

He rang for more bottles, and two very striking girls, whom I hadn't seen before, came in giggling and carrying trays inefficiently.

'The Lithunian contingent,' Dennis explained. 'A discovery of Gordon's. They're to come on for night duty when Frau Gessler's staff departs.'

'Do we need them?'

'I should think we do. We must build up this place, it has great possibilities. We should get hold of a chef and a barman who've been on one of the transatlantic liners, a *Luftwaffe* mechanic for the cars—just think of the skilled labour that'll be available once demobilisation sets in. We might even have a private orchestra. And it'll be doing them all a favour at the same time. They'd be wasted cooking bacon and eggs in an officers' mess.'

Walter had been talking to one of the girls, and when they'd gone out again, Dennis said, 'I believe you're succumbing at last, Walter.'

'Don't leap to conclusions, my lad.'

'I see that look in your eye.'

'You're in no condition to see any look in any eye. And let me tell you, if I do get friendly with one of these lasses, I won't be going with any Gerry girl, like some do.'

'Is that wrong, Walter?'

'It is in this sense, Dennis, that it's not right to take their women while they're down.'

'You've got a noble soul. I admire you for it.'

'I don't know about my soul, but I do know this. The

occupation's going to make things very different. We're going to stop soldiering and become civil servants, as far as I can see.'

'And you believe in civil servants' home comforts.'

'I wasn't referring to that. You wouldn't understand, Dennis, but it's danger makes a soldier's life dignified, not holding people down. That'll be gone from now on.'

I went through the ornamental arch into the sitting-room, where Norman was helping Cuthbert set up his portable radio. I was thinking about the prison, and how quickly I could get in and empty it. I wanted an ally, and it seemed Cuthbert was the only one who might be interested; and it would be a help to have his scale of values to react against when I wasn't sure what to do.

'You know,' Norman was saying, 'there's one thing I'll miss now the war's over. Did you used to listen to Radio Hamburg at all? There was a girl on it with a voice I used to admire—a sisterly voice, I used to consider it—who put out a musical programme just before bedtime.'

'That Miss Haw-Haw,' said Cuthbert.

'You can call her that, but she used to announce her programmes very endearingly. It was propaganda, I know. But I found it very effective.'

When they'd got the radio going, Norman said to me, 'Has it occurred to you that this is our last chance of getting a ciné-camera?'

'I didn't know you wanted one.'

'It's all I came to Germany for. In a day or two Mil. Gov. and all the rest of them will be here, and what chance will we have then?'

'We'll go and have a look round tomorrow.'

'The Town Hall will be the place. They're bound to have collected some of the cameras in.'

'We'll go tomorrow. Good-night, Norman.'

'I'm not going to bed.'

'I want to speak to Cuthbert.'

'Well, there he is. You mean alone? Oh, very well, I can take hints.'

While Cuthbert searched for stations on his set, I told him of the prison and tried to lure him on with the prospect of dispensing justice. He listened carefully without comment, winding a coil of wire round one hand. 'Well,' he said at last,

'I don't mind coming along there with you, if you think it'll lead to any useful results.'

THE VISITORS

WHEN I WOKE IN THE MORNING, IN THE ROOM I'D TAKEN IN THE office building, I heard a clattering of hooves in the factory yard below. I looked out of the window and saw two German soldiers in conversation, both holding saddled mounts by their bridles. I dressed and went downstairs. One of them was an officer, whose rising high of the cap, projection of buttocks and splendour of top-boots, were those of caricature. When he saw me, he handed his reins to his companion and came up, holding a salute.

'Good morning,' he said, smiling with some big teeth. 'I have been waiting for you. You must take over my horses as quickly as possible.' I looked at the animals. 'Oh no, not these,' he said, laughing. 'There are two hundred of them.'

He explained that he was a Colonel in a Veterinary Corps, with pedigree horses in his care, and that he wanted to hand them over intact to the British.

'I'm sorry, I can't help you.'

'No?' he said, in great surprise.

'Not yet. Later on our people will be glad of them. But we have no one to look after them yet.'

He was very disappointed. 'But the Easterners are already stealing them. As time goes by, I shall lose more and more.'

'Why don't you hand them over to General von Wallwitz?'

He made a noise with his tongue, put his head on one side, and said, 'That gentleman is not a cavalry officer.'

'Not many of our gentlemen are cavalry officers either.'

I asked where his stables were and made arrangements to go riding. Then I walked over to the billet. The *Wehrmacht* sentries were sitting on the bridge in the sun, the park was washed fresh, and a squirrel hurtled across the topmost branches.

We had breakfast on the terrace, and then sat out in the sun doing nothing, as the Captain had said. But while Dennis was reading out aloud to us, from a crumpled English newspaper, an account by a woman reporter of how our men scorned the advances of the German girls, Norman, who had gone across to the office to lay out his files, came back to say a lot of visitors had gathered there. Apparently the news that we were in the factory had spread around the town, and when we all went over we found about twenty people standing in the hall. Some were talking in groups in low voices, and others standing alone with their eyes lowered, or glancing at one another. After a short discussion, we stationed Cuthbert at the office door and told him to sift out their stories and send in anyone who had something interesting to say.

The first person he allotted to me was a young Hungarian officer, who came in saluting his way across the main room. When I took him into the Captain's office next door, he said he wanted transport down to Austria to see his fiancée, who had been staying there when last he'd heard from her. 'Of course,' he said, 'I realise it cannot be just at once, but I am determined to see her, and as I do not want to walk there, I thought it best to appeal to you to arrange it directly things are settled.' He was gracious and condescending, treating me as Bonnie Prince Charlie might have done a clansman. I told him there was nothing doing. He was surprised, but not offended.

I went out and found Cuthbert. 'Don't send me in any more like that. Who else have you got?'

'Well, perhaps you should see this person,' he said, and he pointed out a woman in her thirties with big hips and swelling breasts, whose copious hair was swept across her forehead like a turban.

'What can I do for you?' I asked her.

'I should like to speak to you alone.'

'What about?'

'As you prefer, but I should like to speak to you alone.'

I led the way back into the Captain's room. She waited till I'd closed the door, then came closer till she was almost touching me, and looking up with her eyes half closed and her mouth falling open, she said, 'My husband is in the Gestapo.'

'And?'

'And he is here.'

Her breasts heaved beneath my eyes.

'Where?'

'You have a pencil?'

She took it from my hand, raised one knee, throwing her weight onto the other leg, and wrote a name and address in block letters on a magazine she was carrying. Then she looked up again and stretched her mouth sideways in a slight grin. 'But quickly,' she said.

'All right.'

She nodded her head slowly, handed me back the pencil, brushed down her skirt which clung to her thighs, and walked out through the door into the hall where she went to a chair and sat waiting with her legs crossed.

I gave the magazine to Dennis.

A grey-haired man in overalls stepped forward, and told me he was one of Gessler's foremen. 'Here is the tailor with your flag,' he said, pointing to another man who was standing expectantly with a brown paper parcel. I asked them both through to the inner office, and the tailor, after glancing at us with a 'Hey Presto!' look, cast aside the wrappings and seizing the flag by one end, flung it open so that it spread itself out on the table. Except that the blue was rather pale, he'd got all the details right. The foreman looked at the flag curiously, with his hands behind his back, but the tailor handled it as he might have done a suit of clothes.

'Thanks very much,' I said.

'Not a bit,' said the tailor. 'Perhaps if there are other orders, not necessarily flags, of course,'—he smiled—'you will remember me? Here is the card of my shop.'

'You're short of cloth, I expect?'

'Well, yes, but I still have some decent materials, not many,' he went on, glancing at the foreman, who had pricked up his ears.

I sent him out to Gordon to get paid, and when I got back, I found the foreman fingering the edge of the flag. 'And where is it to be put?' he asked.

'I'm not sure yet. At the front gate, perhaps.'

'Here might be a better place.' He led me over to the window and pointed to a flagpole on the factory roof.

'Is it difficult to get up there?'

'Heavens, no. Shall I put it up for you?'

'Oh, I'll get one of our people to do it.'

'As you wish.'

I asked Norman to do this, and watching from the office window, I saw them cross the yard to the factory entrance, the foreman carrying the flag under his arm. Some minutes later, they reappeared on the roof, the foreman moving resolutely forward and Norman stepping cautiously behind. They reached the pole, and the foreman hoisted the flag into the breeze and stood looking up at it. It struck me this was the first time I'd seen a Union Jack since we'd left Brussels.

But now I heard the sound of loud feet and voices in the next room, and went out to find two Belgian soldiers, armed with German rifles, who were standing on either side of a young man who towered above them. 'We have brought you an S.S. man,' one of them was saying to Gordon. 'We were forced to work on his father's farm, and he turned up there a week ago and hid his military equipment.'

'What can we do with him?' asked the other, fingering his rifle.

The German stood bolt upright, gazing straight ahead. His body was massive and swollen, filled with strength, and his face was like another limb—expressive as hands and feet are.

'What is your rank?' Gordon said.

'*Oberscharführer*.'

'Where did you serve?'

'Holland, Belgium, Poland,' he shouted, looking over the top of Gordon's head.

'And what was your job?'

'Not understood!' he shouted.

'Your Unit, your formation.'

'Shock-troops and occupation duties.'

The Belgians watched us, gripping their weapons. 'Did you have trouble getting him here?' I asked them.

'We said, "You—come"!' one of them answered, making a gesture with his rifle.

'You'll have to take him back to the farm and put him under house arrest,' I said, and explained the position to them.

They didn't answer.

'You're under house arrest,' Gordon barked at the prisoner.

At this he abandoned his rigid posture and ringing tones, and said in a soft voice, 'My father needs me, because the workers have all left. He needs me out in the fields.'

'Take him away,' we told the Belgians. They looked at us reproachfully, and marched him off, very dissatisfied.

The tailor had been watching this scene from a corner of the room. 'A powerful youngster,' he said. 'Yes, that is a generation I can no longer speak to. They are ready to die, admittedly, but what is the use of that? Ten years more, and all our young men would have been like him. They would have devoured the rest of us.'

The last visitor I saw that morning was a Flying Officer from the small British party on the airfield. He was a lean man with a perpetual frown, and he came through to the inner office with Walter, carrying a haversack.

'We're all alone here, and we've got to stick together,' he said. 'Take a look at this.' He pulled out from his haversack a piece of chain about three feet long. 'They've started their tricks, as we expected. This is part of what they stretched across the road last night.'

'Who did?'

'Fanatics, I suppose. That's what I want you people to help me find out.'

'Was anyone hurt?'

'Luckily not—not yet, that is. But if they're going to begin that sort of thing, not one of us will be safe out on the roads.'

We asked for more details. He said that on the evening before, three trucks had come up from beyond the boundary line carrying guards to reinforce the airmen who'd landed previously. One of these trucks had fallen behind, and as it was approaching the airfield, the driver had felt a bump and, getting out, had found this length of chain hooked on a tree.

'Was there any more of it?' said Walter.

'No doubt there was. But by the time we came back with a search party, it had disappeared.'

'The driver was sure it was right across the road?'

'Look here, Sergeant, it's not me you should be interrogating, but the men who did it.'

'Could we speak to the driver?'

'Yes, if you like, he's downstairs. I've been round to see the German police about it, but they're no use, they'll try to protect the criminals.'

The driver showed us a dent two inches deep on one mudguard, and when Walter asked him to describe his speed and how great the shock was, he became vague, and glanced at the officer, 'Well, you've got the facts,' the officer interrupted. 'What about some quick arrests?'

Walter said he'd go with them to see the place where the accident had happened.

Norman reminded me about the cameras, and we went round together to the Town Hall. We found the police Colonel in his office, leaning against the mantelpiece, paring his nails. He hadn't the jauntiness of the day of our arrival, and the honorary S.S. flashes had been removed from his tunic.

We told him what we wanted, and he detailed a policeman to take us down to the basement. This man opened a door on an Aladdin's cave of cameras—the room was piled knee-deep with them. Norman began making a selection. 'I'll take one for each of us,' he said, in tones that suggested he wasn't going to be greedy.

He stepped about like a gardener plucking strawberries. The policeman took the cameras Norman chose, held them together in his arms, then laid them out in two little piles in the corridor. Norman stared at this suspiciously. Pointing to one pile, the policeman said, 'These I would not take. They are not the best.'

'Well, which are the best?'

'Have I your permission?'

The policeman went on his hands and knees, turning over cameras as a child searching for crabs on a rocky shore. From time to time he handed one back over his shoulder. Then he stood up again and brushed himself. 'These are all excellent,' he said.

Norman examined them, and gave me one that had a wooden ticket on it with the owner's name and address to ensure its safe return. 'This is for you,' he said.

We took them upstairs to the car. As we were driving off, the police Captain came running out of the building and pushed his head through the window. 'In respect of the report of attempted sabotage,' he said. 'My force is in action, and I shall notify you at once of an arrest.'

'You think you'll make one?'

'If there is a culprit, we shall find him.'

We got back to the billet, and were parking the car, when we heard the noise of shrill voices coming from the house. The Gessler girls were standing in the garden looking anxiously over their shoulders, and as I went in by the back door, I saw the Lithunian maids peering eagerly into the kitchen. I went in there. The room was crowded with people. There were Gordon and Cornelis, Frau Gessler, her lady-help and all her domestic staff. Frau Gessler was clasping a large white dish in both hands, and Gordon was standing with his fists on his hips, looking at her disdainfully.

'It is insufferable! Here in my house, it is insufferable,' Frau Gessler was saying, white with anger.

'Come, Frau Gessler, let us go,' said the lady-help.

'They take my house, that is their right, but not to introduce such people beneath my roof!'

'We haven't taken all your house, you're luckier than most,' said Gordon.

'I would rather sleep in the woods than have such immorality underneath my eyes.'

'You'd better be careful.'

'I speak my mind. These two creatures did not go last night to their own chamber, but were seen this morning coming from your rooms.'

Gordon smiled, and turning away from her, came out with Cornelis. 'She doesn't seem to realise her position,' he said to me. 'If she likes to be all that superior, it's the last time she'll go in that kitchen.'

'We'd better arrange for them to cook somewhere else,' I said, as we went into the sitting-room.

'We'd better put them out altogether, I'm beginning to think. It was all right on the way up, but it's different now that we're going to live here for good.'

Dennis was lying full length on the sofa. 'It's the thought of what her two innocent daughters might see that upsets her,' he said.

'Upsets her, does it? She says she wants to sleep in the woods—well, let her.'

'We must live and let live, Gordon. If she doesn't like our morals she can go elsewhere, but if she accepts the situation, she should be allowed to stay.'

'Why can't you take your women somewhere else?' I said.

'You think it more convenient to put yourself in the office building out of sight.'

There was an unpleasant silence.

'It's not a bad idea, that, you know, Gordon,' said Dennis. 'What if we got ourselves a separate flat in town? A frat.-flat.'

'Why bother?'

'Well, the Captain may have closed his eyes to the glimpses he saw on the way up, but he's bound to become more regimental again as things get settled. But if we got a flat, we could put our concubines in it and settle down to a matrimonial life.'

Dennis poured out some drinks. I asked him about the Gestapo man he'd been to look for. 'Yes, he's from a town beyond the Kiel canal,' he told me, 'the second-in-command there. He admitted it all, and gave me a list of his colleagues.'

'Where did you put him?'

'In the police lock-up. Not in the State prison you told me about, but in the local jail. The police Captain was very unfriendly to him.'

'Did he know who'd denounced him?'

'The subject wasn't mentioned, but I fancy he had an idea.'

As we sat down to lunch Walter came in, and he was sceptical about the chain across the road. 'That driver had hallucinations, in my opinion,' he said. 'He and his officer are suffering from werewolf mania.'

I drove round to the office and parked the car in the factory yard. There was a group of crippled soldiers there, sitting in the sun. One of them came over on crutches. He had purple-coloured skin and a face with big, curved features and bones. We talked about car speeds and fuel consumption, then I asked him who he and his comrades were.

'We? We're the ruins. When the army had finished with us, they sent us here to work.'

'You live here?'

'We have a dormitory. We learn manual tasks in the factory to fit us for the future, so they say. But will we have our pensions now, or medical help?'

Some of the others came over and gathered round the car. An airman explained his medals to me. 'And you have none?' he said.

'No.'

'You have not been in combat?'

'No.'

They looked at me curiously. 'Well, we have fought more campaigns than you,' the airman said.

'And lost more,' said another.

'What, Erwin! Germany has never been defeated, so long as the conditions were equal.'

'Conditions are never equal. War is not a boxing-match.'

'In total war, military valour counts for less. Material factors become decisive, as we now see.'

'Military valour we have always had.'

'But war is not a boxing-match.'

Some of them laughed sardonically.

'Tell me,' said one. 'Will it be possible to fight the Japanese?'

'Haven't you had enough fighting?'

'Oh, us here, we're finished. But healthy men will be ready to volunteer.'

'Not for me. The Japanese are fanatics.'

'So were the Russians.'

'He was at Stalingrad,' someone said.

'That was a bitter struggle.'

'It was also a great achievement. Say what you like, it was one of our greatest achievements.'

Some of the others nodded. It seemed they regarded this battle as a victory of the kind we had felt Dunkirk to be.

I said, 'For us Stalingrad changed the whole course of the war. That is why we're grateful to the Russians.'

'If you knew them as we do, you would not be grateful.'

'But we don't. We know them as allies.'

They shook their heads over this. 'Now admit it, Sergeant,' the airman said. 'You people fought on the wrong side.'

The man on crutches called out as I was going into the office block, and came hobbling after me again. 'Listen,' he said. 'Can you help me over my leg? At the hospital, they keep telling me they can't give me one. But there is a man here in the town who can make it, if I can get the money.'

'Have you told them that at the hospital?'

'They say I must wait till they themselves can supply one. But until I get it, I cannot go home, you see? I can't travel there with these things.'

'Where is your home?'

'In East Prussia. I shall go back there if I can. The people in this region treat us as if we were foreigners.'

I arranged with him to come over to the billet after supper and see Dennis.

In the hall upstairs, I found two men walking up and down as though they were on board ship. One of them looked like a public figure, an orator. His companion, who was much older and had only one arm, came up to me and said, 'We are leaders of a democratic party here. We wish to ask, is public activity now to be allowed?'

'Which party?'

'We are Communists. My comrade has recently reached home from Buchenwald.'

The younger man answered my questions about the life in the camp as if he didn't expect to be believed or disbelieved, or much care either way. His face had a sullen, emphatic expression, and he ran his fingers through his hair and pushed it restlessly back from his forehead. The older man was interested in practical details. I said we'd had no directive about political parties.

'And may I ask,' he said, 'what has happened in other cities? Have democratic parties been supported?'

'No parties have been supported officially yet.'

'Is this not a mistake? For war does not exist without political ideas, and to encourage the rapid emergence of democratic parties would be a means of winning it. But that is not the view of you gentlemen?'

The younger man, who had been staring out of the window, broke in, 'Their attitude, you may be sure, will be hostile to us.'

'Is this forecast correct?' said the older man.

'The official attitude will be unfriendly,' I told them.

'Then who is to rule us? Foreign soldiers? Or once again the Nazis?'

'Well, it will make no difference,' the younger man said, 'since we shall in any case continue with our work.'

He began walking up and down for distances of about three yards. The older man glanced at him solicitously, then took hold of my arm with his one hand and said, 'Understand. The Nazis have destroyed our wealth and corrupted our people, and we know that Germany is hated and mistrusted now in the entire world. All those who are defeated are hated.' Here he tugged at my arm. 'But we admit there are reasons for this hate, which arise from the actions and crimes of those who have ruled us. Believe me, the misuse of German ability is the world's greatest tragedy. It will take years of endless work by such as ourselves to regain the confidence of those outside.'

The younger man stepped forward and broke in again.

'If Germany has had faults, different from those of other nations, that is undeniable, but it is also due to the facts of our historical development. And in these present circumstances, it is we who must take things as they are and transform them. In this task it is ourselves, Germans, and not the British authorities who must make the essential decisions.'

The older man nodded, and let go my arm. 'Naturally,' he said, 'we wish to co-operate with you so long as this is to be possible. We hope it will be so.'

Somebody could be heard coming up the stairs, and he stopped suddenly. The younger man looked quickly over his shoulder, then shook himself and put one foot up on a chair to roll his woollen socks. It was Norman. He frowned at them and went into the office.

'If you come again,' I said, 'I'll tell you if we've heard anything.'

'And meanwhile?'

'Meanwhile is for you to decide, isn't it?'

He smiled, blinked his small eyes, and said, "All right, Sergeant.'

'About the prison here,' I asked him. 'Have you people in there?'

'Naturally.'

'Are there many German political prisoners?'

'Some hundreds, I should say. All categories. Even Nationalists have recently been arrested.'

'And Allies of ours—Dutchmen and so forth?'

'Doubtless. Well, really, one cannot know who is in there now. Even the officials themselves will not know this. So many have been evacuated, transferred, sent hither and thither in the last weeks. You are going there?'

'Yes.'

'Make haste.' He gave me his one hand turned the wrong way round. I went down with them to the front door.

A young Easterner was sitting on the steps there with a girl. He gave me a friendly smile, and told me he'd come for new clothing. 'Look at these things,' he said, 'they are not fit to be worn.' He tore a piece off his coat and handed it to me.

'I've got no clothes, I'm sorry.'

He shook his head in total disbelief. 'You can get some for me from the Germans. Or a uniform like yours would do.'

'You can't wear that. You'd get into trouble.'

'Give me one,' he insisted, as if demanding his due.

I went up to the office, unlocked Gordon's store, got out a battledress and took it down to him. He pulled it on over his rags. It was too big. 'And boots?' he said.

When I came down again with these, the girl was making a tuck in his trouser leg, and he was carrying the blouse over his arm.

'How much?' he said.

'It's a present.'

'I can pay.' He held out the money.

'It costs nothing.'

'Then a present for you,' he said, giving me some of it.

He went off arm-in-arm with the girl. The crippled soldiers watched them disapprovingly.

I shouted up to Norman I'd be away for an hour, and I got in the car and drove out to the country. It didn't take long to reach, for it wandered into the suburbs in the form of market gardens. Soon I came to a village scattered about a group of hills which jutted up suddenly out of the plain. I climbed an earthy track with the wheels spinning, and came onto a hilltop with an unexpected view over miles of woods and fields, set in rows one behind the other. A thin strip of the sea was shining on the skyline.

I sat on the mudguard smoking. Birds rose, fell, turned and rose, never colliding. There wasn't a soul in sight.

Driving back into the town, I noticed yellow posters stuck up on the walls. They were covered with thick, black lettering and exclamation marks. The third time I saw one (on the gates of the prison), I got out and read it. It was General von Wallwitz's proclamation. I peeled off a copy to keep as a memento. Two women passing stopped to watch me, and went off whispering together.

Walter was alone in the sitting-room, drinking tea. 'I was wrong about that chain, it seems,' he said. 'They've caught the man who did it.'

'Who caught him?'

'The German police Captain. He sent word round to the office just now, and Dennis has gone over to join in the questioning.'

'You were sure there was nothing in it.'

'I must have been mistaken. This man's confessed.'

'Confessed? Let's go round there.'

The police Captain was leaning against his office filing-cabinet, looking detached. Two of his assistants were hovering in the background. Dennis was browbeating the prisoner. He was a young German with a crafty, bewildered look. Some of his answers were clear, others voluble but quite indefinite. After each answer his head fell on his breast, but he shot glances at the police Captain, who rarely caught his eye and said nothing. When we'd watched five minutes, I said, 'Pack it in, Dennis.'

Dennis frowned, but got up and said, 'Let's step into the next room.'

'They've framed him, haven't they?'

'Yes. He's done something, but not the chain.'

'You're quite sure?'

'Positive. He's the fatted calf for the sacrifice. They don't believe in this chain any more than we do. But it's simpler to deliver up a victim to the British than to have us taking sanctions against the town.'

'Who is this man?'

'They've got him in on some other charge. They must have persuaded him to confess.'

'Persuaded. Well, I'm going to turn him loose,' said Walter. 'Any objections? And I want you two to have a word with that police Captain.'

'I agree to the first, but not to the second,' Dennis said. 'You'd never pin it on him, and if you're going to use this police force, you can't interfere with their methods.'

We took the prisoner and drove about a kilometer down the highway. Walter stopped the car, opened the door, and said, 'Skip it.' The prisoner, when he understood, got out and started walking back towards the town. Dennis laughed and said, 'He'll be back in the jail tonight.'

'Perhaps he's going to his home,' said Walter. 'But why didn't he beat it out of town while he had the chance?'

'Policemen and jail-birds are like man and wife,' Dennis

told us. 'They may fight each other, but they're bound together by ties of habit.'

We found our Captain at the billet when we got in. He was very annoyed about the reception he and the chemical expert had been given. At first, nobody was interested at all. Long-distance calls had been made in vain and then, just as he was getting ready to start back, orders had come through for him to take this man immediately to a distant headquarters.

'Apart from all that,' he told us, 'Corps weren't pleased when I told them where we were. Major Bane says we're to lie low and pretend we're not here until the troops move up. Though I gather you've found that difficult.'

'When will the troops be moving up?'

'He's not sure, but it'll be soon.' The Captain led me into a corner under the picture of Goethe meeting Napoleon. 'You were right about that prison, you know. I went and had a look round there on my way back. I had a tremendous reception.'

'From the prisoners?'

'Yes. I came in as they were having a meal, and they cheered me to the echo. I spoke to a Dutchman, an intelligent sort of fellow, who said he was an officer. According to him, there are hundreds of Allied civilians in there.'

'What did you tell him?'

'I said I'd lay something on immediately.'

'What are we going to do?'

'That's the question. I spoke about it to Benedict-Bane, and he said it's not our pigeon, which I knew full well. It seems there's a special Mil. Gov. team to deal with prisons, but he doubts whether they've crossed the Rhine. So I told him if something wasn't done, there'd be a riot.'

'Something should be done at once. We've been here two days now.'

'Yes. Well, I explained all that to Major Bane. He said if there's danger of a riot, to take matters into our own hands, but unofficially.'

'What does that mean?'

'Go along and screen them and let out the deserving cases.'

'They're probably all deserving cases.'

'We don't know that yet. Anyway, you can go along and see.'

'What do we do with them when they're let out?'

'We can face that problem when it arises. A Mil. Gov.

Major will be moving up here tomorrow ahead of the others to spy out the land, and Major Bane tells me the future Garrison Commander of this town may be coming up, too. We could try to get them interested.'

'They'll lay on some sort of camp for these people?'

'In due course, I hope so. I spoke to this Mil. Gov. body about the prison, but he seems to think he'll have too much on his hands, which I can well believe. He said he'd leave it to us, but unofficially.'

'Unofficially.'

'Yes, that's right, so you might as well go ahead tomorrow morning.'

THE PRISON

CUTHBERT AND I DROVE UP TO THE PRISON AND ASKED TO SEE the Commandant. The gates were opened, we turned into the courtyard and parked the car by the entrance to the centre block. Warders were hurrying about and there was an atmosphere of suspense, as in a siege. We were taken up to the first floor and asked to wait in a corridor while our escort knocked at a door. He took off his cap and went in, and we could hear a conversation going on.

A man came out of the room and stood in the doorway, looking at us. He was perhaps in the sixties, with cropped hair, a bulky figure that had once been military, big red hands and a face that was heavily lined, sad and brutal in an uncomplicated way. He wore a civilian uniform and jack-boots.

He came forward and stopped at attention two paces from us. He half bowed with his hands hanging at his sides, looked at us as if we might suddenly explode, or disappear, and said, 'Are you the English Commission?'

I said we'd been sent by them.

'I am Colonel Bruhmer, the Commandant. The English General has ordered us to await the arrival of the English Commission.'

I told him we were there to evacuate Allied nationals at once. He gave me a look which I took to mean, 'May I assume that you take responsibility for what you will tell me to do?' I nodded, and he ushered us into the room from which he had just come. It was full of officials, and one was the tall, anxious man of the evening before last. He and the rest all stood stiffly and examined us from top to toe. The Commandant led us up to his desk, stood aside as he reached it and waved me towards his chair. I sat down with Cuthbert on one side. The Commandant remained at the end of the table, and the other Germans massed themselves on the far side, facing us.

'Who are these?' I asked the Commandant.

As he named them one by one, each man lowered his eyes or moved his head with an expression suggesting he was a responsible person who would be glad to be of service to us.

The two standing nearest the window, and slightly forward from the rest, were also prison Commandants. The younger one with the bald head, large eyes, curved mouth and spuriously puzzled expression, was Eberhard, who had retreated with his prisoners all the way from a jail by the Rhine. The older one with the rounded shoulders, smart blue civilian suit and smile which showed teeth with gaps between them, was Albinus, whose Provincial prison had also been evacuated to this town just before the capitulation.

'Then men from three prisons are in the building?' I said.

'Yes, indeed.' All three shook their heads to imply the inconvenience and irregularity of an arrangement forced on them by circumstances.

'And there are fourteen hundred men in all?'

The three looked at one another.

'Perhaps fourteen hundred,' the Commandant said. 'That would be the approximate figure.'

'What is the capacity of this prison?'

'Normally, seven hundred.'

'Yes, well, go on.'

The other men present, the Commandant told us, were members of the prison staff proper. The tall, scared man Rose was the assistant director. The very small, shrimp-like man with pointed shoes and a surprisingly loud voice, who wore a large key hanging round his neck, was Krampff, his deputy. The remaining man carrying a bundle of files was the prison Secretary.

'Please take note of these instructions,' I said.

The Commandant beckoned to the Secretary, who stood with his pencil poised. The rest glued their eyes on me.

'All Allied nationals will be released as soon as we have arranged accommodation, which will be in a few days.

'Two representatives of each Allied nationality, to be chosen by the prisoners themselves, are to visit us at this office in half an hour.

'Let us have, by this afternoon, lists of all persons in the prison, showing names, nationalities, the date and length of their sentence and the reason for it.'

There was a silence. The officials looked at one another and started whispering.

'Address your remarks to me.'

'May I firstly ask,' said the Commandant, 'whether Allied prisoners remain subject to prison discipline until they are released, and whether the warders may continue to carry arms. May I also ask whether it is your intention for the Allied criminal prisoners to be released as well as the Allied political prisoners. I would further enquire whether, in view of the overcrowding'—he looked round at the other two Commandants—'you will agree to the return by road of prisoners under the charge of Dr. Albinus to his Provincial prison, as this is not far distant. As to the lists you require, these could scarcely be prepared by this afternoon, though we shall begin work on them immediately.'

He said all this in a deliberate, emphatic way, then raised his eyebrows at his colleagues as if to ask if he had forgotten anything.

'The lists must be ready today,' I said. 'We shall wait here till they are completed.

'As regards discipline. These Allied nationals have been detained illegally and must not be considered as prisoners at all. We shall see that they exercise restraint towards the prison staff, but there will be no question of normal prison discipline. No sanction is to be taken against any Allied prisoner without reference to us, and you are to report any dispute with an Allied prisoner immediately. The warders may continue to carry arms. As to your further questions, I shall answer them shortly. That will be all.'

The Commandant opened his mouth, but said nothing. They filed out, beginning to whisper again as they reached the door.

Cuthbert sat down opposite me. 'That's all very fine,' he said, 'but they may lose their grip.'

'We'll have to hope they don't. But we must leave them in nominal charge until we find out who's here. What would you have said?'

'I'm not criticising what you said, it was a very good effort. I only wonder if it's realistic. Well, what happens now? Are you going to look around?'

'No, I'm going to stay here. I think we should work through the Germans and the Allied representatives. If we talk to the prisoners, they'll twist us round their little fingers. Remote control is best.'

'So long as it's not too remote. I've got an idea, you know. Let's get hold of that Secretary by himself. He'll probably tell us more of what we want to know than anyone else.'

'Yes, go and fetch him back, Cuthbert.'

I got up from the Commandant's desk and looked round the room. On one wall was a photograph of Bismarck, and beside it, an empty space where another picture used to be. Two reproductions of water-colours by Hitler hung nearby, and next to them were framed tables of prison statistics. At the far end of the room was a large glass bookcase, containing the warders' library.

I was examining the books when Cuthbert came back with the Secretary. He was a man in the late thirties, and as we talked to him to gain his confidence, we learned he was a soldier who had been posted to this job on account of war wounds. He seemed knowledgeable and open, and didn't seem to think the prison as important as the other officials did.

'Those lists needn't be typed,' I told him. 'We must have them quickly.'

'Very well. We shall copy the details from the Personal Acts of each prisoner.'

'What are they?'

'The prisoner's individual dossier.'

'Have you dossiers for every prisoner?'

'For most of them, we have. But many were lost on the different journeys here.'

'Let us see those Acts when you've finished with them.'

'There are many hundreds of them, you know.'

'We'd like to see them.' He nodded. 'What's the distinction you make between a criminal and a political prisoner?'

'That is not easy to define.'

'Give us examples.'

'A political crime is, well, for instance, conspiracy, disloyalty, subversive action and so on. A criminal act is more generally such a thing as murder and theft principally, but there are also other categories.'

'Most of the Allied nationals would be political prisoners?'

'Most, but not all. Perhaps seventy per cent of them are political.'

'And are the rest murderers or thieves?'

'Not necessarily. Illegal slaughtering of meat is, for instance, a criminal offence. Or some cases of sabotage.'

'Isn't sabotage a political matter?' said Cuthbert.

'Not in all cases.' Cuthbert looked at him suspiciously. 'You will understand,' the Secretary added, 'that I am not expressing a personal opinion, but trying to answer your questions.'

'Of course. All right, thank you.'

But the Secretary paused before going to the door. 'You know that there is an Englishman here?'

'No, is there? Send him in right away, will you?'

'Certainly. There is another thing you should know.' His face assumed an expression of tolerant scorn. 'Many German prisoners from the East zones have now declared themselves to be Poles. Likewise, a number from the West state themselves to be Dutch or French. Which nationality am I to put on the lists?'

'Put both, the second one in brackets.'

'Yes. I have also been asked to deliver you this letter. It is from a Pastor who is in prison here.'

'A German?'

'Yes.'

I took the letter. 'Was this handed to the Commandant, or directly to you?' The Secretary smiled slightly. 'All right, thank you,' I said. 'Send us in the Englishman.'

The letter was written in pencil on a piece of squared paper. It read, in translation, as follows:

> To the English, French or American Authority:
>
> I, Pastor Dr. Schwedler, of the parish of Ganderhausen, beg to bring to your notice most urgently the following.
>
> I was arrested on 25th May, 1943, on the charge of disloyalty to the State, and have been held ever since without

trial, namely for approximately two years in disgraceful circumstances.

My only crime was to say, from my pulpit (on the preceding Sunday), *May Heaven forgive us all*, which remark was noted and formed the subject of a denunciation.

I, a Minister of the Reformed Church, consider myself to be imprisoned without cause, and wish to draw your attention to my case as well as to those of countless others concerning whom I beg you most earnestly to grant me an immediate interview.

'Pastor or no Pastor, he'll have to wait till we've seen the Allies,' said Cuthbert.

'All the same, we'll look into the Germans too.'

'You're not going to let any of them out, are you?'

'I don't see why not. Cases like this man's, for instance. And a lot that will be more deserving still.'

'You may start letting out the murderers.'

'Not if we go through the Acts he spoke of.'

'Well, just as you like, but it's outside our terms of reference, isn't it?'

'We haven't got any terms of reference.'

'I mean it's not our business.'

'Let's make it. If we don't get some of them out now, they'll be in weeks and months before the Mil. Gov. people arrive. They may not get out even then.'

Cuthbert raised his brows. 'Well, provided we see to the Allies first.'

'Oh, of course.'

The Secretary knocked again, and the Englishman was shown in. He was a thin young lad with curly hair and a wary, rather stupid look. Cuthbert and I gazed at him with some disappointment as we asked him to sit down and gave him a cigarette.

'Where are you from, pal?' I said.

'The Channel Islands.'

'Oh yes, which one?'

'Jersey.'

He spoke with a near-Birmingham accent.

'Are you a Channel Islander, then?'

'No, I was living there, you see, working, like.'

'And what did they put you in for?'

He looked at the floor, then up at us as if he found the question tactless. 'It was over some cattle meat,' he said.

'How was that?'

'They said I stole it and flogged it off to one of the locals.'

'Well, not that it matters, did you?'

'That's what they said. I don't know how it was, myself.'

'And how long have you been in?'

'I dunno. They sent me over to France and interned me. Then they let me go, then they pulled me in again and sent me up here. What are you going to do for me? I don't want to go back to Jersey.'

'You'll be coming out today. Wait outside, will you? We'll send you off to where they'll look after you.'

'Who?'

'The Army. They'll send you home.' He looked at us doubtfully and got up. 'Do I have to go on wearing these?'

'We'll get you other clothes. Just wait outside, will you?'

'All right, I'll do that, thanks for the fags.'

'I didn't much like the look of him,' said Cuthbert. 'He ought to be enquired into more fully.'

'We'll get somebody to run him over to Corps tonight. They can do that.'

Shuffling of feet and the noise of voices could be heard outside the door. The Commandant knocked, opened it, stood on the threshold and said, 'The Allied representatives are now here.'

About a dozen men dressed in prison clothes came in. They gathered in two groups, one near the window and the other near the door. Most of them said their names as they shook hands, and they looked at us in a way that suggested they wanted to be matter-of-fact about the interview. They sat down with a decided air, as if to say, 'Let's get on with it.' But an immense sigh seemed to fill the room.

Cuthbert called out for more chairs and handed round cigarettes. Some of them took one with a precise, deliberate gesture that proved they weren't in a hurry. Others held the cigarette up between a thumb and finger and showed it to a friend with a slight smile of content.

'I want to make a note of your names,' I said.

A fair-haired, wiry looking man, the only one in normal clothes, said, 'Some of us do not speak English. Perhaps you would like me to translate.' He had a quiet, authoratitive manner, and stood in front of the desk as one sure that his gift for leadership entitles him to get his way.

'What different nationalities are represented?' I asked him.

'I am Captain van Lansberghe Telders, this is Lieutenant Geerling, and we are Dutch. Here you have M. de Tournay, a civilian, and the naval Commander Laguarrigue, who are French. This is Major Goethals of the Belgian army.'

Each of these persons slightly rose in their seats, or made some expression with their faces.

'Of these other gentlemen,' Captain Telders went on, indicating the group nearer the door, 'I do not know all the names.'

I looked at the other group, and so did those just mentioned. 'What are the nationalities of you gentlemen?' I said in English, then in German.

A lean young man said quietly, 'I am Hayek, Czech, a lawyer by profession. Shall I introduce? The Polish Captain Wisniewski . . .' he indicated a grizzled man with a disillusioned face ' . . . two from Yugo-slavia—Dr. Bogdanovic . . .' an elderly man of scholarly appearance '. . . and Mr. Filipovic . . .' a much younger man, with a fierce, disdainful look. The Czech presented them all in a decided way; then sat waiting self-containedly.

I wrote down all the names. It was agreed we would speak in French, with a repeat in German.

'First of all,' I said to the French-speaking group, 'I want to be sure you are the representatives of the prisoners: that there is no question of anyone here being appointed by the Germans.'

They smiled and brushed this emphatically aside. 'That sort of thing is over,' the Dutch Lieutenant said.

I then told them much the same things as I had said to the Germans. I asked them to take charge of their countrymen, and to be responsible for them while they were still in the prison. I told them to interfere with the Germans as little as possible, and to refer any disputes to us. I said that each of the representatives would have a pass to move in and out of the prison. They nodded and seemed to agree.

When I repeated all this in German to the group near the door, there was a certain amount of muttering. I asked for questions.

The Polish officer said, in a dignified, irritated way, that some of his men refused to obey him. I asked him to prepare a list of those who did, and for whom he would be responsible.

'And the others?'

'Please ask the others to choose another delegate and send him to us here.'

'There is no such man with a rank that entitles him to lead.'

'We want somebody the men will agree to. Will you ask them?'

He gazed at his boots. 'I cannot be accountable for such a decision.'

'You do not have to be accountable.'

'All right. Very well, I shall tell them.'

The elder Yugo-slav now spoke. Glancing at his companion with what seemed amiable contempt, he said that they, also, would prepare separate lists of persons for whom each would be answerable. I asked the younger man if he agreed to this, and he said, 'Yes, I accept that for the moment.'

I asked the Czech if he had the support of all the men in his group. He said yes, they had all agreed to him, we could ask them if we liked.

Then they had a talk among themselves, the Czech apparently acting as translator. At last they all got up and said they'd go and prepare their lists.

While these discussions, which were lengthy, had been going on, the men in the French-speaking group sat looking rather bored. And when the others had left the room, the naval Commander looked after them with an expression of aloof commiseration and said, 'Ah, the Balkan dust.' This Commander had a flat, oriental face and a fastidious manner.

M. de Tournay now leant confidentially across the desk and, tapping the ash off his cigarette, said, 'Tell me, old fellow, are there any arrangements for rapid evacuation in special cases?' He was a small man with a pink head, wisps of grey hair and sunken eyes. 'What sort of special cases?' I asked him.

He didn't answer, and the Commander also leant forward and said, 'My friend has been severely ill.'

'I don't know, I'll see,' I told him.

'Well, we're glad to have met you, old chap,' M. de Tournay said. 'As for me,' he went on, fingering his blue prison clothes, 'I've got a good mind to go straight back to Paris dressed as I am. I'd like to appear at the next board meeting in this rig-out.' He spoke in a precise, agitated fashion, as if he was at a cocktail party. There was a sharp tremor in his voice.

'He did wonderful work,' the Commander whispered to me as they got up. 'He has lost his health and they have treated him with particular malice.'

He put his hand on his friend's shoulder and they went together out of the room. The two Dutchmen and the Belgian looked after them in a tolerant way. 'Too much temperament,' the young Lieutenant said. But Captain Telders frowned slightly. His look implied that the prison party should keep some sort of solid front in relation to ourselves.

'Well, is there anything else just now?' I said.

'Yes, there are several points,' said Captain Telders. 'First of all, you will not mind if I offer you some words of advice? Do not on any account trust the Germans. They will be out to deceive you.'

'We'll be on our guard.'

'You have not experienced what we have. You cannot know them as we do.'

'No, that's true.'

'I should like to tell you something about the officials here—those that I know of.'

'Yes, I wish you would.'

'Firstly, Bruhmer, the Commandant. He is a German of the old school, without understanding and a disciplinarian. But he will obey an order. You will have no trouble with him.' I lit Captain Telders' cigarette, and he went on, 'He has a certain respect for me, you know. He tried to make me work in the factory, where parts for small-arms are made. I said, "Colonel Bruhmer, you cannot ask a Dutch officer to make arms to be used against his allies." He said, "You will do as you are told like any other prisoner." I said, "If you are a man of honour, you will not insist on this"—and he capitulated.'

'He has not altogether caught up with the times,' the Belgian Major remarked. 'But he is stupid, and a stupid man with power over others is dangerous.'

He said this in a worldly-wise way, making a grimace with

his lips. This Major seemed the most relaxed and cheerful of those we'd met. His unassuming, self-confident face gave a strong impression of practical good sense.

'Then Krampff,' Captain Telders went on. 'Krampff is a nobody. He is exactly the same as the key hanging round his neck. Bark at him, and he will run and do your bidding.'

'And Rose?'

'Rose has lost his nerve. He foresees that the Allies will shoot him. However, these are not the dangerous men. The dangerous men are the Commandants of the two other prisons, Eberhard and Albinus.'

The others nodded vigorously. The Dutchman reflected, as if to make sure he would give the most damning facts in the concisest form.

'Eberhard we know best,' he began, 'since we were in his prison before it was evacuated here. Eberhard is'—he paused—'is a man unfit for the firing-squad. He is, in the first place, a murderer of prisoners.'

We waited for him to go on.

'Have you visited the prison hospital here?'

'No, not yet. Are there many men in it?'

'There are quite a number, and I hope you will see what you can do for them. When you have been there, you will know why.'

'I'll go there at once.'

'Eberhard is a murderer and torturer of prisoners.' He said this with great bitterness.

'However, if you talk to him, you may find him quite pleasant, as he has his agreeable side,' the Belgian Major added.

'Albinus,' Captain Telders continued, 'is, among other things, an official of the *Sicherheitsdienst*. He is an intelligent and vicious creature, not a brute like Eberhard, but a would-be Machiavelli.'

'What will you do to these people?' the Lieutenant asked.

'Nothing, yet. For the present, we must get the prison cleared.'

'You won't let them go?'

They looked at me sharply.

'Give us affidavits about them,' I said. 'Put all the facts in them, and they'll be used later on. We can't do anything more about it yet.'

They got up to go, and when Cuthbert and I were alone again, he said, 'What are we to believe of all that?'

'Most of it, I expect.'

'I didn't like that naval Commander's remark very much. Even being in prison doesn't seem to unite them.'

I rang for the Secretary. 'Cuthbert,' I said, 'will you find out how they're getting on with the lists? I'm going along to see the hospital.'

The Secretary had called for a warder, who held out his arm and then went ahead of me up the corridor. He unlocked a steel door, locked it again after us, and we passed through the central block of the prison. Four three-storied wings met at right angles round a hall, and there were arrangements of steel ladders like in the engine-room of a ship. The cells were crowded, and faces watched us as we passed. I tried not to catch their eyes.

The hospital ward had about thirty beds in it, all filled, and patients were lying on stretchers on the floor. There were German prisoners in attendance as orderlies, and I asked one of them for the Doctor.

'He is not here, Sir. He does not visit at this hour.'

'Go to the Secretary,' I said to the warder, 'and tell him to have the Doctor fetched at once.'

Those of the patients who could, sat up in bed and gazed at me. In the first bed was a Polish boy with a big, round head and an idiotic expression of bliss. He held my hand and wouldn't let it go. I asked what was the matter with him.

'Fever,' said the orderly.

'What fever?'

'The Doctor knows, I do not.'

In the next bed was a Dutchman.

'Look at me,' he said.

I looked at him with all the sympathy I could.

'No, look at me,' he said, trying to move the blankets.

An orderly pulled them back reluctantly. The Dutchman was so thin that he looked as if he would snap if you touched him.

'Never mind,' I said, 'never mind. Keep going, you'll soon get better.'

'I'm not a pretty sight.'

'Don't you worry. We'll get you well again.'

'I'm finished.'

'Don't believe it. Don't believe it.'

The orderly put the blanket back over him and muttered, 'It is a disgrace.'

There was a French sailor who told me he was from Brest. He had pale ginger hair and blue eyes, and his skin was the colour of grey flour. Emaciation put expressions on his face which his emotions didn't intend.

He seemed to be trying to talk, but couldn't do so. Then he wept and said in a thin voice, 'I can't help it.' It was hard to know what to do. I patted him on the shoulder softly, and whispered what truth and lies I could think of.

A patient suddenly shouted piercingly, 'They are trying to kill us!'

I went over and found that he was also a Dutchman. He looked at me fiercely, and cried, 'They're trying to kill us, and how can you stop them? You can't stop them.' He went on repeating this. He had a cunning, lunatic expression, and I had no real idea of what was passing in his mind.

Another Dutchman in the next bed stretched out an arm and tried to calm him, then called me over with a hoarse voice. He had dark hair, enormous brown eyes and must have been once good-looking. His face was firm but gentle, or perhaps it seemed gentle because he was so weak.

'Don't worry about him,' he said, in good English. 'He is excited. But you'll do what you can for us, won't you?'

'Of course. Straight away.'

He beckoned me closer.

'He had too much, he doesn't mean it. We can't control him any more. Get him back to Holland and he'll be all right.'

'We'll get him back.'

'All right then. Hurry up.'

'What's your name?' I asked him suddenly.

'Maarten.'

'Is that your first name?'

'Yes, my first name.'

I took his hand and said, 'We'll get you all back. I'll come again soon and tell you what's been arranged. All right?'

'Yes, do that.'

The orderlies followed me round to the other beds with a reserved, doubtful look, but one of growing shame and anger.

When I got back to the Commandant's office, I found a notice pinned on the door with ENGLISH COMMISSION written in Gothic letters. I went inside and was glad to find the Captain there with Cuthbert. They were looking through piles of dossiers stacked on the floor. The Captain got up, dusted his hands and offered me a cigarette. 'You look a bit pale,' he said. 'How's it going?'

'Oh, all right. You've heard what's happened so far?'

'Most of it, I think. We may be able to give you some help soon. The Garrison Commander's arrived with an advance party of troops. I've been to see him, and he's an old acquaintance: in fact, the Colonel we went on the night raid with, remember? He's still running true to form. Immediately on arrival, he's evicted the German General from his barracks, and he's made the Burgomaster order the population to take in their white flags and wash them and hang them out again.'

'Did you tell him about all this?'

'Oh, yes. He was quite interested, and said, "Carry on." I expect you'll be having a visit from him.'

'Will he do anything about accommodation for the people here?'

'I went into that with him. He's going to evacuate a hutted camp, and it should be ready in a day or two's time. And he says that from tomorrow onwards, he'll be able to supply transport and so on, to get these people there.'

'Well, here's another thing. There are about forty sick men in the hospital here. Can you get an Army doctor to see them?'

'I don't know if there is one yet, but if so, I'll ask him. How bad are they?'

'They seem very bad. Couldn't we put them in the city hospital?'

'Would it be safe to move them if they're all that bad?'

'I think it would be a good thing psychologically.'

'Psychologically?'

'Some of them seem to be scared stiff here.'

The Captain looked at me with his head on one side. 'Isn't there a prison doctor?' he said. 'What does he think?'

'There is one, but he's not here. I've sent for him.'

'Well, I'll see if there's room in the town hospital and if there's an ambulance. You might let me know when a doctor's seen them. Is there anything else?'

'Yes, the prison's overcrowded. About a third of the people here were evacuated from a Provincial prison about fifteen miles off. I think the thing to do is to keep all the Allied prisoners here, but send the others from the Provincial prison back there as soon as we can. But please tell them at Corps that the Commandant of this particular prison is in the *Sicherheitsdienst*.'

'How do you know that?'

'A denunciation.'

'Well, I'll tell them. How do you propose to get these prisoners there?'

'They came with their own trucks and warders when they were evacuated here, and they can go back again by road. Could you ask the Garrison Commander for an escort?'

'Yes. Just a moment while I write these things down.'

The Captain put on his spectacles and made notes with his fountain pen in his careful handwriting.

'When could this Provincial party leave?' he asked.

'Tomorrow.'

'And the Commandant's name is . . .?'

'Albinus.'

'Albinus? Peculiar name. Is that all?'

'No. We're sorting out the Allies, but there are also a lot of German political prisoners here.'

'Well?'

'We might get rid of some of them too.'

'I don't think so. That definitely doesn't concern us.'

I showed him the Pastor's letter. 'This is probably quite true, of course,' he said, after reading it, 'but we can't tackle all of them as well.'

'There are Germans in here for listening to the B.B.C.'

The Captain took off his spectacles and considered.

'Well,' he said, 'I don't mind what you do, really, provided you get the Allies out first and don't release any habitual criminals.'

I went with the Captain into the corridor to get the young man from the Channel Islands, and saw that several other people were waiting there. One was a big, tall man in a brown suit. The Secretary told me he was the prison Doctor, and when the Captain had gone, I told the Secretary to send him in.

The Doctor had a 'noble' head, like that of a young senator, and although he wasn't smiling, his mouth was built so tightly across his teeth that he appeared to be constantly on the point of doing so. His eyes blinked behind strong lenses, and he stood on the carpet with his fingers locked, bending slightly forward as if to catch the better any remarks I might make.

'Are you responsible for the prison hospital?'

'Yes.'

'Why are the patients in that condition?'

He raised his eyebrows, bent slightly further forward, and said, 'Please?'

I repeated the question.

He opened his hands and raised them up. 'They are ill,' he said.

'They certainly are. How did you allow them to get into that state?'

'Sickness is bound to occur.'

'Of course. But these men have been starving.'

'For patients in their condition, they are certainly undernourished.'

'Well?'

'But we are all undernourished. All Germany is undernourished. It is a consequence of the war.'

'Your soldiers are not undernourished like this.'

'Naturally.'

'Nor are all your civilians. You, for instance.'

He frowned slightly.

'Excuse me,' he said. 'The rations granted to sick prisoners, whether German or foreign, are identical with those given to civilians.'

'I don't believe it.'

He said nothing. A thought struck me. 'Do civilians live on their rations?'

'Oh, no. They supplement them in various ways.'

'While prisoners are unable to supplement them?'

'Of course. Being prisoners, they are unable to do so, as you say.'

'In other words, they are starving.'

'I have already said that I esteem them to be undernourished.'

The Doctor had explained all this patiently, as if to a man of limited understanding; but a note of vexation now came into his voice.

'And what have you been doing to remedy these conditions?'

'I?'

'Yes, you,' I shouted. 'And I didn't tell you to sit down.'

He stood up again, and his face assumed a severe expression.

'I have another question to ask you,' I said. 'Why were you not in the hospital today?'

'Excuse me,' he said, and paused. 'Allow me to explain. I was not in the hospital because I am not engaged as the full-time prison doctor, but only as the visiting doctor, and I have patients of my own, including outside hospital cases, some of whom I have left in order to answer your summons.' He took a deep breath. 'I would point out in addition that certain of the present inmates of my ward have not been for long under my care, since they have but recently been evacuated here. As regards the question of food, I have frequently made clear to the prison officials that the rations are insufficient. You will probably find my reports in the relevant files.'

'And they took no action?'

'Evidently not, since the rations did not improve.'

We stared at each other. He now continued more calmly, 'I have no doubt that the prison officials brought the matter to the notice of the higher authorities. You will understand that we can scarcely do more than this.'

'Then the higher authorities are responsible?'

'I cannot answer that question. It is not within my competence.'

I tried to return from the general to the particular. 'How many prisoners have died in the hospital?'

'In what period?'

'In the last year.'

'The exact figure I could give you from my records, but it would perhaps be between fifteen and twenty.'

'Is that normal.?'

'Normal in relation to what, might I ask?'

'In relation to a pre-war year.'

'The circumstances are scarcely comparable. Before the war, there were rarely more than five hundred prisoners here, few of them political, since those were sent elsewhere.'

'Well, let me have the figures, will you? Names, nationalities, dates of death and causes.'

'Certainly. That should not be difficult.'

'As regards the men at present in the ward. We are evacuating them with the others as soon as possible.'

'I am glad to hear it. I have not the proper facilities for treating them here. Certain medicines are also lacking.'

'Would they be better off in the civilian hospital?'

'Assuredly. Can you arrange this?'

'I hope to.'

'That would be excellent. I have never succeeded in doing so myself. You will understand that our city hospital has rarely vacant beds.'

'I suppose not.'

'A further advantage will be that I shall now have more room in my own hospital for many sick German prisoners who have been awaiting attention.'

'Why is it that all the worst cases in the ward are other than Germans?'

'The worst cases? By no means. Among the German prisoners are also serious cases.'

'As many as among the Allies?'

'Perhaps not so many. But remember: the foreign prisoners came from afar off, and were frequently admitted here in a poor state of health. But if you have seen more of them in the ward, it is because I have recommended that, in the present particular circumstances, everything possible should be done for those of foreign nationality.'

We stared at each other again in silence.

'All right,' I said, 'I'd like to see you again tomorrow, when I expect one of our own doctors to be here.'

'I shall be happy to make his acquaintance. Perhaps he can supply me with various needed drugs.'

'Meanwhile I'll make arrangements with the city hospital. Perhaps you'd see about getting the patients ready. Can they all be transported?'

'Yes, with care. Some are in a critical condition.'

He shook his head, blinking.

'The young Dutchman called Maarten,' I said. 'Is his condition grave?'

'Called Maarten?'

I described him.

'Oh yes, I recall him. His condition is unfortunately hopeless.'

He waited to see if there was anything more, made a little gesture with his open hands, then half bowed and disappeared.

Cuthbert came in with the first of the lists. It was that of the Allied prisoners, and it was divided into two sections, political and criminal.

We looked through the political list. Some men were awaiting the execution of death sentences. Some were condemned for life, or for periods of ten to twenty years. Others had not yet received sentences, though they had been arrested long before. Others again were condemned to terms of imprisonment which would begin only after the end of the war.

I looked to see what some of the Allied representatives were in for. Captain Telders had fifteen years for belonging to forbidden organisations, and had been already detained for two. The Belgian Major had seven years, increased to ten, for operating an illegal transmitter. The Czech lawyer had an unspecified sentence for harbouring persons disloyal to the Protectorate. The young Yugoslav had twenty years for participation in an attempted assassination of a person friendly to the Occupying Authority.

Maarten, the papers said, had been arrested on the Dutch-Belgian frontier, and his documents were marked, 'Detained on instructions of the *Sicherheitsdienst* for further interrogation relative to enemy Desertion Routes.' The date of his arrest was in the same month as that of the Allied landings in Normandy. It seemed certain he was the man I had been asked to look for.

When we came to examine the list of criminal prisoners, it was apparent most of the crimes were not crimes from our point of view; and in any case, the distinction between criminal and political charges seemed a subtle one. Shooting at a guard, attempting to evade deportation, failing to deliver grain—these were examples of criminal charges that seemed to have a political motive. We also noticed, as we went through the list, how the duration of the sentences often bore little relation to the gravity of the alleged offence, and varied widely in cases of identical crimes.

'I suppose there are some criminals among them,' Cuthbert said. 'Look at this one: theft with assault, four previous convictions.'

'Well, they're all going out. We'll hand their documents over to Corps when they've gone.'

'Is that right?'

'Stop worrying about whether it's right. The world's full of people who'll look after that. Follow your own instinct for a change.'

This dashed itself like a futile wave against the rock of his assurance. 'My instinct is to see these people are properly supervised. Will Corps make sure the documents are forwarded to the Allied Missions?'

'Oh, they may do. Or they may sit on them a month, or use them for salvage.'

'Well, I'll arrange their documents in national bundles. After that, they're Corps' responsibility.'.

'That's right. Now, what about the German lists? How are they getting on with them?'

'There are five of them hard at it. They're doing the list of those that are going with Albinus, first.'

'How many would be left here when the Albinus party and the Allies have gone?'

'There's 1400 in all, about 300 of Albinus's Germans and about 500 Allies. That leaves less than half.'

'We'll have a go at them tomorrow.'

Cuthbert nodded non-committally. 'There are one or two other things that have turned up,' he said. 'The Secretary tells me there's a Latvian who claims he's British. And one of the murderers has something important to tell us, and wants an interview.'

'You'd better look after those items. But first of all, find out whether the Captain's made arrangements at the city hospital, and if he has, go over there with all the patients, will you?'

Later in the day I met the Polish officer in the corridor. He pointed sullenly to a man in a torn prison uniform who was standing talking to Filipovic, the younger of the two Yugoslavs.

'That is the Pole who claims to speak for those who will not obey me,' the officer said. 'His name is Kowalski. You will find he speaks no foreign language.' Captain Wisniewski made the stationary jump that signifies a salute, turned, and went away.

I asked the two younger men in to the office. The Yugoslav's attitude was tolerant and supercilious, as if he was taking part in a comedy. He behaved in a protective way towards the Pole, who had a hefty frame and an air of enormous energy waiting to fling itself in some direction.

'He asked me to come along too,' the Yugo-slav explained. 'He prefers me to the other as an interpreter.'

'Does he know what he has to do?'

'Perfectly.'

'Ask him to tell me he understands.'

They spoke together. The Pole nodded vigorously. The Yugo-slav put his hand on his shoulder and said, 'Here's a man who fought in the woods a year before they got him. That is something your English soldiers don't know of, fighting behind enemy lines.'

'They've done a bit of it in Burma.'

'In Burma?' He gazed at me with incurious, intelligent eyes. 'I do not know of Burma, but that could not be the same. These men had poor equipment, and their own country was overrun.'

He was standing by the window, and he laughed and beckoned me over. Colonel Bruhmer could be seen plodding across the cobbles below with his shoulders hunched. He stopped and shouted angrily to someone out of sight. The Yugo-slav turned and said, 'And you still let him go free. If I had my way, he would have changed places with his prisoners by now.'

'That's what he will do'.

'Why not now? What are you waiting for? Some of us do not understand it. We found it difficult to persuade our people you're in earnest. But I explained that you are, in your own English way.'

'What do you know about the English way?'

He smiled and put his hands in his pockets. 'Old England,' he said. 'Old England.'

We smoked a cigarette. 'You don't seem to have had difficulty with your own compatriot,' I said to him.

'Why should I? He is an intelligent man. It makes little difference to me, anyway, whether my group is bigger than his, or his bigger than mine. Once we get out, his will disappear.'

'What is he?'

'He's a professor of some kind, a schoolteacher. Fond of his books, but he doesn't read the right ones.'

'And what are you?'

'Nothing, yet. I was a student when the war started, since then, a soldier.' He beckoned to the Pole. 'We will go back now. Don't be too long over it,' he said to me.

He paused as they reached the door.

'If you could get me a bottle of spirits, I should be grateful. You'll have some whisky, I expect? See what you can do, will you?'

He took the Pole by the arm and they went out.

I rang the bell, and told them to send in Albinus. He had been waiting outside, and came in immediately.

Albinus was by far the most supple and ingratiating of the prison officials. He treated me with such gross deference, flattered so visibly and effaced himself so vigorously, that his personality protruded with unpleasant force. When he smiled his eyes turned up at the corners, and he contorted his head sideways into his shoulders in gestures of self-abasement.

I talked to him about next day's departure. He seemed to have arranged everything admirably. At any suggestion I made, he nodded his head energetically, putting on the gravest air and giving me the strong impression that my instructions would be interpreted or ignored.

'When you arrive there,' I said, 'report to the British Military Governor at once, or as soon as he arrives. I shall see he gets a list of the men you are taking with you.'

'Of course, of course.' He now assumed an expression that was even more grotesquely servile. 'I have a little favour to ask. My wife and family: may they travel in the official vehicles?'

'Why not?'

'Oh, thank you. May I have a paper to this effect?'

'It's not necessary. I'll mention it to the military escort.'

'But may I not have a written permit?'

'Why don't you make one out for yourself?'

'That will be in order? Have I your word for it?'

'Quite in order.'

He got up to go, then paused, and turning his large torso

on his slender legs, said, 'Excuse this personal question: are you a jurist?'

I reflected whether I was. 'Yes,' I said.

'You are specially trained for prison work, no doubt?'

'Yes, carefully trained.'

'You have had other experiences of this kind in Germany?'

'This is the first.'

'Really.' He nodded at his boots; then looked up, bared all his teeth at me, and said, 'May I then congratulate you on your undoubted capacity?'

As he bowed himself out, I asked him to send in Colonel Bruhmer.

The Commandant came in, glancing at the portrait of Bismarck as a martyr might at a holy image, and stood opposite me on the far side of the desk. He carried a folder under his arm.

'Sit down,' I said.

He lowered himself into his chair, put on his pince-nez, and looked at me with his jaw dropping.

'Any problems?' I asked. He looked at me with his mouth further open, and I said, 'Is everything proceeding correctly?'

'Yes. All is being done, I think. There are many minor questions, however.'

'Go on.'

'First of all, I have to report that Mr. Rose has declared himself sick and been admitted into hospital.'

'With what?'

'He would appear to be in a state of delirium.'

'Have you enough staff without him?'

'I have appointed Mr. Krampff to his place for the moment.'

'All right. What else?'

'The regulations state that each prisoner, on release, is to be given a sum of money depending on the length of his sentence, the work he has done and his behaviour while in detention.'

'And?'

'Is this sum to be paid to Allied prisoners?'

'Certainly.'

'In that case, I must report we have insufficient funds.'

'Where do your funds come from?'

'From the Regional Bank. The director there informs me all funds have been blocked by order of the English authority in Hamburg.'

'I'll make enquiries about that.'

'Thank you. Prisoners, on release, are also entitled to the clothes and valuables taken from them at their entry into prison.' He took off his spectacles and looked at me tragically. 'In the case of persons coming from the other prisons, we have not all these clothes and valuables.'

'What happened to them?'

He shook his head despairingly.

'Well, that needn't delay us,' I said. 'Though I'd rather they didn't have to go out in prison clothes.'

'No. These must be retained in the prison, and will be needed for other convicts in the future.'

I stared at him.

'Send an officer to the Burgomaster for the number of suits you need,' I said. 'I'll give you a paper.'

He appeared relieved, and made a note in his agenda book. 'Are Allied prisoners to be issued with the release documents that are usually given?' he asked.

'That won't be necessary. But it will in the case of any German prisoners we release.'

He shifted suddenly in his chair. 'Are German prisoners also to be released?' he said, in an unexpectedly loud and angry voice.

'Yes. I'll speak to you about that tomorrow. Have you anything else?'

He opened his mouth once or twice, then got up rigidly and said, 'May I take my leave?' He walked out of the room as though a ton of lead were resting on his shoulders.

From the window of the Secretary's office, I saw an ambulance driving into the courtyard, and Cuthbert getting out and explaining something to a group of officials. I went down the stone steps and asked him what was happening. 'We took them round to the city hospital,' he said, 'but some of them insisted on coming back here again. They say they thought we were taking them to an English Army hospital. When we tried to off-load them at the local one, these four refused and said they'd rather be back in the prison near their friends.'

Among them was the excitable Dutchman. He gave me a hostile, triumphant look when he caught my eye.

'We'd better put them back in the ward, then. Will you give

the orderlies a hand? I'm going over to the city hospital to see the others.'

'These people are very difficult,' said Cuthbert.

I drove round to the billet and collected a load of rations and the letter Maarten's girl had given me. Then I found my way to the hospital, a large, new building on the outskirts of the town. The lights were already on when I reached it.

In the entrance hall, I met a middle-aged Sister who looked at me with contained distaste. I asked her to have the rations collected from the car, and as she showed me up to the first floor, I explained to her who they were for. 'You'll do what you can for them, Sister, won't you,' I said.

'Oh, we will do what we can. We are not monsters.'

'I know you're not. But do you know what these men have suffered.'

'So many have suffered.'

The ward where they had put the Allied prisoners was a wide room overlooking the fields. Some of them were already asleep, and I found Captain Telders sitting by the bed of the emaciated man.

'I am sorry the others went back,' he said. 'If I had got here in time, I should have stopped them.'

'It doesn't matter. So long as they're comfortable as possible.'

'Of course.'

I asked him where Maarten was.

'They have put him in a separate room. I will show you the way, but you must be careful.'

We walked along a very clean corridor. The nurses didn't look at us, nor did Captain Telders look at them.

'What that prison Doctor says about him, Captain. Is that true, do you think?'

'I should like to hear the opinion of one of our own doctors. If we can get him home, perhaps he may be all right.'

We found Maarten in a small room alone, lying in a position of sleep with his eyes open. He smiled when he saw us, and sat up. 'Now, now, young fellow,' said Telders, going over to the bed.

'I like these white sheets,' he said, as hoarsely as before. 'Did some of the others go back to the prison? It's a pity. Can you get these letters back to Holland?' he said to me.

'Yes, surely.'

'How long will they take?'

'A few days. I'll send them off at once.'

'A few days . . .'

'You should rest yourself, Maarten,' Telders said. 'And now I must say good-night. I must return to the prison to supervise the evening meal.'

'Would you like to take my car?' I asked him. 'The other Sergeant could bring it back.'

'No, it is pleasant for me to walk a short distance in the streets. Till later, then.'

As soon as he had gone, I said to Maarten that I believed I knew friends of his; and told him about my visit to the house of the Dutch doctor at the town we'd started out from in Holland, and how I had met his girl and the other young men there. He sat up again and said, 'She is alive?'

'Of course she is. I saw her only a few minutes, and it was six months ago now, but she's sure to be well. She asked me to give you this, if ever I found you.'

He took the letter and sat staring, waiting for me to go on.

'I wasn't at the doctor's for more than about an hour—it was an accidental meeting, and I never saw her again after that. But she's sure to be all right—the town had been liberated some months by then. She'll be waiting for you there.'

I thought he would want me to go so that he could read the letter, but though he kept glancing at it and held it with one hand against his chest, he asked me to describe the whole evening in detail. I tried to remember all I could, and spin the story out. He kept interrupting, and then I told him about the Seminary Director and the new job the young Dutchmen had been doing.

I got up to go, but he shook his head as he turned on one side and opened the letter. It must have been short, for he read it in a few seconds, stayed a minute with his lips open staring beyond the wall, then put the letter next to his breast and turned round again. He said nothing, but lay looking at me, or rather, not at me, with such joy that I felt I shouldn't go yet, and sat down again. I waited a bit, then asked him what had happened to him after he had been arrested.

'We were taken near the Maas with some pilots,' he said. 'I and the man you saw in the prison hospital—the one in the next bed who was shouting out.'

'How did he get in that condition?'

'They questioned him a lot after we were arrested, and often again since then.'

'And you too?'

'Yes.'

'What happened to the pilots?'

'I don't know—we were separated. They were sent to an airman's camp, I expect. They would be treated as prisoners-of-war, of course, not as political prisoners.'

'You know that lad's one of those who've gone back to the prison ward again?'

'Yes. They shouldn't have put me here in a different room. But we will be together when we all get out of the prison, won't we?'

'Yes, you're sure to be.'

'I have been writing to his parents also, so that they make ready for him.'

'I was looking at the address on the letters you gave me. I think I know his parents too.'

'His father is a lock-keeper at home. You met him as well?'

'With two young daughters?'

'You knew them also?'

'Yes, we had a billet near their house. One of our soldiers used to visit them a lot, and they came to dances we had.'

He asked me all about this, and I told him of our stay in his town, and found he knew most of the people we'd met there. He sat listening with his head on one arm and his eyes getting bigger and bigger.

A nurse came in, put a glass of some fluid on the side table, and began to take his temperature. While this was going on, I thought how, directly I got back to the billet, I'd ask Walter to go straight down to Corps headquarters and find out if Harry was still there and, if so, try to get him to come up to see the brother at once.

The nurse made a mark on the chart above the bed, and told me I shouldn't be there.

'What has she written?' Maarten asked.

'She's made a line.'

'Going up or down?'

'Going straight on, as a matter of fact.'

The nurse stood by the door holding it open, looking at me.

'Come again, won't you.'

'I'll be along tomorrow. Is there anything you want?'

'No. Only send those letters.'

'They'll go off tonight.'

'Come now, if you please, it is time,' said the nurse.

There was great activity next morning in the front courtyard as the prisoners under the care of Dr. Albinus got ready to leave. Stores were loaded onto the coal-driven trucks and trailers, and the warders, carrying slung rifles, were marshalling the men in long files.

A Corporal came up and told me he was in charge of the escort the Garrison Commander had sent. 'What are we supposed to do?' he said.

'Just see them past any German Units or any of our own, if you meet them.'

'We should do, there's a lot of our vehicles coming in this morning. Now what about their arms and ammunition? I've got the ammunition in my truck. Do I issue out some rounds to the Gerry warders?'

'Yes, you'd better. No. No, don't issue them ammunition. I'll tell them your men have got loaded arms, that'll be enough.'

'What if any of the prisoners try to escape?'

'Don't interfere.'

'You mean don't shoot at them?'

'No. Make the warders run after them.'

'You're serious about this, Sergeant?'

'Yes.'

'Well, I wasn't going to let the lads shoot at them, but I prefer to have it as an order.'

'You can have it in writing if you like.'

'I didn't mean that. So long as you'll say the word if there's any consequences.'

'I don't think you'll have any trouble.'

Cuthbert called me over and said Albinus wanted to know if, in addition to his wife and family, he could send his wife's father on the transport. 'No,' I snapped. Albinus, who had been standing expectantly by, looked at me with ill-suppressed malice and turned away. 'You're edgy this morning,' said Cuthbert.

As we watched the officials running about, we began to get the impression that something had gone wrong. They talked rapidly in little groups, sent warders scurrying hither and thither and glanced covertly at Cuthbert and me. I called the Secretary over. 'Is it all going well?' I asked him.

'Oh, yes.'

'Is there anything you're not telling me?'

He drew me inside a doorway, and said, 'They have lost the key.'

'Which key?'

'One of the master keys.'

'Who's lost it?'

He looked away and said he didn't know.

'How many of these keys are there?'

'Six.'

'And what do they open?'

'Everything.'

'Now that's why they carry them round their necks,' said Cuthbert. 'Hadn't we better do something about it?'

But there was no need to. Down a staircase into the sun ran Krampff, brandishing the lost key as though he had found the elixir of life. The officials took heart, joked about it, said their good-byes and the convoy moved off.

The lists of the remaining prisoners had now been completed, and Cuthbert and I went through the personal dossiers of the Germans.

'Of course,' said Cuthbert, 'we've no means of telling whether they've let us know about everybody. There may be people in the prison who aren't on the lists at all. And Albinus may be taking anyone in his party—we don't know any better.'

'We'll check the Allies out of the prison ourselves. And when they're gone, we'll go round all the cells and see who's left.'

'And who will be left?'

'That's what we've got to decide now. We'll let out all the German political prisoners to begin with.'

'All of them?'

'Is there anyone whose papers you've seen who you think shouldn't be let out?'

'What about these people who are in for acts against the State?'

'Cuthbert, don't you realise an act against the Nazi State isn't a crime to us? This man: ten years for printing an illegal pamphlet. Would you keep him in?'

'I wouldn't keep him in, but I wouldn't let them all out.'

We looked through the long list of German criminal prisoners. We found that some had been convicted a great many times over long periods. But as in the case of the Allies, we found others who seemed in the same class as the political prisoners. 'Look at this one,' I said. 'A suspended sentence for desertion.'

'Desertion's a crime.'

'We were dropping leaflets telling them to desert. We can't keep them in because they did. We ought to give them a medal for it.'

'But it is a crime from the German point of view. We're in Germany now, and we can't undo their laws till we've made new ones.'

'Mil. Gov. have revoked a whole lot of German laws.'

'Well, what about this one? An engine-driver in for abetting an illegal operation. That's a crime, isn't it?'

'An engine-driver? Let's have a look. Well, he may be all right. We should see him and find out the circumstances.'

'I see where you're heading. You want to let everybody out.'

'I wouldn't mind. The world's too full of prisons. And there are plenty of murderers and criminals outside, aren't there? Well, aren't there? The world's full of murderers, let's turn a few more loose.'

'Now you're talking wildly. But what we could do, is to make three piles of the criminal dossiers: In, Out and Doubtful. Then we'll go through them with the Secretary.'

'Yes. He probably knows more about the real criminals than we do. He's a practical man.'

'What about these juvenile prisoners? Some of them are sixteen. Here's one of fifteen.'

'Put them all among the ones to go out.'

In the middle of this discussion, the door was pushed open and the 'Beast of Belsen' appeared. He carried his fly-whisk and was followed by his Adjutant. We saluted him.

'What are all these?' he said, pointing with his whisk to the dossiers.

I told him. He walked over and looked at one or two, then carried them to the desk where he sat down in Colonel Bruhmer's chair. 'Have you got one for a man called de Tournay?' he asked. I found it for him. He turned over the sheets with his short fingers. 'He's been pestering me for an air passage to France. Funnily enough, I've managed to get him one.'

He shut the dossier, clasped his plump hands and looked at us. The Adjutant was examining Adolf Hitler's paintings.

'He's not the only person who's been pestering me,' the Colonel said. 'Do you know a Hungarian officer called Hunlady?'

'Hunyady, Sir,' said the Adjutant, turning round.

'Well, him. He visited you, didn't he?'

'The one who wanted to go to Austria?'

'That's the one. He gives me no peace. First he wants to do that, next he wants to give me riding lessons—me!—and then he begs me to stop his Yugo-slavs deserting.'

'His Yugo-slavs, Sir?'

'Apparently there are quite a number who were conscripted by the Hungarians, and they very naturally want to resign and become Displaced Persons. But I can't allow that. A man in Hungarian uniform's a Hungarian, as far as I'm concerned.'

He eyed us as if defying us to say the contrary, got up, and began walking about.

'Well, do you want any troops to help you out here? Don't say yes, I haven't got any to spare.'

'No, that's all right, Sir. But could you . . .'

'The hutted camp for the Allies? It will be ready tomorrow. Ready this evening, as a matter of fact, but don't evacuate them till tomorrow. I'll send you transport at eleven, will that do? Two trucks only, you'll have to move them in relays. Anything else?'

'No, I don't think so, Sir.'

'How many people will be left here when you've finished?'

I hesitated, then said, 'About two hundred.'

'Leaving how many empty cells?'

'The normal capacity is seven hundred.'

'Well, I want one block cleared completely.'

We looked at him.

'War criminals and such like, you know, and no doubt you people will be making your contribution. They'll soon be sending them to my guardroom from all over the province. And I won't like that, it'll mean I can't have any defaulters of my own.'

He smiled at us. We smiled back rather glassily.

'I'd like to see that hospital before I go. My Medical Officer will be along this afternoon.'

He had stopped in front of the warders' bookcase.

'They're an intellectual lot, aren't they. Poetry, too. And politics, of course. Well, never mind. Good-day to you.'

I asked Cuthbert to show him the way, but he was already out of the door, stepping briskly up the passage with his Adjutant. Cuthbert ran after them.

I rang the bell and told them to send in the German Pastor who had sent us the letter. He turned out to be a tall, theatrical looking man with wavy hair and big features. Almost before he could get out a few words, he began to sob on the desk. I told the warder to go.

'I've had your letter,' I said.

'Forgive me, forgive me, you cannot understand. You do not know . . . I . . . I who . . . it is impossible to say . . .'

I went over to the door and told the warder to fetch some coffee. When I sat down again, he suddenly raised his head, pushed it towards me and said, staring, 'For Heaven's sake tell me if I shall be set free. You have been here days now, and still we are locked up.'

I spoke to him angrily. 'You're going out shortly. First our own Allies must be released.'

But he wasn't listening. His face wore an expression of bliss, and he sobbed again.

After a while I said, 'What was it you wanted to tell me about the other cases?'

He had nothing particular to say, except that many were wrongfully convicted, including one of his parishioners. We discussed these cases a bit, and as he went on, he talked to me like a boy to an adult who has exonerated him. At last I gave him a large sheet of paper and told him to go next door and write everything down. He went out clasping the paper in both hands, and he glanced at the warder with a new light of friendliness, and yet wounded self-righteousness, in his eyes.

Cuthbert came in again. 'I've seen the Beast off the premises,' he said. 'We went all over.'

'Did you have any trouble with him?'

'No. He seemed very interested in everything, though. He asked them to show him the executioner's axe, but there doesn't seem to be one here.'

'I've just seen the Minister who sent us the letter. He was very upset.'

'You can't blame him for that, surely. This place *is* upsetting, you know. As I was coming back up the corridor, they started rattling their bars and shouting at me.'

'Who did?'

'They were Germans, I think. They shouted in German. The Allies are allowed out in the yard now.'

'Well, let's see that engine-driver of yours.'

'What engine-driver?'

'The one you want to keep in jail.'

He had a large, spare frame and a box-like head. He sat down, crossed his legs, and waited to hear what we should say.

'I see you were arrested two years ago and sentenced to eight years.'

'Sentenced, yes. But not tried. It was an administrative sentence.'

'Did you commit the offence for which you were sentenced?'

'If it was an offence. In the first place, it was not the real reason for my arrest. But I prefer not to speak of that unless it affects my prospects of release.'

'You'll have to tell us what the real reason was.'

'The woman had been forced without consent by a man with influence who tried to steal her from me.'

'Can you prove that?'

'If certain persons are still living, I can. Otherwise not, but it is as I say. If you insist on hearing more, I shall tell you. But it is a personal matter, and I do not like this habit of informing and denunciation. We have suffered enough from it.'

We had given him a cigarette, but he hadn't lit it. He now held it by the tip and, pointing it at us, said, 'May I ask if you intend to free me?'

'Yes.'

'When?'

'Within the next few days. Before, if possible.'

'I shall know what steps to take about this man when I am free.'

He accepted a light for the cigarette. 'What are conditions like among the German prisoners here?' I said.

'These are naturally bad. Go and see for yourself. They result from insufficient food, overcrowding, poor hospital treatment.'

'The prison Doctor here, he's good, is he?'

'He is competent, certainly, but he is a prison doctor.'

He got up and said, 'One final question: shall I be allowed to do my work again? You saw in my papers that I was perpetually debarred from the railways for so-called drunkenness?'

'Yes, I should think so, once they get the trains going again.'

'Very well. Release within the next two days.'

Cuthbert closed the door behind him. 'And how do you know that's true?' he said.

'I think it is. I got that impression, didn't you?'

'As a matter of fact, I did.'

'Let's have the Secretary in, Cuthbert.'

The Secretary was by now treating us as soldiers like himself who had to deal in a rough and ready way with a mess caused by civilians. We went through all the criminal dossiers with him, and he understood very clearly the sort of classification I wanted. He opened each folder, ran his fingers down the columns, read out scraps of the man's record, commented on it to us, made a recommendation, then put the folder down with a bang on one or the other of the piles. His judgements seemed very sensible.

At one point, he held a dossier open without speaking, then looked up at us. 'This man perhaps should stay,' he said. 'But he is a good fellow. He was a soldier with me. A very good fellow.'

'What's the charge?'

'Repeated assault. But I know the circumstances of one of these assaults.'

Cuthbert looked at us both.

'Listen, Sergeant,' the Secretary said. (He was the only one of the officials who called us 'Sergeant.') 'You know what it is with soldiers. He had a fight and wounded a Corporal accidentally.'

'Look here,' said Cuthbert, in English. 'You've got to call a halt somewhere.'

'We've got plenty of rejects. Aren't there enough for you?'

'Oh, well,' said Cuthbert wearily. 'And it is true the Garrison Commander seems to want the prison cleared.'

'All right, we'll let him out,' I told the Secretary.

He nodded approvingly, and we worked steadily on until we had divided the dossiers into three final piles: the Allies, the Germans for release and those who were to stay. We began carefully enough, but as time wore on we made up our minds more quickly. At first we had each consulted a dossier separately, passing it from hand to hand. But soon we read them all together, leaning over the desk, the Secretary tapping rapidly with his middle finger at the place where the previous convictions were written. We rarely disagreed and, if we did, usually decided on release.

We had just about finished, and were thoroughly exhausted, when there was a knock on the door and Colonel Bruhmer came in. I was ashamed to find myself embarrassed, but calling up reserves of ill-nature, I showed the Commandant the piles of dossiers.

'These are the Allies,' I said. 'They all go out tomorrow.'

'Yes, indeed.'

'Here are two categories of German prisoners.' I put a hand on either pile. 'These will remain—all these will go out.'

He looked at the larger pile for release, then back at me. 'ALL?' he said, with tremendous emphasis.

He stood gazing at the heaps of documents first with astonishment, then with anger and disgust. I could see he was losing any confidence he'd had in our capacity. But at the same time, he looked puzzled, as if there must be some reason for this, some logic of the occupying power he would have to try to understand. At length a huge thought struck him:

'But I shall have more warders than prisoners.'

He looked at each of us in turn as if we or he must be out of their minds. I told him to see about getting more suits of clothes, and to start the German releases immediately.

Dennis brought round a lunch hamper from the billet. He gave Cuthbert a thermos of tea, uncorked a bottle and poured out two glasses of wine.

'Well, here's to the Commissioners,' he said. 'Are you enjoying yourselves in this place?'

We asked him how he'd been getting on. He walked about gesticulating, holding a glass and a sandwich in either hand.

'The troops are moving up in force outside,' he said, 'and we've heard from Corps we're now here officially. Mil. Gov. arrived yesterday evening, and have set themselves up at the Town Hall. But some of the things they've already done are enough to break your heart.'

He put down his food, and pulled a large envelope out of his blouse. In it were photographs that had been taken at Belsen-Bergen.

'I lifted these from Mil. Gov., they've got a stack of them. And what do you think they've done? They've plastered them over the entrance to their office in the Town Hall. I suppose they imagine it'll cause everyone to tremble. But all it does is make their offices look like a derelict Information Room.'

'What's wrong with sticking them up?' said Cuthbert. 'The Germans ought to know about it.'

'Then let them do the thing properly. They should put them on a notice-board and say what they're all about. But what's happened is that a little clerk has fixed them onto a glass door with stamp-paper, and written insults underneath in red pencil in English. Do they think anyone will believe them if they do it that way?'

He glared at us, and poured himself out another glass.

'Well, I shan't lose any sleep over it,' he said. 'I shall put in my six hours a day, and then return to rest at my frat.-flat.' His face grew more cheerful. 'Do you know what I did yesterday? I drove all the way back to the Hotel Pfeufer and brought my steady up here. I've installed her in the new flat alongside the woman Gordon's got himself. It's a very nice place. You must come and see it, and meet our wives.'

'So you and Gordon are going native, Dennis.'

'It would seem so, wouldn't it. Gordon's thinking of marrying here in Germany. That's not a bad idea, I might end up that way myself. At any rate, all I can say is my Rhine-maiden's so attached to me that if ever I go back to England without her, she'll either jump out of the window or follow me there.' He looked proud and rather glum.

'Did you have any difficulty getting her up here?'

'Oh, no. Things are settling down in the rear areas. Jodl's signed the surrender at Rheims, they say, and the war's well and truly over.' He paused, with a note of sorrow in his voice, then frowned darkly, and said, 'As for the things I saw Mil. Gov. doing in that town, they make you despair. In the first place, they've started christening streets after themselves. The The Adolf Hitlerplatz has become the Parsonsplatz. The Hermann Göringstrasse is the Finlaysonstrasse in honour of a Legal expert who's joined them. They tried to call the Town Major's street the Adeaneallee, but he tore down the signs and threatened to put in a complaint.'

'They've really done that?'

'Oh yes, you know how it is. They all get happy at the mess and start picking themselves streets. But what will the locals think? Once you lose the respect of these people, you're done for.' He poured himself another glass. 'But that's not the worst of it. Do you remember the paper factory opposite the mill dam? Well, they've taken the machines out and dumped them in the fields.'

'You're making this up.'

'I'm not. It's the talk of the whole town. You can see the machines there, rotting in the dew.'

'Is there any reason why they're doing it?'

'It's going to be a provincial internment camp for all the people we and our kind arrest. But why can't they use some other place than a factory?' He stared at us indignantly. 'Well, there it is. It makes you realise what's it's like to be occupied. After all, it's a thing that might happen anywhere. We're all getting to be Displaced Persons now.'

He hunched his shoulders and paced gloomily up and down the room. 'And what's been going on at our office here?' I asked.

'Oh, we're arresting right and left. Denunciations are pouring in, and the big Nazis are queueing to give themselves up. In fact, we've discovered one useful thing. There's no need to go out and find them. All you do is send round word that they're to hand over their latchkey and ration-book to their wives, and report up at the office with their small kit and a toothbrush. And round they come, with their rucksacks, like lambs to the slaughter.'

'The Gestapo too?'

'No, not the Gestapo, they need looking for. But the Nazi leaders, yes. They come round as if they were doing penance.'

'Where are you putting them all?'

'In the little police jail. But it's overflowing, and we'll soon be sending them in here, they tell me. And that reminds me. You remember the Flying Officer and his chain? Well, he came round this morning to tell us he's seized fifteen youths he discovered on his airfield. They were committing some more sabotage, he says. I expect they were looking for potatoes in the allotments there. We've refused to take them, but I warn you, he may try to bring them here.'

'Didn't you tell him not to?'

'I tried to persuade him to release them. But it's a waste of breath talking to these amateur enthusiasts.'

Captain Telders came in, and we introduced Dennis to him. He said he had some documents he wanted to show us. But Dennis wasn't interested in hearing about these, so after inviting Captain Telders to come round and drink with him at the billet some time, he left, carrying the empty hamper.

Captain Telders handed us a manuscript report on Eberhard. 'In the annexes, you will find affidavits by some of my countrymen here,' he said.

'And what are all these?'

'Those are documents I have obtained from the prison files.'

'You've been consulting the prison files?'

'Yes. For information I needed.'

'I didn't say you could see the prison files.' He made no answer. 'Who gave them to you?'

'I had them from Bruhmer.'

'Captain, if you've been going to Bruhmer and telling him to give you files, you've been overdoing it.'

'Oh? I am sorry. I did not think to find an objection on your part.' He was very polite and frigid.

'The prison staff are on edge, and if you start giving them orders as well, they won't know where they are.'

'I did not forsee your objection.'

'Please deal with the Germans through us for anything of this sort.'

'Very well, that is understood. Shall we leave this subject?'

'Yes.'

'Well, now. I would like to ask you to have Eberhard in here.'

'Why?'

'I have an accusation to make, and I wish you to witness it.'

'What accusation?'

'That apart from other things, he has personally taken the prisoners' valuables.'

'That's a minor point, isn't it, compared with what you've put down in these affidavits?'

'For the prisoners, it is not a minor point. I wish to confront him with this accusation.'

'No, not now. I don't see that it's necessary yet.'

'Will you have him arrested?'

'We're not going to have anyone arrested till you people are out of the prison.'

'You know he is preparing to leave?'

'No, I didn't know that.'

'He says his duty is to return to his own prison, and he is leaving tomorrow. And do you not see why? Because he is afraid. And if he goes away now, he may easily disappear altogether. That is why I sought to get proof for you by asking for the prison documents.'

I reflected. 'You'll have to wait till after tomorrow before we begin anything of that sort. I'll tell Eberhard he's not to leave.'

'You will tell him, you say.'

'I'll see he doesn't leave.'

I was showing Telders out, when the Secretary brought a Medical Corps Captain over. He was young, and had a well-washed, untroubled look. He said he'd been sent by the Garrison Commander, and wanted to see the hospital ward. I took him along there, and left him with the German Doctor.

As I was returning to the office, the warder who had opened the various doors unexpectedly took me by the arm and said familiarly, 'My name is Hofacker.' He was an elderly man with a sad, wicked face, and his uniform hung on him in folds.

'Listen, Sir,' he went on. 'Please remember that I have always behaved decently to the foreign prisoners. Ask them. They will tell you so.'

'Good for you.'

'Make a note of it. I got them linen, and sometimes tobacco.'

'I'll note it down.'

He patted me on the arm, and let me through the last of the doors.

I now had an interview with Krampff. Standing opposite to me precisely at the middle of the desk, he announced apologetically that the only clothes the Burgomaster could supply were sailor suits from the Naval Depôt. 'Without insignia, of course. The material is satisfactory, but it is proper for these men to wear such uniforms?'

'I don't think they'll mind.'

'Well, as you say. Now to the question of money. I understand you have not yet succeeded in releasing the funds?' he asked politely.

'Not yet.'

'What are we then to do?'

'You can make a token payment.'

'Of how much?'

'Divide the sum you have by the total number of prisoners to be released, and give them that.'

'And the future salaries of our own staff?'

'Keep back enough for a week's pay before making the division. The Allies won't have much use for marks, anyway.'

'Then excuse me, is it necessary to make them a payment?'

'Yes, for the principle of the thing.'

'The principle?'

'Yes.'

'Now,' he said, assuming a determined expression, 'I am sorry to tell you the Polish officer has struck a warder.'

'Why?'

'For no reason.'

'I'll look into it.'

'Thank you. The man has lost some blood.'

'All right, I'll look into it. Is there anything else?'

He eyed me doubtfully, then drawing himself together, his

voice growing even louder and rather higher, he said, 'There is one thing I would like to say. Perhaps you think we have been inhuman in our treatment of the prisoners. May I continue?'

'Go on.'

'It is not so. We have always done our duty to them.'

'That is impossible.'

'I beg your pardon?'

'It's impossible to do your duty to men imprisoned unjustly.'

He pondered over this, but his train of thought remained the same.

'I only want to assure you that this has always been considered a model prison. We have had missions visit us from many parts of Germany.'

'Sit down a minute.'

He sat on the edge of the chair, with his hips spreading over it. He had a curious way of pursing his lips, as if he were sucking a sweet.

'Have you been here long?' I asked him.

'Here in this prison? Oh, no. I am from Prussia. I was transferred here not long before the war.'

'But you've always been a prison official?'

'No, not so. I was previously in the Finance Department.'

'What made you change?'

He shifted in his seat and looked rather embarrassed. Then choosing his words carefully, he said, 'My motives were twofold.'

'Yes . . .'

'On the idealist plain, if I may say so, I became interested principally in juvenile crime, and wished to apply the principle of strict segregation of juvenile from adult prisoners. That is to say, I believed that habitual crime in the case of juveniles must be considered as non-existent.' He breathed out.

'Do you mean you think that only adults can really be criminals?'

'I mean that young offenders, ın my opinion, whatever their records, should in principle be considered as delinquents, not as criminals.'

'And you were able to put your idea into operation?'

'Oh, it is not my idea. It is a generally held idea—that is, among enlightened persons, so I would say. Yes: prior to the waı, our younger prisoners were established in farming and wood-cutting camps. Unfortunately, since the war, through lack of staff and other causes, such cases have in most respects been once again assimilated to the others.'

'I see. Now what about the material plain?'

'You mean?'

'You said you had two motives when you became a prison official.'

He now looked diffident, almost coy. 'Well, this will be evident to you. As a finance officer, I enjoyed my salary: so much, and no more. But now, with the same salary—also increasing, of course—I have numerous additional advantages, such as house, food and various services.'

'What services?'

'Free repair of boots by the prison cobbler, for instance,' he said, pointing to his feet. 'Also free peat, dug by the prisoners in the course of their work.'

'And you like living in the prison?'

He looked at me in a horribly affable way.

'Such things are no doubt a question of habit,' he said. 'It was my wife who at first made objections'—he smiled— 'but she is now as attached to these duties as I am, and she delights in the sharing of my problems.'

A bell rang in the distance, and he picked up his papers. 'Well, you will excuse me,' he said, and touching his key, as a cleric might his pectoral, he went out with it swinging on his neck.

The Medical Officer had returned from his survey, and he looked in to collect his mackintosh. He was leaving without a word, so I said, 'How did you find them, Sir?'

'Who?'

'The men in the ward.'

'Well, they're as comfortable as can be. They seem to be doing all they can for them.'

'Have you seen the others at the city hospital? We've taken most of the Allies there.'

'No. Ought I to?'

'I got the impression they were all in a bad way.'

He stared at me. 'Some are sick, certainly,' he said. 'But as prison hospitals go, this one seems to me reasonably efficient.

They're short of certain drugs, of course, and handicapped by overcrowding.'

'Could you help them with the drugs at all?'

'I may be able to later.'

He began to put on his mackintosh. 'We must give these people their due,' he said.

'For starving our Allies?'

He emerged from his detachment and considered me as a person, but as a distasteful one. 'There's no need at all to speak like that, Sergeant,' he said.

'That's what they've done, isn't it?'

Washing me out of his mind again, he did up the belt of his coat, slapped it, and went out in silence.

As he passed through the door, I saw the prison Doctor in the corridor. He smiled good-bye to the Medical Officer, then knocked and came into the room.

'Those who returned from the town hospital,' he said. 'They will be going also tomorrow?'

'Yes.'

'Prime, prime. We shall all be very busy.'

He now looked at me rather dubiously, and putting his fingers on the edge of the desk, said, 'At the Town Hall they are showing some photographs.'

'So I've heard.'

'Of a place called Belsen.'

'Yes.'

'A question: are these photographs authentic?'

'Yes.'

'You have seen this place?'

'No, not personally.'

He smiled.

'I've talked to people who have.'

He nodded several times, then said, 'In the photographs, it seemed to me there were soldiers in Russian uniforms, standing by the open graves.'

'At Belsen?'

'So it appeared to me.'

I picked up the packet of photographs Dennis had brought.

'Look at them. Those soldiers are British.'

'And that is Belsen-Bergen in Germany?' He took up the photographs one by one and examined them carefully, holding the rim of his spectacles between a finger and thumb. He took his time over each one, and his total lack of expression, other than that of obvious interest, was such that it was absolutely impossible to guess what was going on in his mind.

'These heaps of bodies,' he said at last, 'are what?'

'What do you mean, "are what"? They're men and women.'

'It is difficult to believe.'

He went through them all, then put them back in a neat pile on the desk. He looked up at me, and said, 'Well, understand. We have heard so much propaganda.'

'You think it's propaganda.'

'Since you say these are authentic, no. But we have heard nothing of such places.'

'Perhaps you have not wished to hear.'

'Wished to?'

'And it seems to me,' I said heatedly, 'that if you take the patients in your hospital and multiply them by tens of thousands, then you have Belsen.'

'Multiply them?'

'Yes, multiply them.'

He examined me curiously as I lit a cigarette.

'And if I may speak freely,' he said, 'are there not similar places in other countries? In Russia? In England, possibly?'

'Would that alter anything? If one of us did it, can the other?'

'So it would seem to me, in time of war at any rate.'

He stood quite still as if inviting me, politely, to convince him further. When he saw I had nothing more to say, he changed the subject and we talked about arrangements for the evacuation.

Cuthbert came is as he was leaving and said, 'Well, that Flying Officer's done as Dennis said. He's landed us with sixteen werewolves. They're all down there in the courtyard.'

I got up. 'Is that Flying Officer with them?'

'No, he sent them round with a Provost Corporal.'

'You refused to take them?'

'I refused to take them, but the Corporal refuses to take them back.'

'Go down and tell that Corporal to get out of here with them.'

'But I tell you, he won't go till he gets a receipt.'

'Give him a receipt, and turn them loose. Go on, get rid of them all.'

Cuthbert sighed, I hustled him out of the door. Colonel Bruhmer was standing there like an ancient monument. He said he wanted to see me immediately.

It was evident some last straw had broken the Commandant's back, for he came in nervous and glowering, no longer the automaton of the day before. He stood at the desk and barked out, 'In view of the facts that my warders are assaulted, that the prisoners give me orders, and that I myself am no longer treated with the minimum respect, I have the honour to hand in my resignation.' He placed an envelope on the table, and stood staring with a flushed face.

'Sit down,' I said.

He remained standing.

'Sit down!' I shouted.

He still stood.

I tore up his letter, leaned forward and shouted it again. He sat slowly down.

'A soldier has not the right to leave his post.'

I stuck to that, while he told me his woes. By exhortation and veiled threats, I persuaded him to carry on.

Cuthbert came back, and watched the tail end of this with interest. 'You seem quite attached to the old boy,' he said, when the Commandant had gone heavily out. 'What's going to happen to him?'

'He'll be inside himself in a day or two. An honorary S.S. Colonel and prison governor? His days are numbered.'

'Do you think he knows?'

'I think he possibly does. That may be why he wanted to resign. I expect he'd like to get it over.'

'So he'll go into his own prison.'

'No, I'll try to get him sent somewhere else.'

'So as not to hurt his feelings?'

'I'm not thinking so much about his feelings. I'm thinking about the effect it would have on the warders here. This place will go on, and a lot of the warders will stay. It won't encourage them if they're put to guard one another.'

'And who'll get Bruhmer's job?'

'That'll be for Mil. Gov. to decide, but I shouldn't be surprised if they chose Krampff.'

'Well, they'd better decide soon, or the organisation here will collapse.'

'So long as it doesn't before tomorrow evening. Did you get rid of those werewolves?'

'Oh, yes. But an Infantry Lieutenant has arrived and is moving about the building. He says the Garrison Commander's sent him to get the block ready for the British prisoners.'

'More people being slung inside. It'll never end, will it.'

'But this is different. They're Nazis.'

'Yes, they're on the losing side.'

'Now listen, you're not comparing Nazi prisoners with our Allies?'

'No, I'm not. The cases are quite different. It's this passion for slinging people in jail I find so horrible.'

Cuthbert looked at me. 'We've done quite a bit of that ourselves,' he said.

'I know we have, and it's not finished. But I've never been convinced about it, myself.'

He shook his head, drew himself together and said, 'So long as a man is guilty, it's a matter of duty to see he pays the price.'

'You're certain when they're guilty, aren't you. But apart from anything else, when you think how many phoney charges we've discovered here, are you sure none of that's going to happen now it's we who are putting them in?'

'You can't compare Nazi Germany in war time with British methods in peace.'

'What do you know about British methods in peace?'

'I mean you mustn't go by conditions here. In Nazi Germany, they'd take your freedom away on any pretext.'

'I'm beginning to think most men wouldn't hesitate to take away somebody else's freedom. It seems as if a great many men like putting one another in prison.'

'Not without a valid reason.'

'They may be unaware of the reason. Perhaps the real reason is that most men know it's a matter of chance whether they're in prison or not themselves. There can't be many men who haven't done something they think they ought to be in prison for. An undetected crime, some act without a law against it—or they may be so impressed by power that they think it really is criminal not to believe whatever they're told to. So if they can get another man locked up, they're reassured.

Because, deep down, they feel they've got someone else to serve their sentence for them.'

'But most men have nothing to do with getting other men locked up.'

'Even when they haven't, it's the same. When a man walks past a prison, he feels fear and satisfaction: fear they may get him, and satisfaction they've got somebody else. If he sees the prisoners, he thinks of them harshly because he wants to forget he might be in their place. That's why they dress them up in those sordid clothes, so that everyone can believe they're all criminals. And you hide this from yourself by saying, "They must be guilty, otherwise they wouldn't be in there".'

'I hide it from myself? Excuse me. Seeing this place has shown me clearly how different honest men and criminals can be.'

'Has it? When you look at a lot of the criminal prisoners here, and then think of the men you know outside, can you really see the difference?'

'How could I, in so short a time! And there is such a thing as a real criminal! What do you know about that? It's easy to come along here and take pity on them, but that's sentimental self-indulgence. And do you think they'd thank you for it? Oh, no. They'd rob and kill you and everyone else, once they got out. Some men can be altered, but others are too far gone. It's best to leave these things alone, and let experienced people deal with them.'

'Of course there are real criminals. But they're outside just as much as in. And as for your experienced people who deal with them, hasn't it struck you how like most of them are to the criminals themselves? Well, hasn't it? Think of the jailers here, and the police we've met. The difference between the criminals and a lot of the men who guard and arrest them, is that criminals commit crimes in fact, and the others in imagination, and often in fact too, as we've seen time and again.'

Cuthbert put his head on one side. 'It seems to me,' he said, 'that it's you who've got a guilty conscience.'

'That's what having a conscience is, isn't it? Have you ever met a man with a clear conscience who wasn't a fraud or blind as a bat?'

'And furthermore, you don't seem to realise that so long as there's evil in the world, police and prisons are needed to keep it in check. They're not ideal in themselves, perhaps. But in suppressing crime, they suppress the greater evil.'

'Police forces don't suppress crime. They create it.'

'Oh, come, come.'

'They prevent individual crimes, and increase crime as a whole. The more policemen there are, the more crime there will be. Police forces create criminals.'

'I say the contrary: crime creates police forces.'

'They create each other. They're part of the same thing.'

'Just as you might say a doctor and the sick man he cures, are part of the same thing?'

'Policemen aren't interested in curing, only in catching. And to cure a man, you don't have to be ill yourself. But if you want to know how a criminal works and how to trick him, you must catch his sickness and become a criminal in your own mind. Policemen are criminals who don't commit crimes.'

'If you don't commit a crime, how can you possibly be a criminal? And don't you see that if it wasn't for policemen, there'd be even more crime than there is?'

'I'm beginning to doubt it.'

'Oh, really!'

'Police forces and prisons breed criminals and spread the atmosphere of crime. The way a policeman sees the world is a place inhabited entirely by criminals in jail and out of it. He knows a certain percentage can always be put inside, and when he looks at anyone, he says to himself, "Why not him?" And if he can, he slings the man in the pending file where society drops its unsolved human problems. Police work has become big business, and they're on the look out for clients. They'll make a crime where no crime existed. And they're always on the side of the big battalions. They'll arrest whoever they're told to. They don't care what the crime is, so long as it's called one. Millions support this now, and even those who think they don't, support police forces. All sort of people say they're against police rule, but everyone wants to increase the powers of the men who'll administer it.'

'You might say the same of war and soldiers.'

'I do say it. And it's best to be consistent. If you're going to use war, you must support soldiers. If you're going to have police rule, you can increase police powers. But not otherwise.'

'As to soldiers, I rather agree with you. The bigger armies

have got, the bigger wars have been, of course. And regular soldiers have a vested interest in war, it's true. But police—no. That's smaller stuff.'

'It's not. Soldiers can blow up a thousand cities, but they can't corrupt a community. It's not soldiers who are a danger any longer—their day's past. The danger now is the police power that breeds crime and encourages indifference and irresponsibility.'

'Who do they make irresponsible?'

'Everyone. Is anyone responsible for the crime that goes on? Should they do anything about it? No, the police forces are there, let them look after it. They're the professionals who understand it. So if you hear a cry in the night, you turn over and say, "It's not my business—the police will handle it." A criminal hasn't got the community against him any more—he's got the police force. Dealing with crime's been handed over to them like dealing with your dirty washing to the laundry. But it's we who dirty the washing. It should be our concern.'

'All right. We suppress prisons and we suppress the police. What happens then?'

'We can't suppress either. They'll be with us for generations.'

'But if we could. There'd be anarchy.'

'The choice may soon be whether you have criminals, or organised crime to suppress them. Whether you'll run the risk of being robbed and murdered, or have the third degree and a bullet in the neck to protect you. But even crime is less dangerous than police power. And if men tried to deal with crime themselves, instead of handing over their responsibility to an anonymous police, they might grow to realise it's they who've caused it—that they're responsible for it themselves.'

'How can individuals deal with organised crime?'

'I don't know. But they'd better find out how if they want to remain individuals.'

'Very weak. And what about the criminals if there aren't prisons? What would be done with them?'

'Oh, I don't know, Cuthbert. But a man like yourself—shouldn't you look after them? Bring them home to live with you and cure them? You take it on yourself to condemn them—shouldn't you take on the job of improving them? Of teaching them?'

'Me?'

'Yes, you. They might teach you a lot, too.'

'Take them home?'

'You'd do it for one of your own family, wouldn't you, if he got into trouble?'

'That I might. But not for all and sundry. I don't believe it'd be at all effective.'

'One day, you might try doing something you don't believe in.'

'And moreover, apart from your being quite wrong, I think you've been generalising too much from particular instances you've seen here in Germany. Are you really making out all this applies to us?'

'It's growing everywhere. Here in Germany, everyone thought of prisons. Every man who didn't believe in Hitler in his heart, and who wasn't inside a concentration camp, must have wondered why he wasn't. And those who did believe in Hitler, and used to say that prisons were just the right place for their opponents and the wrong place for themselves— a lot of them are thinking now, "Since we put so many in, it's our turn, and we deserve it." We could reach the same state of mind before long. But imprisoning vast numbers of men is a process that has a growth of its own. The more you arrest, the more you have to. And the more everyone grows to feel they should be arrested themselves.'

There was a glimmer of doubt in Cuthbert's eyes, and for a moment, he seemed defenceless. But it was only for the space of a heart-beat; and as the water in a pump, if it falls, must rise again to the top, so did the familiar look spread over his face again.

'We must be practical about these things,' he said. 'There are bad men as well as good in the world, and until they alter, we must keep their evil instincts in control.'

'You'd be lost if it wasn't for the bad men.'

'I don't quite get that.'

'A lot of men would be lost without their enemies.'

He shook his head and said, 'Well, perhaps you can really only tell about these things when you've been in prison yourself. At all events, cheer yourself up. I've been handing out clothing and documents with the Secretary *ad nauseam*.'

'And what about the politicals in Albinus's party? We should have kept them here, as well as the Allies.'

'Now look here, don't exaggerate. We couldn't have thought

of everything at once. We'll let our people up there know about them, and they'll take action.'

'You think they will?'

'Well, I expect so.'

'We should have let them out while we had the chance. We should have let everyone out. Everyone.'

Cuthbert tidied the heap of dossiers on the table. 'If you'd let everyone out, you know, Corps would have smelt a rat, wouldn't they?'

'I don't believe anyone would have noticed.'

'Still, we've handed in the figures now.'

'Yes. How many of the Germans for release will be gone today?'

'Oh, a good half. After that, we retire from this place, I hope.'

'Before we do that, we'd better see the Polish officer and the warder. And I want to talk to Eberhard. Will you ask the Secretary to find him as well?'

Cuthbert was seeing the warder in another room, and Captain Wisniewski stared at me balefully with one hand gripping each arm-rest of his chair. I asked him how the dispute had arisen, and he said, 'I do not consider I must justify my action. If you have accusations to make against me, you may do so.'

'Did this man provoke you?'

'Provoke me! Our whole existence here has been subject to humiliation and provocation. We have been treated worse than the beasts in the fields.'

'Why did you strike this particular man?'

'I do not know his name or anything about him, and to me he is not a particular man. He is a German warder, that is enough. He dared to give me an order. He was the first who dared to give me an order since their defeat. Therefore I struck him. Somebody should strike them, and I did so. I do not regret it.'

'Oh yes, I see.'

'No, Sir, you do not see. You cannot conceive what these men have done to us. We have had to support insults that are unbearable. There is a limit to what insults a man can be asked to bear in silence.'

That seemed to be all, and I saw him to the door. The

Secretary was waiting there, and he said he hadn't been able to find Eberhard anywhere.

'He's not in his office?'

'No, nor in his living quarters.'

He told me this rather pointedly. I said, 'Then where is he? Has he gone out?'

'Where he is I do not know, but I notice that the drawers and cupboards of his room have been mostly emptied.'

We nodded to each other, and he left without further comment. It struck me Eberhard was a more practical man than his colleagues. I got out Telders' report about him, typed a covering note and put these papers in an envelope for Corps. Then I went down to the courtyard.

Walter drove in to the prison as I was driving out. He drew alongside, and we spoke from car to car.

'Just missed him,' Walter said. 'The draft left for Antwerp yesterday.'

'Major Bane couldn't do anything to keep him, then?'

'I saw Major Bane, and he has his own troubles to think of, besides Harry's. They've sent up a Colonel from Lines of Communication to take over his job, and Major Bane's dropped down to second-in-command. Well, there it is. Young Harry shouldn't have played fast and loose.'

'He might see one of his girls on the way back.'

'He won't see either of them. I spoke to the Movements Sergeant, and he says that now all the roads are clear, the convoys are being routed direct by north Holland. He won't pass through any of the places we were in on the way up.'

'Unless he deserts.'

'Harry? He's got more sense, or at least I hope he has. That never gets you anywhere. No, he won't desert. And perhaps it's a blessing in disguise, this posting of his. He'll have time to think it all out in the jungle there.'

'You don't think love out. You think of love.'

'Maybe. But if you're asking me for a steady guess, I'd say he'd come back to the Dutch girl. That's where his heart lies, really. Or at any rate, his better nature. Though I doubt he'd ever feel the same about her if he does . . .'

Walter turned his car round, and we drove out of the prison together. He took the road to the billet, and I went on to the city hospital.

I found Maarten writing another letter. He moved the things off the bed onto the table as I sat down beside him. I told him what had happened at the prison, and he said, 'And tomorrow we will all be out? It is hard to believe, even now. Did you have difficulty?'

'Not really. It had to happen of itself, when you come to think of it. There was a fragment of the old State left there, and all we had to do was to appear for this last scrap to fall to pieces. It's been the same the whole way up—we've only had to arrive and clap our hands to get what we've wanted. But from now on, it will be different, I expect.'

'They will resist you, you think?'

'I don't know . . . You get the impression that now their gods have been overturned, they've withdrawn into their huts to lick their wounds there. They feel deserted and lost, and sit waiting for some new revelation . . . And what about you? They're treating you all right here?'

'Oh, yes.'

'They gave you a bloody awful time, didn't they.'

'Well . . . these men were caught up in events which got worse by degrees, till they lost control and couldn't stop what had been started. I can't forget what they've done to me and the others. But it's easy to see how it happened.'

He moved round in the bed, not finding a comfortable position.

'We knew we shouldn't be there, and that helped us. But they knew it too, or some of them did. Most were inhuman from the start, but even those who weren't, soon turned into the same thing. They had to do something destructive, and to be able to do it, they had to destroy themselves. They were dragged backwards, and any real human conduct became impossible. Everything they did grew dirty and shapeless, and their whole natures were spoiled and eaten away. It was terrible for us, but perhaps more terrible for them, because we were victims, but they were free, or thought they were.'

'You'd say they're not entirely responsible?'

'I think everyone has responsibility for each act at each moment. But once conditions like that have developed, they take control of the men who believe they're making the decisions. It all swells like a great sickness, and in the end, they become their own victims.'

'I don't think any of the prison officials see it that way. If they feel guilty at all, it's only because of the defeat.'

'Oh, probably they do not see this. But it's not they who count now, they're men who have been ruined, whose lives are the casualties of a great error. There were different Germans in the prison, though. Men inside the cells who kept another life alive, and it was even harder for them than it was for us, because they had to wish for the defeat of their own people.'

'You met many of them?'

'Yes, though it was difficult. There is more mistrust in prison than outside it. Our own people did not like such contacts being made, nor did many of the Germans. But I knew fine men. Some, it is true, were indistinguishable to me from the worst outside. But not all.'

'Then you have friends among the Germans.'

'Yes.'

'You don't hate them.'

'I hate what I hate in them. But when what you love and what you hate exist together, you cannot be entirely an enemy.'

'What is it you love, particularly?'

'Their generosity.'

'You think they're a generous people.'

'Yes.'

We looked at each other.

'It can also be a terrible generosity,' he went on. 'There is still some of an ancient tribal spirit in them, and it was this old, blind will the Nazis could appeal to—to their wild faith and their hidden yearning to surrender their persons and throw off the burden of thought. And when you see the consequence, an S.S. man or a Hitler-youth in the pure state, you feel as if you were looking at a tiger. Their natures have been distorted, and their self-sacrifice abused.

'But they are a people of creators as well as of tribal worshippers who leap up at the beat of a drum. There are two strains intermingled, creative and destructive, and according to the way that circumstances and their own prophets impel them, this energy may be turned in either direction. Their intelligence can become diabolical, and their fervour madness, but it is also the fact that they have this twofold richness, that makes them capable of so much. And either they will try to kill us all again and then destroy themselves, or else they will become truly conscious, and this instinctive force, which so few other peoples have, will be one of the world's greatest gifts. They are not cast eternally in the mould we have known them in. They are not fixed in essence, any more than we. They can shape themselves by their own will, if they are guided in different ways by new men.'

'Which new men?'

'Those who remember, those who will learn to think and those who will be born, and who may teach their parents.'

'And this will happen?'

'I do not know, but it is possible. One cannot say it is impossible.'

He stopped, and drank some of the liquid from the glass. 'They are here, among us, defeated or not,' he said. 'Whatever they do will concern us.'

'So you forgive them.'

'I? No one can forgive anything as big as a nation. And even we in the prison cannot fully pardon what they have done to us. No man can be forgiven until he has learned to forgive himself. It is for the Germans to understand what they have done, and what they must do next. Then they can be forgiven.'

The nurse had come in. She did all her tasks in silence, and when she lifted him up to arrange the bed, her skill was as helpful as kindness, and may have contained it. She didn't speak to me this time, but frowned as she reached the door. I nodded, she went out, and I got up to go.

'And tomorrow we move to the camp,' Maarten said.

'That's right. I'll come round and see you before they take you down there.'

'You've done a lot for us. I expect you know that we are grateful.'

'It's nice of you to say so, but what we've done here has been like what we've done everywhere else. We've followed our inclinations, and sometimes they've led us to do decent things, sometimes not. We've drifted along, into good and evil . . .

'We've come along, dividing the good from the bad like judges, releasing the one and punishing the other. But when you've behaved as we've often done, the only thing that entitles you to blame the enemy is your pistol. That's one thing to be said for soldiering: you certainly get to find out what you really are. And you certainly get to know how parts of your nature were held in check before by fear of the consequences. You soon discover that there's no such thing as a small evil, one dirty little act. They're all the same, they all carry you the same way. Once you're caught up in it, you really are caught up in it. And if you know what you're doing, you begin to fear your own enjoyment.'

I stopped and looked at him. His eyes had little outward expression. 'Well,' he said, 'clearly you can only condemn evil and act against it when you are freed from the evil in yourself. You can only do anything good when that is your strongest desire. And the alternative is always there, it is impossible to do nothing, there will always be the growth we choose to struggle for, or the growth into chaos that is spun out of us if we refuse to struggle . . . Good is harder, because it requires a choice, and a reason for the choice. It isn't enough to help people because it is necessary to yourself, or even because of them.'

'What must you do it for?'

'For a reason common to everyone and everything. You must have a reason that is outside each person as well as common to them all. A reason that holds each one together since, in the end, we are responsible for one another. That is why there must be a reason that is bigger than each one. And whatever it is, you must not only find it, but live it. The struggle to do good must also go on in your heart.'

'In your heart.'

'Yes, what matters is to keep your heart intact, and exercised constantly. Even the best hover on the verge of evil at each instant. It is not relative; if you are not free from it, you are responsible for the worst of it everywhere. The crime in all of us makes crime possible The criminals are what we want to be. We all contain one another's evil.'

The hospital lights went off and on in warning of their being turned out for the night. I went over and took his letters from the table.

'And for everyone, it is the same as for the Germans. Each one must find how to forgive himself. Good night. I hope we shall get back—you, and I, and all who are separated.'

I saw him turn over towards the window as I went out of the room.

The day of the final evacuation was brilliantly sunny with a light wind. I drove down to the hutted camp early in the morning, to see if everything was ready, and found it was partly occupied by released workers from the town. The women were doing the washing, and the men strolling about. In charge of the camp was a young Service Corps Major, and as he showed me round the huts, he spoke of his pleasure at running a purely civilian concern again. But he was treated as a warrior by the admiring inmates, to whom he distributed salutes when they greeted him.

The camp seemed well organised in the short time they'd had. There was a big hospital hut, with nurses and two young Belgian doctors; and a phenomenon I hadn't seen before—a polyglot team of United Nations helpers, with a north-country Englishman in charge. 'This is a grand job, lad,' he told me, when the Major had left us together. 'I'd not get a salary like I do anywhere else, at my age.'

The Belgian doctors had been up to the prison ward and to the civil hospital to see the patients and make arrangements for fetching them later on. I asked them what they thought of the men on the danger list, but they wouldn't commit themselves. One held out a hand and waggled it, the other blew air through his lips, to suggest their doubt.

As I arrived back at the prison gates, a man rushed out carrying a bundle. When he saw me, he raised it in the air and shouted repeatedly, in English, 'God save the King.' I guessed this was one of the released Germans. Two warders were grinning. Another looked shocked.

In the courtyard, half-a-dozen soldiers with purple berets were getting into a truck. They were Belgian paratroops. Their Sergeant explained they'd brought S.S. officers to the Garrison Commander's block. 'It's something new for us to be keeping prisoners,' he said. 'Well, em-bus, gentlemen,' and they drove off, leaving the courtyard quiet in the sun.

The Secretary stopped me as I went into the office. 'Two of them have come back,' he said.

'Two of which?'

'Two of those we released last night.'

'Come back?' He nodded. 'Tell them to get out again. No, just a minute, send them in here.'

They stood in their sailor greatcoats in front of me, looking abashed.

'Why have you come back?'

'But, Sir,' one said, 'we could find nowhere to sleep.'

'Do you think this is a hotel?'

'No, no,' he rebuked me. 'But we were too late to draw our ration cards, and without food and shelter, what can one do?'

'Well, get out of here and never return.'

'But where shall we go?'

'Wherever you wish. Anywhere.'

The Secretary hurried them out. Then he put his head back round the door. 'Do you know what some others have done? They've sold the overcoats we gave them in the market outside the Town Hall.'

'Have they.' He grinned. 'Well, will you ask the Allied officers to come in?'

There was something I'd been meaning to do. I went over to the bookcase and unlocked it. I took out the complete works of Nietsche, some geo-political atlases and an album of views of classical Greece.

Krampff chose this moment to come in. 'Excuse me,' he said, 'that the library has not yet been purified.'

'That's all right. There have been other things.'

'I was meaning to remove the books not now permitted.'

'I'm sure.'

'The Allied'—he checked himself at the word "prisoners"—'officers are now here.'

The delegates filed in and arranged themselves, as before, in two groups. M. de Tournay was of course absent, and the Eastern party had now increased by several members representing national and political sections.

They were amiable but impatient; I could see they regarded me as already belonging to their past. Together we made arrangements for the move. I asked them to check every man in their party, and I said Cuthbert and I would re-check each person with them as he came out of the inner yard.

Captain Telders asked in which order the parties were to leave. I said in alphabetical order, starting with the Belgians.

I asked if all their men had got the clothes and money.

Apparently some had refused both, but most had accepted. I told them each man would get five cigarettes as he left, and that a meal would be ready at the camp.

There seemed to be nothing else, so we all shook hands and they filed out.

I went over with Cuthbert to the Secretary's office, and we collected up the lists. When we saw two Army lorries drive in through the front gates and park there in the sun, we all three went down into the courtyard. There were not many warders about, and none of the senior officials had appeared. One warder was stationed by the steel door leading to the inner courtyard. I told him to open it, and we looked inside.

This was my first sight of all the Allied prisoners together. Hundreds of them were lying or standing on the cobbles, with the air of steadfast patience that you also see in bodies of soldiers.

Captain Telders came up, and I saluted him for the benefit of the warders and the prison staff, who were now beginning to peer discreetly out of the upstairs windows. He said that the Belgians and Czechs weren't quite ready, but that his party was, so why not begin with them? I asked the Belgian Major and the Czech lawyer if this was all right, and they immediately agreed. So Captain Telders mustered his men and brought them forward.

We saw that every group had managed to make a national flag, and the Dutch colours were carried by the first man who passed through the gate. Captain Telders patted each prisoner on the shoulder as he went by, and called out his name, making sure we ticked it off on the list. They went steadily through, and were helped into the lorries by our soldiers. Most of them looked too tired to be happy. A few gave us a friendly look, but some glanced at us as if to say we'd been a long time about it. For the most part, they ignored the Germans.

When Captain Telders had marshalled as many of his men as would go on the lorries, he came back and shook hands again. The other delegates came through the steel door and gathered in the front courtyard, and some of the prisoners crowded at the gate to look through. The faces of the Germans could be seen at the windows above.

'Okay, Sarge?' said the driver.

'Take them away.'

As the lorries moved off, Captain Telders and his Lieutenant, who were perched up on the tail-board, began to intone the Dutch national anthem. I wondered whether they'd get away with it. The others took it up slowly at first, but as the trucks reached the main gate, they passed out into the road singing lustily. I got the impression that everybody watching the scene was in agreement for a moment.

As the lorries came back, the rest of the Dutchmen left, and then the other contingents one by one. Among the Belgians was a Gendarme in tattered uniform, who was booed ironically by his comrades as he drove off. Many of the men hadn't bothered to change out of their prison clothes, and they carried their sailor suits and boots in bundles under their arms.

In the first lorry of each national group there was always the flag-bearer, and they went out, as the Dutchmen had done, singing their song. But the following lorry-loads were less exuberant, and until the men of the next nationality came forward, there was a pause in the singing.

As the courtyard emptied during the day, I expected difficulties might arise when we came to the dissident groups; but there were none. Though one thing did happen which we hadn't foreseen. While the last of the crowd was dwindling away, two men came up who spoke in a language we couldn't identify, and couldn't find anyone to translate. It seemed that no group had accepted them. They repeated their names a great many times, and we hunted for them in the lists and fetched down all the German lists and went through those too. By this time the last party was leaving, so we gave up, and told them to join it.

When the courtyard was quite empty, I went up to the ward to check if all the sick men had been taken away in the ambulance. Then I got in the car and drove round to the civilian hospital, to see whether the patients there had been moved down to the camp as well. The Sister met me on the stairs. 'They have all gone,' she said. 'The Belgian doctors have taken them all away.'

'Did it go off all right?'

'Well, yes. Except that some had colics due to the too rich foods you brought them.'

'How was Maarten?'

'Oh, he was in the number that they took to the airfield.'

'Some were taken to the airfield?'

'Yes. Those for immediate evacuation.'

I hurried down to the car, and drove across the town. When I reached the hangars on the further side, they told me his party had just taken off. Several planes were overhead, and I asked which one he was in. No one could tell me for sure. But looking up at them rising and wheeling in the sky, I felt the elation this sight always brings, and with it a hope for him and for us all.

THE END